Not Your Father's
HORSEMAN

Valerie Griswold-Ford

www.dragonmoonpress.com

Dragon
Moon

Not Your Father's Horseman

ISBN 1-896944-27-2

Dragon Moon Press is an Imprint of Hades Publications Inc.
P.O. Box 1714, Calgary, Alberta, T2P 2L7, Canada

Dragon Moon Press and Hades Publications, Inc. acknowledges the ongoing support of the Canada Council for the Arts and the Alberta Foundation for the Arts for our publishing programme.

Printed and bound in Canada or the United States
www.dragonmoonpress.com
www.v-gford.com

Not Your Father's
HORSEMAN

Valerie Griswold-Ford

www.dragonmoonpress.com

www.vg-ford.com

Acknowledgements

First, to my husband Brian for putting up with the vagaries of a writer for the past two years. I love you, sweetie.

To my readers and friends who bled beside me while I wrote and rewrote: Mom, Beard, Lai, Maridius, Gabriele, Moosey, Kathy, Beth, Tarren, Rob, Mike, Barbara and George. I couldn't have done it without you.

To everyone on FM Chat: bless you! For all the long nights and days of agonizing, for cheering me on and letting me cry on your shoulders.

To my editor, Tina, for helping me put the professional touches to this.

To Gwen and Tom Anderson, for believing in me.

And, last but not least, to Tee, for starting this in the first place. Thanks, I'm enjoying the ride.

Dedication

This book is dedicated to my husband, Brian,
for being my rock.

And to my father and my Aunt Marge, who always
knew I would do this.

Prologue

"Beginnings"

Boom.

The first explosion was barely noticed throughout the labyrinth that was the Gene-Tech Scientific Facility, especially in the secure wing, where the soundproofing and cold steel walls dampened the noise into the background. The lights flickered a bit, and one of the guards at the front desk noticed a small blip on one of his security screens. He was reaching for his walkie-talkie to ask one of his comrades to check out the generators when the lights died abruptly. The sudden silence was broken only by the excited babble that exploded over the walkie-talkies and the buzz of the orange emergency lights as they came on.

"What the hell is going on?"

The strong voice of Alex Masterson, head of the Facility, cut cleanly through the confusing gibberish, and the other voices stopped abruptly. The silence stretched as it became clear that no one had a response for the man who said impatiently, "I want an answer, dammit!"

He was standing in an antechamber deep within the secure wing, his handsome face lit by the hellish orange glow of the lights, the walkie-talkie clenched in one hand as he watched the two junior Mages in the other room finish the final preparatory spells. His dark hair was slicked back, as much by sweat as by gel, and his dark eyes were tense as they strained through the gloom to monitor what was going on in the inner chamber.

The ritual room was barely brighter than the outer room, but by the light of the candles lit around the edges of the chamber, he could see the two breeders strapped to the tables, their swollen bellies revealed and ready for this final session. When no answer came from the walkie-talkie, he threw the unit into the wall with an angry oath and resumed pacing. There was the faintest smell of burnt wires, like brimstone, in the air—some damn fool must have tripped one of the fail safes on the circuits again.

Everything had to go perfectly. There was no more room in the schedule for delays—the breeders were no more than three weeks away from delivering, and his Patron Lords were eager for the births. This was the last session—it had to go exactly according to plan. His patrons, and his pride, would demand nothing less.

He came out of his musings as the door to the outer chamber opened and one of the Mages stepped in. "We're ready to move forward, Mr. Masterson," the man said quietly. "We've repaired all the damage to the spells that Cameron did. Everything is set for the Lords, as soon as they are ready."

"They'll be here shortly. Thank you, Damon." Alex watched the man bow and leave before continuing his pacing.

Damn Cameron and his change of heart. Alex still didn't understand what had happened to his former best friend and chief Mage. What were you thinking, Cam? Alex thought for the thousandth time. You knew how important this was to us! To Gene-Tech! This is the future, and you chose to try and stop it. Why couldn't you understand? There had been several moments, right after Cameron's death, that everyone had thought he'd succeeded in aborting at least one of the fetuses, but they had managed to save all three. Alex's patrons had been most displeased with his lack of control over the project. Alex was still smarting from the lecture Andreas had given him.

This is MY project! He glanced in at the chamber again, savoring the sight of both women tied to their tables. Caran's eyes were closed, her pale lips moving in what he assumed was prayer. Alex sneered at her fear, and then stopped.

Teraisa was looking back at him, her dark blue eyes alien in the flickering candlelight. There was no fear—only a promise of something that stung him. Challenge? Threat? After a moment, he deliberately turned his back on the window, ignoring her stare, although the skin on his back prickled as her gaze continued to bore into him.

His thoughts were interrupted by the faintest whisper of wind moving through the room's still air. Alex moved back towards the window as a dot of emerald light appeared in the semi-darkness of the center of the room. The spot turned lazily, arms of energy spiraling out from the center in ever-lengthening swirls. Alex waited, his arms crossed over his chest and one foot barely tapping the ground in irritation as the portal continued to open.

Andreas always did like to make an entrance.

"Did we rush you?" Alex asked sarcastically, as the two Elemental Lords stepped through the portal slowly. Andreas, the majestic Shadow Lord, ignored him, meticulously settling his dark robes around his tall, athletic frame as the green glow of the portal faded.

"Don't be obnoxious, Alexander," Kymara said softly, gliding over and kissing his cheek. Alex tried to keep his scowl in place, but the slender Dawn Lord smiled up at him, her golden eyes mischievous, and he smiled back, in spite of his irritation at their theatrics.

They were a picture of contrasts—Andreas tall and dark, with hair and features similar to Alex's own, and Kymara, as golden as her name implied, long blonde hair trailing in a cloud down her back, her pale silver robes a stark contrast to Andreas' midnight blue ones. Even in the eerie glow of the emergency lights, Alex fancied he could feel the warmth of the sun coming from her skin as she laid a hand on his arm.

"Have you repaired the damage?" Andreas asked, his robes finally arranged to his satisfaction. "I want no problems."

"The damage has all been repaired." Alex gestured to the other room. "Everything is ready."

"Then let us begin." Andreas opened the door and gestured for the two of them to precede him.

The atmosphere inside the chamber was thick with fear. Both breeders flinched as the door opened. Kymara leaned over the dark-haired breeder Teraisa, trailing her warm fingertips over the woman's cool skin. "Think of what she will do," the Dawn Lord whispered to her. "Your daughter will be the envy of our worlds."

"My daughter will never belong to you," Teraisa replied, her mouth twisted with anger. Alex watched, almost fascinated by the challenge in her dark blue eyes.

"We'll see." Kymara laughed and turned to the other table, where Caran still prayed, her green eyes screwed tightly shut. It was hard to tell which excited the Dawn Lord more: Teraisa's defiance, or Caran's fear. She trailed her fingers over Caran's belly as well, smiling as the woman whimpered, marveling at the twin heartbeats that beat within her womb.

"How do they feel, my love?" Andreas asked. Kymara smiled, running her fingers once more over Teraisa's womb. The energy that surged up from the child still inside sparked along her nerve endings, adding to the excitement she felt welling up inside of her. They were so close....

She shuddered in pleasure and turned back to her lover, who stood glowering in the middle of the room. "Perfect. Once these are born, we should breed Teraisa again for the fourth child. Her blood is stronger." Kymara joined Andreas in the center of the circle painted on the floor and looked over at Alexander. "Are you joining us?"

He shook his head. "I'll watch from the other room. These Magics make me sick."

Andreas snorted. "Why does that not surprise me?" Alex's jaw clenched at the contempt in the Shadow Lord's voice.

Alex refused to rise to the bait, and only the slamming of the door belied his anger at the jibe. Kymara's silvery laugh only made matters worse.

"Come, my love," she said, still giggling a bit. "Let us begin."

She stepped to the very center of the circle and took Andreas' hands in her own. Her voice, light and clear as a church bell, floated up into the darkness above the candles, supported by the deep baritone of Andreas as he matched her chant.

The glass and the wards that kept the spell's power confined also muted the sounds, but Alex knew the words to this final Calling by heart. His lips moved along with the Elemental Lords' as the darkness coalesced and began to move down into the center, spreading shadowy fingers along the wombs of the breeders.

Boom!

This explosion caught everyone's attention. The entire Facility shook—inside the chamber, Kymara's voice faltered, although Andreas continued to chant steadily. Alex leaned against the glass, the smell of brimstone and burning stronger now. What the hell was going on?

Boom!

A brilliant flash of light exploded in the center of the chamber. Even years later, Alex couldn't say what happened. He was thrown backwards by the shockwave that poured out from the center of the ritual chamber, the glass from the window shattering around him. Pain lanced through him as shards penetrated his skin; instinctively, his hands had come up to protect his eyes, but the rest of his body was showered in the bits of safety glass from the window that had been blown out. There were several screams—Kymara's, Andreas' and a guttural shriek that scraped against his eardrums. When his eyes cleared and he saw the nightmare before him, his own scream intertwined in the mix.

Kymara lay in a pool of her own blood, the harsh gargle of her breath scraping out of the hole ripped in her throat. Andreas knelt next to her, his hands clapped over his eyes, blood spattered all over his robes. There was blood on the walls, the floor, and the remains of the window. The candles had been knocked over—now the only illumination was from the emergency lights.

Caran and Teraisa were gone.

After checking himself to make sure he was relatively unhurt, Alex tore into the room, unable to believe what he saw. None of the bonds were intact—it looked as though whatever had stolen his two breeders had claws, not fingers. His brain shuddered away from the implications.

Kymara gave one last shuddering gasp and lay still. Alex knelt beside her and felt for a pulse on her wrist. Finding none, he clenched his teeth, and turned to the Shadow Lord.

"What happened?" he asked, trying hard to keep the harshness from his voice. I need him, remember, he told himself. Especially with her gone. I need him to make this work.

Andreas didn't answer, and Alex clenched his jaw, holding onto his temper by sheer will. "Andreas?"

The Shadow Lord finally lifted his face from his bloody hands, and Alex scrambled backwards hastily, his mouth dropping open in shock. His hand came down on a pool of blood and he fell, trying to get away from the ruin in front of him.

There were two huge slashes across Andreas' formerly handsome face, obliterating not only the dark eyes, but part of the sockets that had held them as well. It was as if some demon had raked his claws across the Shadow Lord's face.

"Find them." There was a wealth of agony and fury in the Shadow Lord's voice, colder than Alex could ever remember hearing from the Elemental. "Find them and make them pay."

Twenty-three years later...

Chapter 1

"Secrets"

"To the future!"

Seven crystal glasses clinked together, as an unobtrusive waiter removed the salad bowls and began to pass out the entrees. The quiet murmur of conversation swirled around the table as the three families enjoyed the elegant dinner party the Kingsley Country Club was playing host to.

Nikki Jeffries savored the taste of the deep ruby Shiraz in her glass as she looked around the table, her mind taking the pictures her fingers were itching to: her best friend Monica Carlin, her blonde hair trailing down over her eight-month-old daughter Rebecca's face as she cooed at the infant, her husband Tom hovering in the background. Nikki's own parents—her mother Lara, dark hair and dark blue eyes so like her daughter's, leaning against her husband's shoulder, her face tired despite its smile. Marc Jeffries, handsome in his dark suit, dark hair going to salt-and-pepper now, leaning back and beaming down at the baby, who was waving her hands in the air. And Monica's parents, Brianna and Doug Wakefield, who were watching their daughter proudly, Brianna with the same blonde hair, although shorter than Monica's, and the same smile.

Doug caught her eye and grinned, leaning over to her. "Penny for your thoughts?" he asked, his green eyes twinkling.

"As if you couldn't tell," she said, grinning. "I was thinking that I shouldn't have left my camera at home."

He laughed. "Afraid you might break it?" Doug owned a chain of camera stores—he'd given Nikki her first camera for her 8th birthday and encouraged her interest in photography. The Nikon that generally was her constant companion had come from his store.

"Something like that," Nikki said.

"So, Nikki, what are your plans now?" Brianna asked, tearing her eyes away from her granddaughter.

"I'm heading up to New Hampshire to start my book," she replied, setting her glass down and picking up her fork. "I've decided that I want to be an author rather than a reporter." She grinned down the table at Monica. "It's more fun."

Monica sniffed theatrically. "It means you don't have to get up at 4:30 in the morning," she retorted. "You can sleep until 4 in the afternoon and still get a full day in."

"Well, there's that too," Nikki agreed, spearing a stalk of asparagus. Monica shook her head as her friend, totally unrepentant, washed the asparagus down with another swallow of wine.

"What kind of book are you writing, Nik?" Tom's deep voice, slow and deliberate, never failed to make Nikki feel like someone had just poured warm maple syrup all over her.

Once again, she surrendered to jealousy for an instant, before she squashed it. Tom and Monica had dated casually throughout his college career—at this dinner two years ago, celebrating his graduation, he'd shocked everyone by presenting her with a diamond ring. She'd compounded the shock by accepting. Nikki shook her head, wondering if she'd ever have the same kind of relationship with someone.

"Nik?"

Tom's questioning voice brought her out of her musing. "Jeez, Tom, I'm sorry. Daydreaming again." She brushed a strand of dark hair out of her face. "It's a book on haunted houses."

Lara shook her head, her gesture mirroring her daughter's. "I still don't understand your fascination with haunted houses and ghosts," she said, a trace of disapproval in her voice. "Where did you get it from?"

"I don't know." Nikki shrugged. "I just think there's so much out there that can't be explained, that should be. And the fact that cameras can pick up things that our eyes can't is just amazing."

"So you're going to be taking pictures as well?" Doug said, and she nodded.

"Taking the pictures and developing them myself. That way, there's no opening for a lab to tamper with them in any way."

"Good plan," he said approvingly. "So I assume you'll be in to stock up on film before you leave?"

"Good assumption." Nikki grinned again, her dark blue eyes sparkling mischievously. "Do you give a bulk discount?"

Everyone laughed at that.

"So, Monica, are you and Tom still planning on opening your own business?" Marc asked when the laughter died down. Monica nodded, glancing at her husband and blushing.

"Yes. We've reached an agreement with Tom's uncle and we sign the papers next week. He'll be the senior partner—Tom will be junior, and as soon as I finish my internship, I'll be coming on as well," Monica said.

"Congratulations!" Nikki raised her glass again, and everyone else followed suit. "To Carlin Associates!"

The rest of the table echoed her sentiment. "I think I'll be coming to talk to you, then," Marc said, once the toast ended. "I'm really beginning to think that my current stockbroker is more concerned about my financing his newest boat than the state of my portfolio."

"We'll make sure you're second on the list," Monica promised, winking at her father.

"Second?" Marc protested, mock-shocked.

"I'm afraid so. Rebecca would be awfully upset if we put someone else before her grandparents."

Marc shook his head, a smile playing about his lips. "Well, I guess I'll just have to settle for second," he said, chuckling.

Nikki and Monica both laughed as Rebecca opened her blue eyes to blink sleepily at them before settling deeper in her seat and going back to sleep. Tom looked over at his wife and smiled.

"Why don't you three take advantage of the fact that the little one's asleep and there's an open bar to go have some fun?" Brianna suggested. "This is supposed to be a party, after all."

Monica looked torn. "I really shouldn't leave Rebecca…" she started, and Tom laid a hand on her's.

"Come on, love," he said. "She'll be fine."

"Yeah, I owe you a drink anyways," Nikki chimed in. "You beat me on grades once again."

Monica allowed her husband and best friend to lead her away; both Lara and Brianna chuckled at the look on her face. "Do you remember that?" Lara asked her softly, once the three were out of earshot.

Brianna nodded, tucking Rebecca's blanket in more securely around the sleeping infant. "My goodness, yes. I don't think I left Monica more than three times that first year, and I worried each and every time."

"Mmm-hmmm." Lara nodded, exchanging a knowing look with Marc. "I was the same way."

※

"Will you stop worrying?" Nikki said, one shot later. "She's not going anywhere."

"I know, but I don't like leaving her alone." Monica fidgeted with one of the shot glasses until Tom reached over and took it away from her.

"She's not alone," he reminded her. "Both her grandparents and her adopted grandparents are there."

"I know, but…" Monica began to twine one long strand of blonde hair around her fingers, a familiar gesture to both her husband and best friend. Tom reached out and gently unwound the hair, smoothing it back before taking her hand firmly in his own.

"No buts." Nikki interrupted her, gesturing to the bartender. "I'm going to get drunk tonight, and you two are going to help me."

"You heard the lady, Pete," Tom chuckled to the bartender. "She's in the mood to drink, and I'm in the mood to watch her drink."

"You're supposed to be drinking with me!" Nikki protested. "Monica's still breastfeeding, so she can't have any more, but don't make me drink alone, Tom."

"Go ahead," Monica told him. "Mom and Dad are driving us home anyways."

Tom shrugged and smiled. "Set them up, Pete."

Two more shot glasses were placed on the bar, filled with pale kamikazes. With the practice born of four years in college, Nikki and Tom downed the shots smoothly and slammed the glasses back on the bar. Two more shots appeared and disappeared in the same way.

"Okay, I can't do any more," Tom said after the third shot. "I'm severely out of practice."

"Wuss," Nikki said airily. "It's only four kamikazes. Nothing."

"Nothing to a reporter. I've seen you guys drink when you go out." Tom shook his head and then grabbed the bar. "I'm done."

Monica giggled. "Yup, you're done. C'mon, big guy, let's get you a chair and something more solid in your stomach."

Nikki watched them go and heaved a big sigh. "Why can't I find someone like that, Pete? Why is it that the only guys I seem to attract are jerks?" She turned and looked up at the bartender. "How about a screwdriver for the road?"

She was halfway back to the table when someone touched her elbow, startling her. The drink in her hand sloshed briefly as she recovered from the surprise.

"Problems?" a deep voice murmured in her ear.

Nikki tightened her grasp on her glass and turned, a tight smile on her pretty face. "No, I know when I've had enough to drink, thank you."

Jack Allen, the dark satin of his tuxedo jacket echoing the darkness of his eyes, slipped a hand under her elbow and returned her smile. "And have you?"

"Hell yes." She stiffened as he slipped his free arm around her. "I'm not that drunk, though."

"C'mon, Nik. We can have one last fling before you leave." Once that voice, smooth as silk oozing down her spine, would have flipped every single hormone in her body into overdrive.

Now, it just made her smile turn even harder. Jack knew exactly how attractive he was and how to use it—the joke at school was that if he decided he wanted into a girl's pants, she had a better chance of outrunning his Porsche than stopping him. That was, until he'd come up against the rock wall that was Nikki Jeffries. After the first whirlwind date that ended up in his bedroom, Nikki had realized she was just another notch on his bedpost and ended it. To say Jack had taken it personally would have been a slight understatement.

Nikki glanced over to where Monica had just settled Tom back at the table; her friend looked up with a "do-you-need-any-help?" expression on her face. The tall brunette shook her head briefly before turning back to Jack and leaning over, allowing him one last look down the front of her black sheath dress. She placed her lips against his ear and said softly, "I wouldn't sleep with you again if God himself leaned down and told me to."

His arm dropped from her shoulders and she pulled back, smoothed her black silk dress and sauntered away. Rather impressive, considering how many kamikazes she'd just had and the fact that the dress required four-inch heels.

"Very smooth," Monica said, as Nikki came up to the table. "So what did you say to him this time to make him give you that look?"

Nikki turned casually, her eyes sweeping up over Jack as she scanned the bar area as if looking for someone before turning back to her friend. Jack's face was purple with anger, and she smiled in satisfaction.

"I told him that not even divine intervention was going to get him back in my pants," she said simply, and drove home the point by swallowing the rest of the screwdriver. Then her face turned green.

"Not smart," Monica said, grinning as Nikki turned and bolted for the restroom. "It's a good thing Jack's looking the other way. Talk about spoiling the perfect exit." She turned to her husband. "Feeling better?"

He nodded carefully. "I think so. The room's not spinning anymore, but I think we'll probably want to head home soon."

Marc and Lara shook their heads. "What are we going to do with her?" Lara asked her husband, who shrugged.

"Ahh, college," Doug chuckled. "Don't look like that, Lara. She's still standing, mostly, and she's not driving. It's her last night to be a free spirit."

"And she'll be paying for it tomorrow," Marc added. "Just think of how much fun you'll have pointing out tomorrow morning how she brought this all on herself."

Doug and Brianna finished putting another blanket around Rebecca and looked over at Monica, who was helping Tom to his feet. "Are you all set?" Brianna asked her, and Monica nodded. "Well, then, we'll see you all soon," she continued, looking at Marc and Lara. "Say goodbye to Nikki for us."

"We will." They waved, and then Marc signaled to the waiter passing by and requested three strong coffees. "How are you doing?"

"Not too bad." Lara looked out at the college kids and their parents and smiled, but Marc saw the lines of pain and fatigue on her face. "I'm glad we came."

"I am too." Marc laid his hand on her's, and she smiled up at him. "I know it meant a lot to Nikki that you were able to come."

"It meant a lot to me, too. It gave me a goal to concentrate on." Her other hand squeezed the top of the teak cane that rested against her chair, a silent reminder of the tragic car accident that had very nearly stolen her from him eight months ago.

The waiter returned with the coffee, disrupting his train of thought and bringing him back to the party. Once the man was gone, Marc leaned over to his wife, enjoying the spicy smell of her perfume, and whispered, "You are the most beautiful woman here. Want to run away with me?"

"Only if we can leave before my husband gets back," she replied, a wicked sparkle in her dark eyes. "Where did you have in mind?"

"If we can leave now, we can avoid my wife and take my car to this romantic little hotel I know of in Acapulco," he said, grinning.

"Get a room." Nikki slid unsteadily into her chair and pulled the coffee to her. "My god, I can't take you two anywhere."

Marc leaned back and sighed. "Busted. Guess we're just going to have to go home and continue this conversation."

"Good." Nikki took a sip of coffee and shuddered. "I feel bad enough as it is—seeing the two of you cooing at each other like that is enough to make me really sick."

Her father chuckled and reached for his coffee cup.

Later that night, as they were driving home with Nikki passed out in the back seat, Lara said quietly, "We need to tell her the truth, Marcus."

One salt-and-pepper eyebrow went up, and he looked quickly in the rearview mirror. Nikki was still unconscious, one hand curled under her cheek as she leaned against the window. "What brought that up?"

Lara sighed, shifting her legs with a wince of pain. "Seeing Monica and Rebecca tonight, for one thing. Seeing Nikki herself as well. She's grown up, Marcus, and I hadn't even noticed until tonight. I've been so busy dealing with the fallout from the accident that I hadn't even seen what a woman my daughter's turned into."

"You nearly died, Lara. You've had other things on your mind, and Nikki knows that."

"That's the other reason." She turned to look at him. "What if I died?"

"You didn't." His arm slid around her, pulling her close against him as his chest tightened. "You didn't, and you won't."

"She needs to know," Lara repeated stubbornly. "She deserves to know. And the longer we wait, the more she'll want to know why we didn't tell her before."

He couldn't argue with that logic. "You aren't going to stop until I agree, are you?"

"No."

Nikki muttered something incoherent in the back seat, startling both of them. Lara turned, but her daughter's eyes were still closed. "I'd forgotten how she talks in her sleep," she murmured.

"Are you sure you want to do this?" Marc asked.

Lara looked out into the darkness. "Yes," she said finally. "We have to tell her. She deserves to know the truth."

He sighed again. "All right. We'll tell her in the morning."

———

The moon was above her, somewhere to the right—not the pale full moon of early summer that it should have been, but the bloated orange moon of autumn. Nikki frowned—something about the moon tugged at her memory; an autumn moon long ago had looked like that....

She shook her head and concentrated on where she was placing her feet. There was a slight mist curling up from the ground—between the mist and the swirling leaves kicked up by the chill breeze that ran icy fingers across her cheeks, the uneven ground was hidden and Nikki didn't want to end the evening by breaking an ankle. She watched her boot tops for several moments before she realized what she was seeing—at some point, she'd traded her silk sheath dress and high heels for her black leather jacket, a tee-shirt, jeans and her favorite leather boots. *Funny, I would have thought Mom would have put me to bed in pjs*, she thought absently.

The wind scraped among the skeletons of leaves that still clung, tenacious even in death, to the lanky limbs of trees that lined the narrow path she followed. Underneath the low moan was another sound, and Nikki paused, straining her ears to catch the elusive music that seemed to rise from the earth itself. After a moment, she identified it as harp music—not the classical harp that her mother enjoyed, but a wilder, more organic sound. The song beckoned her on, each note shimmering on the air around her, will-o-the-wisps leading her farther down the path.

As she listened, a prickly feeling crawled up along her back and she shivered. Turning, she looked back up the hill, wondering who or what was watching her. The breeze pulled a sweet scent across her nostrils, too quickly for her to identify it.

The woman (at least, that's what Nikki thought it was) was silhouetted against the pumpkin moon, wrapped in shadows so deep that nothing except her eyes were visible. Those were emerald, cat's eyes, and they shone in the gloom like precious stones, pinning Nikki in place.

Again, a sense of the familiar rushed through her and then was gone.

Why do you watch me? The thought rose in her mind, and hung between them, rising on the music that was louder now.

Why do you come here? The voice that filled her head was deep and smoky, redolent with images of jazz clubs. Nikki closed her eyes to revel in it for a moment; when she opened them, the woman was gone.

Nikki shook her head, thinking, This place is too weird for me. There was a half-formed suspicion that she was dreaming, but the chill in the air and the feeling of the wind across her face was more real than she'd ever experienced in a dream before. The fragrance was back, naggingly familiar. The whole place was familiar—it was on the tip of Nikki's tongue, and refused to come any further. She moved back down the path in the direction she'd been moving in before she'd seen the woman, listening as the music, a minor key that wrapped around her, began to grow louder.

The trees thinned as she moved further into the darkness, following the notes that beckoned her onward. As she moved over the small hill, Nikki saw the gathering darkness was the shadow cast by a large plantation house that stood on a nearby hill, with lawns sweeping up from the edge of the trees where she now stood to the columns on the porch. The moon hung behind the house, beginning to grow brighter as she moved closer.

It was a wayward tree root that betrayed her, catching her foot as she started to move backwards, shading her eyes against the increasingly bright light. She hit the ground hard, bouncing her head against another tree behind her as she fell. When the stars cleared, the moon was the proper color and in its proper place outside her bedroom window, and the lump on her head was the result of her collision with her headboard. Nikki sat up, rubbing the bump and chewing on her lip, for a very long time.

When she went down to breakfast the next morning, her thoughts were still on the strange dreams that had been plaguing her sleep since midwinter. Her mother was already on the deck, cup of coffee in her hand and the paper spread out on her lap, as was usual. "Good morning, sunshine," Lara said cheerily, and grinned as Nikki grunted and slid into a chair, her own coffee cradled in her hands. The headline on the newspaper screamed, "Forensic Mages Uncover 6th Victim In House Fire."

"Feeling okay?" Lara continued, a mischievous look in her dark blue eyes.

"Feeling odd," her daughter replied, staring into the depths of the cup as if the answers she looked for swirled with the cream. Lara raised one dark eyebrow, and waited.

"Have you ever had a really, really strange dream, Mom?" Nikki asked after about five minutes of silence, looking up at her mother with the blue eyes that had tugged at Lara's heart since the first time she'd held her. "A dream where you were certain your subconscious was trying to tell you something, and you just couldn't grab the one piece of information to make it all make sense?"

Lara set down her cup before replying. "I think so, yes. Why?"

"I've been having this dream." Nikki looked out over the garden, still drenched with dew as the sun was barely up over the horizon. The morning glories were just beginning to open—she drew in a deep breath. "It all seems so unbelievable now."

"Tell me."

"It's dark, but the moon is full. It's an autumn moon, all gold, and the trees are almost bare." Her voice dropped. "I'm in a wood, and there's music, and a scent that I know, but can't place. And then I can feel her eyes on me, and I turn."

"Her?" Lara felt a chill run through her.

Her daughter shook her dark head. "I don't know who she is—I can't even see her, really. Just her eyes." Nikki paused to take a sip of coffee. "They're like cat's eyes—you know, how they glow in the dark when the light hits them just right? Green like that."

"Does she do anything?" Lara asked.

"Not until last night. Last night, she spoke in my head." Nikki smiled mirthlessly. "How crazy does that sound?"

"Pretty crazy," her mother agreed. "But you've always had vivid dreams."

"True. But this one seems different." Nikki frowned. "I swear, I know this woman, but I can't remember where."

Lara chose her next words carefully. "You're sure?"

Nikki snorted. "I'm not sure of anything anymore."

The careless comment tore at Lara's heart, and she knew what she had to say next. Swallowing hard, she said, "You can be sure of one thing—I will always love you."

"I know, Mom." Nikki smiled over at her. "I'm sorry."

"Don't be." Don't be a coward, Lara, she scolded herself. You won't have a better opening. "Are you still planning on leaving in a few days?"

"Yeah. Maybe the dreams won't follow me." Nikki stretched, and raised one eyebrow, a gesture she'd learned from her mother. "Why?"

Lara looked out over the garden. "Have you ever been afraid to open your mouth and change everything, and yet the words are beating at your lips, demanding to be let out?"

"Maybe." The other eyebrow rose to join the first. "Why?"

"Nikki, you're adopted." The words rushed out before Lara could stop them. She bowed her head as Nikki's breath caught in her throat.

The silence that stretched after her statement was broken only by Marc coming through the screen door with a steaming basket full of muffins. The smile on his face faded as he took in the scene in front of him: Lara with her head down, and Nikki staring at her, her jaw dropped in shock.

"What are you talking about?" Nikki whispered finally. "I'm your daughter. You're my mother."

The pain in her voice brought Lara's head back up, and she put a hand over Nikki's ice-cold one as it lay on the table. "Yes, I am," she said, her voice breaking slightly. "I am the mother that raised you. But I am not the mother that gave birth to you, Nikki. You are the child of my heart, not my body."

"I don't believe you." Nikki pulled her hand away. "Why would you say such a thing?"

"Because it's true." Lara's hand fell back into her lap, and she pulled a piece of paper from underneath the newspaper there. She offered it to her daughter, who took it slowly.

The letters were beautifully formed, elegant script that flowed across the creamy paper—parchment, from the feel of it. It said simply, "This is my daughter Nikki. She is healthy, but I cannot take care of her. I know you will give her a good home."

"That's all we found in the basket with you," Marc said quietly, putting the basket on the table and laying a hand on Nikki's shoulder. "I'd gone out to get the paper and there you were on our front step, sleeping like an angel in a basket."

"I'd just lost a baby," Lara added. "And there you were, and when Marc brought you in, you opened those huge blue eyes and my heart ached for you. I knew, right then, that you were meant to be our's."

"Our lawyers drew up the papers, and that was that. It was easier not knowing who your birth mother was, because that way, there was no one else intruding," Marc said. "You are our daughter, Nikki, and always will be."

Nikki pulled away from them, her dark blue eyes full of tears. "So you have no clue who I really am, do you? How long were you going to wait before telling me?"

Lara and Marc exchanged glances, and Nikki's chin trembled. "You weren't, were you? You were just going to let me go on believing a lie my whole life!"

"Nikki, we never meant to hurt you," Lara said. "I just didn't know how to tell you."

"You'll pardon me if I don't believe that either." Nikki turned and ran into the house.

Marc sat down in the chair his daughter had just vacated and looked at his wife. "That went better than I thought it would."

Lara looked over at him, tears starting to fall down her pale cheeks. "And how can you say that?"

"She didn't swear at us, for one thing."

She smiled, despite the tears, and he got up and went to put his arms around her. "Don't worry, Lara," he murmured as she buried her face in his chest. "She just needs to get used to it. She won't leave us."

"But will she still love us?" his wife mumbled.

He had no answer to that.

CHAPTER 2

"EARLY TWILIGHT"

"My Lord?"

The words stirred the twilight darkness in the study, floating across the room to the man who was napping in his armchair. It had grown chilly—not that the Lands were ever truly warm, but once the wan sun went down, his bones began to ache as the coolness of the shadows sank into them, reminding him of how old he was and what abuse he'd put his body through. Andreas sighed, turning his face to the side, trying to sense how long he'd been asleep.

"My Lord? Your guest is here."

Guest? What guest? Andreas shook his head irritably, trying to get the cobwebs of his nap out of his thoughts. I shouldn't have slept, he thought, stretching. It never makes me feel better.

The air currents swirled around him as his butler crossed the room and stirred up the fire that had sunk to coals in the large fireplace. The warmth of the renewed flames chased the last of his fuzziness away, reminding him that he had invited the Dawn Lord Trimaris to dinner. Andreas stretched again and then rose from the chair, his dark silk robes draping around him like living shadows. Andreas enjoyed being impressive, even when no one else was around to appreciate the effort.

"Tell Trimaris I will be down shortly," he said, moving with practiced ease to the desk on the other side of the room. His butler bowed and left quietly. Andreas pulled open the bottom drawer and brushed his fingers over the scrolls in their leather cases. Power stirred along them, waiting for him, and he smiled at the promise implicit in them. This time, there would be no mistakes.

He closed the drawer quietly and turned to the top of the teak desk, where a slender manila folder rested next to an onyx cube. Opening the folder, he ran his fingers over the glossy pictures within—even though he could no longer see with the eyes ruined years ago, there were others who could, and he was certain that the pictures would be the final straw that would bring Trimaris into his web.

Revenge is such a wonderful reward to dangle in front of someone.

"Ah, Trimaris, how wonderful of you to come over tonight," he said a few moments later, as he walked carefully down the stairs, one hand on the ebony railing and the other extended in greeting. The woman waiting at the bottom of the stairs rose gracefully from her chair, setting down her glass of wine before taking the outstretched hand and guiding him to her for a cool, chaste kiss on the cheek. He slipped his arm around her, feeling her stiffen but not pull away, and together they went into the dining room. His butler, ever soliticious, picked up the abandoned wineglass and trailed after them.

"You're looking good, Andreas," Trimaris said, slipping into the chair he held for her and inclining her head at his courtesy. "I'm ... surprised, to say the least. I never expected this invitation."

No, I'll bet you didn't. Andreas covered his smile carefully as he moved to his own seat. This was the informal dining room: the table was small and exquisitely carved, big enough only for three at the most. The rest of the room was equally sized; it was an intimate area, with light green walls and deep bronze trim, a room that encouraged soft voices and leaning in to the other person to share thoughts.

It was the same room Andreas had entertained Kymara in, all those years ago. For a moment, he flashed back to those nights, her golden hair aglow in the candlelight, much as Trimaris' must be now, and her laughter floating on the air with the aroma of roasted meat and vegetables, as she leaned over to touch his cheek, her golden eyes warm with more than the wine...

"Andreas?"

<hr/>

Light, don't let him get all strange on me now; it's not what I need...
Trimaris still wasn't sure what she was doing here, in the house of the man she was certain had killed her younger sister. Not that she and Kymara had ever been truly close, but blood is blood, after all.

When the message had come this afternoon, written in Andreas' strong hand, she had been sorely tempted to throw the thing in the fire and be done with him. Something had convinced her instead to come. Now she was wondering if that was such a good idea.

He hadn't mentioned Kymara's name, not in the invitation nor yet tonight, but she was certain Andreas wanted to discuss her before the end of the night. Am I up to discussing her? She wondered.

Is he?

⸻

Her voice snapped him back to the present. Trimaris was the elder of the two—where her sister Kymara had been a pure soprano, Trimaris' voice was a deeper, smokier mezzo-soprano that flowed over him like late autumn sunshine. It was tinged with concern. He could only imagine the expression on his face.

"Sorry. Just reliving some old memories." He picked up his glass and took a sip, hoping the strong wine would stop the shaking in his hands. "Kymara enjoyed this room very much."

"I'm sure." Trimaris' voice flattened a bit. "Is that why you've invited me here, Andreas? To discuss my sister?"

"In part." Andreas gestured to his butler, who refilled his lord's glass. "But not until after dinner."

He raised his glass to his lips again, using the motion to conceal his small smile of triumph. Andreas could no longer see as normal people could; however, his magic allowed him to see the Power flows and swirls of the world around him, making the loss of his physical eyes a minimal one. No longer able to see details of people's expressions, no, but he could read their auras, and that was sometimes even more telling. People can learn to hide their true expressions. Disguising their aura was a lot more difficult.

Trimaris' aura was a jumble, displaying the emotions she was trying very hard to hide. Flashes of red, blue, green and violet danced around her as she struggled to keep her curiosity and her anger in check.

Twenty-three years ago, when he had returned to the Shadow Lands, Trimaris and her brother had been waiting for him. They knew Kymara had left with him, and they had known, with the searing of their shared blood, when she'd been killed. What they didn't know was why or how.

He'd hidden out at Alex's for several weeks, trying to get his own pain and rage under control while learning to function without his eyes. The time away had allowed him to concoct a tale explaining what had happened. Xavier had accepted his explanation of a spell gone wrong, although his aura had shouted his skepticism, but Trimaris had angrily denounced him. He hadn't been sure she would even come tonight.

Apparently, time had healed even that wound.

"I was surprised myself," he said, as one of the servants laid plates of savory venison steak in front of them. "I didn't expect you to come tonight, to be honest."

"I'm not sure why I did," she replied, and he heard the brittleness in her voice as she spoke. "I still believe you killed my sister."

"Trimaris, why would I have? I loved your sister." I wanted to make her my queen…. He broke off that line of thought; that door was closed to him now. All that was left was to carry on in her memory.

"Did you?" The Dawn Lord paused, looking at him. "Or did you use her, the way you seem to use everyone around you?"

"That's cold, Trimaris. I'm not trying to use anyone." Except my son, and you, but that's a different matter. "I'm trying to avenge her."

"Really?" She didn't sound convinced. "I find that hard to believe."

"Just trust me." Andreas laid his knife beside his plate and began to eat. "After dinner, I will lay everything out and show you that you have nothing to fear from me."

"I doubt that," Trimaris said, but she bent her head over the meal, and the rest of dinner passed in almost companionable silence.

What a challenge you will be, my dear! Andreas thought as he ate, watching the swirls of her aura out of the corner of his eyes. Your sister was all for this project. Convincing you to take her place will be a pleasurable undertaking, I'm sure.

Despite the loss of his eyes, he knew he was still a handsome man, tall and dark, with a solidly built body that he kept in shape. A little wine, some sweet nothings whispered in the dark, and you will be mine, little one.

After the bananas Foster had been served, he called for brandy and invited her up to his study. She sat back, her aura screaming her distrust of him in brilliant yellow.

"Upstairs? Please. Do you think I'll fall as rapidly into your bed as my sister did?" Scorn laced her voice with acid.

One could only hope. "No. I promise you, we're only going to my study. I find it easier to think upstairs. It's quieter."

He could feel the desire to defy him warring with her urge to know what truly happened to her sister and he decided to give her just a little more information. "The files upstairs are what your sister was working on when she died."

"What she was working on?" The scorn melted a little, into skepticism. "My sister never worked on anything."

"Trust me, Trimaris." Andreas rose and offered her his hand. "Kymara had a dream and she died trying to accomplish it. You deserve to know what she was doing."

Suspicion turned her aura light purple. "Why? Why are you telling me this now?"

His shoulders rose in a shrug. "I don't know." Because I need your help. "Maybe because it finally doesn't hurt as much to talk about her now."

It was the right thing to say. He could feel her skepticism starting to falter. "You mean you really did love her?"

"Yes."

"Convince me, Andreas." She stopped and looked straight at him. "Show me by telling me the truth of how she died."

Andreas smiled. "I thought you'd never ask."

She didn't resist as he led her up the ebony staircase, moving with the certainty that comes with time. He didn't stop until they entered his study and crossed to the desk, lit now by soft candles.

"You people all live in the dark," Trimaris complained, and he felt her hand move. Golden Power flashed from her aura to the various candles around the room, and he felt the room warm as the flames leapt up. Andreas chuckled as he sat at the desk and handed her the folder.

"And this is?" She held the folder, looking not at it, but at him. He gestured.

"You'll see."

He sat quietly as she crossed to the chair he had napped in earlier, settling in before opening the manila folder. Alex had been meticulous in documenting the experiment—the photos covered the entire spectrum of the eight months, culminating in the final blood-drenched scene. It was apparent when she came to that part. The flipping of the photographs ceased, and her aura darkened. Kymara had been laid to rest in on Earth; this was the first time Trimaris had seen what her sister's final fate was.

"Light of my ancestors."

The words were scarcely audible, and her aura had turned completely blue-white, the loss of her younger sister draining her of all emotion. Andreas waited, knowing what would come next.

Even though he was waiting for it, he missed the first soft sobs. Trimaris was trying to keep her grief private, but the sight of her sister lying in a pool of slowly congealing blood, her throat torn to shreds, golden hair turning sticky and black, was finally too much. Andreas moved over to her quietly, laying a hand on her shoulder in sympathy. She wrenched herself away from him, and he retracted the hand. Retreating backwards to his desk, he settled himself against the edge and waited.

Ask me. You know you want to.

"You spoke of revenge." When she finally spoke, it was in a voice harsh with tears. "Implying that you know who did this."

"Not yet." But I have my suspicions. "Sometimes, the best revenge is to finish what was started."

The skepticism was back in her voice, and her aura was shading back to purple. "Pardon my doubt, but these pictures were taken twenty-three years ago, Andreas. Are you telling me that you had these two women somewhere in suspended animation, waiting to finish the spells?"

He laughed softly. "Hardly, my dear. However, I do have the resources to start the project again. With your help."

"What project, Andreas?" Trimaris tossed the folder onto the small table beside her. "What were you doing with these women? What were they carrying, half-breeds?"

"Not exactly." Now would come the difficult part. "Kymara and I were breeding soldiers, Trimaris."

"Soldiers." She thought about it for a moment. "Why would you need soldiers, Andreas? Who were you and my sister planning on fighting?"

Everyone who got in our way. "It was an experiment, Trimaris. Kymara and I were exploring options for the next time the Cleansing came."

"Really?" Now her voice shifted from skeptical to amused. "Were you just planning for another apocalypse, Andreas, or do you have information you aren't sharing with the Council?"

Tread softly. "Just planning, Trimaris." He got up and went around the desk. Opening the drawer, he pulled the first scroll out and held it out to her. "We were experimenting with this."

It was a mistake—he saw her aura flare as she took the scroll, flashing to dark purple as touch confirmed what she was holding. "How dare you…."

That was as far as she got. Andreas' hand had moved in the short amount of time it had taken her to react; the onyx cube was in his hand, and shadows sprang out around her, wrapping her in their darkness. Once she was safely cocooned, he laid the cube back on the desk and moved to the sideboard, where his butler had left a bottle of dark red wine and two glasses.

"How dare I, Trimaris?" he said conversationally to the now-silent Dawn Lord as she struggled against his magic. "How dare I take the Summoning Scrolls from their chest in the Council House, and attempt to modify them? How dare I attempt to breed soldiers, imbued with Power no one else can comprehend?" Andreas turned back to her, glass in hand, and smiled. "Or how dare I involve your precious baby sister in so heinous a scheme? Is that it?"

Andreas walked over and laid his hand back on her shoulder, leaning down to whisper in her ear, "I suppose you don't want to hear that Kymara was not only a party to this, but she was a driving force? That your precious baby sister was actively plotting to tear away the façade of a government that is our Council, and replace it with one of our own?" Trimaris made a strangled sound. "I know, my dear. And yet, 'Queen' had such a nice ring to it that she really couldn't resist."

He went over to the mantel and took down an intricately carved box, barely the size of his own hand. The wood was cool against his skin, even after being above the fire that constantly burned in the flagstone fireplace. He had never seen it, or its contents—now, he turned back towards her, and said conversationally, "She was so looking forward to our coronation. You were going to be her first lady-in-waiting, you know."

Holding the box out in front of him, he advanced on the captive Dawn Lord, enjoying the rapid fluctuation of colors in her aura. Fear, anger, shock, horror—they chased each other in never-ending flashes of brilliant color as she sat pinned in her chair, unable to summon her own Gifts to combat the shadows that held her. That was the special power of the onyx cube: it was only good for one use at a time, but any Elemental Lord caught in its grasp was cut off from their Power source. He'd heard rumors of Elemental Lords dying in the cube's prison. Perhaps someday he'd have the chance to test the rumor. Not tonight, however.

"Just think, Trimaris. Instead of Queen Kymara, it could be Queen Trimaris. All you have to do is agree to help me."

A single word whispered under his breath, and the part of the spell holding her silent faded. "Why should I help you?" she spat. "You'll kill us all."

"That may be," Andreas allowed, smiling. "But let me put it to you this way, Trimaris. You can either help me."

He opened the box and heard her gasp.

"Or you can join her."

CHAPTER 3

"JOURNEY OF THE SOUL"

"Are you sure you have everything?"

Nikki slammed the trunk of her dark green Jeep Cherokee, rolled her eyes skyward in a request for patience, and turned to her father. He had asked the same question every time she'd packed the car to return to college, and despite multiple assurances, continued to ask it until she pulled out of the driveway. Why should this time be any different? She thought wryly.

Because now you know that you aren't really his daughter, whispered that little voice in her head that had shown up two days ago, right after her parents had dropped the bombshell of her adoption on her. She shook her head almost angrily; ignoring the voice was the only way she could deal with life right now.

"Yes, Dad," she said heavily, looking into his anxious eyes. "I'm sure."

"But," Marc started, and then stopped as his wife dug an elbow into his midsection.

"Enough, Marc. She'll be fine." Lara limped forward, leaning heavily on her cane, to embrace her daughter. As Nikki stepped back, her mother noted the shadows in her dark blue eyes, shadows that hadn't been there two days ago, and swallowed against the lump in her throat.

As if she could read her mind, Nikki leaned back in and whispered, "Don't worry, Mom. I'll be fine."

"I know." Lara took advantage of the moment to hug her tightly again. "It's just hard to let our little girl go."

"I'm not a little girl anymore, Mom. I'm 22, remember?"

"You'll always be my little girl," Lara said, stepping back to let Marc hug Nikki as well. "Don't forget to charge your phone, and let us know you're alive once in a while."

"I will."

Marc held his daughter as tightly as Lara had. "Are you going to search for her?" he murmured, and Nikki closed her eyes, burrowing her face into his shoulder.

"Not yet," she mumbled. "I need some time."

"I understand." He hugged her shoulders one last time and let her go. "Be good."

"I will." Nikki gave them a last watery smile and slid behind the wheel of the Cherokee. As she clicked her seatbelt snug and her father shut her door, a feelings washed over her—regret, and the certainty that no matter what she found on this trip, nothing would ever be the same.

Of course it won't, she told herself irritably. You can't change the fact that you're adopted.

Nikki stopped the car at the end of the driveway and looked back. The two most important people in her life were standing in the front garden she had helped her mother plant, the morning glories twining in blue and white splashes of color against the dark green of their leaves, the tulips and late daffodils golden in the background. The lilac tree behind her mother had just finished shedding its last dark purple flowers; underneath it, the ground was dark and shadowy, almost a hole in the otherwise perfect scene. Lara and Marc were waving; she waved back, but her mind was on the person that wasn't there.

Who is she? The thought that had been running almost non-stop through her head started up again. Why did she give me up? What about my father? Why didn't they ever try to find me? Should I try to find them? What if they don't want anything to do with me?

"It's not important right now," Nikki said out loud, hoping the sound of her own voice would drown out the one in her head. "I have a wonderful set of parents, and a book to write. I have a contract with deadlines, and a room at an inn waiting for me up in New Hampshire. If she's waited this long to meet me, she can damn well wait another six months." As if to underscore her determination, she turned on the radio, tuning it to her favorite country station. Toby Keith's deep, resonant voice filled the Jeep, and she began to sing along.

She stopped for gas at her favorite station before leaving town. The sun was bright but not too warm for the jeans and pale blue tee-shirt she wore. Her long dark hair was pulled back in a ponytail, and her sunglasses were perched on top of her head as she leaned against the side of her car. As she entered the station to pay, she inhaled eagerly; Mrs. Campbell, who owned the small station, had just finished making a new pot of hazelnut coffee.

"Oh, yum," Nikki murmured to herself, watching the dark liquid fill her cup. "I'm going to miss your coffee, Mrs. C." Then a familiar cologne drove the aroma from her nose and she groaned.

"Why, Nik, going somewhere?" Jack peered over her shoulder, ostensibly looking at her coffee. "Your Jeep's not that full."

Nikki turned and glared at him, grateful she was wearing a tee-shirt so he couldn't get a free look at her cleavage. "Don't you ever give up?"

She tried to push past him to the counter, and hissed angrily when he grabbed her elbow, jogging the cup of hot coffee in her hand. "It's over, Jack. Give it a rest, and get over it!"

"It doesn't have to be." he insisted. "I know your parents didn't like me, but…"

Understatement of the year! Lara and Marc had loathed everything about Jack, from his flashy Porsche to his short black hair, cut in the latest fashion, of course. But it was the wrong thing to say to her now.

"This has nothing to do with my parents!" she snapped, yanking her arm out of his hand and cursing as the coffee spilled on her wrist. Only a quick sidestep prevented her from wearing the rest of it, and supreme self-control kept her from throwing it in Jack's face. He put a hand on the small of her back and she twisted away from him, her blue eyes nearly black with anger. The coffeepot behind her shattered and the fury in her eyes actually caused Jack to back up a step in surprise.

"It has everything to do with the fact that you're a pompous ass, Jack Allen, and I want nothing more to do with you!" she continued, slamming the cup down on the counter. More coffee splashed, but Nikki was too furious to notice. There was a heaviness in her chest that she ignored as she snapped, "And yes, I am going away! Far enough away that you cannot follow me! So maybe I can finally get some peace!"

Jack stepped back again, apparently stunned by her reaction. For a moment, only the drip of Nikki's spilled coffee broke the silence; then Mrs. Campbell stepped into the station from the back room. The older woman took in the scene and asked quietly, "Is there a problem, Nikki?"

Nikki took a deep breath, struggling to get a hold of herself, and dropped the dripping cup in the trash. She picked up a few napkins and wiped off her arm before answering. "No, Mrs. C," she said finally, giving the woman a brittle smile and picking up her wallet. "I guess I just wasn't meant to have coffee this morning."

Jack opened his mouth and she held up a hand in warning. "Don't say anything, Jack, or I'll be forced to hit you, and then I'd miss my appointments, because I'd be in jail."

"Just for hitting me?" he scoffed, starting to get his bravado back now that the fire in her eyes was not aimed directly at him.

She paused at the door to look back at him, her dark blue eyes still full of flames, and he shrank back again. "Who said I'd stop with just hitting you?"

Irritating, narcissistic asshole! She fumed in the car a few minutes later, pounding on her steering wheel in time to the music, hoping it would soothe her. Leaving Kingsley is hard, but there are some benefits. Never running into Jack again is definitely one of them. What did I ever see in him??

Nikki and Jack had dated briefly in high school, when she'd thought he'd shared her love of photography. She'd soon discovered that it was only another way for him to get into a girl's pants, and the relationship had ended almost as quickly as it had begun. Unfortunately, he'd taken her distaste for him as her simply playing hard to get, and not even four years of college and several different boyfriends had convinced him that she wanted nothing to do with him.

I doubt even a husband would convince him that I really don't want to jump back in the sack with him. She shook her head in disgust and changed the radio station. Oh well, I won't be seeing him for a while, at least. No sense in dwelling on my personal past.

Nikki checked the clock; it was nearly 10 am. She'd left later than she'd planned, and the scene with Jack had eaten up more time. Thank God the inn is open late. This trip is going to take a while.

And it did, but part of the reason was that it was a glorious early summer day. Nikki stopped at a small deli somewhere in Central Massachusetts for a sandwich; she ate next to a small lake, her itinerary spread out on the grass around her. She had a list of haunted houses and graveyards to investigate in the White Mountains. She'd been compiling possible hauntings for the past couple of months, and had made appointments to see several in the next week. Her goal was to document the phenomena in the area with black and white photographs and her own words—a small press in Calgary had been interested enough in her proposal to give her a contract for the book. She'd passed up a trip to Europe to save for this; her father had been impressed enough with her dedication that he'd matched her savings penny for penny. Now, sitting in the bright sunlight, the remains of her tuna sub tossed into the lake for the ducks, she wondered how much she'd actually find.

It doesn't matter, she decided. Even if I don't find anything, it's still worth it. Who knows? Maybe I'll prove the existence of an afterlife once and for all!

Grinning at the boldness of that thought, Nikki gathered up her lunch things and turned back to her car … and stopped, fascinated.

A large black cat, easily the size of a small pony, had stepped out of the woods that surrounded most of the lake. She watched, fascinated, as it picked its way delicately among the wildflowers towards the mostly empty parking lot where Nikki's car was parked. The attendant at the deli had recommended this picnic spot to her when she'd bought her sandwich, mentioning that it was a good place to see wildlife; as the cat continued to saunter towards the other side of the lot, she realized that he was right.

I didn't know jaguars could get that big! Hard on that thought came the realization that jaguars weren't native to New England. God above, what is that?

As if it heard her, the great cat paused and looked over at her. Even in the sunlight, its eyes glowed green. Nikki just stared, hoping it wasn't going to charge her.

Lord, what a beautiful creature!

It was a stunning picture: golden sunlight poured over the green swatch of lakeside and dusty dirt parking lot, her dark green Jeep and the black cat in stark relief against the brilliance of the sky. Too bad my camera's in the car!

The cat looked away and strolled into the trees, looking as if it were simply out for an afternoon constitutional. As it melted into the shadows under the trees, Nikki let out the breath she'd been holding. Her fingers trembled slightly as she fit her key into the lock on the Jeep; once she was safely inside and the doors were all locked, the full impact of the scene crashed down on her. It took nearly five minutes before she could control her shivering enough to start the Jeep.

"Hell of a greeting," she muttered, and jumped at the sound of her own voice. Then she drew a deep breath and started out of the parking lot.

The rest of the drive passed in relative normalcy, but with traffic and the small bookstore that Nikki discovered later in the afternoon, it was twilight before she turned onto the small one-lane road that the Connor House Inn was located on. The trees huddled up next to the pavement, and a light mist curled around their trunks as she drove slowly down the winding road. *Okay, if I start hearing harp music, I'm leaving!*

There was a sudden break in the trees, and a large house rose out of the gathering darkness, aglow with welcoming lights. There were several cars parked in the small lot next to the house—as Nikki pulled up to the front steps, a large yellow Lab came bounding out, barking a joyful greeting. *Definitely NOT the house from my dreams. Thankfully.*

Following the Lab, who slobbered his greeting all over Nikki's outstretched hands, was a young woman with long blonde hair, looking like a Renaissance angel in her white poet's shirt and painter's pants. "Welcome!" she called, her light voice cutting across the dog's whines of pleasure as Nikki scratched his ears. "I see you've already met the welcoming committee. Jonathan! Get down!"

Jonathan blissfully ignored his owner, who chuckled and held a hand out to Nikki. "I'm Sarah Connor, your hostess. And you must be Nikki Jeffries."

"Guilty as charged," Nikki grinned, warming instantly to Sarah. "Sorry I'm running late. It was too nice a day to hurry."

"Agreed. Don't worry about it—we're pretty much night owls around here anyways." Sarah reached down and snagged Jonathan's collar, dragging him away from Nikki. "Sorry about that. We haven't been able to convince Jonathan here that not everyone likes to be drooled on."

"That's okay. We had a Lab down the street who used to do the same."

Sarah leaned over and looked at the boxes in the back of the Jeep. "Is this the developing equipment you warned us about?"

"Yup." Nikki joined her next to the Jeep. "Is it going to be a problem?"

The innkeeper shook her blonde head. "Not at all. After we got off the phone, I went and finished up the other bathroom on the second floor. You and Rick will be the only ones on that floor, and I doubt we'll see him very often. Too bad, really—you guys seem to have a lot in common, and he's a cutie."

Nikki ignored the cutie comment politely and opened the back of the Jeep. "I don't know how often you'll see me, either. I plan on being out a lot, and spending the rest of my time writing and in the darkroom."

Sarah took the hint, but smiled. "Rick's a writer too. We seem to be developing our own little arts program; maybe we should explore that market." She looked at the boxes again, and then turned to the house. "Chuck! Come and help!"

Chuck Connor was as blonde as his wife, tall and athletic, with a farmer's tan. Between the three of them, they got the Jeep emptied in about twenty minutes, and then Sarah sent Chuck to park the car while she showed Nikki her room.

"I thought this might be the best, since it attaches to the bathroom," she said, flipping on the light. Nikki, her duffel bag slung over her shoulder and her suitcase in her hand, paused, enchanted.

The room was small, but airy: there was one large window, a dormer window, with a seat set into the bottom that looked out on the back yard. The walls were light blue, with a swirling pattern to the paint that reminded Nikki of clouds. The bed was a four-poster canopy, dressed in a dark purple comforter that looked sinful. There was a desk set against the wall opposite the bed, under another smaller window that Sarah told her looked out over the orchard.

"The window seat looks out on the garden," she said, setting Nikki's laptop bag on the desk. "Will it do?"

Nikki blinked and slowly entered the room. "I'm just wondering if I'll actually get any writing done."

"Is something wrong?" Sarah's eyes were worried, and Nikki hastened to smile.

"No, nothing. It's just so nice…I'm not sure I'll be able to write about hauntings and things like that!"

The worry passed, and Sarah returned Nikki's smile with one of her own. "Sorry, the dungeons are being redone, so this was the best I could do."

Nikki chuckled and then yawned. "Must be more tired than I thought."

"I'll let you finish unpacking, then." Sarah left, shutting the door quietly behind her.

Another yawn and Nikki decided to leave unpacking until the next morning. She pulled a clean tee-shirt and her toiletry bag out and after a quick wash, tumbled into bed.

The crescent moon had risen by now, and it streamed in silver through the dormer window. Nikki leaned back against the fluffy pillows, her eyes already beginning to close. The moon swam against the wispy clouds, changing as she watched it, growing more golden and fuller, until it was a pumpkin moon, hanging behind the tall trees around her. She shook her head, bemused, and the wind that whispered between the branches lifted the stray strands of hair from across her face.

She turned slowly, realizing she was back in the woods as leaves crunching under her boots. Mist curled around her legs, damp even through her jeans, and she shivered. Then the wind passed through again and on its wings, the first harp notes sang to her.

Not again, she thought, feeling slightly panicky. They weren't supposed to follow me—the dreams were supposed to stay home!

The music coiled around her, wrapping her in a cocoon of notes, faint but perfectly audible, a minor key that somehow soothed her and calmed her fear. She turned back towards the moon, looking down the narrow path and could almost see the notes floating on the air, beckoning her on.

Nikki followed the path as it wandered among trees trapped in their skeletal phase, leaves rattling a warning at her passing. Then, as the wood began to thin, the darkness deepened—the moon, always retreating before her, started to fade behind the house that rose up before her. She stepped out of the trees onto the beginnings of the lawn, stared up at the façade, and caught her breath.

It was one of the old antebellum mansions she'd seen in pictures, painted a faded white, with a wide front porch and columns rising along the veranda. It wasn't the house she'd seen the last time but like the other, this one called to her. She started forward, then felt the prickling on her back and stopped.

This time the woman was on the hill to her right, standing next to a single tree that raised its arms to the dark sky. Nikki turned towards her; as before, she was wrapped in shadows. This time they were from the tree that sheltered her; in the dimness, her eyes glowed as clearly as ever.

Welcome back.

Nikki started towards the tree, but a second pair of eyes, green as the first, glowed out of the branches, startling her. She strained to penetrate the shadows; after a moment, she could see a faint outline. A feline body stretched on the branch, one paw hanging down lazily towards the woman beneath it, and her breath caught in her throat.

The cat from the lake!

Indeed. The woman projected amusement. *I was most impressed* with you this afternoon. Most would have panicked and ran.

This is only a dream! Nikki's own eyes narrowed. I don't know what my subconscious is trying to tell me, but I'm starting to get a bit irritated!

And are you so sure this is a product of your own mind?

The simple question stopped her cold. What else would it be?

What indeed.

And as she watched, the shadows began to dissolve, running down the edges of her vision like paint dissolving under a stream of turpentine. Nikki fell back into darkness, reaching out for the steady green eyes that watched her until everything faded to black....

———

"Dr. Richards?"

Dr. Sylvia Richards turned as the young security guard came running up the corridor. "I've got a message for you, Dr. Richards."

He thrust the small slip of paper into her hand, saluted and then ran off again. She stood there in the hall, shocked for a moment.

The security guards don't salute me. They've never saluted me. The piece of paper in her hand stared up at her like a guilty conscience. This is either the promotion I was hoping for, or my pink slip.

Does Masterson pink-slip in absentia?

It would fit with what she'd heard of the reclusive owner of Gene-Tech. He was rarely seen anywhere but the secured wing of the facility: the techs whispered that he'd been terribly injured in the explosions that had destroyed part of the secure wing twenty-three years ago, and had had extensive plastic surgery to cover it. Of course, they also whispered that he was not entirely human, and that black magic was the cause of said explosions. Sylvia usually dismissed the entire conversation; she'd joined Gene-Tech because they were on the cutting edge of combining magic and science, something the rest of the world was only beginning to research. Even though most of the scientific community was now ready to admit magic existed and worked, there was still enough stigma attached to the word in the rest of the world that many of the major institutes were being very slow in initiating their programs.

She turned the piece of paper over and read the brief message scrawled on the back.

"You are being reassigned to a new project. Please gather your personal effects and report to the guard station at the entrance to Delta

Wing immediately."

Delta Wing? That's the secure wing!

The piece of paper trembled. Despite the curtness of the message, Sylvia felt a thrill of excitement run through her. These twenty-six words represented what she'd been working towards the last ten years of her life. She crumpled it in her hand and took off for her office.

Twenty minutes later, a small box in her arms, she presented herself at the guard station. Each wing had its own entrance, manned by a guard; Delta Wing's station had three guards, each carrying a loaded machine gun. She was patted down by one while another held his gun on her; the third went through her box meticulously. The security didn't shock her; what did was the thrill along her senses that told her a magical scan was being run on her as well. She snuck a glance at the third guard; the slight blurring of his edges was a telltale sign that he too was doing magical scans as he went through her belongings.

Where did he find magical security guards? And why? A niggling suspicion that the rumors of black magic might be true tried to rear its head and was immediately squashed by her practical side. Magic was neither black nor white; the caster who summoned the energy determined how it was to be used. Sylvia stood and waited while they checked her against their files; finally, one of them nodded his head and waved her through the wrought-iron gate.

Iron? How paranoid IS this guy?

Most magical facilities tended to shy away from using iron and its derivatives in their construction; its ability to "ground" magical energy made working around it obnoxious to most mortal Mages. Sylvia had heard stories of some Mages being so bothered by the drainoff that they lost all ability to work magic near the material.

"Dr. Richards?"

The guard's voice broke through her thoughts; she'd been staring at the gate bemusedly. Sylvia started guiltily and grabbed her box.

"Sorry."

He shrugged and nodded to one of the other guards. "Please follow me, Dr. Richards."

The corridors he led her down were cold—not just in temperature, but in attitude. Sylvia could feel the lacings of iron through the foundations. Alex Masterson must be very, very worried about magical interference to have spent so much money in security measures. She wondered briefly how it was going to be working in this environment.

"Do you know what project I'm being assigned to?" she asked the guard, more to hear a voice than to get an answer.

"No, ma'am."

And nothing more, she thought wryly. Oh, this is going to be fun.

He stopped suddenly and opened a door; only excellent balance kept her from running into him. He motioned her in; she swallowed, her throat suddenly dry.

"Well, come in, dammit! We haven't got all day."

The well-cultured baritone sounded irritated, to say the least. Alex Masterson, I presume. The tone stung; she straightened unconsciously and entered the room.

The office was huge and paneled in mahogany. A large cherry desk was up against one wall; there were bookcases, filing cabinets and another, smaller desk against the others. A large table dominated the center of the room. Standing beside the table, tapping one foot impatiently, was the man who'd hired her six years ago via a proxy. The man who paid her paychecks but that she, like many of the other younger researchers, had never actually seen. Sylvia allowed herself the luxury of staring at him for a moment.

Alex Masterson was tall, and if he had been injured in the explosions twenty-three years ago, he'd been either incredibly lucky or had phenomenal plastic surgeons. Although she knew he was supposed to be in his sixties, his unlined face appeared no older than a man in his mid-thirties, if that. The whisper of rumor began again and this time, looking at his dark glossy hair and dark eyes, it was harder to quiet, but her will asserted itself and silenced it.

"Does the room suit you?"

The sound of his voice, a baritone that could drown one if it hadn't had the acid edge of impatience laced through it, stung her back to life. She looked around again, seeing the room for the first time.

"I guess. Will I be working here?" Great, Richards, real brilliant. Did you think he invited you down here to talk about the weather?

Masterson smiled ironically. "Yes, my dear Dr. Richards. You will be heading Gene-Tech's newest research project. As such, you now have an office that reflects your station. If you perform well, this is only the beginning of the rewards I am prepared to hand out." He gave the room a brief disinterested glance. "You have the rest of today to get yourself set up. The pertinent files are in the top drawer of your desk. They are not to leave the facility. The rest of your team will be assembled at 9 am tomorrow morning for a preliminary briefing, which will be in the small conference room down the hall. I will be attending most of your meetings, so I expect you to be prepared." Then before she could say anything, he nodded curtly, pushed by her and left the room.

Sylvia stood there for a moment longer, her box in her hands, absorbing everything he'd just said. Well, it sounds like I got my promotion, she thought wryly, setting the box down on the table and going over to her desk. Wonder who the other desk's for?

And why me? I'm not even the most senior! This thought was followed swiftly by, If he thinks he can push me around just because I'm one of the newer members here, he has another thing coming!!

Another one of Masterson's foibles, according to the rumor mill, was a misogynistic streak a mile wide. Judging by her introduction, that rumor wasn't too far off the mark. Which raises the question of how many others are closer to the truth than you thought, Sylvia?

She shook her head and sat down, running her fingers over the glossy desktop, enjoying the feel of the rich wood. "Well, Sylvia, if all you have to deal with is a misogynistic asshole as a boss, and this is the beginning of the perks, I think you'll do just fine." Reaching into the top drawer, she pulled out an aged manila folder, stuffed with bits of parchment. "Good lord, what is this mess?"

The folder looked ready to disintegrate in her hands, and there was a faint musty odor that rose from it as she opened it gingerly. The tag on the top of the folder said "Soldier Project"; as the edge of the folder touched the top of her desk, the tag fell off and floated down to the floor, where it crumbled into dust.

Looking at the pile of dust on the floor, Sylvia felt a slight shiver. Hope that's not an omen. Then she smiled at her own whimsy. Come on, we've got a lot of work to do before tomorrow morning.

Turning back to the folder, she pulled a memo pad and a pen and began to read, jotting notes in bold, black ink. Beside her on the floor, the pile of dust began to fall in upon itself, unnoticed, and vanished into the floor.

Cassandra's Prelude

"Shadow Hunt"

Cassandra sits besides the pool, her dark wood harp a shadow against her silken white robes. Her long dark hair is loose, flowing down over her back to brush against the moonflowers that droop down from their vines, growing over the small scrying pool that someone placed in this grove a long, long time ago, before even this ancient Shadow Lord was a child. The water is very still, almost glass. If there are secrets to be revealed, this is where they will come.

The spell of Foresight is forbidden to all but the most powerful of the Lords—the veils of Time and Space do not take lightly to being pulled aside by those who walk the Realms, even the great Elemental Lords. There is something going on in the Realms, though; something dark is afoot. For the life of her, she cannot figure out what it is, but a suspicion deep within her murmurs that she must try.

She sets fingertips to the silver strings, coaxing the first whispers of sound from the harp that has been her companion since before she can remember. A minor key, a spell for thinning the walls between Times and teasing out the possibilities of what might yet be. A song of potential, of roads that may or may not yet be taken.

The song is complex and multi-toned, yet amazingly simple and achingly pure. It rises above the harpist to float out on the breeze that never ceases to blow through the Shadows, gathering information on single notes and bringing them back to the pool, which has started to swirl lazily at her feet. Cassandra's fingers drop; the harp continues to play the spell as the Shadow Lord watches the results unfurl.

The white clouds grow dark as they coalesce in the pool; the scene shimmers into being, and her green eyes grow shadowed as she watches nine Lords, three from each Realm, gather around a large boulder. There is no sound, but she can see their lips moving as they chant.

They raise their arms; the boulder shimmers and then splits into four figures, figures of legend. Red, white, yellow and black: four horses, with skeletal riders on their back. War, Plague, Famine and Death—once again, the Four Horsemen are summoned to cleanse the land and restore the Balance.

There has not been a Cleansing in many years. Cassandra thinks back to the last; even with all her years, she can barely remember it. As she watches, the Horsemen ride out of the circle, and the scene dissolves back into spinning clouds. The melody plays on; this spell is not yet complete.

The clouds change again. This time, red bloody devastation rolls before her eyes like a cinema gone horribly wrong. The Realms have been destroyed; as far as her eyes can see, there is only scorched earth, curling smoke and faintly glowing rocks. Nothing moves... wait.

She leans forward as two people appear at the edge of the vision. Their faces are blurred, but they wear robes of a fashion she knows as well as her own. These are Lords, but of what, she cannot tell. One is light and one dark, but there is no color in this desolate landscape.

The smoke lowers across the scene. Everything goes dark, and the music begins to falter. The walls between Times are beginning to resist her intrusion; very soon, her song will be swallowed by eternity and the vision will end. Cassandra leans forward, hoping for one more scene, more information that she can use to piece together her uneasiness.

The pool remains dark; she fears that her time is up, and then a single face swims into view. A pale, human face, framed by long dark hair; dark blue eyes stare into Cassandra's green ones, almost real enough for the Shadow Lord to reach out and touch. Shadows caress the face, and it turns, losing its edges as the darkness seeks to embrace it.

There is a loud snap! Cassandra jumps; the song is finished, and one string of the harp hangs limply, broken by angry Time, a price for her arrogance in thinking she could hope to control the future.

The Shadow Lord sits, deep in thought, pondering what she has seen.

Chapter 4

"A Change in the Wind"

"Nothing. Just like the last twenty rolls."

Nikki tossed aside the pictures in disgust, adding them to the growing pile on her desk, and sighed heavily. Outside the bow window, the weather echoed her mood—rain fell steadily, coating the world in grey, more suited to November than June. Below her, the flowers in Sarah's garden bowed their heads against the wet onslaught; the bright colors of the tulips, roses, dahlias and phlox muted now, watercolors rather than acrylics in the beautifully landscaped garden. Nikki leaned her face against the cool glass, fancying she could feel the rain washing away the evidence she was looking for.

A week into my search, and I've found nothing, she thought sourly. *An entire week. Lord, I hope the rest of my trip isn't like this!*

At least I followed my mother's advice, came her next thought. *So when I have an afternoon like this, I can throw in the towel, go downstairs and forage for the Ben & Jerry's that I know Sarah bought yesterday.*

Suiting actions to words, she left the pictures and the rain, ending up in the warm kitchen, eating New York Super Fudge Chunk and pouring out her troubles to her hostess as she made chocolate chip cookies.

"So now I don't know what to do," she finished, watched Sarah scoop out round balls of dough onto yet another cookie sheet. "I've gone through six houses so far. Nothing. Not a single interesting photo. Not even a blip on my light meter. What a waste."

"How far are you into your list?" Sarah asked her, carefully sliding out one sheet from the oven and replacing it with the sheet she'd just finished. There was still a huge amount of dough in her bowl, and an equally impressive mountain of cookies cooling on racks around her spacious kitchen. Nikki licked the remains of a ribbon of fudge from her spoon and regarded the mountain, thinking.

"Well, I have a couple of books upstairs that I need to go through," she said finally. "I've only really scratched the surface. I just feel like I'm treading water and going nowhere."

"That's what usually happens when you tread water," Sarah pointed out dryly. She pulled a warm cookie off the rack in front of her and handed it to Nikki. "Here. Warm chocolate chip cookies solve everything that Ben & Jerry's doesn't."

"Warm chocolate chip cookies?" came a new voice, a male one, and Nikki and Sarah both jumped as a young man with dark amber eyes and dark blonde hair poked his head around the kitchen door, a shy half-smile on his handsome face. "Did I hear warm chocolate chip cookies being offered? I'm in definite need of their healing powers."

"I'll bet you are," Sarah said wryly, handing him a cookie as he came into the kitchen. "I know you, Richard Kinsey Jackson. You can smell cookies a mile away."

"Your cookies, Sarah, most indubitably," he replied unabashedly, the smile spreading to the other side of his full mouth. He took a bite and shuddered in sheer pleasure, then planted a kiss full of melted chocolate on her cheek. "Wonderful, as always. I swear, Sarah, your cookies could stop a war."

"Flatterer." Sarah wiped the chocolate off her face with a hand towel and then snapped the towel at his hand as he took another cookie. "Compliments will not get me to let you eat all of these."

"Why are you making so many, Sarah?" Nikki asked, as her hostess shooed him towards the table and pulled yet another cookie sheet towards her.

"There's a bake sale for the middle school tomorrow," she said, dropping more neat balls onto the sheet. "I'm donating as many as I can."

"You're so charitable, Sarah," Rick said, winking at Nikki. "I swoon in your divine light."

"Some day, Rick, your mouth is going to get you into a situation you can't talk your way out of, and the rest of us will laugh our asses off," Sarah told him, her blue eyes dancing. "Probably your wedding day."

Rick shuddered. "Heaven forbid. I intend to be the old bachelor cousin that hangs around the rugrats you and Chuck are planning on having. I wouldn't wish my genes on anyone."

"In case you haven't figured it out yet, this reprobate is not only our other writer, but he's my cousin," Sarah said to Nikki, who was watching this tête-à-tête with wide eyes. "Rick, this is Nikki, the other writer I was telling you about. Be nice—she's a paying guest, unlike some in this room I could name."

"I'm a paying guest," he protested, winking again at Nikki.

"I meant she's paying to stay here, twit. Not you making me pay every time I turn around." Sarah turned back to her cookies, but not before she too winked at Nikki, who realized that this must be standard operating procedure for the two.

So they're cousins, she mused, leaning back and looking at him as he continued to banter with Sarah. How very interesting. No wonder she's been hinting I should come down and meet him at some point.

Sarah's hints had been fairly subtle at first; but as she and Nikki had gotten to know each other, the hints had gotten less understated, until they'd reached the point of padded bricks being thrown at her head. Looking at him now, Nikki wondered why Sarah thought she had to find her cousin dates; with his long dark blonde hair, pulled back in a careless ponytail that hung to mid-back, and his dark amber eyes, glinting with wicked mischief, Rick Jackson didn't seem like it would take much for him to get a girl, if he wanted.

Maybe he's gay….

She shook her head and grinned. Who cares? I'm here to write, not find a guy!

Although I wouldn't mind waking up next to him one morning….

The line of her own thoughts amazed her. Nikki prided herself on keeping a cool head; even when she was attracted to someone, she tended to step back and weigh the pros and cons of the relationship very carefully before even considering something intimate. That this thought should have popped into her head after only five minutes in his presence was a little startling.

"So, Nikki, Sarah says you're a ghost hunter."

The remark was casual, but she caught a glimpse of his eyes as he said it, and the seriousness in them startled her. "I suppose so," she replied cautiously. "Why?"

He shrugged. "Just making small talk." His half-smile quirked at her again, and she smiled back, responding instinctively to its warmth.

"Sarah's always after me to be polite."

His cousin staggered back in the middle of pulling another sheet of cookies out. "Oh my Lord! You actually listened to something I said!"

"Yeah, well, some things do sink in, if they're said often enough. Even through my hard head," Rick joked, and Sarah tossed the spare oven mitt at him. He caught it deftly and sent it flying back at her; she caught it, shaking her head.

He chuckled and turned back to Nikki. "Seriously, though, how've you been doing?"

Nikki shrugged, a little uncomfortable for some reason. "It's been a slow week," she said finally.

"Where have you gone?"

She raised one dark eyebrow. "Why?"

"Rick's a bit of an expert in this area," Sarah said quickly, before he could respond. "I can't believe I didn't think of asking him to help you!"

Nikki couldn't help it; she winced. The bricks had just lost their padding. The only thing that made the situation a little better was that Rick winced with her.

"Maybe later." The kitchen had just gotten too close, despite its size—Nikki rose and smiled sincerely (she hoped) at both of them. "I think I'll go and see if Jonathan wants to go for a run."

"Real subtle, Sarah," she heard Rick say as she ran out of the kitchen. "Why didn't you just ask her..."

The kitchen door shut behind her, cutting off whatever he was going to say. Luckily, Jonathan was waiting out front for her, almost as if he'd sensed what she wanted. She grabbed his leash and fled, something in the back of her mind wondering why.

"Real subtle, Sarah." Rick shook his head and took another cookie. "Why didn't you just ask her if she's seeing someone and get it over with?"

"She's not. I found that out three nights ago." Sarah glared at him. "Which you would have known, if you'd ever come out of your room. Jesus, Rick, you're a freaking hermit lately!"

"I've got a deadline, Sarah, remember? Books don't write themselves." He shook his head. "I don't have time for dating."

"Oh, and your deadline is when? December?" She shot back. "It's a freaking fantasy novel! How hard can it be?"

"Tell you what, Sarah—you come and write it, and I'll squire your little friend around, okay?" Rick got up and stomped out of the kitchen, leaving his cousin to shout creative insults at his back.

Her voice followed him through the slammed kitchen door to the front door; he slammed that one too, just to prove his point, and then stomped out into the garden, where he threw himself down in a lawn chair.

He jumped up again almost immediately; the rain had stopped, but the clouds were still gathered in the sky above, and the humid air hadn't dried the lawn furniture at all. The invectives that flowed from his lips were almost hot enough to dry the seat of his pants on their own.

Why can't she leave it be! He thought to himself angrily, settling for pacing up and down on the soggy path. She knows I'm not ready for another relationship—not after what Madeline did to me. Christ, she hardly knows this girl! Can she think I'm that hard up already?

"It's only a freaking fantasy novel" Only!!! Rick pounded his hand against an unoffending cherry tree and swore again as cold water dropped down on him from the still-wet leaves. Sarah has no clue what writers go through.

I'll bet Nikki does, though, a small voice teased in his head. Rick blinked, wondering where in the hell that thought had come from. For a moment, a vision of deep blue eyes swam before him, and a frisson of something caught somewhere between fear and desire wiggled its way down his back.

What the hell?

The second feeling came hot on the heels of the first; Rick caught just the edge of it, recognized it for what it was, and dropped to his knees right before the vision hit.

It always hurt less when he had a shorter distance to fall.

—————

Jonathan ran her hard, rejoicing in the fact that Nikki showed no inclination to head back to the inn until they were both breathing so heavily that they couldn't just stop, but had to turn around and walk slowly back. Her dark hair was matted with sweat and the random splashes of water that had fallen from the trees around the road. Her shirt was plastered to her back, and her back and legs were sore, but the run had chased the nagging thoughts of Rick from her mind for the moment, and for that alone, Nikki was thankful.

She ambled back along the quiet country road, Jonathan now content to merely pace beside her, his frantic energy spent for a bit. The air was soft now that the rain was moving out; the countryside was beginning to wake up, moving from November back up to June.

I'm reading way too much into things, she decided, stopping to smell a rain-drenched primrose. Sarah's just trying too hard, that's all. I'll go back and apologize to both of them. I'm sure he's a nice guy.

Her thoughts streamed along like that until she hit the inn's front gate. She opened the door, unhooked Jonathan's leash, and glanced into the garden as he ran inside.

That's when she saw Rick lying unconscious on the wet moss.

"Sarah!" she screamed, dropping the leash and running over to his side. Nikki dropped to her knees; he was still breathing, ragged and hard, like he'd been running, and his face was screwed up in a grimace of pain. His skin was pale and ashy; shaken, she screamed again, "Sarah!"

The innkeeper came bursting out of the house, followed by Jonathan, and took in the scene in an instant. "Don't touch him!" she ordered Nikki, grabbing her hand. "He's fine."

"He's what?" Nikki yanked her hand away, horrified. "He's not fine—he's having some sort of fit or something!"

"A vision," Sarah said curtly, all trace of the meddling cousin gone as she knelt on the other side of Rick and kept Jonathan back. The Lab whined anxiously. "It's a vision. We have to let him come out of it on his own."

"A vision? He's a seer?" Seers were rare; even lately, when it seemed there was a new Mage or psychic discovered daily, seers were seldom found, and once they were, the universities usually fell all over each other in an attempt to gain the chance to study them. Once their talent bloomed, most seers never saw the outside world again.

"Not exactly." Sarah chewed on her lip, watching her cousin intently. "But he has visions every once in a while."

Nikki sat back on her heels, watching Rick twitch and moan. "How long do they take?"

"As long as they take."

Sarah's voice, flat and clipped, didn't invite any more questions. This was a side of the innkeeper Nikki hadn't seen before; she closed her lips on the rest of the questions aching to get out and sat in silence with her.

Their vigil lasted nearly ten minutes; Nikki felt an odd relief wash over her when Rick finally shuddered and opened his amber eyes to stare up blankly at them. Sarah shot her another look, warning her silently to keep her questions to herself; Nikki nodded mutely and helped her pull her cousin to his feet and then into the house.

Sarah guided them both to the living room; Rick was a dead weight between them. After that first look, his eyes had closed again; his feet were moving, but barely. Nikki was reminded of the last party she and Monica had thrown before her friend had gotten pregnant; Tom had really gotten sloshed, and it had taken both of them to get him to bed.

If this is magic, I'm not sure I want any part of it, she thought, studying his pale face. *At least the grey has gone, but he looks like death warmed over too many times.*

"Ready to talk about it?" Sarah asked her cousin once they had him tucked onto one end of the couch, a warm handmade quilt wrapped around him. Rick opened one bleary eye to stare at her and shuddered.

"Nikki, go put tea water on." Sarah shook her head. "There's a small tin of blackberry sage tea in the cabinet. And put a shot of the blackberry brandy in it—he needs to warm up."

Nikki gave her a surprised look, and the innkeeper nodded. "Trust me. He's done this before. I'm just glad you found him as soon as you did—he might not get sick this time."

"Okay." Nikki gave up trying to understand and hurried into the kitchen. Once the sound of water indicated that she was occupied, Sarah turned back to Rick.

"Talk," she commanded. "She's gone. You don't have to worry about her hearing your precious secrets."

"There are no secrets," he mumbled, the one eye already closed again. "We can't afford secrets."

"What are you talking about?" Sarah's voice sharpened with worry. Nikki, about to come back into the living room, paused at the door, not wanting to intrude.

"She's special, Sarah," Rick continued in a voice wrapped in cotton. "We have to keep her safe."

"Safe from what?"

Nikki strained to hear the answer, but the kettle began to whistle. Cursing her luck, she ducked back into the kitchen and poured the tea, adding honey and a generous dollop of the brandy Sarah kept "for medicinal reasons." Then she paused, looking out the window to the back garden.

She didn't want me to hear what he said, she thought, chewing on her bottom lip. Why? Because she's afraid I'll flip out and tell someone? Or just up and leave?

There was definitely something strange going on here. Granted, Nikki didn't really have any experience with magic, but Sarah should have realized that if she was up here hunting ghosts, she probably wasn't going to have a problem with magic either.

Then again, she might think I'm hunting ghosts to disprove or destroy them. In which case, I might have either freaked or called the God Squad in.

Thoughts of that group gave even a mundane like Nikki the shudders. The God Squad was a group of ultra-religious scientists who were looking for a "cure" for magic. They were currently on the run from the authorities for several "experiments" that ended up with the subjects dead, but there were others who were trying to take their place. Not everyone was happy with the new influence magic was wielding in the world.

As if it were reading her mind, the classical station that had been playing on the radio stopped for a news break. "Police are still looking into the clandestine laboratory found in the outskirts of Laconia Friday night. Officials have been reluctant to comment on speculations that the lab had been used by the scientists known as the God Squad, but at least one unofficial source has confirmed that three bodies were found in the building. In other news, Alex Masterson has donated another $3 million to the Children's Hospital in Boston. The money will be used to complete the new cancer wing for children born with magical abilities. Over the past four years, Masterson and his company, Gene-Tech, have donated more than $20 million to the hospital for projects beneficial to what are now being called 'Talented' children."

The tea was cooling in her hands; with a start, Nikki pulled the tea bag out and tossed it in the trash. She brought the tea out to Rick, who was still leaning back, his eyes closed. As she pressed the warm mug into his hands, his eyes opened; for a moment, amber eyes locked with blue, and the world vanished. "Don't go anywhere alone," he said. "Promise me."

"I promise."

The instant the words were out of her mouth, the feeling vanished. Suddenly aware of everything, Nikki and Rick stared at each other, wondering what had just happened.

Sarah cleared her throat, causing both of them to jump. Rick's hands lost control of the mug; it fell to the hardwood floor, shattering into pieces with a retort like a gunshot.

"Shit!" Rick swore, pulling his legs up and trying to get the edges of the blanket out of the pool of tea on the floor. "Jesus, Sarah, I'm sorry."

"Don't worry about it." Sarah shook her head and went to get a broom and some towels after telling Nikki not to move.

"Why did you say that?" Nikki asked, once their hostess was gone.

Rick's color was slowly coming back, but there were huge dark circles under his eyes. "I don't know," he replied. "I just know that I had to." He looked up at her from the couch. "Answer me a question."

"I'll try."

"Who are you, Nikki Jeffries, that just seeing you triggers visions?"

The question, even though it was serious, sounded so like the melodramatic lines that Jack had favored that it tweaked her sense of the absurd. She tried hard to stifle the giggle that welled up inside her, but after a moment, surrendered to it.

Rick looked at her for a moment, but the laughter was infectious. Sarah came back to find both of them doubled over, laughing hysterically. She gave them a strange look, cleaned up the pieces of mug on the floor and then retreated back to the kitchen, as if she didn't want to catch whatever they had.

Nikki finally stopped laughing, pressing her hand to her side. She had slumped into the easy chair across the room, and now she and Rick looked at one another, tears of laughter sliding down their faces. Rick's color had returned; he was curled up on the couch, trying very hard to keep from laughing again.

"I'm sorry," Nikki said. "I know you didn't mean it, but that sounded…"

"Like a bit from a really bad romantic comedy," he finished. "I know. I wanted to kick myself as soon as it came out."

———

Her mouth twitched again, and he watched as she surrendered to the smile. But I was serious, his thoughts continued. Who are you, and why did just seeing you trigger that vision?

He shook his head; time enough for that later. Nikki was leaning back in her chair, much more at ease than she had been before. She seemed to have forgotten the vision and Sarah's matchmaking; watching her now, he was struck by just how striking she was.

The chair was a beige color; her long dark hair lay against it like black silk, showing off her lightly-tanned skin to perfection. She was clad in a tee that proudly proclaimed "Basketball is life. Everything else is details," and a pair of cut-off jeans that showed just how slim her legs were. Her face was dominated by her eyes—deep, clear blue eyes, with just a hint of a shadow in them; eyes that seemed to sparkle when she laughed.

It would be very easy to fall into those eyes and not come out....

No! He shook his head, and she quirked a dark eyebrow. "Problems?"

"Just weird thoughts. Sorry, I tend to zone a lot."

She shrugged. "Comes with the territory." At his questioning look (although he couldn't raise an eyebrow, he could and did do a very good puzzled frown), Nikki clarified, "With being a writer. I zone out a lot too."

Ahh, a safe topic. Rick started to relax again. "So, tell me about your writing. Sarah told me a bit, but you said you were going slowly."

"Only if you tell me about yours," she countered.

"Fair enough."

The clouds began to break up as they talked the afternoon away. By the time the aroma of the meatloaf Sarah was making for dinner snaked its way out into the living room, Rick and Nikki were deep into a conversation about writing habits, ghosts and other things that go bump in the night.

"Are you two coming up for air?" Sarah asked finally, sticking her head out into the living room. "Or should I bring in some TV trays?"

Rick looked at Nikki. "Shall we take this to the table?"

"Will we bore everyone else?" she replied, looking at him.

"It's just the two of you tonight," Sarah said, grinning. "No other guests, and Chuck and I are going to see my folks. So don't trash the place, and turn off all the lights and lock the doors before you go to bed or to write or whatever, okay?"

Rick saluted. "Yes, oh captain my captain!"

She shot him a look of equal parts amusement, exasperation and caution, to which he grinned. "Don't worry, cousin. We won't blow up the house, sacrifice Jonathan or eat all the cookies. I promise."

"You'd better not," Sarah shot back. "It took me a long time to make those cookies."

With that parting shot, she sailed out, and Nikki and Rick lost it again.

When they had finished laughing, Rick looked at Nikki. "Let's eat before it gets cold."

"Agreed."

Once their plates were piled high with homemade meatloaf and mashed potatoes swimming with butter, they settled in around the beautiful oak table in the dining room and resumed their conversation.

"How do you know so much about the haunted houses around here?" Nikki demanded. "I haven't even heard of half of these places, and I have been planning this for a very long time."

Rick grinned at her. "Easy, I grew up around here. I've been interested in ghosts for forever."

"Because of your visions?"

He shook his head. "Nah, those only started happening about five years ago." He started to say more and then changed his mind. "But we lived in a haunted house when I was a kid, and that got me really interested in it."

"No way!" If she'd noticed his hesitation, she didn't comment on it. "Do tell!"

"Well, we lived in a Cape that was built on the site of an old tavern," Rick said, pausing only to wash down a mouthful of mashed potatoes with a swallow of Dr. Pepper. "Legend has it that the tavern keeper's brother was killed there one night—died of a heart attack. Apparently, he came around the side of the building after drinking too much one night and came face-to-face with a moose."

"No way!" Nikki gave him an incredulous look. "He died of fright?"

Rick nodded. "That's the story. Anyways, I was lying in bed one night when I was about 8 years old, and I heard footsteps coming down the hall. I thought it was my brother trying to scare me, so I slipped out of bed and got my whiffle bat and stood right beside the door. I was going to whack him when he came in."

"And?" Nikki leaned forward, totally entranced.

"And boy was I surprised when the footsteps came right through the door, which was still closed, by the way, and went all the way across the room and out the wall!" Rick stopped, remembering the shock and fear that had gone through him that night.

"What did you do?" she asked, bringing him back to the present.

"Ran back to bed, jumped in and hid under the covers, clutching that bat for the rest of the night," he said, grinning unrepentantly. "And boy was I glad when morning came!"

"Wow. I'd love to have experienced something like that." Nikki leaned back, poking her fork idly into the remains of her mashed potatoes. "Maybe then I'd know what to look for."

Rick looked at her for a moment. Do I dare take her to White Mountain Cemetery? That would most certainly get her going in the right direction ... but do I dare?

<hr />

Nikki looked over at him. He's trying to make a decision, she thought. I know that look—I've certainly seen it enough on my dad's face.

"You know a place, don't you?" she said, acting on the hunch. "Please, tell me!"

The look of indecision grew.

"I am not looking to get rid of anything," Nikki insisted. "I just want to find some proof. Please, Rick, help me!"

The plea seemed to decide him. "Okay. I do know a place, but I want to go with you."

Her eyes narrowed in suspicion. "Why?"

Rick sighed. "Because it's ... different. Trust me, Nikki, you'll get proof, but you really don't want to go to White Mountain Cemetery alone."

"Why not? What's so special about it? What kind of phenomena has been reported?" Nikki switched to reporter mode so fast that Rick blinked.

"Well, not the usual," he said finally. "You won't get any pictures of orbs or figures or anything like that."

"So what's there?" she insisted.

"The Guardian."

Nikki looked at him. "The what?"

"Legend has it that White Mountain Cemetery is home to a Guardian spirit, sent there to protect the grave of an old witchwoman who died about three hundred years ago." Rick looked past Nikki, his eyes unfocusing slowly, as if he were looking into the past. "The legend is that if you bring an offering at night to the grave of the witchwoman, the Guardian will answer a question for you."

"And have you tried it?" He has, he must have!

There was a long pause as he stared off, and for a moment, Nikki thought she might have lost him. Then he closed his eyes, opened them again and smiled at her. "Yes, I've tried it."

"And?"

"And there is definitely something there. But it's different for everyone."

"What happened when you went?" she insisted.

"I went down with a couple friends who wanted to take pictures," he said, settling back into his chair. "My girlfriend brought the obligatory bottle of alcohol and asked for proof of the afterlife."

Nikki looked at him, this time with both eyebrows raised. "You're kidding."

"Nope. She wanted proof that she could photograph, too."

"And did she get it?"

"Well, we set up the cameras, and waited. Her friend wandered around a bit, and then we started to hear something coming through the woods."

"The woods?"

He nodded. "There are woods on three sides of the graveyard. The road parallels the fourth. So, anyways, we started hearing something coming through the woods. And then her camera started going off on its own."

Nikki's jaw dropped. Rick grinned at her expression and continued, "It freaked us all out. Especially since the sounds were coming from all three sides at once. So we decided caution was the better part of valor and hauled ass out of there."

"Sounds like a good move." Nikki sat back and chewed on her lip. "Any plans for tomorrow?"

Rick blinked at the abrupt change in topic. "Umm, no, not that I can think of."

"Good." She looked up and smiled. "You made me promise not to go anywhere alone, remember? So you'd better be ready to go tomorrow to this graveyard."

She listened to the words come out of her mouth in shock. *What am I saying? I don't want him tagging along! This is my book!*

And yet, I do want someone there. This afternoon was freaky enough. I never thought about how I might react when I do find the proof I'm after.

If Rick noticed her inner struggle, he didn't mention it. "Nikki, I…"

"Don't." She stood up, plate in hand, and gave him a steely look. "Just say, 'Yes, Nikki, I'll be ready to go' and leave it at that."

He threw his hands up in the air. "Yes, Nikki, I'll be ready to go."

Her mouth twitched again, and she fought the urge to smile. "Good. Where is this place, anyways?"

"Outside Conway. If we leave around noon, we'll get there in plenty of time."

They placed their dishes in the sink in companionable silence, each caught up in their own thoughts. Then Nikki yawned.

"Think I'll head to bed," she said, leaning against the doorway. "Thanks for a great evening."

He gave her a sweeping bow that made her giggle again. "My pleasure, my lady." Then, as she turned to go, he added, "Sleep well, Nikki."

"You too."

Once upstairs, she stripped slowly, wondering what was going on with her. The thoughts continued as she showered, reveling in the hot water. He's cute, definitely. He's a writer, which is a plus. But why am I doing this? I'm not usually like this!

She fell asleep with the thoughts still running rampant. Her last coherent one was that at least with thoughts of Rick occupying her brain, maybe she wouldn't end up in that damn wood again.

Partially right, Nikki thought, turning slowly. She wasn't in the woods, but this was definitely not her bedroom.

The ground beneath her boots was dirt, not moss, and there were no trees in the immediate vicinity, although they marched in orderly rows off into the distance around the edges of the graveyard wall. The breeze was here, as always, and the harp music that was so familiar rose from her left. She turned; in the back of the graveyard, near what looked to be a weeping willow, sat a figure all in white, playing a harp that appeared to be made of shadows. The figure's head was veiled as well and slender fingers caressed the silver strings of the harp.

Nikki frowned and did a slow, 360-degree turn, taking in the scope of the graveyard. It wasn't large, but there was an ancient feeling in the air; the graves were all worn and softly rounded by time, the grass growing long and luxurious, wildflowers poking their heads up wherever their seeds landed. Vines covered the large granite monolith that dominated the center of the cemetery. As she watched, the moon that had been hidden by clouds came out, and the buds on the vine burst into bloom. Pale white moonflowers opened shyly, and Nikki breathed in the familiar fragrance.

That's it! That's the scent! I've been smelling moonflowers!

She started towards the grave, to see what name was inscribed on it. Then a cloud seemed to roll in out of nowhere—when the grey mistiness cleared, there were two clear emerald eyes staring back at her. The large black cat from the lake lay in front of the grave, calmly watching her.

Not yet, child. The smoky voice surrounded her, as did the hazy fog. Time enough for this later.

But I need to know! Nikki started to protest, but the fog was inexorable; it dragged her down into deeper sleep, chased by the voice, which soothed her.

Soon, child. I promise you, soon.

Chapter 5

"Hazy, with a chance of Spirits"

The sun was well overhead when Nikki awoke the next morning, and the warm breeze blew in the smell of pancakes and the sounds of a melancholy harp. She lay in her bed, wondering just what she was going to find when she went downstairs. In the pool of warm sunlight that her bed lay in, the music wasn't as haunted, and her nose told her that not only did Sarah have blueberries in her pancake mix, but there was warm maple syrup involved somewhere. Her stomach rumbled; with a sigh, Nikki threw off the covers and pulled on jeans and a tee-shirt. She headed downstairs, figuring that no matter what weirdness was waiting for her, it would wait until after breakfast.

However, the only weirdness downstairs was the sheer normalcy of the scene. Sarah stood at the large restaurant-style range, cheerfully flipping pancakes and checking to make sure the syrup didn't boil over. The harp music came from the CD player tucked under one of the cabinets; the case was standing next to it, a beautiful redhead and an enormous harp on its cover.

"Good morning!" Sarah said cheerily when she caught sight of Nikki in the doorway. "Come on in. The coffee's fresh and there's fruit salad too. How many pancakes would you like?" Then she saw the circles under Nikki's eyes. "Sleep okay?"

It was on the tip of her tongue to say something about the dreams, but in the bright light of the morning, in the cheery kitchen, the feelings were already fading. Nikki shook her head and tried a smile. It didn't hurt, surprisingly.

"Just not a morning person," she replied, heading over to the coffeepot.

"You and Rick both," Sarah chuckled, opening the oven door and pulling out a pan of bacon. "I think it's a writer's thing."

"I think you're right." Nikki slipped into a seat at the table, cradling her coffee cup in her hand. "Listen, Sarah, about yesterday...."

She looked up to see Sarah already shaking her head. "Don't worry about it. I shouldn't have been shoving you two at each other. If anything, I should be the one apologizing." She put a plate piled high with bacon and blueberry pancakes in front of Nikki, and then set a container of steaming syrup next to the plate. "I'm just worried about Rick, truthfully. That bitch he was with last..."

"Is not going to spoil another meal without even being here, is she?" Rick asked mildly from the door. "Nikki doesn't need to hear about her."

Sarah flushed and turned back to the stove. Nikki raised one eyebrow at Rick, who shook his head warningly as he headed over to the coffeepot.

Yet another day of As the Inn Turns, Nikki thought to herself, shrugging mentally. Do I just attract drama, or find it? Ah well, maybe we can compare hideous exes another time. He might get a kick out of some of the Jack stories I have.

She turned her attention from Rick to the plate in front of her. Sarah's pancakes, like everything else she made, were heavenly, and Nikki soon forgot the rest of her dreams as she savored the sweet cream butter and warm syrup atop the fluffy cakes. When she looked up again, Rick was deep in his own pile; there was a drop of syrup on his nose, and she chuckled, unable to stop herself.

"Are you laughing at me again?" he said, looking up himself. "Didn't you get enough of that yesterday?"

The drop of syrup sparkled in the light as he talked, and Nikki laughed even harder, reduced to shaking a finger at him as he stared at her, puzzlement writ large on his face. Sarah turned around to see what she was laughing at and, noting the drop, sighed and tossed him a napkin.

"I'm glad to see you enjoy my cooking, cousin. I just wish you didn't wear it quite as well," she commented wryly, indicating his nose, and Nikki laughed even harder.

Rick wiped off his nose and then threw the napkin at Nikki. "Go ahead, laugh it up."

When she'd subsided to giggles, he asked, "So, are we still on for today? Or have you decided to go somewhere else?"

Nikki shook her head. "I'm still game if you are. Where did you say this cemetery was?"

"Up past Conway." Rick cocked his head to catch a glimpse of the kitchen clock. "It's only 10 am; we have some time. The Guardian doesn't come out until after dark anyways, and sunset's not until 7ish."

"Yes, but I want to check this place out in the daylight first, and set some cameras up," Nikki said, getting up and stretching. She placed her plate in the sink and refilled her coffee cup before sitting back down. "And we still have to load my car, and get the offering."

"You're taking her up to White Mountain?" Sarah asked Rick, a note of concern edging into her voice. "Is that wise?"

"Probably not, but she wants proof, and she'll definitely get that there," Rick said, looking over at Nikki, who nodded stubbornly. "If I don't take her, she'll probably just go herself, and I don't think either of us wants that."

Sarah sighed. "Just be careful, you two. I remember what happened the last time you tried this, Rick." She looked over at Nikki. "Did he tell you that story?"

"About the camera taking pictures on its own and the sounds? Yes."

"Did he also tell you that one of his friends committed suicide in that graveyard a year later, and that the note he left said he couldn't stop thinking about the Guardian?" Sarah continued.

Nikki blinked, and Rick suddenly was very interested in his coffee cup. "No, he failed to mention that part." She raised one eyebrow at Rick. "Any reason you forgot about that?"

"Matt had other problems," he said quietly. "The note Sarah's talking about was a three-page rambling letter, in which he blamed his problems on everything from the government poisoning him with arsenic to the Guardian to his family trying to get him committed. There's no reason to think we'll have any problems tonight—I'm also a little wiser than before. We'll take precautions."

"Oh?" Nikki's other eyebrow joined its mate.

"I have a friend who's a witch."

"Among other things," Sarah mumbled, and then turned back to her stove when Rick shot her a look.

"Among other things," he amended. "Justin's really good at protective amulets. I've got a couple—they should protect us from anything that might go bump in the night."

"What kind of amulets?" she said warily. *This is getting stranger by the minute—what have I gotten myself into?*

"Just charm bags. They're filled with herbs," Rick said reassuringly. "I promise—no signing your name in blood or anything like that."

Nikki gave him a disgusted look. "Did you really think I was thinking that?"

His return look was pure innocence. "Did I say you were? I was just trying to clear things up."

"How about helping me clear up the table while Nikki gets her stuff together?" Sarah interjected, winking at Nikki. "Then you can help her load her car."

"Great. Now I'm a pack mule," he complained, unfolding himself from his chair and starting to gather the dishes. "Let me know when you're ready to go, Nikki."

Two hours later, he wasn't quite so enthusiastic. "Do we really need all this?" he asked, staring at the pile she had put next to the front door.

Nikki grinned as she came down the stairs with her camera bag slung over her shoulder. "What, having second thoughts?"

"No, but hoping you have a big car." Rick shook his head; his dark blonde hair was loose this morning. "What is all this?"

Nikki shrugged. "Lights, extra film, battery box, laptop, and lenses. And a picnic lunch that Sarah packed for us. And yes, I've got a Jeep Cherokee. Plenty of room."

"Good." Rick picked up the picnic basket and one of the light sets. "Let's go, then. Don't want to keep the Guardian waiting."

What if I'm wrong? Rick thought, looking out the corner of his eye at Nikki as they drove up the highway. To the casual eye, she was fine, but he noticed how her hands were tight on the wheel, and the shadows in her eyes had darkened. He had seen the circles under her eyes when he'd come down to breakfast; it was obvious that she'd had a bad night, and didn't want to talk about it.

He'd been furious that Sarah had brought up Matt. Rick had spent a long time trying to come to grips with his death, and the fact that Matt had been with them in the graveyard when Madeline had summoned the Guardian was something he'd tried to forget. But it hadn't been that alone that had unhinged Matt; Rick had suspected for a long time that his friend was having problems, serious problems—the incident in the graveyard hadn't helped him, but it wasn't the only cause.

As if she was reading his thoughts, Nikki said quietly, "Do you mind if I ask you a question about your friend? The one who died?"

He sighed. "No, go ahead. I should have mentioned him."

"You said you never saw anything that night," she said, keeping her eyes on the road. "So what happened to him? Why did he snap?"

"It wasn't just that night. Matt had a lot of problems. He'd been keeping to himself lately; I hadn't seen him in months." Rick settled back against the seat and leaned his head back, closing his eyes. "We were surprised he even wanted to come; he hadn't wanted to do anything but write up until then." Matt's face swam out of his memories to rest against his closed lids, Matt as he was before he'd gotten paranoid, Matt when he was still a good friend….

Rick shook his head, bringing himself back to the present. "Anyways, it was me, Madeline, Matt and Jason. Matt was wandering all over the graveyard; he was the one who first heard the sounds in the woods, and he was the first back to the car. After that night, we didn't see him again for almost a month."

"Did you try to find him?" Nikki asked, still focusing on the road.

He nodded. "We went to his room; it was locked tight, and if he was in there, he didn't answer. We even got the RA to go in and check on him—she said he was fine, just didn't want to be disturbed. When he finally came back around, he was back to being the Matt we'd come to know: very closemouthed, not interested in the people around him."

He shifted and looked out the window. "After he committed suicide, there were rumors that he'd fallen in with a bad crowd. There were a couple of wanna-be Satanists on campus; they didn't do more than posture, but there was something …icky about them. We heard that he'd fallen in with them, started taking drugs." And doing blood magic rituals, selling his soul, but hey, they were only rumors, right? Rick shook his head again, trying to get rid of that line of thought. We never found any of that stuff in his room, and Shanna swore that she couldn't sense any blood magic residue. But still….

You think too much, Rick.

"So we don't know. His journal didn't mention anything other than the sounds and the camera clicking. And no, we didn't get any good pictures out of it," he finished. "So nobody knows."

Doesn't mean we still don't blame ourselves, though.

"So what do you think will happen tonight, then?" Nikki said, finally glancing at him. "Will we see anything?"

He shrugged. "Something will happen. I can almost guarantee that. Will it be something you can photograph? I don't know. But tonight will not be boring."

Unfortunately....

———

They stopped at a liquor store on the outskirts of Conway, and Rick watched as Nikki prowled the aisles, looking for the perfect offering. She stopped at the cordials section and stood a long time before selecting a bottle full of dark indigo liquid.

"Blackberry brandy?" she asked him.

"Sounds good to me."

After they paid for the brandy and climbed back in the Jeep, he directed her to a narrow road leading into the forest. The trees hung heavily over the Jeep. Even though it was late afternoon, it was already twilight under the cover of the branches.

"You weren't kidding about how far out this place was, were you?" Nikki observed, as the Cherokee slowed to a crawl. "How much further?"

"Not far enough."

The edge in his voice distracted her from the road, and she stopped the Jeep to look at him. His face was pale and set, his eyes closed; when he felt the Jeep stop, he opened them and looked at her. She was struck by the shadows in his eyes: the shadows, and the fear.

"We don't have to do this," Nikki said quietly. "We can still turn around."

Rick shook his head violently. "No. I have to go back. It's the only way to get over it." Then he gave her a weak version of his half-smile. "Besides, you need your proof, remember?"

"Rick..."

The smile got stronger. "Don't worry, Nikki. I'll be fine."

Nikki gave up and started the Jeep moving again. "Just don't pass out on me before we get there, okay? I'd hate to have to try and find this place myself."

He chuckled. "It's not that hard from here. Just keep going until you see the graveyard on your left."

It wasn't far, but with the slow pace the Jeep was kept to (Nikki was being very careful with her photographic equipment in the back), it took them another thirty minutes to get to the graveyard. Once they got there, Nikki guided the Jeep off to the side of the narrow road and parked it. Then she looked up, and it was her turn to gasp and turn pale.

"What's wrong?" Rick asked, concern driving the fear from his eyes as he looked at her.

Nikki didn't answer; she got out of the Jeep in a daze and walked into the graveyard, leaving the iron gate hanging open behind her. Rick, a little alarmed at her sudden change in behavior, followed behind her.

It can't be. Her thoughts were racing around her mind in circles, like trapped mice. It was just a dream, there are lots of graveyards like this, I was just dreaming…

But no, there's the monument and there's the stone where the harpist was sitting… what is going on?

"Nikki?"

Nikki jumped and let out a little shriek as Rick touched her on the shoulder. Her dark blue eyes were wide with fear; she shrank away as he reached out to her again, shaking like a leaf.

"Nikki, what's wrong?" Rick pulled himself up with a visible effort as she continued to back away from him, obviously upset.

"I've been here," she whispered, her voice thick with her fright. "I've been here before, but it wasn't like this, the cat was there, and there was music…"

This time, she let him touch her when he moved towards her— suddenly she had the need to feel something warm and human around her. Rick pulled her into his arms, surprised at how protective he felt. "It's okay, Nikki, it's okay. Calm down."

After a moment, he felt her draw a shuddering breath and dropped his arms. "Sorry," she said, not looking up as she turned away. "It's just…I dreamed about this place last night."

"A cemetery like this?" Rick looked around. "It's a pretty traditional design. I'm not surprised you've seen something similar before."

"No," she replied, looking at the center monument, the one that had

had moonflower vines over it in her dream. "It wasn't one like this, Rick. It was this one." She pointed to the monument. "Is that the one where the Guardian is?"

He nodded, and she moved over to examine it more closely. In the light of the mid-afternoon sun, the white granite glowed with a pale light. The writing had begun to fade on most of the graves, but this one still had the name of the witchwoman inscribed on its face with bold letters.

"Polly McDavid," she read. "Born 1723, Died 1795. Wow, she lived to be a ripe old age, didn't she?"

"Yup." Blinking a bit at how quickly she seemed to have recovered, Rick joined her at the stone. "Some said she was a witch, some that she just had good luck and some medical knowledge. Legend has it that she delivered every baby in the area, right up until she died."

"Do they know how she died?" Nikki ran her hands idly over the stone, amazed at the coolness of the granite, even on this warm summer afternoon.

"Nope. That's part of the legend. Supposedly, one of her daughters had a dream that her mother came to her and told her that it was time for her to take over her patients, as the time had come for her to move on." Rick squinted up at the top of the monument, where a single star was carved into the stone. "When the daughter went to her mother's cabin, her mother was laid out on the kitchen table, dressed in her best dress, stone dead."

"Creepy." Nikki turned away from the stone, fighting the urge to look into the corner where the figure had been with the harp. "Well, let's get started."

They set the lights up in the clearing around the center monument. Rick watched as Nikki wired everything with practiced ease. Once the lights were up, she shot a roll of film, seemingly at random, from various points in the graveyard.

"What was that for?" he asked when she was done.

"Control shots," she replied, replacing the spent roll with a new one. "Okay, I'm going to need your help in a bit."

Rick looked warily at her Nikon. "Please tell me it doesn't involve that monstrosity."

Despite herself, Nikki chuckled. "Not exactly. I want you to stand in front of the monument, so I can focus these two. Then, all you'll have to do tonight is hit the button and keep taking pictures."

"Okay." Rick stood in front of the monument, striking silly poses while she focused both cameras on their tripods, trying not to giggle too much at his faces. Finally, she declared herself set and showed him the button she wanted him to push.

"There are sixty photos on each roll," Nikki told him. "As soon as you finish one roll, switch to the other camera. You advance the film like this."

They practiced for a bit, and then she pronounced him fit to man her cameras.

"Just one thing," she said, as they crossed back to the Jeep to get the picnic basket.

"What?"

"If you break my cameras, I'll kill you. Capisce?"

Rick looked over to see if she was joking. "I'll be careful."

Nikki leaned in the Jeep's window, looking for her notebook. "To quote George Lucas, 'you'll be dead!'"

He looked at her, the faintest hint of panic in his amber eyes, and she couldn't help but grin. "I'm kidding, Rick. But those are very expensive cameras. I don't want them getting hurt."

Rick breathed a little deeper. "Gotcha."

Sarah had packed them a full basket of goodies, including some of the chocolate chip cookies she'd been making the day before. As the sun sank below the trees, Nikki and Rick checked their flashlights and made their way back to the monument. Nikki switched on the lights; the monument flared into pale luminescence against the darkness of the graveyard.

So help me, if I hear harp music, I am so out of here. Nikki tightened her grip on the bottle of brandy, nodded to Rick and moved into the pool of light. At the base of the monument, she knelt and placed the bottle on the grave; then she stood up and said clearly, "Guardian of the Night, a penitent draws near. Spirit of Darkness, answer my prayers."

As she finished the last word of the rhyme, a breeze sprang up, rustling the leaves on the trees around her. From behind her, she heard the camera start to click. There was a heaviness in the air—suddenly, Nikki felt like she was breathing smoke, or fumes.

What the???

She backed away from the bottle, watching as something dark and misty curled up out of the grave around it, darkness creeping up the stone to form a cloud at about eye level with her. Red eyes opened within the darkness; she stumbled and fell on her butt, eyes wide with shock.

God, I hope he's getting this!

"Child of Shadows, why do you bother me?"

The voice, dark as velvet, flowed over her, eerily similar to the one in her dreams. Nikki sat blinking, trying to find her tongue.

"I...I have a question," she stuttered finally.

"Ask."

Nikki blurted out the first thing that came into her mind. "Is my mother still alive?"

"More alive than not, more dead than most, but part of this world forever."

Something surged through Nikki: hope, elation and fear, bundled into one. She started to say something else, but the air grew heavier still, and she blacked out.

———•———

Rick kept shooting, even as the Power surged up around him. He'd switched to her other camera, hoping to get as many pictures as he could while trying to ignore the red eyes that glowed in the darkness. Then Nikki slumped over onto the ground, and he abandoned the camera to leap forward.

The mass of darkness flowed up the monument as he got closer, as if allowing him to get to the girl crumpled at its base. The eyes turned on him—Rick froze, unable to move.

"Guard her well, for she is the hope of you all." The words, heavy with the same feeling as his visions, sank into him. He stood gaping at the cloud as it dissipated. Once the final wisps of darkness were gone, he shook off the paralysis and knelt beside Nikki.

Touching her skin, he gasped and yanked his hand back. Cold Power surged through her, as if she were a battery. Christ, no wonder she passed out! That had to hurt!

Steeling himself, Rick touched her neck again, searching for a pulse in the midst of the Power that battered up against his shields. Thank God Shanna taught me to shield; otherwise, I'd be down on the ground with her. His fingers finally found what he was looking for: her pulse was strong, which settled his nerves a bit. That last surge must have overloaded her system, that's all.

Not surprising, especially since there was still a massive amount of Power running through her body. Rick shifted his hand to her arm and settled down on the ground; lowering his shields gingerly, he began to drain off some of the Power from her.

Cold...this is Shadow Magic, he mused, watching the color come back into her face. And the Guardian called her "Child of Shadows." I wonder if she's got some Shadow Mage in her background.

Nikki's eyelids fluttered; he clamped off the flow of Power and pulled his shields back up as she opened her eyes.

"Take it easy, champ," he said, as she moaned and tried to sit up. "That was quite the Power surge you took. Lay back for a moment."

"Power surge? Is that what that's called?" Her voice was foggy.

"Yes." He put a hand on her shoulder as she tried to sit up again. "Trust me, you want to lay back."

Nikki stopped struggling and lay back, closing her eyes again. "It felt like a Mack truck."

"Usually does, when you don't have any kind of defense."

Nikki suddenly sat bolt upright. "My film!"

Rick grabbed her as she swayed. "Is fine. I took pictures up until you passed out." There was a scratching somewhere at the back of the graveyard, and they both paused.

"Tell me it's not a cloud," Nikki whispered, closing her eyes and leaning her head against Rick's shoulder.

Rick peered into the darkness at the back of the graveyard. Two emerald eyes gleamed back at him, and another whiff of Power tickled his senses. "Not unless it's changed its eyes to green."

Nikki raised her head and looked in the same direction he was staring. "I've seen those eyes before," she whispered, and then shuddered. "In my dreams."

Definitely need to talk to her about these dreams she keeps mentioning, Rick thought to himself as he helped her to her feet. The eyes simply watched; as he looked out again, the darkness formed a shape around them, coalescing into the form of a large black panther.

"Why are you following me?" Nikki muttered rebelliously, and Rick looked down at her in surprise.

She was staring at the cat, her blue eyes narrowed dangerously. As he watched, she shook off his arms and stalked over to her camera.

This time, you won't get away, she thought angrily. I'll take your picture if I die trying.

"The one on the right still has film," Rick called, and she altered her route to the proper camera. The great cat simply lay on the bench in the back, watching her line up her shot.

Nikki could have sworn the damn thing was laughing at her.

The floodlights were throwing odd shadows across her shot; with one practiced pull, she killed them by yanking the wires from the battery box. Darkness fell around them; the emerald eyes continued to glow, and she lined up her camera based on them.

Be sure to get my good side. I don't want to have gone through all this trouble for nothing.

The warm, sultry voice, so very familiar, made Nikki grit her teeth.

I'm hallucinating. I hit my head on the ground when I fell. Cats with green glowing eyes, made of shadows, do not talk.

The ridiculousness of that statement hit her as she took the shot. I definitely hit my head.

The great cat yawned, stretched and then simply faded away. Nikki let her hand fall away from her camera as she stood up.

"It was there, wasn't it?" she asked, her voice a little wobbly.

"Was that the proof you wanted?" Rick's voice was full of astonishment.

"I'll let you know when the pictures come out." A wave of exhaustion broke over her and she swayed. "Let's get this stuff cleaned up and get out of here."

Chapter 6

"Colors"

Rick eased open Nikki's door the next morning, peering around the edge to see if she was still asleep. They had gotten in very, very late the night before, but he'd had the suspicion that she was not going to go to sleep any time soon. Her eyes had been a little wild when she'd wished him good night, and the lights in her room had stayed on for most of the night. They'd still been on when he'd gone downstairs at dawn to get something to drink, but she hadn't answered his soft knock on her door.

Now, he wished he'd checked in on her sooner. Nikki was curled up against the window on the window seat; one hand tucked under her cheek, the bright crocheted blanket Sarah had made last winter while she was sick draped over one shoulder. The lights in the room were still on and the dark circles under her eyes indicated that she had fought sleep as long as she could.

Poor kid; you got way more than you were expecting last night, didn't you?

Moving as quietly as possible, he padded across the room on bare feet and lifted her into his arms, blanket and all. She murmured something, but barely stirred as he laid her on the bed and covered her again. Then he shut off her light and padded out, shutting the door quietly behind him.

He'd been headed downstairs for breakfast; he could smell the coffee Sarah was making, but something made him detour back to his own room and grab his journal. Then he headed down to the kitchen, wondering what he was doing up so early.

The birds were still singing a morning song; the clock in the hall read 8:30 am, a time Rick usually tried very hard to avoid. He was a night owl:

his genre was dark fantasy, and for some reason, he found it hard to write about things that go bump in the night when the sun was shining.

To his surprise, it wasn't Sarah, but Chuck who was puttering around the kitchen. "What, no Sarah?" he asked, pouring himself a cup of coffee.

"She's not feeling well this morning," Chuck said quietly, putting together a tray with a pot of tea and some toast. "I told her we'd take care of things."

"Everything okay?" Rick asked, a little concerned. Sarah tended to mother everyone around her so much that it was hard to remember she was only human too.

Chuck nodded and smiled. "She's just overtired, that's all. Her mum's not doing too great, and she's worried. I think a day in bed, and she'll be fine."

Rick watched as he left the kitchen, balancing the tray in one hand while he held the door to keep it from slamming. Chuck was more than content to let his wife be the one to stand in the spotlight—unlike many artists Rick had met, Chuck preferred to simply paint and draw in his studio, and let Sarah market his work. But when she got sick, he would immediately drop everything to care for her.

Someday, I'm going to find a person like that, Rick thought, taking a sip of coffee and shuddering at the strength. Chuck liked his coffee strong enough to eat the polish off of spoons. Rick got up and added both sugar and cream to his, watching the cream swirl into oblivion as he stood at the counter. Someone who does their own thing, but is there when I need them.

Someone like Nikki, maybe? The small voice in his head whispered, and he gave a grim smile.

Hell, if she doesn't hate me after last night, she just might be the one!

Shaking his head to cut off that train of thought, Rick rummaged through the shelves until he found the instant oatmeal Sarah had bought for him. His kitchen skills were minimal at best: he could boil water, make coffee and operate a microwave, which had been enough when he was living with Madeline. Once they broke up and Sarah saw the way he lived, she had raised holy hell until he'd agreed to move into the inn. Technically, it was a temporary move.

He watched the kettle steam as he sipped his coffee, still trying to reconcile what had happened last night with what he knew of magic and Nikki. He'd thought she'd had some experience with magic and ghosts; most ghost hunters did, but apparently she'd been one of the few that hadn't. Once they'd gotten back on the road, she'd succumbed to a fit of the shakes that it had taken most of the ride home to stop.

Granted, most haunted houses do NOT contain that kind of Power. Talk about a welcome!

He wondered how the pictures came out. Nikki had mentioned wanting to develop them as soon as possible; maybe that was how she had staved off the sandman. He shrugged—no doubt he would see them at some point.

Wonder if she'll give me credit for taking them?

The kettle began to whistle; he hastily pulled it off the heat before it got too loud and poured the hot water into his oatmeal. Then, with bowl in one hand and mug in the other, he retreated to the kitchen table and opened his journal. Between bites of oatmeal, he recorded what had happened last night.

I sincerely did not expect an actual manifestation, he wrote, the black ink glistening against the paper. Nor did I expect the Power level. There was nothing like that the last time we went—could it be that Nikki is a latent Mage? That would account for it.

She's been having dreams, too, it appears. I wonder if she's just a late bloomer. Dreams, Power surges—that's what Shanna used to look for when she was on the scent of a potential Talent. Could that be what triggered everything last night?

He paused, chewing on his pen as he thought about that. What if that was the problem with Matt? Maybe something did follow him home...that might explain his weird personality changes.

The kitchen was bright and warm. The only sounds were the birds outside, the drowsy ticking of the grandfather clock in the hall and the scratching of his pen against the paper of his journal. Rick refilled his coffee cup once; the inn seemed lost in time, waiting for someone to start the clock again.

Around 11, the kitchen door opened, and Nikki stumbled in, yawning. She tossed a pile of glossy photos silently in front of him and then headed straight for the coffee pot.

"Watch out, it's strong," he said absently, staring at the photos in fascination. They were in order; he flipped through them, noting the detail from her cameras. "I thought you said we used black and white film."

Nikki sat down across from him and took a sip of the coffee, shuddering. "We did."

"That's impossible." He flipped to the photo where the Guardian's eyes had opened. The red eyes glared up at him from the picture. "How are these red, then?"

"You tell me. You're the expert on magic." She looked at him; the circles under her eyes made her look like someone had punched her.

He shook his head. "This is beyond my knowledge. I'm no Mage. But I would say you have your proof."

Nikki gave a mirthless laugh. "Yes, yes I do."

Her reaction startled him. "I thought that was what you wanted."

She sipped her coffee again, her dark blue eyes unreadable. "So did I."

Nikki sipped at the coffee, trying to organize thoughts that raced around her head in laps. *He was as surprised as I was at the photos. I guess that means I'm not going crazy.*

Or we're going crazy together. I'm not sure which thought is less-comforting.

She'd developed the film as soon as they'd gotten back to the inn. Even with every light blazing in her room, she'd begun seeing things out of the corner of her eyes. The last thing she remembered was sitting on the window seat. Someone, probably Rick, had moved her to her bed at some point, as she'd woken up there.

"Those aren't the only ones," she said now, as he was still staring at the pictures of the Guardian. "Take a look at the ones at the end."

He obligingly flipped to the end of the pile, to the pictures of the cat. It had been a dark graveyard, especially after she'd cut the lights. Her flash had been disabled while she used the lights. So a black cat in a dark graveyard shouldn't have come out at all. At most, she'd hoped she'd gotten the eyes.

Rick stared at the pictures, shock in his eyes. "These look…"

"Like it was as bright as it is now," she finished for him. "And the damn eyes are green."

They were. Every detail of the cat and the stones around it was visible, as if the picture had been taken in broad daylight. The eyes glowed an emerald green as the cat lounged on the granite bench.

Nikki swore the damn thing was still laughing at her.

Rick swallowed, his face pale. "Nikki, I have never seen photos like this." He looked up at her, letting the pictures fall to the table. "Is there Shadow blood on either side of your family?"

She shrugged, ignoring the lancing of pain that shot through her as she answered calmly, "I don't know. I'm adopted. Why?"

"Because that might explain these photos." He indicated the pile. "This is way beyond just coincidence."

As he glanced down at the picture again, he gasped. Nikki looked down too—as she watched, the cat finished its stretch, yawned and winked at both of them. Then it rose from the bench and sauntered from the scene, vanishing at the edge of the picture.

"Okay, that's just plain wrong!" Nikki burst out, jumping up and shoving her chair back in an effort to get away from the table. Rick hastily followed her example, obviously wanting to get as far away from the photos as she did.

"Pictures do not move," she said, her voice trembling. "Not even ghost pictures." She looked over at Rick, her eyes begging him to tell her that what had just happened was a hallucination.

"No, most pictures don't," he agreed slowly, confusion writ large on his handsome face. "But these are not most pictures."

She watched as he moved back towards the table, picking up the top picture and frowning. This is so not fair! Why isn't he as shaken up as I am?

"Why are you so calm?" Nikki asked accusingly. "You act like this happens every day!"

"Not every day," he replied, picking up the rest of the photos and shuffling slowly through them again. "And you don't know anything about your mother? Your birth mother?"

"No," Nikki said, confused by the change in subject. "What has that got to do with anything?"

"Hmm? Oh, sorry. Magical Talent is passed on the maternal line, unless your father happens to be a Shadow Lord."

"A what?" Nikki walked back to the table and picked up her coffee, hoping the caffeine would shock her back into a world that made sense. "Speak English, please."

Rick finally looked up, the fog clearing a bit. "You really don't know anything about magic, do you?"

"Nope," Nikki admitted, sitting down again. The caffeine wasn't helping—the world was still weird. "So tell me."

Rick sat as well, and took a long drink from his coffee cup before answering. "Well, I can't tell you a lot. There are a couple of different types of magic—Shadow Magic, Light Magic and Earth Magic are the main ones. There are some others, but I don't know much about them."

"How do you know as much as it is?" Nikki asked. "You said you weren't a Mage, but you did something to me last night, didn't you?"

He looked surprised. "I can't believe you remember that. You were pretty out of it."

Nikki shuddered, putting the memory in one of her mind's closets and shutting the door firmly. "I remember," she said. "So what did you do?"

Rick just stared at her amazed. Fear still looked back at him from her dark blue eyes, and yet she was still looking for answers.

This is one tough kid! He thought admiringly.

"Are you going to answer me or just stare at me?" Nikki said finally, when the silence had stretched between them for several minutes.

He shook himself mentally before answering. "Sorry, but most of the people who went through what you did last night wouldn't be interested in what I did. They'd rather forget what happened instead."

"I'm not like most people. I'm a reporter," she replied. "I'm not saying I'm comfortable with what happened last night; I'm not." She shuddered again. "Far from it. But you don't get the good stories by staying where you're comfortable. So tell me."

But how much can you handle? He wondered and then mentally shrugged.

"All I did was drain some of the excess Power from your system," Rick said honestly. "You were overloaded. That's why you passed out, I think. I'm not really sure—I can see the energies, but short of just draining them off, I can't really do anything."

"How can you see them? What do they look like?" Nikki leaned forward, her face interested.

Rick shrugged. "I just can. And it looks…well, Shadow Magic looks like shadows, Light Magic is like sunlight, and Earth Magic has this greenish tinge to it."

And Blood Magic is reddish, and Demonic Magic is purplish, and hopefully, I will never run into either again.

"What do you mean, you just can?"

"I'm what they call a Sensitive. I'm sensitive to magical energy: I can see it, can feel it, but can't use it." Thank God.

Nikki looked over at him, digesting this information. *From the way he's acting, he's been around people using magic before,* she thought. *I wonder how.*

"Interesting," she said out loud, then blushed as her stomach rumbled. "Jeez, I'm sorry."

Rick looked up at the clock and swore. "No, my fault. I didn't realize it was almost noon; the conversation was so stimulating." He smiled at her and despite herself, she smiled back. "Sarah's not feeling well— what say we forage for sandwich stuff?"

"Sounds good, but what's wrong with Sarah?" Nikki asked, getting up and following him to the refrigerator.

"Chuck said she's just tired," he said, pulling out lettuce, tomatoes, cheese and roast beef. "Sarah gets so involved taking care of others that she forgets to take care of herself sometimes."

"Ah."

They built their sandwiches in companionable silence, each lost in their own thoughts, and then retreated to the table.

He's so easy to talk to. Maybe that's why I'm attracted, she mused, looking at him over her sandwich. *There aren't too many guys I could sit and have this kind of conversation with. Even Tom looked at me funny when I started talking about what I wanted to write about.*

Now, I'm not so sure they weren't right.

Her train of thought was dragging her mood right down. Nikki set her sandwich down, no longer hungry.

"Penny?" Rick said, and she looked up to see his dark amber eyes full of concern.

"Just wondering if I really am cut out for this," she said quietly. "I mean, my first real experience with magic, and I black out. Great reporting instincts."

"Nik, what happened to you last night doesn't happen every day," he said, getting up and taking their plates to the sink. "That Power surge was stronger than almost anything I've experienced—I only remained standing because I have mental shields that diverted the Power. Don't beat yourself up over it."

"Maybe." She stood up, stretched and went back to the refrigerator. She snagged a Dr. Pepper, hefted it in the air and cocked an eyebrow at him. He shook his head; she shut the door and stretched again. "I'm going upstairs to write up what happened. And I've got to see where else I'm going this week."

"So you won't give up?" he asked, settling back down at the table with his journal.

"Not yet."

"Don't forget these," he said, holding up the pictures.

Nikki took them gingerly, almost afraid they were going to do something else strange, like bite. They lay in her hands, cool and glossy, simple photographs.

She wondered if anything would be simple again.

"Nikki," Rick called as she left the kitchen. She turned at the door.

"Don't be afraid to come and talk again," he said. "I've got a good shoulder."

She smiled. "Thanks."

Once upstairs, Nikki placed the photos in a special box that she'd brought for evidence and then pulled out her journal. Curling up on the window seat, she noticed that there were vines stretching green fingers up around her window casing. How odd. I didn't notice those before. Sarah's thumb must really be green!

Dismissing the vines, she began a meticulous description of what she had seen and experienced in White Mountains Cemetery, as well as noting the information Rick had given her about magic. The sun was sinking towards the western horizon as she finished, and the window seat was bathed in a pool of golden sunlight. Sitting in the midst of it, Nikki looked down at her journal and shuddered. Not even the warmth of a June sun could drive away the cold that seemed to have settled into her bones.

I have never felt anything like that, she thought, looking out over the garden. It was like ice water being poured through me. Like it was February, in the middle of a deep freeze, not June.

I wonder if that's how it feels to Rick. And if the other magics feel different.

The setting sun was hovering over the edges of the trees, sending last loving fingers of warmth over the scene. As Nikki watched, several of the buds on the vines outside her window swelled and burst. The sweet scent of moonflowers drifted up to her.

"How odd. I didn't know Sarah planted moonflowers this year."

Rick leaned around the edge of her open door. "Chuck sent me up to tell you that Sarah's feeling much better, but doesn't want to cook, so we're ordering subs. Would you care to join us?"

She smiled and tossed her journal on the bed. "Love to."

After dinner and an enjoyable evening playing Scrabble with Chuck and Sarah, Rick walked back upstairs with Nikki, both intent on their own projects. At her door, he stopped for a moment.

"Have a good night, Nikki. Good luck on the writing." Rick reached out and brushed a stray lock of her dark hair from her face. His fingers trailed gently across her cheek; without thinking, she turned, so his hand cupped her face momentarily. Then she stepped back into her room, a little surprised at her reaction.

"Thanks, Rick. You too." She managed to keep her voice steady, surprising herself. She even managed a smile, which he returned.

He was still standing there when she shut the door gently.

Nicolette Marie Jeffries, what are you doing?! Talk about encouraging him!

Nikki stripped down and threw her tee-shirt on the floor, too distracted to think about a shower. She was still tired from the night before—her eyes closed almost before she hit the pillow, even though she knew the dreams would probably follow...

"There has got to be a way to stop this," she said under her breath, calming the horse between her legs with a pat to its neck. The great black horse stamped one hoof and blew out a gusty breath, but stopped dancing beneath her. The horse calmed, Nikki looked around.

Once again, it was twilight, a dusk so velvety that it seemed tangible. Mist curled around the horse's fetlocks, weaving gentle fingers up along its girth. The saddle beneath her creaked as she turned, looking for the others she knew should be with her.

The hounds howled, off to her left—without a thought, she turned the horse's head and sent him off with a click of her tongue and a tap of the black riding crop she held in her right hand. He turned and set off obediently across the field.

This is a hunt, she realized, but what are we hunting?

That thought continued to nag at her as she was joined by three other figures, indistinct in the mist that continued to swirl around them. The music was back, too—wilder than the last time, seemingly whipping the fog that spread across the field, separating Nikki from the other riders. One of them turned back, as if to help her, but the fog surged between them and the figure vanished. The fog rolled over her, pushing her from the back of the horse, down into darkness that finally claimed her.

When she awoke the next morning, the riding crop was still tightly clenched in her hand.

Interlude 1

"Shadows of Change"

It was the wards that first alerted her.

She drifted in sleep, wrapped in shadow, until the first stirrings of wards long dormant disturbed her rest. Opening eyes dark as late twilight, she moved through the ancient house towards her workroom, wondering if what she felt was truth or only a bitter hope.

Surely he wouldn't be that foolish, would he?

The center of her workroom was dominated by a large onyx ball, clasped in the silver claws of a great gryphon statue. Teraisa glided over to the ball and passed one hand over it, the tips of her delicate claws barely brushing the dark surface.

The great bulk of the Gene-Tech Facility gradually came into focus in the ball, stark contrast against the gently sloping sides of the dale it nestled in. Teraisa watched, concentrating on narrowing the focus of the spell to the new wing that was pushed directly into the rear valley wall.

The foundation, where her wards had been laid twenty-three years ago, was the only part of the original secure wing that Alex Masterson had kept when he bulldozed the entire thing after the disaster that had ended the Soldier project. Teraisa had watched as the new construction had consumed the better part of six years—Alex was taking no chances with his new project, it appeared.

Lucky for me his Mages didn't think to look for Lord Magic.

It still amazed her that they had pulled it off. Once again, she blessed the Darkness that had sent the Shadow Lord to help her and Caran Masterson escape. Without the distraction of the blown generators, they wouldn't have had a prayer.

Once they had escaped, Caran had emptied her and Alex's joint account, and disappeared. Teraisa supposed she could find her, if she wanted. Very little was hidden from her now.

It didn't surprise her that she really didn't care about where the other breeder had ended up. In all honesty, the only thing that did surprise her a little was that she remembered her name.

I have turned into a cold bitch.

She'd retreated to the Shadows after her daughter was born and placed with a suitable family, setting up this enclave where she could watch over the Facility. It was hard for the former Shadow Mage to remember the idealistic young researcher she had been when she'd started on the Soldier project.

It was getting hard to remember many things from her past. The Shadows that she lived in were wrapping tighter around her each year, squeezing her humanity from her little by little. In a few years, she feared she would have nothing left from her past at all.

Perhaps it is best that he make his move now, while I still care enough to intervene.

Spell walls were going up around the secure wing of the Facility as she watched—multi-layer protections, designed to keep out demonic and mortal Shadow Magic. Apparently, Alex thought whatever had destroyed his experiment twenty-three years ago had a connection to the mortal plane.

How very interesting.

She watched in the crystal until nearly midnight, when the spell flows appeared to settle into place. By this time, the shields were a solid geodesic dome over the entire Facility—Alex was taking nothing for granted.

Except for the fact that those who wish to see him stopped might not be human.

Once the Facility had settled down, Teraisa left her enclave and headed for the great building, retracing steps she had not taken in years. By habit, she had shifted form; the great black cat form was easier to travel in than her own.

The scent of mortal spells, sealed in the Mage's own blood, hit her sensitive nose as she crested the final hill and looked down upon the Facility. Teraisa had chosen the site for her enclave carefully: barely three miles from Gene-Tech, hidden deep in the Shadows, warded from all eyes, mortal or Lord. Since the spells had changed her, her magic held a flavor neither was very familiar with.

Not Lord, not really mortal anymore—what am I truly, other than shadow?

She ignored the faint pain of that thought as she padded down into the valley, keeping to the Shadow Realms as long as she could. Once she was within the Facility, she slipped back into the mundane world, a wisp of black that moved along the shadowed corridors, hardly noticeable for the few researchers still up. Only the guards might have noticed her, but Teraisa had perfected the art of going unnoticed among mortals. It took patience and time, but what was time to one who had the rest of eternity to look forward to?

She settled into a dark alcove near the security station that guarded the entryway to the secure wing, putting her chin on her front paws as she considered the best way to get through. The fact that Alex had gone through the trouble to hire Mages as guards was amusing; of far more interest to her were the secondary wards that she could sense now that she was in closer proximity—wards set to repel Earth and Light Magic. She could also sense the iron that wove through the very walls of the building.

Paranoid much, Alex?

The guards at the station were a minor annoyance; once she was sure there was no one else about, Teraisa began to weave the shadows about her, imbuing them with a deep feeling of lethargy and sleep. Once it was dense enough, she pushed it out into the corridor, watching it creep along the floor to the station and start winding its way up. Subtle enough not to disturb the wards, it was too strong for the guards to resist. Within moments, they were nodding at their station. She waited until they were just asleep and slipped through the door; once through, she released the spells. No sense in leaving any traces of her magic.

She roamed the halls, knowing that she would eventually end up in the main lab, the last place she and Caran had been held before they escaped. There were still magical resonances coming from the lab; Teraisa slipped quietly into the room and settled into a corner, noting the similarities with a mental shudder.

He really is insane. He's trying again.

There were four stretchers, with restraints for wrists and ankles, which brought back feelings she'd thought long buried. Two junior researchers, still new enough to amuse her, flanked a young woman who was setting secondary wards beneath the ones that had alerted Teraisa. She was powerful, despite her youth, and was setting the shields with a delicacy that spoke of long practice—Teraisa was impressed, and wondered where Alex had managed to recruit her.

She's very nearly as good as Cameron was. I'll bet she's his new lead.

The young woman finished setting the ward and frowned, as if something were encroaching on her concentration. She looked around the room; Teraisa shrank back deeper into the shadows as her hazel eyes swept the corner. She was sensing something, perhaps a leak from Teraisa—the former Shadow Mage decided to leave before she was discovered.

She slipped into the Shadow Realms carefully, closing the hole in the shields quickly, before she could be followed. Once safely in the Realms, she retreated to her enclave, more disturbed than she wanted to say. Gene-Tech was restarting the Soldier project. That meant that at least one of the Lords had survived.

Going over to her desk, she pulled out a piece of parchment and a long black quill pen. She dipped the tip of the quill into her inkwell and began to write.

"It has begun. We must meet."

Signing it with a simple T, Teraisa laid the quill down and dusted the words with sand. Blowing carefully, she let the ink dry while she considered what she had seen. Then, with a wave of her hand, she sent the letter to her contact.

The message sent, Teraisa turned back to the onyx globe. Images stirred, but she was too preoccupied to see them.

Alex, what are you up to now?

Chapter 7

"Misgivings"

There were files littering the tops of both desks in the office, but Sylvia wasn't reading any of them. Instead, she was bouncing a rubber band ball off the far wall, thinking about the strange Power signature she'd encountered last night.

She hadn't even been sure it was there. In fact, she almost dismissed it for a ghost trace; if it hadn't been for the momentary flicker in the wards, signaling a small portal being opened, she probably would have missed it all together. Neither of her juniors had sensed anything—whoever it was had been very, very subtle.

And that was worrying. Sylvia had seen the end result of the last Soldier project; the blood splattered pictures had been anything but conducive to a good night's sleep. She hadn't known a body could bleed like that.

So what was watching us last night? She tossed the ball against the wall again, barely hearing the hollow thunk. If I were superstitious, I'd say it was the Dawn Lord's ghost come back to haunt us. Do Elemental Lords leave ghosts when they die violently?

That was not a comforting thought.

With a sigh, she tossed the ball onto the table and went back to her own, where the dusty files of the last lead researcher, Cameron, lay in a box. The files were in complete disarray, as if whoever had gone through them last was trying to find something in a hurry and failing utterly. There were blood stains on some of the pages; whether from a cut finger or something else, Sylvia wasn't sure, and didn't really want to know.

After about 15 minutes, she had the file in some semblance of order, and she'd discovered a treasure in the bottom of the box: Cameron's diary. The small book, bound in green leather with a Celtic knot engraved in silver on the front, had been tossed in the bottom of the box, almost as an afterthought, she mused. There was a faint magical residue on it; Sylvia frowned and opened the book.

Every single page was blank.

What the?!

The magical residue tugged at her memory. She cleared the rest of the papers off the desk and laid the small book down in the center. It mocked her: the worn cover indicated that it had been used extensively, but the blank pages were pristine. Sylvia opened her drawer and pulled out a slender silver wand, tipped in onyx and bound with moonstones.

Let's see what you've done here, my friend.

Chanting under her breath, Sylvia watched the onyx begin to glow greenly from within as it absorbed the power of her spell. She touched the cover of the book and then cried out as Power flashed around her.

That sonofabitch! He locked the damn thing!

Narrowing her eyes, she laid the wand aside and took the book in both hands. The tenor of her voice changed as she recited the standard unlock spell she'd learned from her mentor—the Shadows wrapped around the book, infusing the pages with Power. There was no flash this time; she breathed a sigh of relief as the Shadows retreated, the spell complete.

She opened the book again—to find blank pages.

"This doesn't make any sense," she muttered, flipping through the pages quickly. "Cameron was a Shadow Mage. That unlock spell is good to unlock anything that a mortal Shadow Mage has locked. Unless he had a Lord lock it…."

Then on the last page, Sylvia found five words in a strange script, written in a dark green ink. "Everything comes from the earth," she murmured. "What the hell does that mean?"

A sudden knock on her door made her jump. Slipping the journal into her pocketbook, she called out, "Come in."

The door swung open, and Alex strode in. She stiffened; the man paid her, but she'd learned over the past week that the rumors regarding his misogynism were all too true.

Behind him was a short man with dark skin and no hair. His eyes were dark as well and burned with a strange light. Sylvia stood as they came in, unwilling to give Alex any height advantage at all.

Now what? She watched as the dark man gathered up the files on the other desk and deposited them on the table.

"This is Tony Ashcraft," Alex said abruptly. "He'll be your second. Fill him in—I want to start the preliminary spells next week." He nodded to Tony and left.

Asshole! Sylvia watched Tony set his desk up with quiet efficiency, fuming. I don't need a second! This is my project!

Tony watched Sylvia steam out of the corner of his eye as he set up his desk, privately pleased at the turn of events. Andreas wanted no problems. He'd approached the Shadow Mage about working on the Soldier project before he'd gone to Alex to restart the experiment. Tony had leapt at the chance to use spells he'd only heard rumors about.

Now, looking at the lead researcher, he felt supremely confident that in very short order, he would be running the project. Just as the Shadow Lord wanted.

"Alex had his chance the last time, and both leads he chose were disappointments," Andreas had said in his deep voice. "I want nothing to go wrong this time. He has chosen a young woman to lead his team—you will go and make sure she has no ... change of heart."

Don't worry, my Lord, Tony promised silently, setting the onyx cube Andreas had given him out on the desktop. There will be no problems this time.

She had been very comfortably spread out in the office; her displeasure at his presence was palpable. She waited until he stopped pulling things out of his bag before she walked over, her hand outstretched.

"I'm Sylvia Richards and I'm in charge, no matter what Alex Masterson told you," she said icily, shaking his hand once and then dropping it like she'd found something distasteful in her palm. "So don't even think about stealing my project, understand?"

Completely. Tony bowed his head, not saying a word. She eyed him suspiciously, then turned to the table and began rifling through the papers.

With her back to him, Sylvia let the snarl she was holding in stretch across her face. She'd had everything in some semblance of order before he'd tossed them all on the table. Now, it took her several minutes to find the papers she was looking for—time she used to get both her face and feelings back under control.

She turned back to him, expressionless, only the fire in her eyes hinting at the emotions she was trying to hold back. "Here are the preliminary spells. Learn them according to this schedule," indicating the sheet tacked to the wall, "and be ready to go next week. You heard Alex."

Picking up her pocketbook, Sylvia walked to the door. At the doorway, she stopped and turned back to him. "And remember what I said. This is my project."

Then she turned and walked out.

How dare he? We didn't need anyone else! I was doing just fine! She pounded her fists against the leather steering wheel as she waited for the Jag XK8 convertible to warm up. The Jag was her baby: the divorce settlement had paid for it and the small cottage she'd bought up here. Considering what Paul had put her through, making him pay for these was small consolation.

Just listening to the motor purr calmed her down. It was a warm night; one touch of a button, and the roof slid back, letting the slight breeze ruffle her short blonde hair as she backed out of the spot. As she shifted into first, her pocketbook fell from the seat and against her leg, and she saw the top of Cameron's journal.

"All things come from the earth," hmm? *What games were you playing, Cameron? And why did you lock your journal and then try to abort the very project you started?* Sylvia shook her head. *I've got too many questions and no answers. Like where are the records on the autopsies of the breeders and the fetuses from the first project? If they were killed by flying glass shards, like the reports say, why aren't there any pictures of the bodies? They certainly got enough of the Dawn Lord's body.*

And that was another thing. Sylvia had looked over the pictures of Kymara's corpse until she could see it against her closed lids, and the marks on her throat did not look like they were made by flying glass.

It looked like something ripped her throat out. And what about Andreas' eyes? Why wasn't the rest of his face ripped up too?

Her entire ride home was spent wrapped in these cheery thoughts. Too tired to cook, she made a sandwich and poured a glass of wine. She sank into her favorite chair and chewed thoughtfully, still lost in thought. The book taunted her from her purse on the couch; she leaned over and picked it up again. The words in the back nagged at her; where had she seen them before?

"I'm too tired," Sylvia said out loud, once she'd finished her meal. "I'll figure this out in the morning."

However, the morning brought nothing but bleary eyes. Her dreams had been disturbing scenes of devastation that she was being chased through by several figures on horseback. There was a pounding in her head that a hot shower did nothing to abate, but it did give her a clue into the five words that had been running through her consciousness all night. She got out, toweled off and headed to her study.

There were tons of books scattered around her library, mostly dealing with the Shadow Realms, but she headed straight to the small bookcase in the right-hand corner. This bookcase housed the smattering of books on other disciplines that she'd studied under her mentor, who had insisted on exposing her to all the types of magic that she knew of.

"That's stupid," Sylvia had insisted. "I'm a Shadow Mage. I can't use the other disciplines. Why should I study them?"

"Knowledge is never wasted," Hesper had replied. "You never know when you might need it."

Now, Sylvia blessed her teacher's foresight. *If she hadn't forced me to study Earth Magic, the words wouldn't have meant anything to me. But how did a Shadow Mage get his journal locked with an Earth spell?*

For that's what the words meant. They were the key to the Earth Magic version of the spell Sylvia had cast. They stared at her from the page, raising more questions than they had answered.

She sank into her desk chair, the Earth magic book open in front of her. "Alex only works with Shadow Mages," she said slowly. "Earth and Light Mages aren't even allowed into the Facility, except for the Dawn Lord they've recruited, whom I've not seen yet, come to think of it. So where the hell did Cameron get an Earth Mage to cast this spell?"

Unbidden came the thought that perhaps Cameron had cast the spell himself, but her logical mind rejected it as it crystallized. *Magic does not cross genetic boundaries like that. If you are born with Shadow Mage genes, you cannot use the other Magics, except for Blood or Demonic Magic. It's been scientifically proven that magical* aptitude is carried on the genetic level, dammit!

And yet, we're playing with the genetic level. What if the spells leaked? Sylvia felt a cold breeze filter across the damp hair on her neck and shuddered. I need to get this journal unlocked.

She called in to the Facility and left a clipped message for Tony, letting him know that she wasn't feeling well and was taking a sick day. She'd call tomorrow and let him know if she was coming in. Then she made another call, to someone she hadn't seen since she and Paul had shredded their marriage and their friendships.

Goddess, please let her still be there, Sylvia pleaded silently, holding the cordless phone against her ear as she pulled on jeans. She's the only one I can turn to ….

"Hello, Sylvia. I've been expecting your call."

Vashti's warm voice, so much like a mother's, suddenly boiled out of the phone at her, and Sylvia flushed, feeling very much the wayward child. "I'm sorry, Vashti—it's been a rough year."

"Indeed. But that wasn't what I meant."

Sylvia paused, the laces of her left sneaker dangling in her fingers. "What did you mean?"

"The spirits told me you'd be calling this morning. They say you have an interesting problem." Sylvia could hear something hissing softly in the background. "When are you coming over?"

She tied her sneaker numbly. "Right now. I'll be there in about 15 minutes."

"Good, breakfast will be ready by then." There was a pause, and then Vashti said softly, "I'm glad to hear from you again, child. I've missed you."

Sylvia swallowed against a rush of emotion. "I've missed you too."

Ten minutes later, the Jag purred its way up the dirt road that led to Vashti's farm. The Earth Mage was waiting for her in the doorway, dressed in a long dark red robe that warmed up her chocolate skin. Vashti was smiling—a welcoming smile that Sylvia returned as she climbed out of the Jag.

"What a beautiful car," Vashti commented. "One of Paul's going-away presents?"

Sylvia nodded. "I decided I could be frugal and put my settlement away, or have some fun. After the hell of the divorce, I opted for fun."

"I don't blame you." Vashti led her inside after giving her a warm hug. "Come, Morgan has breakfast ready."

Sylvia followed her through the overgrown entranceway to the outdoor kitchen, where Vashti's brother was busy dishing out scrambled eggs onto three plates. "Sylvia!!! Good to see you again!"

"Hello, Morgan. It's good to see you too." Sylvia sat in the chair Vashti indicated and smiled at the slight black man as he put the empty pan into a nearby basket. "I've been way too negligent of my friends in the last year."

"You have gone through a trying time. We knew you would come back when you were ready." He returned her smile, his white teeth brilliant against the dark velvet of his skin. "Eat."

She dug into her breakfast, tasting the bite of cayenne and jalapeño explode against her tongue, a contrast to the smoothness of egg and cream. The bacon was crisp and hot, with a faint taste of apples—home smoked, she knew. Morgan and Vashti ran a small produce stand in the summer months; during the winter, they sold Christmas trees and wreaths. The chutney for the eggs was full of vegetables from Vashti's garden; Sylvia sighed in contentment, feeling the easy joy of the house surround her.

"You have begun to heal, child," Vashti said, smiling at her over her own plate. "You look much more content than you did last year."

Sylvia nodded. "I'm finally putting Paul behind me. And I've got a new project at work—I've been promoted."

Morgan and Vashti exchanged unreadable looks that Sylvia missed as she bent back over her plate. "You are still working at Gene-Tech, then?" Morgan asked finally, his voice carefully neutral.

Catching the note of control, Sylvia looked up and cocked her head. "Yes. Why?"

"That's a bad place, Sylvia. You would do good to leave there," he said firmly, and rose to clear the table.

Vashti waited until her brother had left the small outdoor area, carrying the dishes into the house to be cleaned. "He still remembers," she murmured, then stopped.

"Remembers what?" Sylvia asked.

Vashti shook her head. "Old history, child. Long before you were there. Let's just leave it at that."

Sylvia wanted to ask again, but something in the Earth Mage's eyes held her back. Instead, she reached into her pocketbook and pulled out Cameron's journal. "Can you help me unlock this?"

Vashti's face registered shock for a split second, and then went back to her customary impassiveness. "Probably."

What was that all about? Sylvia wondered, getting up and following the Earth Mage back to the small garden oasis that was her workroom. If I'm not mistaken, Vashti's seen that book before.

"You know whose journal that is, don't you?" she asked softly. "You helped him seal it."

"I've seen it," was the only response she got. "I didn't seal it."

"What?" Sylvia's mind worked fast. "Did Morgan?"

Vashti turned and looked at her, dark eyes full of something Sylvia couldn't identify. For a moment, the familiar Earth Mage was gone, replaced by something alien and far more powerful. "No. The owner of the journal locked it."

"That's impossible!" Sylvia blurted out. "He was a Shadow Mage!"

"Once, he was." Vashti turned back to her work table, a granite slab that was worn with years of use. "At the end? That was anyone's guess."

The sorrow in her voice shut down any other questions Sylvia was about to ask. Instead, she took a seat on a convenient rock as she watched Vashti sprinkle various powders on the book, marveling again at the differences between the various magics.

Shadow Magic and Light Magic took their strength from the Realms that had spawned them. The current theory in magical genetic circles was that the original genetic material for Shadow Mages and Light Mages was provided by Shadow and Dawn Lords that had come among humans in their past. Earth Magic, however, was firmly rooted in this Realm—it took its power from the very substance of the Earth, and its practitioners were usually well-versed in subjects like herbalism and shamanism. There were rumors of Earth Lords, elementals similar to the Shadow and Dawn Lords, but the Earth Mages would neither confirm nor deny their existence, and no one else had ever seen one.

Vashti finished with the powders and laid a sprig of holly berries on top of the book. Then she laid her hands on the granite on either side of the journal and began to chant in a language Sylvia had never heard before: guttural, earthy and harsh, like the cold ground one digs up after a first frost in the autumn. The berries began to waver and melt, like a heat mirage. Sylvia watched, fascinated, as they and the powders sank into the cover of the book, sending up the ghosts of aromas: bay, basil, rosemary and garlic.

The chant ended; Vashti stood a moment longer, and said something else in that strange language. Then she handed the book to Sylvia.

"Before you return to that place, you need to see what he found," she said, that alien look back in her eyes. "There is much that you need to see."

Chapter 8

"Explorations"

"No!"

Rick lurched out of his bed, nearly knocking himself out on his headboard as he slipped on a stray sock. After righting himself and drawing a deep breath to calm his racing heart, he looked around for the source of the sound that had catapulted him out of a strange dream. Vague images flashed randomly in front of his eyes—Nikki had been there, and there had been horses. He shook his head as the sound blared again. This time he was able to identify it as his cell phone.

Excavating it from the pile of papers on his desk took him to the next ring cycle; he blinked at the phone number that showed up and clicked the phone on.

"Took you long enough."

"Sorry, most people are asleep at this time in the morning," Rick responded, shuffling back over to his bed and squinting at the clock. "Please tell me that you calling at 4 a.m. does not mean that the world's falling apart again and you need my help to put it back together. I'm a little busy at the moment."

Shanna Greystone's rich laugh belled out of his phone and filled the room. "Not this time, my friend. I just wanted to check on you, actually. Fiona's had some weird dreams lately, and she's a little worried about you."

Why doesn't that make me feel better? "She's not the only one." Quickly, he filled her in on the situation, including the dream Nikki had had about the graveyard, and what had happened there.

"I don't like the sound of that," Shanna said finally. "Do you really think she's a latent Shadow Mage?"

"I don't know what else she could be," he replied honestly. "In all the pictures, she has this dark aura around her. And the Shadows were just drawn to her in that graveyard. You've been there, Shanna. Did the Guardian ever appear for you like that?"

"Yes, but I was expecting it," she told him, and he blinked. "This sounds serious, Rick. Are you still up at the inn?"

"Yup. And she's staying here too."

"Good." He heard something move in the background. "I'm going to ask Justin to come up; if she is a latent, he'll be able to help her at least construct shields until we can find her a teacher. He should be up later today."

Rick felt a wave of relief break over him. Justin was Shanna's younger brother: a talented Earth Mage, and more than capable of dealing with just about anything that came up, including a stubborn Nikki.

"I'd come myself, but I've got to go deal with something else," she continued, and he felt a stab of fear at the subtle change in her voice.

"Everything okay there?"

"Here, yes." The unspoken was that it wasn't somewhere else, but she didn't seem inclined to open up, and he knew better than to push.

"I'll tell Justin to keep me informed. Let's not have another Matt, shall we?"

Definitely not. He stretched after they hung up, and tossed the phone back onto the desk. Lying down, he noted that it was almost 5 a.m.—the sun would be breaking over the horizon far too soon. I've been seeing way too much of mornings lately.

Just before he drifted off to sleep, there was a tentative knock at the door. Groaning, he reached out mentally, wondering if he could pretend to be asleep, and encountered Nikki's familiar touch. Damn.

"Hang on," he called softly, reaching out for a nearby pair of sweatpants. Once decent, he padded over to the door and opened it.

———

He's probably not even up. Why am I bothering? Nikki thought, standing awkwardly in front of the door. Then she heard movement; before she could bolt away, Rick opened the door and she stared.

He was wearing only a pair of dark blue sweatpants. His chest was sculpted, much more athletic than most writers she'd run into before. Nikki didn't realize she was staring until he surprised her by chuckling.

"Did you stop by just to stare, or did you have something else you wanted to do?" he asked, giving her that shy, sexy half-smile.

Lots, but not now, she thought, clamping down hard on the heat that rose from her groin. "I needed to talk," she said out loud. "I know it's late, but ...."

"Let me guess, you had another dream." He stood aside and motioned her into the room. "The bed's probably the safest place. I know nothing on it will bite."

She bit back the obvious remark and scrambled up on the bed. She hugged a pillow, watching him kick the dirty laundry into a semi-pile by the closet and excavate the chair. Damn, it is so not fair. He even makes cleaning up look sexy....

"So, what did you dream about this time?" Rick asked, dropping one last pair of white silk boxers onto the pile and then straddling his desk chair. Nikki pulled her mind out of the gutter and sighed.

"It's changing now. It used to be this dark landscape, shadows and mist and cold, and this woman, made out of shadows, watching me." She told him of the dreams, starting with the ones back when she was still in Connecticut and following up through the most recent one. She didn't mention the riding crop, which was still sitting on her desk in her room.

"And I realized tonight that I've been smelling moonflowers, all the way through the dreams," Nikki finished, hugging the pillow tighter. "You saw the vines outside my window, Rick. They weren't there when I got here last week. Moonflower vines can't just appear in a week. I don't care how green your cousin's thumb is—it's not possible."

She hunched her shoulders. "I keep thinking that I should be able to put this all together, to make it make sense—and I can't. I hate that!"

Rick got up and came over to the bed. He settled in beside her and put an arm around her. "I know. Magic has a wonderful way of screwing up everything you think you know about the world. Trust me."

She leaned against him, enjoying the spicy smell coming from his skin. "How did it screw you up?"

His laugh vibrated against her cheek as it lay on his shoulder. "Oh, Lord. Well, let's see—it broke up my relationship, caused my mother to pitch a fit and throw me out of the house, and pretty much left Sarah and Chuck as the only family that would acknowledge me for a while."

"Wow. That's harsh."

"Yeah, well, most of them came back around. I'm not the official family outcast anymore, although family gatherings are pretty interesting." Rick chuckled again. "But magic does some pretty amazing stuff too."

"Like what?" Nikki was in the mood to just listen to his warm voice spread over her and feel his solidly muscled arm around her. He's so well-put together; much better than Jack, her inner self mused, not listening at all when she was told to knock it off. I could definitely get used to sitting like this.

"Well, I met some of the best friends I have ever had," he said, not aware of the inner monologue she was fighting. "And I've seen things most people only dream about."

"I'd rather not dream about shadows any more," she murmured, and his chest shook with his laughter again.

"There's more to magic than shadows, Nikki. There's achingly beautiful music that spins out of nowhere on a summer morning, sung by faeries. There's the sight of a newborn unicorn, taking its first steps while its mother watches protectively." He stopped for a moment, lost in his own thoughts. "There's so much more to magic than what you've seen. The best part is sharing it with someone."

It sounded like his inner thoughts were mimicking hers. I really should stop this. I can't deal with these feelings now. Let me figure out what's going on with me first.

The problem was, while her head understood that line of logic, her heart and body showed absolutely no interest in following her head's instructions.

"Nikki," there was hesitation in Rick's voice. "Don't take this the wrong way, please."

Oh, this ought to be good.

"I really like you, but … it's too soon." Relief poured through her; Nikki smiled, even though he couldn't see it.

"I'm glad to hear that, Rick. I was afraid I was going to have to be the one to say it." She raised her head, her blue eyes unshadowed for once. "I do like you, too, but I'm not the type that just hops into a guy's bed as soon as I meet him."

Rick made a big show of looking around the two of them, sitting together on his bed. "You can't say that any more, I'm afraid."

Nikki grinned and hit him with the pillow she was still holding. After a moment of shock, he grabbed the other pillow off the bed and smacked her back. The awkward moment passed in a flurry of thumps and giggles, which ended when she got a great overhand swing past his defenses. Rick, already perched on the edge of the bed, fell backwards and hit the floor with a loud thump!

"Oh, no!" Nikki scrambled to the edge of the bed and peeked over to where he lay on his back on the floor. "Are you okay?"

For a moment, he didn't answer. His eyes were closed, and she, afraid he'd been knocked out, leaned over farther. "Rick?" she whispered.

Then she squealed as his pillow came up and smacked her on the head. "Hah!" he grinned, opening his eyes. "That should teach you to knock me off!" She scrambled back from the edge, trying to ward off his blows as he climbed back up, intent on exacting revenge.

"You know, it's a good thing Chuck and I are early risers, and the only other guests aren't coming until tonight," Sarah commented from the doorway. "You two are making enough noise to wake anyone up."

Nikki could only imagine how it looked to the innkeeper: she was bent nearly backwards on Rick's bed, dressed in a thin tee-shirt and soft grey cotton shorts. Rick, bare to the waist, was kneeling over her, pillow raised for another strike. Not the most innocent scene, no.

"I'm going to put coffee on," Sarah continued. "If you two are finished, feel free to join me."

She closed the door, leaving Nikki and Rick to stare at each other, fighting to control their laughter. Nikki gave up first, dropping her pillow to clutch her sides; Rick followed soon after.

"Oh, ow," she gasped. "I can't stop."

Eventually, she ran out of laughter and just lay there on her back, looking up at his ceiling. "Rick."

"Hmmm?" He was lying near the head of the bed.

"Sarah's never going to let us forget this."

He sighed. "You're probably right. I'll be hearing this story when I'm eighty."

Nikki heaved herself off the bed with another sigh. "I'm going to get dressed. Coffee sounds good."

Rolling over on his stomach, he squinted at his clock and groaned. "It's 6 a.m."

She glanced at the clock. "Yes, yes it is."

"I hate 6 a.m."

Yet another thing we have in common. "I'll tell Sarah you went back to sleep." His eyes were already closing.

"Thanks," he mumbled, pulling one of the pillows over his head.

Nikki paused at the door. "Hey, Rick?"

"Mph?"

"Thanks." Then she went out and closed the door gently.

Walking back to her own room, Nikki looked at her own bed. The pillow fight had definitely tired her out again, and this time, she thought she might be able to bypass the dreams and go directly to sleep. Her body was moving before she completed the thought; she was asleep as soon as she hit the pillow.

When she woke up, light was streaming in through the windows, and her clock said 11 am. Nikki felt oddly refreshed—she actually started humming in the shower, and only the sight of the riding crop, still propped up on her desk, dampened her mood at all.

Toweling dry her hair, dressed in a bra and jeans, she considered the crop. It was on top of her desk, holding open one of her books.

Funny, I don't remember leaving any books open. Nikki dropped the towel onto her bed and went over to the desk. Moving the crop, she picked up the book and gasped.

The house from her dream stared up at her from the book, triggering a strange fear/desire in her. Nikki dropped into her chair, still holding the book, and reached for her notebook and a pen.

"Rothman House, in Rockland, New Hampshire," she read. "Built by Edgar Rothman in the late 1800s. His great-grandson, Robin, hung himself in the attic. Supposedly haunted by Robin and his great-grandmother, Daphne."

Nikki put the book down and stared out the window. "Well, I dreamed about the graveyard, and got the best pictures of my career. Maybe I should follow this." She looked back down at the book. "But how did this get open? I don't remember opening it at all."

Pondering the improbabilities, she shrugged and reached for her phone.

"Hello, Rothman House." A young but cultured voice answered.

"Hello, may I speak to…" Nikki checked the book. "Francesca Childers, please?"

The voice hesitated. "This is Francesca."

"Francesca, my name is Nikki Jeffries. I'm writing a book on haunted houses, and was wondering if I could come investigate your home."

There was a small pause. "Rothman House is open to the public, Ms. Jeffries. I can help show you around. But I'm afraid staying here is out of the question. The Historical Society doesn't allow it."

"But I could come over tomorrow." Nikki was already making notes in the margin of the book.

"Yes, I'll be here tomorrow."

"Good. I look forward to meeting you, Francesca."

Once she hung up the phone, Nikki grabbed several other books, looking up references to Rothman House. Sarah stopped in once around 1 pm, to bring her a sandwich, and pointed out gently that she might want to finish dressing before she got too much more wrapped up in her research.

"Huh?" Nikki said, looking up blankly.

Sarah grinned and tossed a tee-shirt at her. "Here, Einstein. Last thing we need is you catching cold."

Nikki pulled the shirt over her head, already being pulled back to her book. "Thanks, Sarah."

"I'll bring a tray up," Sarah said, rolling her eyes. "I'm sure we'll see you at some point."

"Uh-huh," Nikki mumbled, reaching out blindly for the sandwich Sarah had placed near her.

"Hey, sleepyhead, wake up!"

Rick's head slowly emerged from the pile of pillows and blankets. "Is it past noon?"

"Yes, actually. It's almost one." Sarah went over and mercilessly yanked up the shade. Rick moaned and burrowed back into the darkness of his bedding. That lasted all of a minute, as Sarah pulled off the covers with a practiced hand and dumped Rick back on the floor. "You've got a guest downstairs."

"You could have just said that," Rick complained, rubbing the lump on his head that had gotten larger with each time it had connected with the floor. "Who is it?"

"It's Justin." Sarah turned around and gave him a frosty look. "What's going on, Rick?"

Rick had risen slowly to his feet and stretched. He missed the coldness in her voice as he stumbled over to the dresser, blinking against the sunlight. "I don't know what you mean, Sarah."

"On the last occasion Justin was here, by the time it was over, there was a dead body involved, and you weren't yourself for weeks," Sarah snapped, fear sharpening her voice. The emotion finally sank through Rick's fog; with a sigh, he turned back to his cousin, who had her arms crossed in front of her and worry warring with the fear in her eyes.

"We're trying to prevent that, Sarah. Justin's here to help." If he can't, then we're all in trouble.

"That's what you said the last time," she accused. "And look what happened to Matt."

"That's not going to happen again. I promise you that."

Sarah still looked mutinous, and he sighed again as he took her hands. "Trust me, Sarah. It won't happen again."

She pulled her hands out of his. "I hope not. I'm getting tired of putting you back together once they use you and dump you off here." With that parting shot, Sarah left him standing in the middle of his room.

Once the door had shut on her, Rick shook his head and grabbed some clothes. He wanted a shower, but something told him that he'd better get downstairs and protect Justin from Sarah. I didn't realize how upset she was last time. I didn't think I was that messed up, but maybe I was wrong.

Justin Greystone was leaning against one of the porch's columns when Rick came down the stairs, watching a ruby-throated hummingbird feed among Sarah's flowers. The young witch was dressed in his normal soft black pants and pale blue silk shirt; as always, he looked slightly rumpled and yet quietly classic. His short brown hair was naturally curly and per normal, looked as if he'd just woken up, but his hazel eyes were clear and just this side of mischievous. Shanna was usually quite serious—it was as if Justin had inherited both her sense of the absurd and his own.

Then again, Justin doesn't have quite the responsibility his sister does, Rick reminded himself.

"Thank god," Justin said, responding to the unspoken thought with a quirky grin. "I think I'd shoot myself."

Rick chuckled, despite himself. "That's the truth. Although we should all thank god that she is. I can think of a couple of times she had to pull our asses out of the fire."

"Only a couple?" Justin joked. "More than that."

"True."

As they went into the kitchen to grab lunch (Sarah being occupied elsewhere, to Rick's great relief), Rick filled his friend in on what was happening. Justin listened gravely, only interrupting to clarify what had transpired in the graveyard.

"The pictures all had a dark aura around her, you said?" he asked, one half of his roast beef sandwich forgotten in his hands as he stared at Rick. "But she hasn't manifested any other powers? And she's how old?"

"Twenty-two. But what if she's a latent, Jus?" Rick fiddled with the ring tab on his Dr. Pepper can until it broke off in his fingers. "And what if I triggered something by bringing her to White Mountain?"

"If she is a latent, something would have triggered it sooner or later," Justin pointed out. "At least you were there if something went wrong."

"True." Rick gave up on his sandwich and dumped the remains in the trash before putting his plate in the dishwasher. Justin came over with his; he loaded it as well and then looked at his friend. "Ready to meet her?"

Justin gave him his quirky grin again. "That's why I came up."

The door to Nikki's room was shut, and Rick and Justin exchanged grins as Rick raised his hand to knock on the door. "Nikki?" he called.

"Go away." The voice was distracted and barely sounded like Nikki. Rick frowned and knocked again.

"Go away!"

Rick and Justin were suddenly shoved back away from the door by a cold force that almost slammed them into the opposite wall. They stood there after the force dropped away, staring at Nikki's door in utter shock.

When Justin spoke, there was worry laced through his voice.

"That is not the touch of a latent."

"Did you want me to try again?" Rick asked, half-hoping Justin would say no.

"Yes." Justin suited actions to words by knocking himself. Rick braced himself against a repeat of the shove.

Instead, there was a crash from inside and then stomping. The door was almost yanked off its hinges; Rick shrank back involuntarily as Nikki glared at them. "What part of go away don't you understand?" she growled. "I'm busy." And before they could say anything, the door slammed shut again.

"Fascinating." Rick's eyebrows went up at the oddly delighted tone in Justin's voice, and the witch laughed at the expression. "She's as cranky as you are when she's working."

"Very funny. So what do we do now?" Rick tried to speak evenly and failed.

"We let her work." The smile on Justin's face was pure mischief. "Let's go."

"I give up." Rick followed Justin down the hall, wondering what would happen next.

Chapter 9

"Approaching the Border"

God, this is just like my dream.

Nikki peered through the light grey mist that blanketed the road and wondered if this was normal for northern New Hampshire in the early summer. It's only been nice for a couple of days, she thought, then mentally shrugged. Maybe it's just a wet summer so far.

Rothman House was set way back from the main road, its private road barred by gates halfway up the hill that she could sort of see through the fog's filmy fingers. Her Jeep was parked next to the gatehouse at the bottom of the hill: it was here that she'd arranged to meet Francesca Childers, the current tenant of Rothman House.

As she waited for Francesca, Nikki scanned the area and remembered what she'd read. Built by Edgar Rothman. The last Rothman to live here was his great-grandson, Robin, who hung himself in the attic. And now the house is supposedly cursed— there have been at least 3 disappearances in the 70 years since Robin died and the house went up for sale. Creepy.

And perfect for ghosts.

Her attention was pulled back to the gatehouse as the front door opened and a slender young woman, dressed in jeans and a cream-colored sweater, came down the steps. Francesca Childers looked to be about Nikki's age, but her long dark hair was pulled back into a sophisticated French braid and her face was so expertly made up that it appeared to have no makeup on it at all. Her riding boots were polished to a shine, and as she came up to the Jeep, Nikki caught a whiff of Spellbound by Estèe Lauder, just enough to let her know it was there.

Wow. What is a woman like this doing here, in the boondocks?

"Hi, Nikki, I'm Francesca." She offered a perfectly manicured hand; Nikki took it out of habit, still bemused.

"Hi." She managed to say. Francesca grinned at her—the sophisticated image shattered, replaced by a young woman with a lively streak of mischief in her. Her delicately shaped hazel eyes were expertly lined and filled with a strange combination of shadows and humor. Nikki covered her confusion by waving her over to the Jeep's passenger side; once they were both in, she started the vehicle up the winding drive, while trying to frame her questions.

"Well, um, how much do you know about the history of the house?" she decided on, hoping she didn't sound as flustered as she was.

Francesca's laugh was rich, but there was a brittle undertone that piqued Nikki's curiosity all over again. "You mean, what's a sophisticated city girl doing out here in the boonies?"

"That too," Nikki admitted, steering carefully around a weeping willow that overhung the narrow drive. The gates were looming ahead of her: tall, iron structures, standing coldly against the filmy mist, rust tainting the air around them with a metallic tang that reminded her of blood. "So why are you here?"

"I'm an architectural historian. I'm working on a book on late Georgian mansions in New England." The flat undertone in her voice puzzled Nikki; it almost sounded like fear, a fear Francesca didn't seem to want to acknowledge. The fear, however, fit in perfectly with the dreary day. The dampness seemed to suck all the life out of the area, only heightening the isolation of the great house that loomed above them on the hill.

Stop that! She scolded herself, putting the brake on as Francesca hopped out to unlock the gates. This is not some crazy stalker movie— Jason and Freddy aren't going to burst out of the woods at us. Just chill out, okay, brain?

Francesca waited until she'd driven through and then closed the gates and climbed back in. "Go straight. The house is hidden by all these oaks most of the year. You actually come upon the main house first. Farther on are the stables and the coachman's house."

"Wow, the Rothmans must have really been wealthy to afford all this." Nikki started the Jeep forward, watching the oaks march down on either side of the road in majestic lines. "How did they make their money?"

"Horses. They raised Thoroughbreds and Arabians," Francesca replied, keeping her eyes straight ahead. The edge was back in her voice and stronger—Nikki thought about that as she passed the last tree. Then she caught sight of the main reason she was here and all other thoughts vanished from her mind.

Lawns ran gently up to the skirts of a tall, cold house that shouldered its way up into the grey sky. A small lake rolled iron-grey to the left of the house, a gazebo and another small stone building perched precariously on its banks. A huge oak tree stood to the right of the great house, near a smaller house that Nikki assumed was the coachman's house Francesca had mentioned. At the end of the driveway (which ended in a small parking lot) stood the massive stone bulk of the stables. Something deep within Nikki's soul stirred, reacting to something about the somber house that gazed down upon her.

"Wow. Now this is what I'd do if I had a bunch of money," she murmured, gazing at the tall Georgian, with its stately brick facing and multiple chimneys silhouetted against the grey clouds. Francesca chuckled, a harsh sound, and Nikki jumped. The landscape had made her forget her companion for the moment.

"That's what most of them said," she said, coming over. "Even though the Georgians were mostly built in the 18th century, old Edgar decided that he wanted a Georgian. The story goes that he hounded the architects until three of them quit—the fourth stuck to it and Edgar rewarded him handsomely when the house was done."

"Four architects? Damn." Nikki shook her head and then went to go get her camera. She pulled her film bag out of the car, threw it over her shoulder and pulled the lens cap off her Nikon, then looked expectantly at her guide. "Well, shall we start?"

Francesca, however, grabbed her arm before she started toward the steps. "No, we can't go inside today."

"Why not?" Nikki raised an eyebrow. Francesca was slowly turning pale, her eyes widening with fright. The other girl swallowed, looking suddenly far younger than she had before.

"You don't want to go into the main house on a cloudy day," she explained, her voice sinking with each word. "They come out on the cloudy days."

"They?" Nikki stared at her for a moment. "The ghosts."

Francesca nodded slowly, her skin matching her sweater, and her makeup standing out against her chalky face. "The main house is creepy enough on a bright day. Dark days are when the weirdness truly takes over."

"Well, I am here to get ghost pictures," Nikki reminded her gently. "So I think we should go inside."

This time, the brittleness lay on top of Francesca's laugh, rather than under it. "This whole area is haunted. Trust me; just walking around out here today will get you some good photos." She glanced up at the house and shuddered. "It's supposed to clear up tonight and be sunny tomorrow. I'll show you the grounds today and you can come back tomorrow and we'll explore the house, okay?"

Nikki glanced back up at the house, feeling the same sort of tug as she had in the graveyard, then she looked back at Francesca, who was practically radiating terror at the thought of going inside. Turning back to the house, she regretfully decided that dragging her guide inside was probably not the best idea, especially if she was serious about the phenomena acting up. She turned reluctantly away from the front steps, and Francesca's sigh of relief was audible.

"Well, where do we start?" Nikki asked, trying not to let the disappointment running through her come out in her voice. If they are more active on cloudy days, maybe tomorrow will be cloudy too ...

Francesca looked around as if to orient herself. "Well, there's the gazebo. It's the scene of a double murder. Or the coachman's house: Daniel Rothman, Edgar's son, had the coachman hung in that giant oak tree. And the stables have their own tragedy: Robin Rothman, the last Rothman to live here, beat a stableboy to death there."

"Charming family," Nikki commented, lining up a shot of the oak. "What did they do for entertainment?"

"You mean besides kill each other?" The fear still lingering in Francesca's voice robbed the dry remark of its humor. "They were all avid hunters, according to legend. And they threw one hell of a party."

Nikki was about to make a comment when she finished focusing the lens and actually saw what her camera was picking up. Among the green leaves of the massive oak, swaying in a breeze that seemed highly localized, was a body, hanging from a rope.

Ice ran through her veins. Take the picture. You can figure it out later, her rational mind whispered, prodding her numb fingers. Besides, it's probably just your imagination.

She managed to snap three pictures before lowering the camera and looking over at the tree, which stood in quiet glory, leaves still and nothing more sinister than a length of wild grape vines trailing down from a branch. "Looks like the grapes are going to do well this year," she murmured to herself.

"Hmm?" Francesca had been studiously avoiding the house. "What was that?"

Nikki shook her head. "Nothing, just thinking out loud." She turned away from the tree. "So, how about the coachman's house?"

Francesca nodded and led the way past the oak to the smaller house. "This house was the lodging for not only the coachman, but the stable-master and anywhere from two to four stableboys."

"And this is where the coachman that Daniel had hung lived?" Nikki lined up several shots, ignoring the fluttering of the curtains. There is no breeze, dammit! I just have way too vivid an imagination!

"Yes." Francesca led her into the small house, and pointed out the various rooms. "His wife Julia was having an affair with the coachman, so the stories go, and Daniel went insane with jealousy when he found out. He accused the coachman of plotting to steal one of his studs and had him hung."

"Charming." Nikki followed Francesca up the stairs and into a small bedroom.

"This was the coachman's room. Julia locked herself in here after her lover was hung and died of a broken heart." She gestured to a window overlooking the paddocks. "You can see her here sometimes, standing by the window."

Since that was exactly what her camera was showing her, Nikki gritted her teeth and snapped several shots. Just before the last one, the woman at the window turned towards her; the sorrow in her dark eyes flooded over Nikki.

Great, now I'm feeling sorry for the phantoms my mind is conjuring up. Nikki, this is it: you are now certifiable. She waited for the fear to show up; but apparently it had the day off. Or maybe the graveyard had sucked it all out of her. All she felt was the ever-present desire to get into the main house.

Back outside, Nikki shook her head as she changed out her first roll. "How about the stables?"

"Robin beat a stableboy to death in front of them," Francesca replied, pointing to the spot. Nikki obligingly took several photos, trying hard to ignore the little boy that stood in the doorway of the stables, blood running from several open cuts. It was the bruises that really tore her heart, though. Geez, what did he beat him with, a saddle?

"His riding crop," Francesca answered when Nikki asked her. "Then he tossed the kid's bleeding body into a group of half-broke horses in the paddock. The horses trampled the poor kid while Robin watched and listen to him scream."

"These guys just get better and better," Nikki remarked, her mouth twisted in a wry grin. "Did they have any redeeming qualities?"

"That depends. According to the stories, Robin gave nearly a thousand dollars to the boy's mother." Francesca led Nikki past the main house towards the lake. "And you haven't even met the ladies yet."

"Oh?"

"Yup. But we'll come to them in a second." Francesca stopped her and pointed to the crushed gravel path they were standing on. "According to the legends, when Edgar died, his faithful companion, a large black dog, ran down to the lake and drowned itself. The dog can still be seen on moonlit nights, running down to the lake."

At least it's not another damned cat! Nikki thought, looking through the lens at the great black dog that lay on the path, its tongue lolling to one side. And no green eyes. That's good. That's definitely good.

They continued down the path to the gazebo, where Francesca stopped Nikki before she mounted the steps. "Get some pictures from down here. That way, you can get the whole interior," she said. "This is where Jacqueline Rothman, Edgar's daughter, stabbed her fiancé and his mistress to death on her wedding night. Then, rather than face her stepmother's wrath, Jacqueline drowned herself in the lake."

Damn, talk about rough wedding nights! As Nikki looked through the lens at the blood-spattered shade in the tatters of her wedding dress, she wondered, Was it worth it?

To not have to live with the fact that he took my honor and made a mockery of it? To not have to see his face every day and know that his heart belonged to another, while he held mine in his uncaring hands? The cool voice in her head caused her fingers to freeze on the camera. Aye, it was worth it.

Nikki couldn't move as the shade of Jacqueline Rothman floated towards her, down the steps and through both her and Francesca on her way into the lake. Nikki couldn't help herself; she turned the camera to follow the tragic shade.

Jacqueline turned and looked back at her. Tell me, Shadowborn, can you say the same?

And then she vanished.

Several hours later, back at the inn, Nikki pulled the last print from the water bath and hung it up with the others. Then she stepped back, turned on the light, and hugged herself, trying to figure out just what the hell was going on.

They were all there—every single image she'd seen through the lens of her trusty Nikon, staring back at her in stark black and white. Julia Rothman, a study in sorrow at the window in the coachman's house. The stableboy, his clothes rent by the riding crop and horses' hooves. And Jacqueline Rothman, coming towards the camera in the remains of her wedding dress, her unfaithful fiancé's blood spattered all over her, her pale eyes lit with a strange fire.

This has gone beyond weird into downright creepy, Nikki thought, trying hard to keep the shivers that were racing up and down her backbone from developing into full-blown shudders. How could I have seen these?

She was trying very, very hard to forget Jacqueline Rothman's words.

"Ghosts from the 1800s that you can only see in a camera do not talk to you," she said out loud, as if the vocalizing of her thoughts made it true. It didn't even sound good to her.

"To hell with this. I need some answers."

Nikki grabbed the still-damp photos off their lines and marched through the door to the hall, headed for Rick's room. From the murmur of voices coming from inside, he had a guest, but she was too caught up in her own emotions to stop.

—◦—

Rick and Justin looked up, startled, as Rick's door banged open and Nikki stormed in. "Explain this," she said, in a voice dangerously close to either tears or fury, as she threw a handful of pictures down on his bed in front of Justin. "Explain how the damn camera took every single damn image I saw. Explain how the damn bitch knew I was there and what I was thinking!"

"Easy, Nik, easy." Rick got up from his desk and put his arms around her as Justin picked up the photos and began to look at them silently. She fought him for a moment, and then collapsed against his chest, her shoulders moving in barely controlled sobs. The fury of her emotions battered at his shields: fear/anger/uncertainty all chased each other around her in ever-increasing circles. He looked over her head at Justin, raising his eyebrows in a silent plea for help. Unfortunately, Justin's head was bent over the photos Nikki had thrown in front of him.

"But she spoke to me," Nikki whispered, shivering almost uncontrollably. "How did she know I was there?"

"Jus…" The emotions were starting to wear his control down; another couple of moments, and Rick wasn't sure if he was going to be able to keep conscious.

The young witch looked up, startled, and then hopped off the bed to help. He gently peeled Nikki's fingers off of Rick's shoulders and pulled her away from the Sensitive, guiding her back to the bed and throwing mental shields up around her to cut off the storm of emotions. Rick sank back against the wall, pulling himself back together as Justin started calming Nikki down; just watching his friend work was soothing.

⸻

He's so good. He must have been working with the Healers again, Rick thought. *Either that or his Empathy's been tested a few too many times.*

Both, actually, Justin replied absently, both of them slipping back into the easy mental communication that had grown up in their group over the years. It was a product of several things; proximity and the fact that they had all nearly died together a couple of times having a large part in forming it.

Nikki was starting to calm down under Justin's influence; her shoulders had stopped shaking, and the silent sobs had been reduced to a few stray tears. She swallowed the final bit of emotion and closed her eyes for a moment, trying to center herself.

"Now, tell us what happened."

⸻

Well, first I went crazy….

Nikki shook her head and opened her eyes. Both Rick and his friend were waiting for her to start—it was the friend that had spoken, his

113

voice quiet and full of concern. She suddenly realized how it must have looked and flushed.

Boy, talk about a winning first impression!

"Don't worry about it," he continued. When she stared at him, shocked, he chuckled. "When you think that loud, it's very, very easy for me to pick up your thoughts, and responding out loud to them is just habit. I'm sorry if I startled you."

Just habit. He says that so casually. Is this what magic does to people?

"Nikki, this is Justin—he's a friend of mine from college," Rick said. "He's a witch."

"If you say anything about little dogs, I'm running screaming out of here," Nikki said to Justin, who gave her an amused grin.

"I promise there'll be no little dog comments, and I left my green-striped socks at home, so we're all set," he replied, and despite herself, Nikki smiled back at him.

"Now, let's talk about these," Justin said, picking up one of the photos from where they were lying on the bed. Nikki glanced at it and shuddered: it was one of the stableboy, blood streaming down the side of his face from several gaping wounds, the walls of the stable faintly visible through him.

Justin picked up the photo and shook his head. "These are incredible. And you took them all today?"

She nodded and told them about her trip to Rothman House. When she got to the part about Jacqueline, though, her voice faltered again.

"She spoke to you?" There was a sharp note in Justin's voice that brought her head up. He was looking closely at her, as if trying to see something that no one else could.

"Yes. Like you did before. She answered the thoughts running through my head and walked right by me." Nikki shivered again, remembering the feel of Jacqueline walking past her, regal and elegant in her bloody wedding dress. "She asked me if I could say the same."

Rick gave her a puzzled look. "Huh? The same about what?"

"What exactly did she say, Nikki?" Justin said, shooting Rick an unreadable glance. Rick responded with a frown, but then turned to Nikki, waiting for her answer.

"Francesca had just told me what had happened at the gazebo—how Jacqueline had murdered her fiancé and his mistress, then killed herself. I'd wondered to myself if it was really worth it, and she said yes.

Then she walked right by us. Francesca didn't even notice." Nikki closed her eyes, trying to remember Jacqueline's exact words. "Then, right before she entered the lake waters, she stopped and turned to me and said, 'Tell me, Shadowborn, can you say the same?'"

Rick looked as if someone had just slapped him: his amber eyes were wide, and his jaw had dropped. It was absurd, but Nikki was suddenly reminded to never play poker with him as a partner—she had the idea his bluffs were all but transparent.

It was Justin's reaction that interested her, however. The witch's hazel eyes had widened briefly, and then a wall had come down in them, shuttering his inner thoughts behind an expressionless, unfocused gaze as he sat back against Rick's headboard. Nikki was reminded briefly of Ben Kenobi, mulling over Princess Leia's message in Star Wars, but Justin seemed a little young for the image.

"You're sure she said Shadowborn?" he said finally, looking up at her. She nodded.

"And you have no information on your birth mother?" he continued. "Nothing at all?"

"I was left in a basket on my adopted parents' porch, with a note saying I was healthy and my name was Nikki," she told him, a little sharply. "Nothing else."

"Okay, sorry. It's just that if the ghost recognized you as Shadowborn, you're probably a Shadow Mage." Justin chewed on his lower lip for a moment. "Do you mind if I try something?"

"Will it turn me into a frog?" The moment the words slipped out Nikki winced, wishing she could stuff them back into her mouth.

Luckily, Justin seemed to have as good a sense of humor as Rick; he just laughed quietly. "No, I'll leave that to my sister. This is just to satisfy my own curiosity—to see if you really are a latent Shadow Mage."

"Your sister turns people into frogs?" Nikki had a sudden image of herself small and green.

"Only if they irritate her," Justin said, exchanging a look of amusement with Rick, who had gotten himself under control. "She's gotten better about that."

"Okay, remind me not to irritate your sister." Nikki pulled her legs up underneath her, so she was sitting Indian-style on Rick's bed. "What are you going to do?"

"You won't feel a thing," Justin promised, imitating her. They faced each other, and he smiled. "Just close your eyes."

Nikki did, wondering very privately what she had done to make her life turn so weird so fast.

Sitting this close to her, Justin marveled at the incredible clearness of her dark blue eyes; despite the shadows that swam in their depths, they seemed to go on forever. He wondered how long the shadows had been there; they seemed to hint at something deeper, perhaps a personal tragedy or loss that she wasn't yet ready to deal with.

He shook his head as she closed her eyes, trusting him with an innocence he hadn't sensed in a long time. Despite her age, Nikki still felt very young in some respects. Either she'd had a sheltered life, or he was getting jaded again.

Knowing me, probably the second. I need to take some time away again.

Justin had actually been planning a vacation when Shanna had called and asked him to help Rick out. He'd figured that this would only take a few days, and then he could bum around in northern New Hampshire, maybe check out some bookstores and just generally take it easy.

When will I learn that when she asks me to do something, it's never that easy?

Shaking his head to clear his mind, Justin settled himself more deeply on the bed, grounding himself to the solidness of the earth below. Then he closed his own physical eyes, and looked at Nikki with magical Sight.

She pulsed with Shadows, dark purple and black forms that writhed around her aura, shot through with the crimson that spoke of a formidable talent. Justin was unsurprised; as he had thought, this was not the touch of a latent.

His spirit form rose from the bed and circled her, inspecting the aura for more clues. Normal Shadow Mages had the purple and black shadows, Earth Mages dark green and brown, and Light Mages amber and gold. Underlying the Shadows in Nikki's aura, however, was both the amber and the green of the other colors—something he'd only seen once before. And there was a very good reason for that....

Sweet Lady of Light, please don't let us have another StarChild on our hands! I don't want to know what kind of world-ending catastrophe would require two StarChilds—I don't think my heart could handle it!

But Nikki's aura felt different from Shanna's—in his sister's case, the colors swirled equally, a kaleidoscope that was constantly changing. The Shadows definitely dominated Nikki's makeup—Justin was struck by their strength.

Whatever else she is, she is definitely the child of a Shadow Lord.

And that's just not good news. Not at all.

Justin sat back, chewing on his lip, wondering what he was going to do now.

CHAPTER 10

"INTO THE DARKNESS"

Brilliant sunshine splashed color all over the Rothman gatehouse the next morning; Nikki could hardly believe that it was the same place she'd seen yesterday. She looked at the scene with a photographer's practiced eye as she leaned against the side of the Jeep, waiting for Francesca to join her.

Grey stones that had blended into shadows and mist yesterday now almost glowed against a sapphire blue sky, streaked by only a few tiny white clouds, and the jade green of the oak trees that marched up the hill towards the main house. The rain from last night had washed the gloom away from the entire scene—Nikki only wished it could have washed away the weirdness she had somehow fallen into.

After Justin had finished his spell, he'd retreated to a corner of Rick's room and meditated, apparently trying to understand whatever it was he'd seen. Rick hadn't been much help either; while she'd been sitting, letting Justin work his spell, Rick had opened his laptop and been quickly sucked into his novel. In the end, after a couple of moments that she spent trying to be quiet, Nikki had let herself out of the room, taking her photos with her.

Back in her own room, she'd first called her mother, needing to hear a familiar voice. Lara had been thrilled to hear from her; Nikki thought guiltily that she really needed to call more often.

But then, I've had other things on my mind.

Like magic.

Nikki stuck her hand in the left pocket of her sweater and felt the small fabric doll Justin had given her at breakfast. Her name was Pouka;

he'd insisted she take the little doll, and Nikki hadn't been able to say no, although she normally didn't carry things like this in her pockets.

"She's all the protection I can give you now," he'd said, his hazel eyes very serious.

"I'm hoping I don't need protection," she'd replied lightly, but her sally failed to lift the heavy atmosphere around the table. Rick had hardly said three words to anyone, and ate as if in a fog; Sarah's eyes had been troubled, and she too barely said anything. It had been Justin who'd spoken to her, and even his voice was hushed, as if he didn't want to disturb something or someone none of them could see.

"So do I, Nikki, but I'm afraid that you might, and sooner than we all think."

Not the most encouraging words for starting out on a ghost hunt, no.

The front door banged open, interrupting her thoughts, for which Nikki was glad. She smiled; once again, Francesca looked as if she'd stepped directly from the pages of a New York fashion magazine. Her jeans were tucked into the same hunting boots she'd worn yesterday, but today she had on a white man's shirt, open at the collar, and a beautiful scarlet silk scarf with gold embroidery was twisted casually around her neck.

"Ready for the main house today?" Francesca asked, her smile bright but forced. Once again, Nikki sensed the fear that lived in Francesca; and once again, as she had last night, she wondered why she stayed here.

"Definitely," she answered her guide, whose mouth twisted in a brief grimace before it smoothed back into the smile. They both climbed into the Jeep and retraced their steps from yesterday.

This time, the air was soft and clean, not oppressive, as they climbed the hill. Rothman House was a young woman raising a newly-scrubbed face to the smiling sky, her green lawns spread smoothly around her. The pond sparkled like a gem set in an expensive ring—the pastures rolled on to the woods in an unbroken sea of emerald. There was none of the oppressive atmosphere that had surrounded the entire area yesterday.

Given her last two weeks, Nikki didn't trust it for an instant.

Francesca waited as she checked all her equipment again: camera, extra film, light meter, notebook, pen and extra flash. Then, when she looked up and nodded, the historian squared her shoulders and led her up the front steps.

"Welcome to Rothman House," she said, opening the front door.

"Oh my Lord," Nikki breathed, as Francesca led her into the Great Hall and flipped on the lights.

Marble glowed under the cool fluorescent bulbs, courtesy of a crystal chandelier that hung from the ceiling three floors up. The entire floor of the Great Hall was a huge rosette, done in green, red, black and white marble; the background of the design was white marble. The black marble was echoed in the banisters that rose up either side of the sweeping staircase that faced the entrance; the stairs were carpeted in dark green, complementing the tapestries on the walls, all of which showed various ladies and gentlemen in hunting scenes, mostly in forest locales. Nikki's sneakers didn't make a sound, but Francesca's boot heels cracked like gunshots as they walked across the room.

"How many floors?" Nikki said softly. To speak louder than a murmur seemed almost sacrilegious; the great house seemed to be more mausoleum than home.

"Four, including the attic," Francesca replied, her voice also hushed. "Bottom floor has the informal parlor, the banquet room, the kitchen, the pantry and the family dining room." She pointed to the doors leading to the rooms as she listed them off; Nikki wrote them down and then looked at her.

"Lead on," she said.

As they moved to the left, into the informal parlor, Nikki caught a flicker of movement out of the corner of her eye. Puzzled, she stopped and turned back towards the grand staircase; for a moment, she thought she saw a shadow move at the second floor landing, but dismissed it as she turned back to Francesca, who was waiting politely. She snuck her hand into her pocket again as they entered the informal parlor; just the weight of Pouka in her hand gave her a sense of protection.

⸺

"Magnificent."

He leaned over the railing, watching her from the safety of the Shadow Lands as she entered the informal parlor with the historian he'd been eying for the past six months. The historian was beautiful, the kind of classy lady he'd kept company with while alive. She would be another fine addition to his collection.

But the other...

"A true Shadowborn," he whispered to himself, feeling desire well up inside him, warming essence long gone cold. "A Shadowborn that I can keep."

"Are you sure this is wise, Robin?"

Robin Rothman turned to his grandmother, his blue eyes bright with arousal. "Wise? Maybe not, but think, Anthea. She'll be the jewel of my collection."

Anthea Rothman shook her white head. "Stupid, Robin. Let her go, and take the historian you've been lusting after. Remember what happened the last time you tangled with the Shadowborn. You ended up dancing from the end of a rope."

"Yes, and without that, I couldn't have done all I've done since," he reminded her sharply. "You'd still be here under your father-in-law's thumb if I hadn't died then. Remember that."

"My father-in-law's thumb, your thumb, what's the difference? I'm still trapped here," she snapped back. "Maybe this time, your death will set us all free."

"I doubt it." He turned back as the two young women came out of the kitchen and entered the family dining room. "Look at her, Anthea. Look at how the Shadows follow her. I must have her."

Anthea muttered something, but Robin was too caught up in his admiration of his quarry to hear her. "You'll be my ultimate prize," he murmured. "You'll live forever here, caught in the prime of your life, and I shall enjoy the taste of you until the Shadows dissolve into the Dawn Lands."

Two words, and one of the minor specters that served him appeared beside him, hovering expectantly. On a tray was a small black teak box; Robin opened it and pulled out the parchment scroll.

And then he waited.

When they came out of the family dining room, Robin spoke four curt words. Anthea sighed as the World Walls thinned between the Shadow Lands and the Earth, forming a vortex that sucked the two mortals through.

"And now you're mine, both of you," he said smugly, replacing the scroll in its case and waving the specter away. With Anthea following slowly behind him, he raced down the stairs like a child on Christmas morning, anticipating the presents he would find below.

She had crumpled to the marble floor after the vortex had spat them both out in the Shadow Lands, curled possessively around her camera.

Her long dark hair was beginning to escape the simple ponytail that held it back from her face; he knelt beside her and stroked one slender strand that was curled down over one cheek. Her porcelain skin was warm beneath his cold fingertips; he shivered in anticipation of the heat she'd bring to him.

"Are you going to take her here, or show a little decorum?"

Anthea's acid remark cut through the red haze that filmed Robin's eyes. With a sigh, he sat back on his heels, knowing she was right. His position as head of this household was based in no small part on how the others regarded him; while taking the Shadowborn here on the floor of the Great Hall would satisfy his urges (for the moment), it would show the others, in particular his great-grandfather, that he couldn't control his own passions.

Besides, think of how much sweeter it will be to let her realize she can never get out... Despair is such an aphrodisiac.

"Prepare them rooms," he said to Anthea. "This one goes in the master bedroom."

"As you wish." Anthea withdrew to the third floor; Robin smiled again and turned back to the Shadowborn.

Leaning over and closing his eyes, he laid chill lips to her warm ear and whispered, "I can't wait to taste you." The sweet smell of brown sugar and vanilla rose from her flesh; the combination, with the softness of her skin, elicited a groan from him. Pulling back just a bit, biting his lip, Robin opened his eyes to find her dark blue ones staring up at him.

For a moment, time stopped. Blue bled into blue, desire recognized desire and Shadows called to Shadows. With effort, Robin pulled himself out of her spell, to find his lips hovering inches above hers.

In pleasant shock, he twisted the Shadows around himself, willing himself upstairs to where he could watch her in private. Watch, and relive the pleasure of her touch.

"This is a dance that I cannot wait to continue," he murmured, feeling the tingle of her magic in his blood. "And, unless I mistake me very much, neither can you, Shadowborn."

Nikki lay on the floor, breathing hard, wondering a) who the handsome young man was who'd been about to kiss her; b) where the hell he'd gone; and c) where the hell she was.

It was still the Great Hall of Rothman House. Now, however, the bright sunlight that had streamed in from the surrounding rooms had dulled to twilight, and the June warmth had leached from the air, leaving a chill she was familiar with from her dreams.

This is not possible. I am not dreaming. The lump throbbing on her head was proof of that. She sat up, easing her camera gently to the floor (and noting with wry amusement that she'd fallen in such a way as to protect the expensive Nikon), and looked around. *This hurts too much to be a dream.*

Francesca was lying not far from her, the scarlet of her scarf pooling around her head like blood. Nikki crawled over to her, not trusting her legs yet, and gently shook her shoulder.

"Francesca," she whispered, shaking the historian a bit harder. "Wake up."

Moaning a bit, Francesca opened her hazel eyes. "What happened?"

"I was hoping you could tell me." Nikki offered her a hand; Francesca grabbed it and let the other girl pull her up to a sitting position as well. "Tell me this has happened before."

"Not to me." Francesca looked around the Hall, much as Nikki had done. "It's too dark. What happened to the sunlight?"

Nikki shrugged. "I don't know. Feel up to exploring?"

Wincing, Francesca nodded slowly, and they both rose to their feet slowly, like two drivers after a fender-bender. The cold was seeping into their bones; Nikki was suddenly very glad for the sweatshirt that had seemed unnecessary this morning. Francesca was already shivering, the thin cotton of her shirt not much protection against the chill.

Nikki turned slowly in a circle. "Where do you want to start?" she asked, and then her eyes widened as a scent drifted across her nostrils.

Not the moonflowers she was half-expecting, but turkey: roast turkey, basted in butter, sage and rosemary. Francesca's wide eyes told her that she smelled it too; as Nikki continued to inhale, her nose picked out other smells that reminded her of Thanksgiving, of all things: rolls baking, corn and carrots, and stuffing.

"I don't suppose it normally smells like a holiday feast," she remarked to Francesca, who shook her head, hazel eyes wide.

Be careful, it could be a trap, whispered a tiny voice in Nikki's head, a voice she didn't recognize.

Nikki stood still, wondering what else could go wrong. Her hand slipped into her pocket, and then she got another shock: the doll nestled itself into her hand.

She pulled it out and stared at it. "Pouka?" It sounded stupid, but Nikki was beyond caring.

Why do you think Justin gave you to me? Even with a stitched-on smile, the small cloth doll managed to frown at her. *He knew you'd need help.*

"You can talk." Francesca was watching her, the fright in her eyes obvious, but Nikki ignored her for the moment. "He didn't say you could talk."

I couldn't. Not until you came here.

"What's so important about here?" Nikki's head was really starting to pound; in the back of her mind, she wondered if hearing voices was an end result of multiple concussions. *It's definitely a possibility.*

Pouka sighed, a mental sound like a bell. *Can't you tell?*

Nikki looked around her. "It looks like where we were, except colder and darker," she replied. "So what?"

Of course it does. The doll's voice dripped with sarcasm. *It's always dark and cold in the Shadow Lands.*

"Shadow Lands?" Nikki stared at the doll, feeling she ought to know what Pouka was talking about. The term sounded vaguely familiar, but she couldn't place it.

"What are you doing?" Francesca asked finally, daring to break in. "Why are you talking to that?"

"Because she's talking to me," Nikki replied absently, still puzzling out what the small doll had said. "What are the Shadow Lands?"

"You tell me." Francesca craned her neck to look at the cloth doll in Nikki's hands. "That looks like a worry doll. Where did you get it?"

"A witch gave it to me." Pouka wasn't answering; with a sigh, Nikki put her back in her sweatshirt pocket and squared her shoulders. "Well, guess we're on our own. Check out the kitchen?"

"Why not?" Despite the cold and her fear, Francesca managed a small smile. "What's the worse that could be there—flaming roast turkeys?"

Nikki giggled, despite her own worries. "Mashed potatoes from hell?" she joked back, and Francesca laughed.

Just keep your eyes open, came a last warning from Pouka. *Someone wanted you here. Gates to the Shadows don't just open on their own.*

Thanks for the comfort, Nikki retorted mentally, not wanting to share the doll's last comments with Francesca, who was heading towards the door to the banquet room.

When they had been in the room earlier, Francesca had pulled back the curtains so the sunlight had sparkled on the dusty crystal and silver on the twenty place settings on the long oak table. The historian had explained that the settings were only dusted once a month: the settings had a habit of "biting" anyone who tried to clean them.

Now, the settings were perfectly dusted, and the whole room danced in the light of the candles set in sconces around the walls, and the oil lamps on the table. A fire roared in the fireplace; even with the huge logs in it, the heat barely warmed the room.

"This damn house is so cold all the time," Francesca muttered, shivering, as she headed over to the fireplace. Nikki followed, and they both stared at the logs, neither wanting to be the first to voice the obvious questions.

"You'll soon get used to it."

Nikki and Francesca spun around as an older woman, dressed in a long purple gown, swept into the room. She favored them with a condescending smile; her mouth was painted in crimson, like blood.

"Luckily, the warmth of your skin will bleed out quickly," she continued, her voice thick with contempt for them. "Sooner than most, if I'm right. You both have the looks Robin likes."

"What are you talking about?" Nikki demanded; Francesca had shrunk against the fieldstone mantel. "Who are you?"

The woman drew herself up arrogantly. "Daphne Rothman, and while you are in my house, Shadowborn, you will address me with respect in your voice!"

"Respect is earned, not demanded!" Nikki snapped back. "And I am tired of people calling me that, and talking over my head, and not fucking explaining things! So, Miz Rothman, why don't you tell me what the fuck is going on here, or get the hell out of my way!"

She stopped, more because she'd run out of breath than any other reason. All the frustrations of the past couple of days had finally come to a head; Daphne's grey eyes had widened in shock, and her mouth moved soundlessly for a few moments as she absorbed what Nikki had said to her.

Nikki doubted anyone had ever spoken to her like that.

Recovery was swift, though. Daphne's mouth closed with a snap; her eyes narrowed and she hissed, "I hope he breaks you first, Shadowborn! Robin loves spirit—the more they have, the harder he rides them!"

Daphne turned and flounced out, the door slamming behind her, cutting off any response from Nikki. "Bitch," she muttered, gesturing rudely at the door Daphne had left through.

"What was she talking about, though?" Francesca asked, fear threading through her voice. "We have the looks Robin likes?"

"I don't know," Nikki said, her eyes dark with anger, frustration and a bit of fear of her own. "But if that was Daphne Rothman, then I have the sinking suspicion that the Shadow Lands are a lot more dangerous than we know."

"Could she really be Daphne?" Francesca's voice dropped. "Daphne Rothman's been dead nearly 125 years."

Nikki looked at the sparkling tableware. "Maybe time doesn't mean as much here." She shook herself, like a dog shedding water, trying to get rid of the sick feeling in the pit of her stomach. "Come on. If Daphne's here, maybe there are some others who can help us."

With Francesca following her, Nikki headed into the informal parlor, where a young girl dressed in a dark burgundy dress sat on one of the sofas, a piece of fabric spread over her lap. She was embroidering, her sharp needle flashing in the light of the oil lamp by her shoulder. Her eyes were dark as she paused and looked up at them.

"I'd heard there were mortals wandering in the house," she said pleasantly, her light voice warmer than anything they had encountered so far. "Welcome."

They just stared at her; she smiled and motioned to the chairs scattered around the room. Francesca sank into an armchair; something within her told Nikki to remain standing.

Just in case.

"You can sit, Shadowborn. He's upstairs; he doesn't like to come in here." The girl picked up her project again and placed another tiny stitch. "This room is too domestic for him."

There was faint scorn in her voice, but Nikki also picked up the undercurrent of fear in it. "Really? And who is he?"

She looked up again, surprised. "Robin, of course. The lord and master of Rothman House." The scorn was stronger this time.

Nikki shook her head, trying to make sense of it all. "Okay, wait a minute. Who are you?"

"Marietta Rothman. Robin's aunt."

Francesca gasped. "Marietta Rothman died when she was sixteen. A sudden illness, the records say."

Marietta gave a ladylike snort. "Illness, indeed. Helped along by my loving mother and the poison she fed me."

"Poison?" Nikki's head was spinning. "What kind of family was this?"

Biting off her thread and pulling the thread loose, Marietta laid it in her basket and considered her options for the next flower. "A sick one," she said finally, and sighed. "Very sick. My mother wanted only males to pass on the family name. I was not in her plans, and when I refused the man they'd picked out for me, she was furious. So she put hemlock in my tea."

"Nice. Going for mother of the year there." The flippant remark covered the chill going down Nikki's spine. What are we doing here?

"You've been collected," Marietta continued placidly. "Robin does this every so often, when a young lady or two catches his eye. He must be very pleased that he caught you, Shadowborn. Mages aren't usually that easy to catch."

"I'm not a Mage," Nikki corrected her. "And my name is Nikki."

The ghost shrugged. "As you wish. I suggest you get comfortable. You're going to be here a while."

"Not if I can help it," Nikki said darkly.

CHAPTER 11

"THIS WAY LIES MADNESS..."

Justin and Rick were sitting in the garden, trying to enjoy the sunshine and failing miserably. Even in the midst of brilliantly-colored tulips and roses, perfume heavy on the air, Rick couldn't get rid of the nagging feeling that something was about to happen.

Something they weren't going to like.

It laid a chill layer over the garden, dulling the sunlight and hanging like a shroud over him. Judging by the sour look on Justin's face, it was hanging over him as well.

"Something's just not right," Rick announced suddenly, and Justin grunted.

Rick looked over at his friend: there was a tightness around the witch's face that bothered Rick more than the oppressive atmosphere. "Jus?"

"Something's definitely not right," he replied, gritting his teeth. "I can feel it. Powers are…NO!"

Justin suddenly lurched out of his chair, grabbing his chest and turning grey. "Pouka!"

Rick grabbed his friend before he crashed into one of Sarah's prized rose bushes and eased him to the ground. He'd felt the energy snap around Justin, although he didn't really recognize it; now, all he could do was sit and watch while the witch tried to pull himself together.

Lying on the gravel, his pale face sweaty and his hands trembling, Justin gasped for air, his eyes closed. Rick waited, gritting his teeth and knowing, somehow, this whole episode had something to do with Nikki and the doll Justin had given her that morning.

"They're gone." The words croaked out of Justin.

"What?" Rick blinked. "Gone where?"

"Pouka said the Shadow Lands. Then I lost contact."

The chill that had hovered around him solidified into a block of ice in Rick's stomach. "Oh no."

Justin took him by surprise by heaving himself off the ground. Rick scrambled back, astonished at his recovery; even now, the grey was fading back to normal.

Duh, idiot, he's a witch—an Earth Mage! Of course he's going to recover quickly: he can just pull energy from the ground!

"And I've had a bunch of training," Justin reminded him, a sour grin on his face. "If you can't recover quickly when you're out with my sister, you get left behind."

"True." When Shanna got going, there was no stopping for anything short of a nuclear bomb. Rick felt in the pocket of his jeans; his keys rattled reassuringly. Looking over at Justin, he asked, "Ready to go?"

Justin nodded. "Let's go save the world."

"You can't escape." Marietta looked at Nikki with faint amusement. "It's impossible. Robin controls the Gates here."

"I don't care what Robin controls," Nikki said levelly. "I'm not staying."

Marietta laughed softly. "Oh, this should be good. I cannot wait to see the battle of wills when he summons you."

"Summons me? Like his prize bitch?" No freaking way! "He's in for a surprise if he tries."

"I can tell." There was satisfaction in Marietta's voice as she took another stitch. "This should be most amusing."

Nikki stared at her. "You're as sick as the rest of your family. How can you just sit there and sew?"

"What else is there to do?" Marietta looked up, surprised. "I am no Shadowborn. I cannot hope to challenge Robin's power." Her eyes returned to her project as she continued, "In truth, I hope you do succeed, Nikki. Perhaps then, we can all rest."

"Is he holding you here?" Despite herself, Nikki felt a pang of sympathy for the pale girl.

"The Shadow Lord he works with is." Marietta continued to stitch while Francesca and Nikki looked at each other.

"Okay, I'll bite," Nikki said finally. "Who's the Shadow Lord?"

Delicate shoulders lifted in an uninterested shrug. "I do not know. What good would the knowledge do me? I cannot face my own nephew—how could I hope to best a Shadow Lord?"

Nikki threw her hands up in the air, exasperated. "So you just give up and accept it? Sorry, sister, not this bitch!" She threw a look at Francesca. "Are you coming with me?"

"Where are you going?" the historian asked softly. "If she's right, we can't leave."

"That's her opinion. I'm going to explore the rest of this damn house, and I'm going to find a way out." Nikki strode out of the room, not even looking to see if Francesca was following.

She ended up in the Great Hall again, staring up at the staircase. As Francesca joined her, Nikki picked up her camera from the floor where she'd left it (funny, she'd thought she'd grabbed it earlier), and put it on a side table. Somehow, she didn't think she'd need pictures after this.

Suddenly, that looming deadline is much less important than I thought…

"So we're going to try and take on Robin and this… Shadow Lord, whatever he is?" Francesca asked her, looking up to the next landing as Nikki joined her at the foot of the staircase.

"That's the plan." Nikki drew in a deep breath. "You in?"

Francesca's shoulders lifted in an elegant imitation of Marietta. "What else is there to do? I left my knitting at home."

The thought of Francesca sitting in front of a fireplace, curled in a chair, knitting, wasn't as much of a stretch as Nikki would have thought. "Then let's go."

"So, what is a Shadow Lord?" Francesca asked as they climbed to the second floor.

"Some sort of elemental spirit, born in this world and powerful, I guess." Nikki looked around the landing. "After that, I can't tell you much more. I just learned about them too. What's up here?"

"Library, men's smoking room, couple of guest rooms, and the ladies' parlour," Francesca replied. "The family rooms are on the third floor."

"Any other ghosts that I should know about?" Nikki asked, turning slowly in a circle, trying to decide where she wanted to go first. The Power that lurked in the shadows called to her, a call she was trying very hard to ignore. *Wonder if that's part of being Shadowborn?*

Again, the elegant shrug. "I didn't know about Marietta. There could be a ton of ghosts here that never show themselves. I can think of some candidates, though." Francesca tapped a finger against her cheek, thinking. "Edgar, maybe. Obviously, Robin. Perhaps Anthea or Dorian."

"Edgar and Robin, I recognize." Nikki found herself facing the men's smoking room again and raised an eyebrow. "Who are the others?"

"Anthea and Dorian are Marietta's parents. Dorian was Edgar's only son; he married Anthea and they had Marietta and Daniel."

"And Anthea murdered Marietta, so she says." Nikki shook her head. "What a screwed-up family." She looked over at Francesca. "Shall we start in here?"

"Sure, if we're allowed in." Francesca smiled at Nikki's upraised eyebrow. "The men's smoking room was just that—women weren't allowed, not even to clean. The Rothmans had a footman take care of that."

"All the more reason to go in," Nikki said, and marched off, muttering something about chauvinists under her breath. Francesca, chuckling, followed her.

Nikki pushed open the heavy oak door and the first hint of pipe tobacco hit her. Her father smoked a pipe on rare occasions (usually when Doug brought over some of his 20-year-old scotch), and she loved the smell of his tobacco: spicy vanilla, usually, with undertones of apple. This tobacco was more of an herby scent, with hints of spice and pine; it wrapped around her as she opened the door wider and stepped inside.

The room was paneled in dark wood; leather armchairs were scattered about the room, and long green curtains hung in the windows. There were several small tables as well, holding such manly games as chess and backgammon. The walls were hung with more of the ever-present hunting pictures; in fact, the wall to the right as they entered was completely covered with a massive fresco of an English hunter-jumper, leaping over a green hedge, chasing a pack of hunting hounds.

"Welcome to my humble home."

The sardonic voice came from a gentleman sitting in a large chair by the window, the source of the pipe smoke. He was older, perhaps in his mid-fifties, dressed in proper hunting clothes: the red jacket, tan jodhpurs and Hessians polished to a higher shine than Francesca's. His face was weathered and tan, the face of someone who was outside for most of his days; the smoke from his pipe wreathed around his head, an improbable halo.

"Edgar Rothman." Francesca's voice was awed. "The man who built this house."

He inclined his head. "Indeed. This house, this room—this prison."

"I can think of worse ones," Francesca responded, moving past Nikki, who stared at her incredulously. "At least this one is comfortable."

"But cold," he replied, his dark eyes lighting up. "I'm glad you enjoy it, though."

"I've been studying it for the past six months," she replied. "It's a magnificent house."

Nikki was still staring at her. *What is she doing?*

She's attracted to him. Pouka surprised her by answering. *I think he's part of the reason she came here in the first place.*

To what? See some guy who's been dead for over a hundred years? Nikki shuddered and looked away. *That's creepy, bordering on gross.*

Who can tell with love? The little Earth spirit's voice was amused.

I was wondering if you were still there, Nikki said suddenly. *You've been quiet.*

There's heavy Shadow Magic around—I'm trying not to attract attention. Pouka sighed. *But I've been listening. If the young lady downstairs is right, it's going to be very, very difficult to get out of here.*

But not impossible.

Nothing is really impossible, Pouka replied. *I did manage to let Justin know something's happened, but I'm not strong enough to reach very far through the World Walls.*

Nikki remembered the feeling of being dragged through something right before she'd passed out. *Is that what happened? Something pulled us through the World Walls?*

Pouka's voice was amused again. *How else do you think you get to the Shadow Lands?*

Ignoring the amusement, Nikki shook her head and looked back over at Francesca, who had taken a seat near Edgar. The two were deep into a discussion of, of all things, fireplaces; apparently, the set-up of Rothman House's fireplaces was an interesting topic to architectural historians. She cleared her throat, and they both jumped in surprise.

"I hate to break this up, Francesca, but we need to find a way out of here, remember?" Nikki said, raising one eyebrow when the historian frowned at her.

"Go and look," Edgar said, leaning back and puffing contentedly on his pipe. "There's no way out."

"Why do people keep saying that to me?" Nikki complained. "I don't care. I'm going to find a way."

"Ah, the optimism of youth." Edgar looked over at her, then did a double take and set his pipe down. "On second thought, perhaps you will be able to find something."

Nikki, her hand on the doorknob, turned as Francesca joined her. "Why the sudden change of heart?"

"Because you're Shadowborn. The last Shadowborn Robin faced off against killed him." Edgar's dark eyes were bright. "You just might be the one to send my arrogant great-grandson to his well-deserved reward."

"Don't hold your breath. I don't know anything about being Shadowborn," Nikki told him, and watched his face fall. "As far as I know, I'm just a normal mortal, and not this Shadowborn that everyone seems to think I am."

"You are Shadowborn." The words were said with absolute conviction. "You can see it in the way the Shadows react to you."

"That's great. And when I figure out what that means, maybe I'll be a threat." Nikki turned back to the door.

"There's nothing to learn, Shadowborn." Edgar's voice followed her out of the room. "You just are. Tell the Shadows what you want."

A way out of this madness. A lump rose in her throat. A time portal back to a month ago, so I could blot out everything that's happened since that graduation party.

Remember what I said about nothing being impossible? Pouka's voice was very small. You just found the one thing that I think is.

Figures.

Nikki drew in a deep breath and turned at random down the hall. The hallway branched off at the landing; she turned right and stood looking at the two doors.

"Right side is the library," Francesca told her. "Left is a guest bedroom."

"I'm not really into bedrooms at the moment," Nikki said, firmly squashing the image of Robin's eyes that rose into her head. "So the library it is."

She pushed open the door and the smell of books, years and years worth of words, rushed over her. Nikki loved libraries; Lara and Marc were both avid readers, and one of the first memories Nikki had was of receiving her first library card. "This is definitely my speed," she murmured, stepping into the softly-carpeted room, with its floor to ceiling bookcases. There were more of the ubiquitous leather chairs, and the fireplace was glowing with warmth.

"You mean he found a literate one? Shocking."

"Does every room in this damn house have a ghost?" Nikki demanded, hands on her hips and the books forgotten as she watched yet another male appear, this one in a soft tailored suit and with a cigarette trailing smoke in one hand. His features were similar to Edgar's, but while the older man's face had character, this one's simply held the aftereffects of a lifetime of dissipation.

"It's our house, my dear," he said, smirking at her. "Why shouldn't we move as we see fit?"

"Daniel Rothman," Francesca whispered in Nikki's ear from behind her. "Marietta's brother."

"The one who had the coachman hung because he was having an affair with his wife?" she whispered back.

"Yes."

"Ah." Nikki looked at Daniel with disgust. "Charming."

"I'm glad you think so." Daniel smiled at her and sauntered over, ignoring her shudder of distaste as he cupped her cheek in his hand. "Maybe when Robin gets bored with you, he'll let me have you for a while."

"And maybe both you and Robin will be looking for your balls first," Nikki replied sweetly, and kneed him in the groin.

As Daniel lay on the ground, gasping, Nikki looked over at Francesca. "Let's go—the air in here is sour."

———

"Tisk, tisk, Father—you should have known better."

Robin stepped from the shadows where he'd been watching the entire episode, a smug smile on his face. He knelt beside his father, who was still curled around his damaged manhood, and shook his head. "She's a Shadowborn, Father; how can you have hoped to even touch her before I subdued her?"

Daniel muttered something, and Robin laughed. "She is spirited, isn't she?" The lust rose again, and he reveled in it. The Shadowborn was making him feel more alive than he had in many, many years.

He made a snap decision and patted Daniel on the shoulder. "Suck it up, old man. It'll only hurt for a little bit." Then he rose and strode back into the shadows.

She and the historian were in the hall again, trying to decide which bedroom to try first. Too bad all of them on this floor were taken—he'd have made that choice very easy for them if there had been an empty one.

Robin drank in the sight of her, eyes still bright and face still flushed from her encounter with Daniel. *Is this what she'll look like after I ride her?* The question heated his blood even more, as did the image it brought with it: Nikki on her back, lying on the satin sheets of his bed, dark hair tangled with sweat and lips parted softly, full and heavy from kissing. Her top did nothing to hide her breasts—small, but well-formed and pert, the way he liked them.

Imagining himself lying between her bare legs was driving him insane with waiting. As she turned to go back down the hall, he stepped out of the shadows in front of her, blocking the way.

"Going somewhere, ladies?" he asked, smiling down at her.

———

It was just like last time. Nikki looked up into his eyes and felt herself fall, diving into a blue that went on forever. She was barely aware of the world around her; the only real thing in her world was Robin, leaning forward to kiss her. Her lips parted in automatic response; his taste was deep, smoky and male, and elicited a groan from deep within her.

This is the way it will be, his voice whispered inside her head seductively. *Just you and I, together. No one else will intrude. Nothing else will matter.*

Her body moved forward, molding itself to his as she began to surrender to him. His arms slipped around her, bringing her in closer, and the Shadows began to wrap around them as she felt him start to gather his Power.

Then Rick's eyes, clear dark amber, like sunlight caught in a glass, swam through the darkness in her mind. Nikki heard his warm baritone voice, as he'd spoken to her two nights ago, when she'd gone to his room for comfort. The chill pleasure that Robin's touch promised faded as she realized what he was offering: a lifetime in his home, trapped in the Shadows.

Part of her longed for that prison, yearning for it with an intensity that frightened her. With a groan that was half fear, half desire, Nikki yanked herself out of Robin's arms and away from him. She sank back against the wall and stared at him, the back of one hand pressed to her lips, eyes wide with shock at how close she had come to succumbing to him.

Am I really that easy?

Robin chuckled, a supremely confident smile on his handsome face. Resist me, Shadowborn, the seductive voice threaded through her mind again, and Nikki moaned. It only makes the chase that much more enjoyable.

And then he melted back into the Shadows.

His voice, however, continued to murmur, Let me share the Shadows with you. This is where you belong. Your heart knows it.

"Get out of my head!" Nikki shouted, turning and slamming her fist into the wall, scaring Francesca, who had been moving towards her. The pain lanced through her fingers up her arm, clearing the last of Robin's webs from her head. She took a deep breath, trying to stop her body from shaking, and looked over at the historian.

"Feel better?" Francesca asked, her face pale. Nikki nodded, not trusting herself to speak.

Francesca looked around. "Mind if I try a little theorizing?" she asked, and Nikki shook her head. "Do we know what this Gate thing looks like?"

Nikki frowned. "No, actually."

I do, Pouka told her.

"Pouka does, though," Nikki continued, and Francesca pursed her lips.

"This Gate is going to be something valuable, I'd think" she said, and Nikki, after conferring silently with Pouka, nodded her head. "So wouldn't it make sense for Robin to keep it somewhere safe? Somewhere he can protect it?"

"Protect it from what?" Nikki asked. "It sounds like everyone else here either follows his orders or is helping him."

There are those in the Shadow Lands who would view this as a very strong defensive position, Pouka told her. The fact that Robin has a Shadow Lord protecting him is the only thing that keeps this house from being disputed, I would imagine.

So where would he keep it? Nikki asked her.

"So where would he keep it?" Francesca said at the same time, her forehead furrowed in thought.

Somewhere he is comfortable. Somewhere he can defend, Pouka said.

Nikki repeated that out loud, and Francesca's frown deepened. "Somewhere he is comfortable," she mused. "Master bedroom?"

Heat flashed through Nikki as her brain connected Robin and bedroom in a decidedly naughty fashion, but she firmly pushed the emotion back down. *I do not want to spend the rest of my natural or unnatural life as someone else's whore!* She told herself sternly. *No matter how good a kisser he is!*

How about his lover? Robin's voice was back, the promise in it winding around the base of her spine and sending spurts of lust shooting through her. *His life, his world?*

No!

Nikki closed her eyes and ground her teeth together, forcing his voice out of her thoughts by sheer will. When she opened them again, she was sweating, as if she'd just run several miles. *There has to be some way to stop him from doing that,* she muttered to herself.

Maybe I can help, Pouka offered slowly. *I'm not as good at it as physical protections, but I might be able to keep his mind out. Justin's going to have to teach you to do this yourself, though. But I'll need your permission.*

Do whatever you have to, Nikki told her. *I can't concentrate with him doing that.*

That's the point, Pouka told her, amused. *He wants you to be thinking with things other than your brain.*

Just make it stop, please! Nikki begged, and the little sprite chuckled. *Give me a moment.*

Nikki waited, feeling Francesca watch her but not wanting to open her eyes. Then it felt like a wall dropped around her; cautiously, she opened her eyes, waiting to see if anything else would happen.

There was blessed silence in her head—even the Shadows' voices were gone, and the pull of the Power waiting there had been reduced to a mere distraction.

I don't know how long I can keep this up, Pouka warned Nikki. *You'd best find that Gate soon.*

What are we looking for?

Something that looks like a vortex. The Earth spirit's voice was a bit distracted. *Trust me; you'll know it when you see it.*

"Okay, she says we'll know it when we see it," Nikki said to Francesca, who was watching her with the same kind of expression people use when watching tigers pace in their pits at the zoo: wondering if they could really get out and attack.

"If you say so." The historian's voice was dubious, but she followed Nikki up the stairs.

———

Robin was lying on his bed in the attic, enjoying himself immensely as he continued to stroke the Shadowborn's emotions to a fever pitch. It was a skill he'd exercised throughout the years after his death; usually from the protection of the Shadow Lands, as the lady who had caught his interest lived in the house on the mortal plane. Once he'd provoked her passion, he'd withdraw and wait; the hunger he'd kindled would continue to grow, resulting in the lady usually begging to be taken. Then, with her permission, he'd take her to the Shadows, where she would warm his bed until a new lady caught his eye.

But the Shadowborn—oh, the Power that sang in her! It called to him, igniting a fire like he had never felt before. Even as she struggled against him, trying to ignore him, he could feel her yearning for what he had to offer. Never before had a woman so matched him in strength— it excited every fiber of his being, driving all thoughts from his mind.

This was one woman Robin was going to take a very, very long time to enjoy.

Her scent, pulled in on the Shadows he'd spun around her to connect them, lay heavily on top of him. He reveled in it, letting the sweet smell of vanilla curl around him, imagining what he was going to do with her.

And then it was gone.

He sat up, the heat in his loins gone as if someone had thrown him in to the pond in the midst of winter. Somehow, someone had broken his connection to the Shadowborn.

Someone was in his house.

"Dorian! Daniel!" Robin roared. His father and grandfather appeared abruptly.

"Someone has entered the house and broken off my connection to the Shadowborn," he informed them acidly, getting up off the bed and pulling his boots back on. "Go and fetch the historian and the

Shadowborn, and make sure they don't escape."

"You-you want us to go against the Shadowborn?" Dorian faltered, shrinking back from his grandson's glare.

"Yes, old man." Robin speared his grandfather with a piercing look. "She's not even begun to use her gifts; she should be easy enough. I'll deal with the intruder." He swung around to Daniel, who was smirking. "And no sampling, either, Daniel. Remember how she treated you last time."

The smirk vanished.

"Now go."

As they disappeared, Robin gathered his Power around him. No one broke into his house.

No one.

————⊱⊰————

Nikki had just put her foot on the final step when there was a hollow-sounding crack above her. The air around her was suddenly cold and slimy; she heard Francesca scream as Shadows wrapped around her.

Pouka! What's going on? The thought rang out in her head as she struggled to breathe. The world was going dark.

They're trying to knock you out, Pouka said. My shield's blocking some of it, but I can't keep it up much longer: they're stronger than I am.

Who are they? Nikki struggled against the tightening Shadows, feeling panic start to well up inside her.

Two of the ghosts. One is Daniel; I don't know the other. Pouka's voice was starting to fade as well.

What do I do, Pouka?

There was a long silence, and Nikki's panic grew. I can't let them take me!

The Shadows surged around her, crushing her as Pouka's shields crumpled under the pressure. Nikki could hear the Power calling her again, from somewhere beyond the suffocating pressure of the two ghosts, and in desperation, she reached out, trying to find something she could hold on to.

Icy Power suddenly flooded her body, a stream of cold that shattered the Shadows Daniel and his companion had wrapped around her. Nikki floated in a sphere of frost, Power singing around her, encouraging her to surrender to its song, leaving the mundane behind...

You have to focus this, Nikki! Pouka's voice was suddenly loud within the confines of her skull, drowning out the seductive song. Find a focus!

A what?

A focus! Something you want this Power to do! The sprite's voice was a line Nikki clung to. Hurry!

A single image formed in her mind—Rick, his face concerned. She reached out to him, focusing only on him. Help me, she begged him. Find me.

The sphere contracted and then shimmered as it expanded. Nikki had a brief glimpse of Daniel and another older man, similar in features, backed up against the walls of the landing, and of Francesca, slumped on the stairs behind her, before everything brightened to the point of blinding light.

And then, there was nothing.

Chapter 12

"Twilight Hope"

"Lord and Lady."

Justin and Rick sat in the truck, staring at the house before them in fascinated horror. The locked gates in the drive had been only a minor annoyance; Rick had produced his trusty set of lockpicks and teased the lock open. Now, they sat in the parking lot, just contemplating the mess in front of them. Justin's breathed invocation summed up Rick's feelings on the subject nicely.

It was a beautiful, bright June day: birds sang in the trees, the sun was warm and the breeze smelled faintly of wildflowers as it blew through the truck's open windows. In short, a typical early summer afternoon.

Right up until one hit the edge of the lawn.

The Shadows that boiled around the house darkened the sky, reminding Rick of the final scenes from Ghostbusters, right before Gozer the Gozerian was destroyed.

Egon, where are you? He thought irreverently, wishing for a blaster pack.

"I think we're going to need more than that," Justin said slowly, looking at the darkness in front of them. "That's one hell of a Shadow enclave." He turned to Rick. "Stay here. I'll go in and find them."

"Like hell you say." Rick was already climbing out of the truck. "There is no way I'm letting you go in there alone."

"That house is so far into the Shadows now that you'll never come out, Rick," Justin argued, also climbing out. "I'm not having that on my conscience!"

"And I'm not going to tell your sister how I let you get killed by going in there by yourself," Rick retorted. They squared off at each other in front of the truck, both handsome faces twisted into stubborn snarls.

Help me! Find me!

The mental plea hit Rick like a ton of bricks, right before the ground shook, and both he and Justin instinctively dropped to their knees. The Shadows roared; then everything stopped.

When Rick opened his eyes again, there was nothing to disturb the sunlight. Rothman House stood above them, serene in the June sun, its windows sparkling. The grass was warm beneath his cheek; he'd fallen on his side, and his arm ached from the impact.

"What the hell was that?" he muttered, sitting and rubbing his arm.

Justin looked as shaken as Rick had ever seen him, a more alarming fact than that the Rothman House had gone from creepy to cozy in less than sixty seconds. "Someone shifted the Balance," he murmured, and Rick's blood turned to ice.

Most people didn't know about the Balance. However, running with Shanna had given Rick some insights into the magical force that controlled the three Lands—for it to have shifted enough to knock them both over meant something very, very powerful was at work in that house.

And that was a very, very bad sign.

As one, Rick and Justin rose to their feet and sprinted into the house. Rick felt Nikki's presence as soon as he entered the Great Hall, somewhere above him; he took the stairs two at a time, Justin hot on his heels.

She was crumpled on the stairs just below the third-floor landing, unconscious. Her aura glowed icy black, cut with flashes of white and green, but Rick dismissed the inconsistencies as he knelt beside her, looking frantically for any sort of wounds. Thankfully, she appeared to have been knocked out when she came back through the World Walls; Rick couldn't find anything more severe than a couple of bruises on her cheek where she'd fallen. But her face was white when he turned her over, paler than he'd ever seen, and her breathing was deep, as if she were a sleeping princess waiting to be roused by her prince with a kiss.

He lifted her gently in his arms and looked over at Justin, who jerked his head down the stairs. "Let's get out of here," the witch said tersely. "I don't trust this place."

As if to underscore that, the hall darkened briefly. Rick hugged Nikki's body close to him as she moaned, somehow reacting to the Shadows that were starting to swirl above them again.

"Move!" Justin shouted, giving Rick a push down the stairs. "They're coming for her; we've got to get her out of here!"

Thankful that he had continued to run after he'd graduated college, Rick stretched his long legs and his endurance as he bolted back down the stairs, Justin moments behind him. Whatever was hiding in the attic howled in fury as they pounded down the stairs; Nikki shuddered in his arms, her face going even paler as she struggled against him.

As they came down into the Great Hall, the front door slammed shut, and Shadows from either side began to coalesce into a solid figure. Rick stopped, unsure of what to do but not willing to risk trying to run through the Shadows with Nikki, who had fallen still again in his arms.

"Now what?" he hissed to Justin, who pushed ahead of him to confront the Shadow.

"Let us pass." There was no room for compromise in the witch's voice.

Let her stay, the Shadow demanded, and I will let you leave.

"Not likely," Justin replied, his hazel eyes narrowing.

The Shadow laughed, a sound like ice cracking in the ocean. You would challenge me here, Earth Mage? In the Shadows? You are more of a fool than I thought.

"This house hasn't moved fully into the Shadows yet, ghost," Justin said coldly, his aura beginning to glow a dark green to Rick's eyes. Usually, his Sight wasn't this sensitive, but the overload of magical energy in the house was causing it to flare, layering magical images over the normal ones everyone saw. The Power that arced around Justin surprised Rick a bit; he backed up, not wanting to get caught in a firefight.

Don't go any farther, whispered a female voice in his head, and Rick spun around to see the faintly glowing shape of a young woman standing in the doorway to his right. She shook her head, warning him not to say anything.

He's trying to frighten you into going back farther into the house, she said softly, motioning at the Shadow menacing Justin. If you retreat much farther with her, he'll draw the whole house back into the Shadows again.

What do you suggest I do? Rick snapped back at her. Charge him? He won't be expecting it…

She faded from the doorway, but her warning rang in his head. Gritting his teeth (and thinking he was going to need major dental work after this), Rick turned back towards the burgeoning fray, wondering how the hell they were going to get out of this one.

Justin, apparently, had a few ideas.

Rick had never truly seen his friend in full attack mode. Justin tended to remain in the back, letting his sister throw the fireworks while he tended to the fallen. However, the Shadow had managed to provoke the witch and it turned out that when provoked, Justin had just as bad a temper as Shanna did.

His hazel eyes narrowed even further, and he raised both hands above his head, clenching them together as he chanted in a language Rick had never heard before. Red fire leapt from his clenched hands to the Shadow, which engulfed the fire and answered with darkness.

Justin unclenched his hands and batted away the ball of night contemptuously. His right hand stabbed at the Shadow and green light flashed, temporarily blinding Rick. He heard a horrific shriek; when his sight cleared, Justin was standing in the doorway, wreathed in sunlight, a frown on his face. Nikki hadn't stirred; Justin motioned Rick out the door, and breathed a sigh of relief once they were all standing on the lawn.

"Now what?" Rick asked, as Nikki began to move in his arms. Her blue eyes opened slowly; once she realized who she was looking at, she burst into tears and wrapped her arms around his neck.

"Let's get her away from here," Justin said quietly. "I managed to get us out, but that ghost has a lot of Power built up here. He wants her, and he's not going to let her go that easily."

Nikki heard the words, but they didn't sink in until Rick carried her over to the truck. She felt him reach for the door, and she realized they were taking her away.

"No!" she cried, trying to wiggle out of his arms. "We can't leave! Francesca's still trapped in there!"

Rick had to fight to keep from dropping her; in the end, he let her legs drop down, but grabbed her wrist as she tried to run back into the house. "Nikki, we barely got out of there!" he shouted, trying to get her into the truck. "You are not going back in!"

She hissed angrily at him, fighting to free her wrist, but he was stronger. He half-dragged her back to the truck, managing to avoid most of her kicks to his legs and groin area.

"You don't understand!" she screamed, tears streaming down her face. "He's still got Francesca!" One of her kicks connected with Rick's knee; he let go of her wrist as he went down against the truck, and Nikki turned back towards the house. She got two steps before a wall of force stopped her; furious, she reached for that Power she'd found before.

"Don't, Nikki."

Justin's calm voice cut through Nikki's fear and anger; she turned to face him, her dark blue eyes anguished. "We can't leave her there—she'll die!"

"She's already dead."

The flat statement hung in the air between them, creating a tableau that would haunt Nikki for years. Rick leaned on the truck, holding his injured knee, watching the battle of wills between Justin and Nikki.

"She's not dead," Nikki said stubbornly, dashing tears from her eyes with the back of one hand.

"She's mortal, and she got sucked into the Shadow Lands. She's dead," Justin repeated, crossing to her and taking her gently by the shoulders. "I'm sorry, Nikki. There's nothing we can do."

The finality in his voice was underlain with deep sorrow. She looked up at him; his hazel eyes were troubled. "I can't leave her to him," she whispered. "I can't."

"You already have." He put one arm around her and led her back to the truck. "Let's…"

His voice trailed off incredulously; Nikki raised her eyes from the ground in front of her to see what had startled him.

The great black cat was sitting in a patch of sunlight, her green eyes strangely intent on Justin. He stared at it for a moment, then shook himself and turned to the others.

"Let's head down to the gatehouse. I need some time to think."

"You let her escape!"

Dorian and Daniel cowered in the corners of the room, ducking frequently as Robin's wrath caused various objects to fly around the room. He stood in the center, Shadows curling around him, his handsome face purple with anger. The Power he generated snapped around them, sending dark sparks up when it connected with either of the two shades.

"I had a chance to break a Shadowborn, to make her mine, and you two idiots let her escape!" he ranted, pointing at them. "I could have solidified my position in the Shadow Lands, without needing a Patron! I could have finally had a consort worthy of myself!"

"She-she called a Gate!" Dorian protested weakly, and ducked again as Robin turned on him. "What were we supposed to do?"

"You were supposed to knock her out!" Robin raged. "She has no control of her gifts—how hard could it be?"

Daniel snapped back, "Something protected her long enough for her to figure out how to tap into your Power reserves."

"Then you should have tried harder!" Robin roared, snapping a strand of Power at his father. "She's a girl, for Heaven's sake!"

"Calm down, Robin." Anthea's voice, from the safety of the doorway, cracked across her grandson's temper tantrum. Robin snarled, but subsided at the look on her face.

"Not all is lost," she continued, moving into the room. "The historian is still here—apparently the Shadowborn didn't know how to move both of them through the Gate."

"I don't want the historian," Robin snarled. "I want the Shadowborn."

"Use your head rather than your balls!" Anthea snapped at him. "Use the historian as bait! Do you think the Shadowborn won't try to rescue her?"

Robin opened his mouth to reply hotly and then closed it again, the fire in his eyes fading as he considered what his grandmother was saying. Slowly, an evil smile spread across his face. Dorian and Daniel straightened up, aware the storm was passing.

Anthea nodded as understanding bloomed across Robin's face. "Good, you are thinking. I was beginning to worry the Shadowborn had stolen what was left of your brains."

"Where is she, Anthea?" Robin asked, ignoring the dig.

"In the Lady's Chamber," Anthea replied, matching his smile with one of her own. "And scared."

"Just the way I like them," Robin purred.

"What about the Earth Mage?" Daniel asked, now that Robin's attention was elsewhere. "You can't believe that he'll let her come back without him. And you couldn't keep him here."

Robin's eyes darkened again, and Daniel shrank back, afraid he might have triggered another explosion. "I wasn't expecting him. That's the only reason they escaped," he snapped. "And I'll make sure he doesn't do it again."

He spoke four words, and one of his servants, one that actually looked human, appeared beside him.

"Tell Lord Andreas that I need his help," he said, and then added, "Respectfully, of course. And do not mention the Shadowborn."

The servant bowed and vanished.

"That should take care of the Earth Mage." Robin smiled viciously, his blue eyes glittering. "Now to take care of the rest."

Francesca sat on the canopy bed, her knees hugged to her chest as she looked around the room. Normally, the Lady's Chamber was one of her favorite rooms—one of the few rooms in Rothman House that she didn't feel watched in. The delicate lace curtains usually let in plenty of sunlight; the walls were papered in a pale rose pattern, matching the rose carpet and the handstitched lace hangings on the bed. The pictures on the walls were of ladies hunting, of course, but they were more fanciful than in the rest of the house: the ladies were dressed in silks and carried hawks. Francesca's favorite picture, of a lady attempting to catch a unicorn, was on the wall across from the bed; she stared at it now as she tried to figure out what she was going to do.

The door was locked; she'd already been up to try that. The Lady's Chamber was on the third floor of Rothman House, and the ivy wasn't strong enough to hold her weight. And the windowpane had been cold to the touch ; the land outside was a nightmare copy of the grounds she'd come to know so well in the last six months. So she had retreated to the bed, where she considered what options she had.

The last thing she remembered was following Nikki up the stairs to the third floor. Then darkness wrapped around her; she couldn't breathe, and an icy cold seeped into her bones. And then she'd woken up here.

"Francesca?"

Francesca's eyes widened as something shimmered at the foot of the bed. Slowly, as if not to attract attention, Edgar's form solidified, his dark eyes concerned.

"What are you doing?" she whispered. "Did you lock me in here?"

He shook his head. "That was my darling daughter-in-law. They're holding you here in hopes that the Shadowborn will come back to rescue you, so Robin can either offer to exchange you for her, or simply take her as he took you."

"Why is he interested in her?" Francesca asked, confusion on her face.

"Because she's Shadowborn. She can control more Power than Robin could ever hope to. If he can control her, he won't have to worry about whether or not his Shadow Lord patron will come and help him defend the house." Edgar came around the side of the bed and sat down. He looked around, as if seeing the room for the first time in a long time. "I'd forgotten how much like Rachel this room was."

"Rachel?"

Edgar sighed. "My first wife—Dorian and Jacqueline's mother. She died in a hunting accident when Dorian was 10. This was her room; Daphne didn't change it much."

"I like it," Francesca confided, smiling shyly. "It's always been one of my favorite rooms."

"It suits you," Edgar said, looking at her and answering her smile with one of his own.

That smile, the one she'd seen in various portraits, the one that had led her to Rothman House in the first place, warmed the entire room. Despite her fears, Francesca felt like this was what she'd come to Rothman House for: to find this man.

Edgar leaned in and touched her cheek. "Francesca, I need to tell you something."

"Yes?"

The word hung between them as Francesca and Edgar gazed into each other's eyes. He looked as if he were trying to figure out a way to tell her something; she smiled again, silently willing it to be what she wanted to hear.

"Francesca, what would you say if I asked you to stay here?" he said finally. "Here, in this house, with me?"

Her heart leapt, but she shook her head, knowing it wasn't possible. "I can't, Edgar. I'd love to, but I'm not Shadowborn or a ghost. I'm still human."

His hand covered hers on her knee. "And that is why you cannot leave, my dear."

"What do you mean?" The icy chill that permeated the house settled into her bones. "I can't stay here."

"Mortal humans are not meant to be in the Shadow Lands," he said, his voice sorrowful. "Once you crossed the threshold into the Shadow Lands, you..."

"I died. Is that what you're trying to say?" Francesca whispered, drawing back from him, her pale face white. "I died."

The awful finality of those two words sank into her soul, and her eyes filled with tears. Turning her back on him, she curled into a ball of misery. "Go away," she choked, when she felt his hand on her shoulder. "Just go away."

Wave upon wave of anger and fear crashed upon her, with homesickness and a longing to see the sun again. Six months ago, when she'd first come to Rothman House, Francesca had looked up at the house and wished with all her heart to never leave. But now, with no other options and knowing who the true master of the house was, she wanted nothing more than to escape back to the small apartment she'd shared with her best friend in Manhattan, even with the loud neighbors and the crazy traffic of the city.

The faint scent of lavender and roses filled her nose as she buried her face in the pillow. It was yet another reminder of the world she'd left behind; Francesca gave into the tears and cried until she had nothing left. When she was done, Edgar was gone.

She raised her head, eyes sore, and looked out the window at the pond. Daylight in this world was twilight; she wondered dully what night would bring.

"True darkness," came a light voice from behind her, and Francesca jumped. "Night is always black here."

Rolling over on her other side, Francesca looked over towards the closet, where the voice had come from. A faint shimmer, golden in the candlelight, hung like a heat haze there; Francesca strained, but couldn't make out any features.

"Wh-what are you?" she whispered, fascinated in spite of herself.

"One who can sympathize with your situation." The voice floated like a spring breeze out of the glow. "One who can offer hope."

"There is no hope here," Francesca replied bitterly.

"There is always hope, especially for one who still has a part to play." The shimmer floated out of the closet, moving towards the bed. Francesca watched, unable to move, wondering privately if death caused madness as a side effect.

"Madness is not your destiny, Francesca," the voice said softly, and she closed her eyes as a warm glow filled her, driving the chill from her bones. "You still have a part to play. Do not despair. The light has not forgotten you."

And then the shimmer was gone.

Francesca slowly pulled her knees up to her chest again, hugging them tightly, trying to keep the warmth within her.

That was how Robin found her: lying on her side, curled up around herself, very nearly asleep. The sound of the door pulled her from her drowsing; she opened her eyes to see him standing over her, a satisfied smile on his handsome face.

"This room suits you," he said. "Elegant, feminine: everything you've always wanted."

"You know nothing of what I want," Francesca whispered, and Robin laughed.

"On the contrary, little historian, I know exactly what you want," he murmured, coming closer and leaning over her. "You want to return to the sun—to be out of this nightmare."

She returned his look levelly. "And since that is impossible, I repeat: you know nothing of what I want."

The look of shock on his face was almost worth the loss of her freedom. Deciding that it didn't matter what he did, Francesca rolled over again, deliberately turning her back on him.

After a moment, she felt a cold hand on her shoulder and stiffened. "Don't worry, I'm not interested in your treasures," he said, and the some of the charm had gone out of his voice. "You may be trapped here, but that doesn't mean you can't serve a purpose. And once I've lured the Shadowborn back with this," and he took the scarf from around her neck, "perhaps I'll let Daniel have you. It might slake his lust for a bit."

She shuddered, remembering the slimy ghost she and Nikki had encountered in the library. Robin chuckled, a harsh sound full of things Francesca didn't want to imagine, and stroked her hair again. "Did you like that idea?" he whispered, wrapping strands of her long dark hair around his hand and pulling her head back towards him. "Should I tell Daniel you'll be ready for him?"

"You can tell Daniel to go to hell," she murmured, trying to pull her head back. "And you can join him."

Robin chuckled again and let her go. "We'll see. You're mine now. Just remember that, little historian."

As the door shut behind him, a wave of drowsiness broke over her. Her last thought before sleep claimed her was that at least she'd be rested enough to fight back if Daniel did show up.

Then she slept.

Chapter 13

"Dances of the Past"

Days like this were to be gloried in.

Alenya niNyx ran, stretching her legs as long as they would go, the wind of her passing slicking her fur to her sleek body. The moss was soft beneath the pads on her paws; the scent of summer flowers flowed past her nose, reminding her that on the Earth, the seasons had turned once more. In the timelessness of the Shadow Lands, it could be hard to remember that there were changes happening elsewhere.

The moss of the forest she ran in gave way to grass as she crossed a meadow, then faded back into moss again as she re-entered the trees. Ostensibly, she was out hunting, making sure there were no lost souls caught in the Shadow Lands by accident.

In truth, it was simply an excuse to run.

There was a trembling in the air around her, a frisson of Power that vibrated along the slender whiskers on either side of her face. Alenya paused in her run, one paw uplifted, trying to sense the direction from which the Power was coming. Someone or something had just entered the Shadow Lands, and she, like the cat she was, was instantly curious as to what was going on.

Sitting down on the moss, she closed her emerald eyes and sent her mind out, looking for the source of the tremor. The scent of flowers darkened briefly; she furrowed her forehead in puzzlement, and then caught a whiff of what she was looking for.

Fear, the stale odor of sweat and terror, tickled her delicate nostrils, and her lips drew back in a feline grin. Time for one of the sweeter duties of a younger Shadow Lord.

She tracked him by the odor: he was dripping fear like water as he ran through the woods, running from something that apparently only he could see. With her tongue lying on one side of her mouth, Alenya ran, chasing him for the sheer joy of it, knowing that she shouldn't toy with him like this, but enjoying herself enough that she ignored the niggling of her conscience for a while.

He broke through the trees ahead of her, heading for the stream Alenya could hear in the distance, and she saw why he'd wandered into the Shadow Lands. Usually, the only spirits here were those who deserved it; occasionally, the spirit of one who had died in violence or before they were supposed to got caught in the Shadow Lands, rather than heading to the Dawn Lands where they belonged. It was up to the younger Shadow Lords to patrol the Lands for these spirits, and to send them back to where they belonged.

Splashing into the dark water, he paused, blood streaming from the ruins of his face. Judging from the torn uniform, he'd been a police officer, shot in the line of duty, she supposed. She slowed, giving him a moment to rest, knowing that he wouldn't truly rest until she freed him. That was the other problem with spirits that got lost on the wrong side of the Balance: they never got a chance to heal, but were trapped in the pain and horror of the moment of their death.

"Don't come any closer!" he shouted, his hand reaching for the gun that was no longer holstered at his side as she stepped out of the trees, although she didn't know how he could see her—his eyes had been destroyed by the blast that had taken his life. Backing up, he slipped into the cold water, staining the dark water even darker.

I will not hurt you, Alenya said silently, her emerald eyes beginning to glow. The smoky mental voice, full of Shadows, wrapped around the fallen officer, smothering his fear with the promise that she would send him to where he belonged.

Long white incisors sank into the collar of his jacket; the sharp metallic taste of blood and death filled her mouth as she dragged him from the stream. She kept the Shadows around him as he lay on the bank; it was easier to send them on when they didn't move.

Releasing his collar, she sat next to him and laid one large paw on his chest. Slipping easily into his mind, she quickly found what she was looking for: the last few moments of his life.

"Jesus H. Christ," he muttered, unsnapping the holster lock on his gun as he and Malone sized up the situation. The shooter was holed up in the remains of the grocery store—there was glass everywhere on the sidewalk in front of the store, sparkling on the ground like a deadly snowfall. In the midst of the glass lay the body of one of the store clerks, a young African-American male with his jacket still on. The rain had stopped minutes before the shooting erupted; blood mingled with rainwater on the young man's leather jacket.

Hank shook his head and glanced at his partner, who nodded, and they both drew their guns. According to dispatch, the shooter had two more clerks inside the store, and possibly one other patron—there had already been several more shots heard. There were two other cars on the way, but if they were going to save any of the hostages, they had to go in now.

Malone led the way, crunching carefully over the glass. One of the clerks had managed to lock herself in the storeroom with her cell phone; that was how they'd gotten the scant information they had. One shooter, she'd said, armed with several pistols and a shotgun. Hank glanced at the body of the clerk as they went by—there was a huge hole in his chest, and his brown eyes were open wide in shock.

They stepped cautiously into the store, dark now except for the lights from the freezer cases, the emergency lights and the streetlights outside. Malone gestured to catch Hank's eye; once he had his attention, he motioned that he was going to work around to the outside aisles. Hank nodded and began to circle the other way.

He went by the bakery, the smells of fresh bread mingling with the metallic tang of blood and the acrid smoke of gunpowder. Today's bread of the day was sourdough; his nose caught the distinctive tang of the bread and unaccountably, his stomach rumbled.

It had been a long time since the bagel he'd scarfed down at the beginning of the shift.

Glancing behind the bakery counter, he saw feet sticking out from behind a rack and detoured over to investigate. The baker had been shot once, at point-blank range; the bullet hole in his forehead ringed with black powder.

Hank's head jerked up as there was another spat of gunfire from the back of the grocery; he heard Malone curse and then a gurgled scream.

"Officer under fire!" he snapped into his shoulder radio, crouching behind the bakery case and scanning the aisles in front of him. The grocery settled into an eerie quiet after the brief burst of shots—which made the dispatcher's voice, distorted by the radio, doubly loud as she advised him *that backup and paramedics were less than a block away.*

"Wonderful," he muttered, moving slowly out from behind the case and down one of the aisles, trying to figure out where Malone had been.

Cereal spilled on the floor under his feet; the brightly-colored marshmallows mixing with a red streak that snaked its way down towards the back of the store. The blood was still tacky: someone had dragged himself or herself down the aisle. Or had been dragged; he couldn't tell.

As he peeked around the corner at the end of the aisle, Hank's eyes widened. The shooter was sitting down; her back propped up against the freezer case. Around her were scattered three pistols and several cases of soda; she had her feet propped up on the body of another store clerk and the shotgun cradled like a child in her arms. The clerk's body was still oozing blood; her face was turned towards him, and a thin line of blood snaked from her left nostril. Her eyes were blue: they stared foggily at him, death already glazing them with white.

Malone lay a few feet away, where the blood smear ended. She had shot him several times, hitting the legs and shoulders, the places where the vest didn't cover. Once she'd dragged him out from the aisle, she'd finished him with a single bullet in the center of his forehead. Hank had to admire her coolness—so far, it looked as if she hadn't wasted any of her shots.

Ironically, it was the radio that betrayed him. He'd forgotten to turn it down after dispatch had advised him of the backup and paramedics, and it burst into sound as he was trying to line up a shot, hoping to take her out without a fight.

As the radio beeped, the shooter's head whipped around, followed very quickly by the shotgun. She must have reloaded after shooting the clerk outside; his last sight was the flash when she pulled the trigger.

Pain exploded in one horrific instant; his last thought as he went down was of his daughter; her birthday was Saturday, and her gift was in his locker. He hoped someone would retrieve the charm bracelet and give it to her.

Alenya sighed, disengaging herself from his mind gently and taking her paw from his chest. She'd been right: he should have gone on to the Dawn Lands, but the violence of his end had routed him here. The shotgun blast had ripped through his face—whoever the shooter had been, she'd indeed been skilled; by avoiding anywhere covered by his vest, she'd spared him a long, lingering death.

Alenya had killed enough in her life to appreciate the mercy of a quick death.

She sighed, looking down at the cop as he lay quietly on the ground, her Shadows taking his pain away for the moment. With one swift movement, she leaned over and ripped out his carotid artery, warm blood spraying over her face and chest. Then the Shadow Lord moved back quickly and sat down again to watch him leave.

The cop's body had convulsed once as his brain shut down, deprived of blood from her quick strike. Then it began to glow with an amber light; Alenya closed her eyes as the light grew, and his body exploded, shattering into bits of golden glow that faded out of existence even as they drifted to the ground.

The Balance restored, Alenya looked at the blood turning sticky on her fur. *At least I'm near the stream this time*, she thought ruefully, padding down to the stream and shivering a bit as she slipped into the cold water. *You'd think they wouldn't spurt after they'd already died once.*

It was one of the things she didn't understand. As the current of the small stream washed the blood from her fur, she pondered the vagaries of humans—even after they died, their spirit bodies clung to what they felt should be the way they were; they bled, they hurt, they died. It was part of what made them both fascinating and vulnerable to the denizens of the Shadow Lands.

Alenya swam, enjoying the feel of the water on her skin, until she felt she might be clean. Then she climbed out and shook herself, splattering the nearby trees with water droplets.

I wonder what else I should do with my afternoon, she mused, stretching. *Kith won't be done with his experiments until evening, and the Darkness only knows what Mother is up to now. Come to think of it, I haven't seen her in a few days. I wonder...*

The thought was broken as the entire Shadow Lands gave a huge lurch. Alenya was thrown to the side as the Lands shuddered—when the quake was over, she scrambled back to her feet, emerald eyes huge with shock.

What in the name of anything holy was that?

The shock waves continued to rumble—someone had done a major shift in the Balance. After a moment's fumbling, she caught the direction of the epicenter and took off running towards it.

Following the scent of the explosion was easy; whoever had shifted the Balance wasn't being very subtle about it. Which meant one of three things—either they were new to their gifts, they were in trouble and trying to summon help... Or they just don't give a shit what the

Council thinks of this, she thought grimly as she ran. And that's just something I don't want to think about.

Distances in the Shadow Lands were distorted. There were stretches of forest that connected the various enclaves that dotted the Lands, homes of powerful ghosts, Shadow Mages and Shadow Lords, as well as the other creatures that lived in the Shadow Lands. The forests were as big or as small as they needed to be, and Alenya had long ago learned the trick of shrinking the distances she needed to travel.

The forest ended and a lush lawn began, rolling up to a large house that Alenya immediately recognized as a mortal home. A haunted house: still physically on the Earth plane, but with a strong presence in the Shadow Lands as well. She paused at the end of the lawn, her whiskers quivering as she tried to sort out the layers of Power around the house. There was mortal magic; most likely the ghosts that haunted the house, but there was a heavy scent of Shadow Lord around the property as well.

A Lord protects this house, she mused. How interesting.

There was another layer as well: one neither Lord nor mortal-flavored, but a strange combination of the two that triggered something, a memory of a similar feeling. She shook her head and padded down the lawn, past the large dog lying beside the pond. The dog looked at her, but was smart enough to let the Shadow Lord pass without incident.

Wise move, little one, Alenya told him, her emerald eyes calm. I'd hate to have to kill you.

Her attention was diverted by the front door opening. Three people came out, one of whom she thought she recognized. They were surrounded by a faint green glow that meant they were physically on the Earth plane; haunted houses were always like this, one of the places on the Shadow Lands where the two worlds were close enough to see into one from the other. She stayed back and watched as the two young men tried to leave, but the young woman with them had other ideas. As she tried to run back into the house, one of the young men stopped her, and Alenya instantly recognized that particular flavor of magic.

Justin?

Her foster son's head whipped around as she called his name, and his hazel eyes widened. Not now, he sent.

The odd scent she'd noticed earlier was stronger now; she came closer, looking at the young woman Justin had his arm around. Her features were strangely familiar; another face swam before her eyes, with the same stubbornness, begging for her help. Alenya couldn't help it; she extended a tendril of Shadow, trying to see if she was right.

Justin's magic blocked her. *I promise, I'll come talk to you later*, he said curtly. *Tell the Council I'm taking care of it.*

Come to the house—I think there's more going on here than you know, Alenya replied, a chill snaking down her spine.

Wonderful. Justin's mental voice was dry. He shook his head and hustled both his charges into the truck parked in front of the house. She watched them drive off, and then turned her attention back to the house. Without the distraction of the strange young woman's magic, another scent came clear: another Shadow Lord, and not the one that had the house under protection. This scent Alenya knew well.

Why were you here, Mother? She wandered around the outside of the house, picking up her mother's scent at various places, although the elder Shadow Lord had been very careful to stay outside. There was an amazing amount of ghosts here; this was once a very unhappy house.

Yet another thing I don't understand about humans. Why do they feel the need to force their ideas on their fellows?

Shadow Lords for the most part were solitary creatures, living out their long lives in their enclaves, surrounded by their research. Alenya was considered an aberration by her peers; she shared her home with not one, but two other Lords: her lover, Kith, and her mother, Cassandra.

Not only that, but I am far more interested in the affairs of mortals than I should be, as my father has told me on more than one occasion, she mused, finally heading back into the woods. *In fact, I believe the last occasion was when I took Justin and Shanna in.*

Andreas had been furious with her, descending in all his Council glory, demanding to know what she thought she was doing, taking an Earth Mage and a bastard Mage that didn't even know what her gifts were into her home. Although, given what had happened, she wasn't sure sometimes that she didn't see his point.

What's done is done. Now, I need to decide what to do with the young woman Justin has found.

Those dark blue eyes rose again in her mind, so very familiar. Alenya sped towards her own home, suddenly very certain that her life was about to change again.

Chapter 14

"Battle Cries"

Justin watched Rick help Nikki out of the truck at the bottom of the hill, his hazel eyes troubled. Even here, her aura was flaring, a reaction to the Shadows that still pulsed through the house above them on the hill. She probably wasn't even aware of what she'd done.

And that makes my job that much more difficult.

As the other two went into the gatehouse, he turned back towards the truck and pulled the phone that had been vibrating anxiously out of his pocket. Glancing at the phone number displayed, he sighed and answered it.

"Tell me you have this under control."

His sister's voice was full of emotion that she was trying very hard not to show. Justin could picture her perfectly: standing leaning against something, one strand of her flaming red hair twined around her finger, her blue eyes narrowed in concentration.

"I have everything under control," he repeated obediently, and she snorted.

"Now say it so I believe it."

Justin let out a gusty sigh.

"That's really not building my confidence, Jus," she said tartly.

"Shanna, what would you say if I told you I found someone with a similar aura to you?" Justin looked back at the gatehouse, but Nikki and Rick were still inside.

There was dead silence on the other end of the line. "Please tell me you haven't found another StarChild," Shanna said finally, and the strain in her voice was evident. "Tell me it's not that bad."

"I hope not. Her aura is weighted towards the Shadows, so I don't think she's another StarChild. But who else do you know besides you with all three Spheres represented in their aura?" Justin waited for her to answer, knowing she couldn't. "And there's more."

"Light, what now?"

"Alenya's here." The appearance of his foster mother was still shocking. Alenya normally left the Earth plane alone, unless she was hunting, and Justin hoped fervently that she wasn't hunting today.

At least, not hunting one of the two in my care right now.

"What's she doing there?" Shanna asked. "Investigating the Balance shift? And do you know what caused that, by the way?"

"Yeah, the same problem you sent me up here to investigate. She opened a Gate." Justin winced at Shanna's curse.

"And that shifted the Balance that much?"

"She's totally untrained, Shanna. And way more than a latent. Think of yourself about 6 years ago." And think of how the Council is going to react when they find out about her. That's so not going to be fun.

That's probably why Alenya wants a full report tonight. Wonderful. I hate dealing with the damn Council again.

Shanna was talking again, pulling him out of his thoughts. "Do you need any more help?"

"Not unless you know someone who can figure her out faster," he replied evenly, and then sighed. "Sorry, that was rude."

"Not a problem—I knew what you meant." She echoed his sigh. "So now what do we do with her?"

———

Nikki and Rick had ended up in Francesca's living room, a pleasantly open room that was full of mid-afternoon sunlight. She sank into the armchair beside the fireplace, still looking very pale. Rick wandered into the kitchen; when he returned with a peanut butter sandwich and a can of Dr. Pepper that he handed to her, she looked at him with blue eyes full of anguish.

"I really did kill her, didn't I?" she said, her voice harsh with emotion, ignoring the food. "I left her in there to die."

"No, whoever pulled you through the World Walls the first time killed her," he replied, trying to hand her the sandwich again. "You were lucky to get out."

"She got grabbed because he wants me," Nikki retorted, curling up in a ball. "That sick bastard wants me to join his little harem."

And you want to, whispered the small voice that she hadn't heard from in a while, the nasty voice that had shown up after she'd learned she was adopted. You liked his kisses, and you'd hop in his bed in a heartbeat.

Would not. Nikki resolutely tuned the voice out.

"There's nothing you could have done, Nikki." Rick put the plate and can on the table next to her and knelt down in front of the chair. He put his hand under her chin, forcing her to look him in the eyes. "You have no training—I'm amazed you could even get yourself out. Don't blame yourself for what happened to Francesca." He nodded towards the sandwich. "Eat. You expended a lot of energy; now you need to replace it."

Nikki looked at him for a moment longer, wanting nothing more than to dive into his eyes and never come out. That thought reminded her of Robin's blue eyes, full of promise; with a deep breath, she pushed that thought away as well and, to humor him, picked up the sandwich.

The creamy peanut butter melted in her mouth, the taste bringing her back to warm summer afternoons when she was a child, sitting in her mother's bright kitchen, a tall glass of chocolate milk ready at her elbow to wash the sandwich down. Nikki smiled at the memory, her legs sliding to the side so she was sitting up, not curled anymore. Rick echoed her smile, encouraging her to finish the sandwich.

When the last morsel was gone, he asked, "Feel better?"

She nodded. "Much. Thank you."

His smile quirked again. "No problem. I'm used to putting fledging Mages back together. You guys never know how to refuel after a major output of power." The smile faded. "And creating a Gate is a major output."

"Do you want to know how I did it?" she said quietly, her lower lip trembling just a bit.

He nodded, not taking his eyes from hers.

"I asked you to help me," she admitted. "Robin's strong, but he couldn't compete with you."

It was out in the open: Nikki listened to the words come out of her mouth and wondered how he was going to react.

Rick's amber eyes widened, and then a slow burn began in their depths. "And did he kiss you?" he asked, leaning in towards her.

She nodded, not willing to say anything more.

"And he couldn't compete?" His mouth was close enough to hers that she could feel his breath caressing her lips. "Watch it, Nik—you'll stroke my ego to untold heights."

"I'd rather stroke something else," she murmured, wetting her lips with just the tip of her tongue and wondering just when her body had taken control of her brain.

"I thought we were going to go slow."

"So did I. Then I thought I'd never see you again."

Even watching him, she almost missed the beginning of the kiss. He leaned just a little more forward; she felt the electricity of his lips and her eyes closed.

He tasted of peanut butter—either he'd stolen some as he'd made her sandwich, or there was some left on her lips; she wasn't sure, and didn't care. Under the nutty flavor was warm masculinity, not cold Shadows; Nikki felt herself drowning in the sensations flowing over her.

Lips opened; she was never sure later whether she initiated it or he did, but suddenly their tongues were exploring each other's mouths, a slow, sweet, intimate search that wiped out all outside sensations. Nothing existed but she and he; their mouths were the only point of contact.

Heat was building around them; so different from Robin's kiss. She felt new Power rise through her; the sphere building around them flared in various colors.

Should this be happening? She wondered somewhere in the back of her mind.

Does it matter? Rick's thought was amused; she shuddered as it wrapped around her.

No…

"Think you can handle this?" Shanna said finally, and Justin heard the concern in her voice.

"I hope so." Something niggled at him; he turned back to the house and his jaw dropped.

She was saying something else, but he missed it as he stared at the house.

"Shanna, I'll talk to you later."

He hung up, not even caring that he cut her off. The gatekeeper's house was glowing: multi-colored flames leapt up from all available surfaces, but there was no heat. Justin stared at the mage lights, utterly speechless, one small part of his mind wondering just how powerful she was.

The rest of him decided that he really didn't want to know.

Shaking himself out of his self-induced trance, Justin went into the house, wondering what had set off this display. *It's warm colors and I don't feel fear, so that leaves only one thing…*

Yeah, that's what I thought.

Rick was kneeling in front of Nikki's chair; both of them were far too wrapped up in each other to even notice his entrance or the flames burning merrily around them. As Justin had suspected, Nikki was the source of the flames; what he hadn't expected was how Rick's aura was meshed into hers.

How very interesting. Well, at least he's stable. Now all we have to do is make sure she is.

But first he was going to have to get their attention. Justin looked around and noticed that there were some large architectural books on the side table near him. *Perfect.*

———

Crash!

Both Nikki and Rick jumped when the book hit the ground. The flames around her vanished; she felt very wobbly all of a sudden.

"Are you two done?" Justin's voice was dry; Nikki flushed, feeling like a schoolgirl caught kissing a boy for the first time by her father. From the look on his face, Rick felt about the same.

"Not that I wanted to interrupt you, but the light show was starting to attract the neighbors," the Earth Mage continued.

"Light show?" Rick looked over at Justin, frowning. "What light show?"

Justin glanced at Nikki, who flushed again. "Let's just say we're going to have to teach someone a little more control before you two should try that again."

Wonderful. Now I can't even control myself.

It's not really your fault, Justin's mental voice soothed her. *You don't have any training, and a really, really powerful gift, from the looks of it.*

It's nothing we can't fix.

Nikki stared at him. *Is it always like this? People talking in your head?*

"No," he answered her out loud. "Shields can keep most people out."

"Most?"

"I don't want to say all," he said. "You never know when there might be someone out there stronger than you."

Nikki remembered the feeling of calm that had descended upon her when Pouka had blocked Robin's insinuations. "Can you show me now?"

Justin looked at her, as if measuring her up. "It's not something that's easy to explain," he warned her.

"I don't care. I have to go back in that house, don't I? I'm not letting him start whispering in my ear as soon as I walk in." She watched his hazel eyes; there was a start of surprise, then he pulled his emotions back behind a wall again.

"Why do you think you need to go back?" he asked her, his voice carefully neutral. Rick was looking back and forth between them, his face confused.

"Because you wouldn't have stopped here if we could just leave," she replied. "You wanted me to leave—then the cat showed up. The only explanation is that I need to go back. You tell me why."

There was grudging admiration in his hazel eyes now. "You're the one who shifted the Balance. We have to right it."

"And how do we do that?" Nikki was struggling to keep her voice steady. "Just go back in?"

Justin shook his head. "I wish. No, I think you're going to have to face the main ghost in there, Nikki."

Cold sweat and heated longing chased each other up Nikki's spine at the thought of facing Robin. *Even after Rick's kiss, he can still do this to me? How am I supposed to face him?*

———✦———

Justin watched her struggle to control herself—his Mage Sight was much more powerful than Rick's, so he saw the flares of emotion throughout her aura.

Interesting that she flares into the Earth Magic colors when she gets emotional, he thought to himself. *I would have expected her to flare into the Shadows, considering the amount of Shadow Magic in her makeup. Then again, Shadow Magic tends to be colder…*

But she was right about one thing: she had to go back into the house to set the Balance straight. He'd hoped he could shift it back on his own, but Shanna had been adamant on that fact.

"It's got to be done by her," she'd said. "If she caused the shift, she's got to set it right. You know that, Jus."

"And what exactly has to be done?" he'd asked her sarcastically. "She was kidnapped by a ghost. What does she need to do, destroy the ghost?"

"Probably. Especially if there's now a mortal dead. You know how it works, Jus—the Balance needs to be preserved."

He hadn't been able to come up with a rebuttal for that.

So now I have to try and do a crash course in magic to a Mage who's probably at least as powerful as my teacher, and do it in less than 12 hours, because the Council is going to be breathing down our necks in about that long. And there's no way we'll be able to convince Rick to stay behind, so I'll have to worry about him too.

Sometimes I hate my life.

Justin shook his head to get rid of these thoughts and gave her a wry grin. "Well, it goes like this…"

This is harder than I thought!

Nikki was drenched in sweat and shaking by the end of the first hour, and Justin was beginning to look a little ragged himself. Still, his patience hadn't wavered at all. She wondered dryly if he was bucking for sainthood.

"I'll settle for you learning how to shield," he replied, and she bit her lip as she realized that once again she was thinking out loud.

"Just try again," he encouraged her, running a distracted hand through his brown curls. "You've almost got it."

Rick had curled up on the couch to watch them; she glanced over at him and saw he'd fallen asleep. Lucky dog, she thought, then sighed and rearranged her legs beneath her again.

She was seated Indian-style on the floor, the better to "ground herself," according to Justin. She wasn't quite sure if she was grounded yet, but the flames hadn't shown up around her again.

Okay, I'm going to do it this time!

Drawing in a deep breath, Nikki closed her eyes and tried once again to feel the warmth of the Earth Magic Justin seemed positive she could control. And once again, it wasn't warmth, but the icy chill of the Shadows that blossomed up inside of her. And once again, she heard Justin sigh, and the Power drained away.

"I don't understand," she complained. "Why can't I build my shield out of Shadow Magic?"

Justin was chewing on his bottom lip when she opened her eyes. "I think you might have to, Nikki. The only problem is that Robin might be able to use it against you."

"What do you mean?"

"Shadows can work with Shadows: he might be able to wrest control of your shield away from you if you aren't careful, and trap you in it." Justin's hazel eyes were worried. "But you can't seem to consciously tap the Earth Magic yet, and we can't let you go in there unprotected. So try again, this time with the Shadow Magic."

She closed her eyes again, and this time willed up the icy chill. Shadows swirled against her eyelids, purplish-black; Nikki imagined a wall, encircling her, made entirely of the Power. It pulsed around her, a bruised battlement—she felt Justin's gentle touch against the shield, and felt his approval.

"Very good, Nikki. Now let's see how it holds."

The next moment, Nikki landed on her back, the Shadows still around her, but cracks beginning to appear in her wall. As she tried to clear the stars from her head, Justin hit her again; this time, the shield shattered.

"Not bad. You kept one bolt out."

Justin's hand appeared above her; she grasped it and he pulled her to her feet. "I'll never get this right," she muttered, and he chuckled.

"Please. Just some practice and you'll be fine. Most of my students couldn't stop one of my bolts after only one hour." The praise in his voice lifted her spirits.

"Students? You mean you do this for a living?" Nikki cocked her head at him, wondering.

Justin shook his head. "Not for a living. I program websites for a living. But I'm a little more patient than my sister, so I get to train most of the newbies we get."

"What, turning them into frogs doesn't get them to learn?" Nikki joked; despite himself, Justin chuckled.

"I hope you don't meet Shanna anytime soon; she'll kill me if she thinks I've told you she turns people into frogs," he said, and motioned her to take a seat again. "Let's try this again."

By the end of the second hour, she was successfully keeping most of his powerful magic bolts out. He still managed to knock her on the floor after a bit, but acknowledged it was probably due more to her exhaustion than anything else.

"There are probably guest rooms upstairs; why don't you go and crash for a bit?" he said, giving her a hand up. She was going to argue, but a wave of sleepiness crested over her and she yawned, making the argument moot.

"What about Robin?" Nikki asked, as she headed up the stairs. Justin smiled.

"Whoever built this house shielded it from Shadow Magic—Robin will stay up on his hill tonight," he reassured her. "Don't worry."

Which tells me that whoever built this house knew that his or her employers were messing with Shadows, he thought, watching her go up the stairs. Rick was still passed out on the couch, but Justin knew there was more he needed to do before he too could sleep.

He stepped outside, to the late afternoon sunlight. June in New Hampshire—the sun still had at least two hours left before setting, but Justin had determined that he wasn't taking Rick and Nikki back up into the main house before morning.

Oh yes, let's go and challenge the powerful ghost in his own domain at night. Brilliant! He snorted, knowing that in his younger days, that would have been exactly what he would have done. Thank the gods for having lived long enough to become older and wiser.

Besides, Nikki's dead on her feet, and she only knows how to shield. I still need to teach her how to attack. But that's going to take time, and time is what we don't have. Not with the Council demanding answers, which I assume they are.

He looked up into the clear blue sky and wondered again what a normal life was like.

Not that I'll ever have to worry about dying of boredom. I guess that's the tradeoff.

Shaking his head, Justin pulled out his cell phone again and checked it. Surprisingly, there weren't any messages from his sister; he thought there should have been at least one message from her. Which means she's distracted. Wonder if that's a good thing or a bad thing?

Considering what he had on his plate, Justin decided not to worry about it. I've got enough to deal with.

He dialed another number on the phone—as it rang, he wondered who would answer this time.

"Good evening, Master Justin." Farnsworth's voice was as stuffily polite as Justin remembered it.

Ah, the joys of calling home. "Is Alenya in, Farnsworth?" he asked.

"Just a moment, Master Justin."

The phone was set down; Justin heard a murmur of voices, and then the velvety, smoky voice of his foster mother flowed down the line. "I thought you were coming over tonight, Justin."

"I don't want to leave them here," he said, leaning against the building and enjoying the warmth of the sun. "With my luck, Nikki would decide to go up to the house by herself and try and fix things. No thank you."

"She's very powerful, if she's the one who shifted the Balance." He heard the creak of leather and guessed she was sitting in the library; it was logical, considering there were only two phones downstairs in her house. "What do you want me to tell the Council?"

Justin breathed a sigh of relief at her tacit offer to run interference with the Council of Nine for him. "Tell them I'm working with her. We're going back into the house tomorrow to right the Balance; I already talked to Shanna about it. However, Nikki's exhausted. I'm not taking her back into that house now."

"So you're taking care of it."

"For the moment. She's going to need another teacher, someone stronger and more knowledgeable than me." He debated for a moment. "Alenya, don't tell the Council this, but she's carrying more than one Sphere in her aura."

"Are you sure?" She didn't sound surprised, which shocked him.

"You know what she is."

"I think I know who she is," Alenya corrected him. "And I think you should probably bring her here, once this is over."

"You're holding out on me," he accused.

"Of course I am." Her amusement only fueled his sudden irritation. "That's my prerogative as your mother."

"Great. Dare I hope you'll share your wisdom?" Sarcasm sharpened his voice.

Alenya laughed, and Justin was once again reminded of jazz singers in smoky clubs. "Fix the Balance. Then I'll share my knowledge, such that it is."

Justin knew better than to beg; his foster mother loved to play the mysterious Shadow Lord, even as she berated her own mother for doing it. He promised to come after this was all over, and she promised to distract the Council until then.

After he hung up, he stood outside for a while, leaning against the warm stone and drinking in the sunlight, trying not to think about how long it might be before he had another peaceful moment like this.

Then he sighed and went inside to rest as well. The morning was going to come sooner than any of them wanted.

Chapter 15

"Enchanted Lady"

"Well, are you ready?"

Justin looked at Nikki, who was staring up at the great bulk of Rothman House. Today, like yesterday, the house was wreathed in morning sunshine. Standing on the grounds, feeling the warmth of the sun on her back, the house didn't look at all as scary as it had before.

She wasn't fooled for an instant.

Justin's question hung in the air between them. She stood on the grass, Rick's hand clasped in hers, contemplating exactly what was going to happen once they stepped inside.

"Robin's made it very clear that you're his objective," Justin had told her early that morning, when she'd come downstairs, following the alluring smell of coffee. "He's going to pull us all through as soon as we enter that house."

"So what should I do?" she'd asked, accepting the coffee mug he'd handed her. Rick had trailed in behind her, lured in by the same scent that had dragged her from bed.

"Well, I'd suggest not pulling up your shield until he starts to bother you," Justin had said. "It takes a lot out of you at first and you're not used to carrying it up all the time. Once we're done with this, I have a friend I'd like to recommend as a teacher for you. I'm not sure I'm up to it."

The conversation had dragged from there. None of them were morning people, but neither had they had felt comfortable lying in bed while the house loomed over them on the hill above.

After coffee, Justin had pulled Rick aside and spoken to him in another room. Nikki wasn't sure what he'd said, but Rick's face was calmer when they came back.

She wished her morning had been that easy.

"You know how to shield," Justin had said. *"Now you need to learn to attack."*

He'd run her through some small drills until her head was aching again. Then, over a light breakfast, they'd discussed strategy.

"I can't teach you to be a major Mage in five hours," Justin had said honestly. *"What I can do is teach you to start to protect yourself. And, if you'll let me, I can help you try and defeat him."*

"How?"

"Nikki?"

Justin's voice pulled her out of her musings. "It's not going to get any easier, you know," he said gently. "At some point today, we have to go in."

"I know." Nikki shook her head and smoothed the silk shirt she'd borrowed from Francesca's closet; they were about the same size and build, although she'd worn her own jeans. Pouka was nestled in one of her jean pockets; the little Earth sprite was a comforting presence in the back of her mind, yet more evidence of how much she'd changed in just a few days.

Just underneath the surface of her skin, she could feel the chill of the Shadows, waiting for her to release them. They called to her, beckoning her in—and this time, she was going to follow them.

Once I go in there, that's it, Nikki thought to herself somberly, not caring who heard her. I will no longer be the girl I thought I was. I guess this is how magic truly changes you.

It does, came Rick's voice softly. But not all the changes have to be bad. And his fingers tightened around hers.

She smiled her thanks at him and then drew a deep breath. "Let's go beard the dragon."

Robin's head came up suddenly. His wards shimmered as she walked through the front door, a tingling over his skin that caused him to shiver in anticipation. Just as his grandmother had said: the Shadowborn had returned.

He rose from his desk and hurried out to the landing, looking over the railing and through the World Walls. As expected, she had the Earth Mage and another mortal with her; Robin dismissed them both, as he had already dealt with them. It was her, glowing with Power, who drew his eyes, as before. Now that his kiss had awoken the true potential in her, she blazed, inviting him to drown in her in a way no woman had before...

He pulled himself out of the trance she was weaving without even knowing it, refusing to allow himself to be lost in her glamour before she was his. But soon, little Shadowborn, he purred. Soon nothing will stop us from enjoying each other for lifetimes without end.

Returning to the master bedroom where he had been working, Robin picked up Francesca's scarf and ran his fingers along the edge, enjoying the smooth silky feel and imaging what else he could do with it. No, for the Shadowborn, it should be dark blue, like her eyes, he thought, shivering slightly at the thought. Dark blue, against her white skin...

The shiver became more pronounced, pleasure crawling over his skin, and he gave into one shudder before controlling himself. Then he spoke the words to open the vortex. As the three were pulled through the World Walls, Robin smiled.

Welcome back, my dear. This time, you won't be leaving.

                             ⸻

Nikki was expecting the vortex this time, thanks to Justin's explanation. She didn't pass out, although the cold and swirling colors were more disorienting than the sudden blackness. There was a brief, horrid sensation of being squeezed and then she stood again in the chill that was the Shadow Lands, looking up the staircase towards the second floor.

There were other, subtle differences this time, changes she perceived with the new senses that had awakened, especially the Power that flowed over everything. The scent of turkey roasting was gone: a new scent, vanilla overlaid with spice, floated on the air. It was vaguely familiar, and Nikki frowned.

That smells like that body wash I've been using, the one Mom gave me for Christmas last year, she thought, as the fragrance filled her nostrils. *How bizarre.*

Justin touched her arm, distracting her. Nikki looked at him; he pointed up and behind her, and she followed his finger. Her dark blue eyes narrowed and a shaft of lust shot through her; pushing it aside firmly, Nikki raised her chin and stared defiantly back at Robin.

"Welcome back, my dear," he called down, his voice smoothly wrapping around her. Rick's fingers were still entwined with hers; the pressure of his warm hands helped her resist the invitation in Robin's voice.

"Where's Francesca?" she asked icily, drawing strength from both Rick and Justin standing to either side of her.

"Where I'd like you to be," Robin replied. "In bed."

Nikki's nostrils flared as an image inserted itself in her head: a large four-poster bed with darkly-red sheets, and herself lying upon it, dressed in something short and black. "Haven't you ever heard of subtle?" she retorted, squeezing Rick's fingers as a hunger started in her groin. "That is so not going to work this time."

And why not, Shadowborn? His mental whisper stroked against her skin, soft fingers of icy Power that fanned the fires his first image had started. It's what you want, isn't it? You know what I offer. My experience is far wider than the infant whose hand you hold. Leave the child and let me show you how only a real man can satisfy you.

His mental touch spread, trailing Shadows across nerve endings she didn't know she had, trespassing in areas none of her boyfriends had ever even imagined. The heat in her loins grew; she closed her eyes, reveling in the sensations for a moment longer.

"Nikki?" Rick whispered in her ear, and she smiled.

You're right, Robin, she murmured mentally back to the ghost above her. Only a real man can satisfy me.

And with a single thought, her shields went up, throwing him out of her mind.

She felt his surprise and anger; with his intrusive touch blocked, the heat turned to ice, and all Nikki felt now was slimy. The fire in her eyes was cold; she locked her gaze on Robin and allowed her smile to turn triumphant. "Now that we've established that, why don't you give me Francesca and we'll leave."

"Do you really think it's going to be that easy, my dear?" With her shield blocking his charm, his voice was harsher, colder than she remembered. "Francesca cannot leave this place."

"I don't believe that." Nikki's voice was flat.

"Ask your pet Earth Mage," Robin sneered. "She's mine forever."

Nikki didn't even bother looking at Justin. "I still don't believe it. Nothing is impossible, so I ask you again. Where is she?"

"Come and find her." Robin tossed something over the railing; as it floated down to her, Nikki recognized Francesca's crimson scarf. She reached up and it coated her fingers; when she looked up again, Robin was gone.

"Bastard." She shook her head and started up the stairs. Rick's hand stopped her, pulling her back.

"What are you doing?" he asked, amber eyes wide as she slipped her fingers from his. "That's where he wants you to go!"

"And that's where Francesca is," she replied, showing him the scarf. "And yes, I know she can't leave the Shadows, but I will be damned if I leave her in his hands. And besides, I can't bloody well kill him if I don't go after him, can I?"

"True." Justin's voice was amused. "And I think you've surprised him."

Nikki's grin turned vicious. "Wait till he sees what I've got planned for later."

Both Rick and Justin gave her puzzled looks and her grin softened. "Don't worry—I'll let you know when I work out the details. Now come on. The bedrooms are all upstairs."

As she climbed the steps, though, Nikki's thoughts were a lot less confident that she was projecting. What was I thinking, taunting him like that? She felt the icy Shadows running through her veins and shivered at the promise there.

Power corrupts, remember? Keep it cool, Jeffries, and you'll be fine.

That sounded more like herself; Nikki drew comfort from that and continued to the second floor.

"That bastard."

Robin paced the master bedroom, Shadows trailing in his wake, fuming. Somehow, the Earth Mage had corrupted his beautiful Shadowborn, turning her abilities against him.

"I want him," he growled, looking at Dorian and Daniel. "I want him in pieces, do you hear me?"

"But, how are we to get him?" Dorian whined. "He's an Earth Mage...what are we..."

"I don't care how you do it!" Robin thundered, whirling around on his grandfather. "Just do it!"

"If I may," Daniel interposed, and his son snarled.

"No! Just do it!" Robin's eyes glowed with fury. "I want him gone. Completely and utterly. He's in our world now—let's remind him of that fact." He glared at the two men. "Now get out, and don't come back until he's dead."

"And the Shadowborn?"

His grandmother's voice was smooth and neutral; it grated against Robin's nerves. "I'll deal with her," he snapped.

"Why don't you let me soften her up for you?" Anthea suggested. "Wear her out. Then you can step in and do with her what you will."

Robin stared at her for a moment, her suggestion whirling with the fury in his mind. Then a slow smile began to crawl across his face, and he nodded.

Once they hit the second floor, Nikki looked over at Justin. "Is there any way we can try and magically find her before we just go nosing around?" she asked.

He shrugged. "You can try and use that," he replied, gesturing to the scarf Nikki still held in her hand. "But all the spells I know are Earth spells. It's very unlikely I'll be able to find her with the Shadows swirling like this."

"Can I use the Shadows to find her?" Nikki's eyes were intent.

"You can, but what good would it do? Nikki, let's just find Robin and go." Rick's voice was troubled, and Nikki looked over at him.

His handsome face was twisted, as if something in the very air pained him. As she looked, he flushed and looked away, trying to avoid meeting her eyes.

"What's wrong, Rick?" she asked quietly, and watched his jaw clench.

"Nothing." The word was dragged out of him. "I just want to get this over with."

It's the Shadows, Nikki realized. For a Sensitive, this must truly be hell. I can only imagine...

His jaw tightened even farther. "I'm fine."

"Fine." She turned back to Justin. "How do I search for her?"

He opened his mouth to speak, but a scream from upstairs cut across the conversation. All three of them whipped around to look up the stairs; another scream echoed through the house, and Nikki's face went pale.

"Francesca!" She bounded up the stairs, intent on finding the source of the screams. As Justin and Rick moved to follow her, Daniel and

Dorian appeared to either side and jumped them, dragging them off to the side rooms.

Nikki paused in the center of the stairs, torn between helping the guys and finding Francesca. And then a third scream ripped through the air; Nikki decided that Rick and Justin could take care of themselves and tore up the rest of the stairs to the third floor.

"I'm coming, Francesca!" *Although what I'm going to do when I get there is anyone's guess…*

<hr>

Rick gasped for air, flailing against the bony hands clenched around his throat. The two old men had appeared out of nowhere, attacking him and Justin from both sides, and his got in a lucky grab. Now the old man was dragging him into one of the rooms off the corridor; Rick caught a glimpse of Justin, struggling with another, slightly younger man, before the door slammed shut.

"Going to make sure his lady is safe," the old man crooned, his bony fingers tightening around Rick's throat, steel cutting off his airway. "The Shadowborn will protect us, once he's broken her. Protect the house."

The old man's eyes were distant, as if he didn't even see the person he was strangling. "Going to be safe," he continued, as Rick thrashed beneath him. "No more worries, no more Shadow Lord. All safe and sound."

Darkness was closing in on him; unfortunately, the old man had dragged him to the center of the room, with no tables or anything he could use as a weapon within reach. Rick's struggles grew smaller; as he was losing consciousness, the hands abruptly vanished.

Rick gasped, pulling oxygen into his tortured lungs, his vision clearing slowly. He became aware of two things: the nut who was trying to kill him was now prone on the floor next to him, and there was a gentleman who looked very similar to the nut standing over him, a brass fire poker in his hand.

"Don't just sit there," the man with the poker said irritably, when he saw Rick sit up. "Get up and grab his arm."

"What?" Rick stared at him, bemused, one hand still on his throat.

"Grab his arm," the man repeated, and showed him. Rick shook his head and climbed to his feet, then grabbed the other arm.

"Good. Now help me throw him out the window." They dragged the old man to the window, which was already open.

"Looks like you planned this," Rick grunted; the old man was heavier than he looked.

"Anything to spike Robin's plans," the other man muttered as they heaved the prone body out the window. There was a plaintive cry as the old man found himself airborne; Rick winced at the impact of the body hitting the ground below.

"Ah, good, he fell in the rose bushes." The satisfaction in the other man's voice caused Rick to stare at him in astonishment. "That should take him a while to recover from." Then he saw Rick's face. "What? It didn't kill him—just made him damned uncomfortable for a while. At least until he pulls all the thorns out."

"Who are you?" The question spilled from him like an overturned jug of water. "And why did you help me?"

"Because it will irritate my great-grandson, mostly," the other man said honestly, dusting his hands off and closing the window. "And because if I helped you, maybe you'd help me."

"Do what?" Rick's suspicions were beginning to stir.

"Help me get my house back." The gentleman turned and looked him squarely in the eyes. "I'm Edgar Rothman."

Nikki rounded the corner of the third-floor landing, and looked around, eyes narrowed. Francesca was up here somewhere; the screams had come from this level of the house, she was sure of it.

But where?

"Shadowborn."

An older woman, her face lined with anger and jealousy, stepped out of a door across the landing. She and Nikki stared at each other across the opening of the stairwell for a long moment, and then a vicious smile, similar to Robin's sneer, spread over the other woman's face.

"So this is the one my grandson lusts for." The scorn in her voice was thick, like molasses. "What a waste."

"Excuse me?" One of Nikki's eyebrows climbed up. "Look, lady, I don't know who you are or why you're here, and I don't care. I've got things to do, so stay out of my way."

It stung, though. What right do you have to look down on me?

"What makes you think you'll be any different?" The older woman sneered. "He'll break you, bind you to him and leave you in my care. Just like all the others."

"Not likely." Nikki worked her way slowly around to the opposite side of the hall, wondering what the woman wanted. *Is she holding Francesca behind that door?*

"So worried about your friend, how charming," the woman said, her smile turning triumphant. "He's already tasted her, you know—you've already dropped down to second. You're just like all the rest: just a flash in the pan. Once he's satisfied himself in you, he'll move on."

"So what?" Nikki's voice matched the scorn in the other woman's, tone for tone. "Lady, if you think I'm going to cry over that idiot, you've got another thing coming."

"And once he's done with you, he'll give you to me." The woman continued as if she hadn't heard anything Nikki had said. "He gives all the girls to me, because I can keep them in line."

"What are you, Mother Hannigan?" Nikki eyed the distance between them. *Maybe I could knock her over the railing...*

The woman's eyes narrowed angrily. "I am Anthea Rothman, mistress of this house! And you will keep a civil tongue in your head, chit!"

Chit? Chit? Now this is getting personal.

Nikki suddenly ran down the hall, bearing right down on Anthea, who laughed and waved a hand. The rug moved under her feet; Nikki landed on her back hard, the air knocked out of her lungs. Suddenly, a weight landed on her chest; she writhed beneath it, trying to breathe, as Anthea walked down the hall and stood over her, one hand hooked into a claw that was slowly tightening.

"You're not as tough as I thought," the woman crooned, kneeling down and leaning over the struggling girl. "One small thought and you're on your back, just like all the others. I could call him now and you'd be all ready for him."

"Not...bloody...likely," Nikki ground out, trying to fight the spell that held her down. Justin's voice echoed in her head against the growing darkness...

"If you build your shield of Shadows, he could use it against you and trap you in it."

She's using my shield!

Knowing that, however, didn't stop it from wrapping tighter around her as Anthea clenched her fist even smaller. Spots danced in front of

Nikki's eyes as her lungs begged for air; in desperation, she withdrew into herself, focusing on the grounding that Justin had tried so hard to teach her.

There has to be a way to break this!

Take this! Pouka appeared in the darkness of her mind, holding out a green oak branch wreathed in mistletoe. Nikki reached for the branch as her lungs screamed; the darkness wavered...

Warm Power poured through her, laced with the feel of Pouka's own Magic, shattering the Shadows that were wrapped around her. Anthea's cries of pain were music to Nikki's ears; she lay on the floor, gasping, as the woman was lifted bodily into the air and slammed into the door behind her.

And that is how you break a shield. Pouka's voice was weak but satisfied.

Thanks for the help. Nikki hauled herself up to a sitting position, sweat standing out on her face, looking over at the crumpled pile of clothing in front of her.

That's why Justin asked me to go with you, Pouka reminded her and Nikki grinned.

Anthea moaned and raised her head, hatred in her eyes. "You will never leave," she spat, blood dripping from her split lip and mixing with the dust on the floor beneath her. "My grandson will enjoy breaking you."

"Yeah, well, he's gotta get me first," Nikki replied, using the railing to pull herself to her feet, the warmth of her new shield skimming the very edge of her skin. She wasn't sure why she could pull it up now, but saw what Justin had meant about the drain. Her legs were still wobbly, and it wasn't all from what Anthea had tried to do.

There was a pounding on the stairs; she turned, still clasping the railing, as Justin, Rick and Edgar, of all people, came running up the stairs. Justin and Rick both stopped short and stared at her as they hit the third floor; Edgar, coming up behind them, nearly knocked them to the floor as he ran into them.

"You did it," Rick whispered, and she knew he could see the velvety green and amber shield that snuggled against her. She nodded tightly, wondering how much longer she could hold it up.

"Not long," Justin said, but she could hear the quiet pride in his voice. "How did you get it?"

"Pouka helped me," Nikki said honestly, and Justin smiled.

"Let her help you with this!"

Anthea had been pulling herself up while the others had been talking; now she launched herself at Nikki, fingers extended like claws. Before she could brace herself, the old woman hit her; the momentum flipped them both up and over the railing, sending both Nikki and Anthea plummeting towards the marble floor of the Great Hall, three stories down.

"Nikki!"

Rick's anguished cry echoed in the hall, mingling with another horrified scream. After a moment, Nikki realized it was coming from her own throat…

And then everything stopped. Nikki hung there in mid-air, shaking, screaming and watching Anthea's body lying in the middle of the Great Hall, blood streaming in thin lines in every direction, a spider web of crimson.

It felt like she was lying in a similar web. Power pulsed in the air around her, strands that cradled her in warmth, suspended over the floor.

Now what? She wondered, still shaking.

Now you wait. Justin's voice was strained; she very nearly didn't recognize it.

※

I so did not want this to happen!

Justin's back muscles rippled as he fought to hold Nikki in mid-air, knowing that without some extra Power, he was going to lose her. *And there's no way she'll survive a drop here…dammit!*

"Rick," he ground out, and the Sensitive next to him jumped.

"Pull her up!" Rick urged, panic in his eyes.

"I'm trying to," Justin grunted. "Do you still have a pocket knife on you?"

"What?"

"A pocket knife," Justin repeated. "Do you have one?"

Rick fumbled in his pockets; a small silver Swiss Army knife tumbled into his hand, and he held it up for Justin to see. The Earth Mage nodded and Rick flipped open the blade.

This is going to be so much fun to explain later… "Cut me."

"What?" The shock in Rick's voice caused his concentration to slip a bit, and Nikki tumbled a bit further down before he caught her again.

"Just do it! I'll explain later!" He put a bit of command into his voice; Rick shook his head but come closer.

"Any particular place?" The Sensitive's voice shook.

"Anywhere you can hit." Justin braced himself, murmuring words under his breath as Rick raised the knife.

Warm blood spurted as Rick drove the knife into his shoulder; Justin's knees buckled briefly before he grabbed the Power generated by the Blood Magic and hauled Nikki up slowly. Rick stepped back from him, looking at the blood on his hands in shock and horror; it was Edgar who grasped Nikki's hands and pulled her over the edge of the railing to lie on the floor, shuddering. Still whispering, Justin reached over and grabbed the knife handle; grimacing at the pain, he pulled it out slowly, feeling the blood slow as he used his Healing gift.

There are some advantages to the way I grew up, he thought ruefully, wiping the blade off on his pants. Of course, now I get to try and explain this...

But first things first.

He closed the knife and handed it back to Rick, or tried to; the Sensitive backed away from him, refusing the knife. Justin sighed and slipped the blade into his own pocket and then reached out to Rick, intending to smooth away the edges of his shock.

"No!" Rick shoved him away. "Don't touch me!"

All three of them looked at him. There was a rough edge in his voice, very foreign: Justin had seen Rick upset before, but not like this.

What the?

"Rick?"

Nikki had risen from the floor; now, with a soft note of questioning in her voice, she reached out to Rick. He shook his head violently, holding up his bloody hands to ward her back.

"Don't," he said, his voice ragged. "Just leave me alone for a moment."

Nikki and Justin exchanged glances, each thinking the same thing. We can't leave him here, Justin thought, wondering just what to do now.

"Leave him here with me."

Nikki and Justin whirled around as Marietta came up the stairs; she threaded her way deftly between them and went over to Rick.

Surprisingly, the Sensitive didn't object to her; as her arms went around him and he buried his face in her shoulder, Nikki felt a small spurt of jealousy.

Oh, knock it off, she told herself irritably. It's just shock on his part. Let her care for him. I've got to go and kill Robin, remember?

"Marietta will be good to watch him," Edgar said, startling her. She'd forgotten the older man was there.

As long as all she does is watch him...

Nikki stifled the thought and even managed to give the girl a nod in appreciation. Marietta's eyes were amused as she held Rick; Nikki stiffened as the ghost sent a mental reassurance to her.

He will be fine in my care. I will watch and let him weep, no more.

You'd better not hurt him, Nikki replied.

"You go to kill Robin." It wasn't a question. "Do you know how?"

"I'll figure it out." Nikki's voice was level.

"Let me offer a bit of advice." Marietta looked directly at her, amusement gone. "In order to destroy Robin, you have to break his hold on himself." She nodded over the railing. "Else all you will do is buy yourself a little time."

Nikki looked down; Anthea's body was gone.

"She will take a bit to heal, but Robin will help her," Marietta said, and Edgar nodded.

"So how do I break his hold on himself?" Nikki asked, looking back at the ghost.

"He must die, again. You must finish what the other Shadow Mage started." Marietta smoothed Rick's hair. "I will bring him downstairs. You can collect him on your way out."

She led Rick past Nikki and Justin and down the stairs. Nikki watched until they hit the second floor; once they passed beyond her view, she turned to Edgar.

"What did the other Shadow Mage do to him?" she asked, her voice still very carefully controlled.

"She got him to hang himself in the attic," he replied. "Quite a neat job, actually— except that he'd been fooling around with Shadow Magic on his own, and gotten in touch with a Shadow Lord, who showed him how to drain her to capture her Power as he died."

"Interesting." Justin was frowning. "I'd heard that was possible, but never run into anyone who had actually done it."

"Well, he did it." Edgar shook his head. "Then he proceeded to make himself master here."

Nikki chewed on her bottom lip thoughtfully. "So in order to kill Robin, I basically have to pull that Power out of him, right?"

Justin nodded. "Put rather simplistically, yes. It's going to be a bit more difficult than that. I think you might have to force him to give it up."

"Lovely." Nikki straightened her shoulders and looked over at Edgar again. "How do I get up to that attic? I'm assuming that's where he's hiding."

Edgar pointed down the hall. "Through the servant's quarters. And be warned: his Shadow Lord has sent a Mage to help him."

Nikki shrugged. "Hopefully he'll have sense enough to stay out of it." She looked at Justin. "Ready to go and kill the bad guy?"

"Are you ready?" he replied. "This is your show now."

Nikki looked back down the hall. "I have to be."

CHAPTER 16

"IRREPARABLE DAMAGE"

"She's coming."

Anthea blotted the blood from her lip again, sniffing her anger into the silk handkerchief she held. Dorian and Daniel were still missing; Robin only hoped that meant they had taken care of the Earth Mage.

Maybe they got themselves killed in the process—that would keep them out of my hair for a while, he thought viciously, looking over at the silent Shadow Mage Andreas had sent to help him.

The Mage looked over, an unspoken question in his dark eyes. He'd barely said ten words since he'd arrived; Robin could only hope he was as talented as he was quiet.

Now, he simply looked away when Robin said nothing, going back to his introspective musing. Except for his grandmother's sniveling, the attic was quiet.

Too quiet.

He looked over into the corner that he normally avoided, hoping the familiar unease of seeing the place where his physical life had ended would shake him out of the anxiousness the silence was building in him. He was so close; if all went well, in the future he would not have to rely on the capricious Shadow Lord to help him defend what was his.

I will make sure she is loyal only to me, and bind her to me.

But first I must make sure to catch her.

The corner was even more Shadowed than the rest of the attic, as befitted a place where a suicide had taken place. Robin even fancied for a moment that he could see the rope that had taken his life still hanging there, swaying as if a body still hung from it.

There was a flicker, deep within the Shadows; Robin frowned as a very brief golden luminescence flared, almost a warning... And then the door was opening, and he pulled his eyes away as the young woman who had suddenly become the focus of his entire existence came into the room.

She was still lovely, but the amber and green Power that floated over her shocked him: yet another indication that the Earth Mage had stolen her away. And, to add insult to injury, the Earth Mage stepped in behind her; obviously, both his father and grandfather had failed him. Again.

Robin's lip curled into a sneer; promising himself that he would deal with his errant forebears later, he swaggered up to the Shadowborn, intending to remind her of exactly what he was offering her...

And came crashing up against a wall, before he got half-way across the room. The wall was Earth Magic, but harsher than he remembered. He stared at the Earth Mage, who raised his chin and glared back at him. There was blood on the Earth Mage's shoulder; Robin raised an eyebrow and acknowledged the Blood Magic with another, lesser curl of his lip.

I should have known. Tainting my beauty, playing with Blood Magic—you Earth Mages are all the same. Robin threw the thought at the Earth Mage; the young man's only response was a sardonic smile.

Shaken a bit by the lack of response, Robin turned back to the Shadowborn, who stood with her eyes flashing and her jaw clenched. Just the sight of her inspired a heat that spread from his loins outward. She was a magnificent creature: he was going to enjoy this very, very much...

The tableau in the attic was an eerie one. There were two people standing behind Robin, one being his grandmother, still with blood spatters over her clothing and her neck at a twisted angle. The other was a dark man, bald, with eyes that held Shadows behind them; Nikki assumed he was the Shadow Mage Edgar had referred to.

It was Robin that she focused on now. The ghost was leering at her, had attempted to touch her; thankfully, something had stopped him before he reached her. Probably Justin, she realized, since he had glared over her shoulder at the Earth Mage right after he stopped.

Good. Because I'm not sure this shield would hold up to him touching me.
She still wasn't sure what she was going to do.

Remember what Marietta said, Justin murmured in her mind. You have to force him to repeat his suicide.

Any suggestions? Her thought had a bit of tartness coloring it.

See if you can keep the Shadow Mage out of it, he replied. You and I are not ready to go up against a trained Shadow Mage, and he's very well trained.

How can you tell?

Trust me. He's trained.

Wonderful. She pulled up her chin. "This is between you and I, Robin. Tell your friend to stay out of it."

Robin glanced behind him briefly, and then turned back to her, his eyes amused. "I will if you will."

Nikki nodded, and Justin stepped back. She felt his wall come down and straightened her shoulders. "Now it's just you and me."

He walked up to her and cupped her cheek, just like Rick had the first night they met. His fingers were chill; despite her shield, she shivered as he whispered, "That's the way I've always wanted it to be."

"I'm sorry," she said quietly. "I can't give you want you want."

"You can," he insisted, moving his hand down to her shoulder. She stepped back before it could go lower, and Robin's eyes darkened.

"So be it," he said angrily, summoning Shadows around himself. "I had hoped to make this easy for you. You've chosen to deny your heritage by wrapping yourself in the Earth Mage's filth. I'll have to remind you exactly who and what you truly are."

The Shadows swirling around him suddenly arrowed for her; Nikki raised her arms in an automatic defensive position, and the Shadows grew sharp edges. She cried out in alarm as the edges sliced through her shield; one particularly sharp edge scraped along her cheekbone, opening her skin to the bone. Warm blood leaked down her face; tasting it, Nikki's eyes darkened.

Shreds of Earth Magic fell around her, sparkles of emerald and amber that shattered on the floor at her feet like miniature fireworks. She drew herself up, Shadows flowing from every corner of the room to cloak her in darkness.

"That," she said evenly, "was really, really stupid."

Robin looked at her, standing in front of him, shrouded in Shadows, and lust shot through him, filling him with longing for the creature before him. She crackled with Power; her dark blue eyes were flashing, and the Shadows writhed around her, barely controlled.

He had to taste her. Forgoing caution and any sense of self-preservation, he grabbed her and dragged her to him, drinking deeply of her lips. She responded eagerly, filling him with her intoxicating taste; greedily, he opened his mouth wider, his tongue searching her mouth frantically.

Taste me, her voice murmured in his head, as his hands came up to tangle in her dark hair. *Drink deeply.*

Robin groaned, trying to meld his body with her's, forgetting everything he had planned to do to her. She laughed, a rich sound that stirred him up even more, and ran her fingers lightly over his face, pulling her lips back teasingly. His hands, still tangled in her hair, tried to keep her near him; she let him pull her back into his embrace, crushing his lips to hers again.

Promise me to never leave, he demanded, his tongue thrusting its way into her mouth again. *Promise me.*

She laughed again, thrilling his senses. *Promise me one thing, and I will.*

Anything.

She tried to step back again, and this time he let her. *Face your fear, conquer it, and I will stay.*

Nikki watched Robin turn to the corner, where a noose already hung, the one part of her that was not caught up in the swirl of the Shadows wondering how she was doing what she was doing.

Don't question it! Came Justin's curt thought. *It's working—we'll figure it out later.*

Robin was heading over to the noose, his eyes glazed with the lust she'd somehow conjured up in him. Her senses were reeling as well, but whether from his kisses or the Power swirling around the room, she couldn't tell.

Her eyes were darkened; somehow, she knew it was because of the Shadows she'd called up. She could feel everything Robin was experiencing, but this was different from before; she was the one now pulling the strings.

Nikki followed him to the corner and helped him to adjust the rope around his neck. He pulled her to him for another deep, searing kiss; once again, she felt herself drowning in him, reaching deep for the Shadows he'd gathered within himself. The scent of his maleness filled her nostrils; she groaned, unable to help herself.

We will be together forever, he whispered, his fingers once again trailing along her cheekbones, skimming the slash, and then tangling in her hair again. Forever.

Suddenly, she felt a click deep within her; she touched the Power coiled within him and it swam along the channels towards her. Robin jerked back suddenly, suspicion and horror in his eyes; with a swift move, she yanked the rope.

A sick crack filled the room; Robin's eyes bulged and his fingers clawed frantically at his neck as Nikki fell to her knees, the rope still in her hands. Power flowed into her; he slumped against the noose, so she released the line and drew a deep breath as he slumped to the floor.

Anthea screamed; Nikki looked at her as the old woman's form shivered and then burst into shards. Robin's body continued to sink; after it hit the floor, it melted into the Shadows, a dark stain that stretched across the room and then vanished.

Nikki rose from where she was kneeling, feeling the Power that had come from Robin swirling within her, a strangely arousing feeling. It still had traces of him; it was almost like he was kissing her from somewhere deep within her. She shivered, enjoying the feel of him beneath her skin.

Justin stared at Nikki as she rose from her knees, feeling a flutter that was very close to panic start somewhere deep in his belly. This, of all things, was not what he was expecting.

Shadows swirled around her madly, but instead of being shot through with the dark purples of normal Shadow Mages, her Shadows contained streaks of emerald, amber and gold light.

What kind of Shadow Mage manifests her Shadows in more than one Sphere?

No kind, came Edgar's voice. She is no Shadow Mage.

Justin couldn't disagree. Nikki stood before them, a glorious sight; her dark hair tousled from Robin's fingers, Shadows coating her in a cloak of living darkness, shot through with jeweled color, Power streaming from every pore in her skin.

Funny, she looks more like Alenya after a particularly successful hunt than any Shadow Mage I've ever seen. Or Shanna, after she's done a really big magic. Shit, she isn't a StarChild after all, is she?

He shook his head and looked over at the other Shadow Mage, who was staring at Nikki as well, a surprised look on his dark face. Once he felt Justin's gaze on him, he closed his mouth and the impassive mask fell back down; he cleared his throat, and all eyes went to him.

"Congratulations," he murmured to Nikki, giving her a mocking little bow. She raised one eyebrow; he smiled and spread his hands. "I have nothing more to do here. This house is no longer under my master's protections. With your permission, I will leave."

Nikki turned and looked, not at Justin, but at Edgar. "This is your house, Mr. Rothman," she said, and even her voice was richer, full of Power. Justin sighed, feeling very old all of a sudden, as she continued, "What say you?"

"Tell your master Rothman House has no further need of his protection," Edgar said, his deep voice reverberating in the attic. "I will protect what I built."

The Mage bowed again, just as mockingly. "I will pass your message. Farewell."

And he vanished.

Back to his master, Justin thought bitterly. *Just what we need.* He looked at Nikki, who was still shedding Power and Shadows like stardust. "Ready to go?"

"I didn't feel a shift this time," she murmured, Power singing along in her tones. "Did we correct it?"

Justin prodded the Balance experimentally; it had shifted, but only a bit, and he frowned. "I'm not sure. I think there's still something that needs to be done, but I'll be damned if I know what." Then he looked at Nikki again. *Then again, maybe it's right in front of me.*

Then another thought hit him. "Francesca," he said, looking over at Nikki. "She's still here, and still alive. That's the remainder of the Balance."

Nikki's eyes darkened again. "I have to finish what Robin started." Justin nodded, surprised at her intuitive grasp of the problem.

I have to kill Francesca.

Normally, Nikki would shy away from something so repulsive. Normally, however, didn't seem to be a word that really applied any more. Not to me, at least.

She licked her lips, a bit frightened at the sensations roiling through her. What scared her the most, though, was how aroused she was; this was more than Robin's kisses intoxicating her.

I am a sick bitch, if I get off on killing people, she thought unhappily. *Maybe this wasn't such a good idea after all.*

Oh well. Not much I can do about it now.

She turned to Edgar. "Where's Francesca?"

"The Lady's Chamber—probably waking up now," he replied. "Let me show you."

The house felt alive as she moved through it; all her senses were sharpened by the Power she'd released from Robin. As they went down the stairs, Nikki realized the Power felt cleaner now than it had; as if it had come to a proper place.

Marietta said he'd stolen the Power from a Shadow Mage. But didn't I do the same?

Not really. Pouka's voice, hushed in the silence of her mind, startled her. *You are some form of Shadow Mage; he was not. The Power rightly belongs to you.*

Even though I killed for it.

Welcome to the Shadows. The Earth sprite's voice held no censure. *This is a land of death, Nikki. Don't deny what you are.*

The room Edgar led them to was a stark contrast to the rest of the house. Shadows hung very lightly here, and the entire room was delicately dressed. Edgar's face softened when he entered; Nikki sensed it was not only because of the woman standing beside the window, but the room and the memories it held for him.

Perhaps what I'll offer her is not as bad as I thought, she murmured to herself, watching as Francesca turned and saw Edgar. The historian's face lit up; for a moment, Nikki felt uncomfortable, as the two gazed into each other's eyes.

Then Edgar murmured something to her; Francesca's eyes darted to Nikki, who flushed, remembering whose shirt she had on.

"Don't worry, I won't need that anymore," Francesca told her, and her voice cracked a bit.

This is going to be hard, Justin warned her, as he stepped in. *I can't do this for you—you need to be the one to end this.*

Me?

Yes, you. The presence in her mind did nothing to stop the butterflies in her stomach. *It's almost the same thing you did to Robin. Reach in and pull the essence that is Francesca out. If I'm right, she won't go very far anyways.*

Nikki turned and gave him a puzzled look, and he smiled. *Just call it intuition.*

Okay. She gave a mental shrug and turned back to Francesca, who was standing next to Edgar, pale but resigned. "I'm sorry, Francesca," Nikki said quietly, moving over to them. "I never wanted to have to do this."

"It's just a formality, really," Francesca whispered, a single tear brightening her hazel eyes. "If what Edgar has told me is correct, I died as soon as I crossed the World Walls."

"You didn't, actually, and that's the problem," Justin said, coming up behind Nikki. "Robin pulled you through alive, and that's why the Balance is still skewed. Mortals aren't meant to remain here."

Francesca looked puzzled. "So now what? Do I get to go home?"

Justin shook his head sadly. "You've changed too much, Francesca—you've been here over 24 hours. Your body is addicted to the Power in the air here. If we took you back to Earth now, you'd go through an instant withdrawal. There's just not enough magic there to sustain your need."

"What would happen?" Francesca asked, horror staining her face even paler. Edgar slipped an arm around her, wan comfort.

"You'd slip into an immediate coma," Justin said. "And then, very slowly, your body would die. Your soul would most likely remain here, but only as a shade, incapable of anything but wailing."

Francesca shuddered. "And the alternative?"

Nikki felt sick as the Power within her surged, sensing she was about to use it again. *This is so wrong…* "I can finish what Robin started," she said out loud.

Francesca looked at her. "Can you make it painless?"

"I think so." *I hope so. Robin didn't look like he suffered, until I broke his neck.*

The historian hesitated, looking up at Edgar. "And I'd be … a ghost? So I could stay here? And still be myself?"

He and Justin both nodded, and she looked again at Nikki, the single tear tracking down her pale cheek. "Then do it."

The Shadows rose in Nikki again, darkening her vision; she stepped up to Francesca and took her face in both of her hands. Tilting her head towards her, Nikki laid cool lips on Francesca's forehead, closing her eyes as she did so.

Once again, she felt as if she were drowning. This time, it was the sweet smell of Francesca that filled her senses; roses and lavender and the sun, all swirling around her. Nikki dove into the morass of emotion and scent, looking for the essential spark that was the core of the historian.

Deep within the girl, she suddenly saw a single, opulent orchid, white at the tips, shading to a dark purple heart. Nikki reached out and plucked it; as she retreated to her own body, the orchid safely held against her, Francesca's physical body slumped out of her hands and settled down to the floor.

Her spirit, however, still stood before them, an astonished look on her face. Gradually, it solidified, and Nikki stood with her face in her hands again, her lips pressed to chill flesh.

Nikki stepped back, still feeling the new Power from Francesca mingling with the Shadows within her. That wasn't so bad.

You did very well, came Justin's approving thought.

Francesca drew a deep breath, her fingers coming up to her face. "I don't feel that different," she whispered, looking down at the body she had recently shed, then looking up at Nikki. "Thank you."

Nikki nodded uncomfortably and stepped back, suddenly not wanting to be here. *I want to go home! Back to a place where I'm not a killer!*

Justin touched her arm; looking up at him, she saw compassion and understanding in his hazel eyes. *We all need to do things that we don't want to,* he murmured. *That's the nature of being a Mage.*

And if I don't want to do this anymore? She didn't have any hope that she could walk away, and his next words confirmed it.

I'm sorry, Nikki. It's nearly impossible to resist using the magic once you've unlocked it.

Yeah, that's what I thought.

Francesca had turned to Edgar during this exchange, her hazel eyes shimmering with tears. "Now I can stay."

"I would hope so," he replied huskily, taking her into his arms. "And this house will be happy again."

They gazed into each others' eyes, her hand creeping up to rest on his cheek. Tears filled Nikki's eyes suddenly; Francesca and Edgar looked to be starting something that it appeared she would never have the chance to experience.

Never say never, Justin said to her softly. No one knows what the future brings.

As they made to leave, Edgar and Francesca came back to themselves. "Nikki," Francesca said, disentangling herself from Edgar's arms and running over. To Nikki's surprise, the historian threw her arms around her and hugged her fiercely. "Thank you," she whispered. "Thank you for doing what I couldn't ask you to do."

Edgar joined them as Nikki was staring at Francesca. "Know that if you need it, you will ever have a home here," the elder ghost rumbled. "None in this house shall bother you."

"Thank you, Edgar." Nikki managed a smile. "I'll remember that."

They found Rick sprawled in one of the chairs in the parlor on the ground floor; his feet were up on a fat ottoman, and his eyes were closed. Marietta sat near the fire, her needlework back in her hand.

"Congratulations, Shadowborn," she said quietly, setting her sewing aside as they came in. "This house will be much happier now."

"So why are you still here?" Nikki asked, frowning. "Robin's gone."

"Aye, but you wouldn't have liked to see your friend left here alone, would you?" A shy smile lit Marietta's pale face. "And I believe I still have things to do. I'm not ready to go on yet."

Justin started forward, but Nikki laid a hand on his arm. She shook her head as he looked at her; one eyebrow quirked, but he let her go over to the sleeping Sensitive.

"Can we transfer him through the World Walls without waking him?" she asked softly. "He's not comfortable here. Too much magic, I think. It overwhelms his Sight."

"We can, if you can keep him asleep," Justin said after a moment's thought. "I can transfer us through, but you'll have to deepen his sleep."

"How do I do that?" she asked, and he sighed.

"Like this." He touched her forehead; the knowledge rose in her mind, and she shuddered. "Sorry. It's just the fastest way to show you right now. I'll give you the long explanation later."

"Thanks." Nikki carefully wrapped a length of Shadow around Rick; he murmured something and sighed. She looked up at Justin and nodded.

———

Justin closed his eyes, looking for the Earth locus that would guide them back to the plane he had called home for the past six years. It beckoned to him, floating green and amber in the darkness of his mind. He carefully wrapped Earth energy around himself, Nikki and Rick and gently moved them from the Shadow Lands to Earth. The passage through the World Walls barely stirred him anymore; sourly, he realized he'd done more interplanar travel than normal travel in the past two days, and it showed. Despite himself, he yawned.

Gotta stop pushing myself like this…

Sunlight streamed in through the window again; the furnishings were older, dustier, more faded. There was no fire in the fireplace; the chair Rick dozed in emitted a small cloud of dust as Nikki rose from where she'd been kneeling next to it. Justin watched as she uncoiled the Shadows from around Rick and drew the energy back into herself; already she was beginning to control the overflow, not shedding the energy like faery dust like she had before.

It's uncanny, he thought uneasily. She uses it instinctively, like a Shadow Lord. But I've never seen a Lord who could use more than one Sphere. It's like she's something entirely new.

He kept circling back to the unhappy conclusion that she resembled his sister more and more. Even if she isn't a StarChild, she's damn close. And I'm not qualified to teach a StarChild.

Time to talk to the only person I know who is.

Rick's eyes opened slowly; he blinked against the sunshine a couple of times, and then saw Nikki standing there and a slow smile spread across his face. "Hey, beautiful, did we win?"

Justin watched her eyes light up, the same way Francesca's had when Edgar had taken her in his arms, and smiled inside. Perhaps her happy ending isn't as far away as she thought.

"Yeah, we won," she murmured, holding a hand out to him. "Did you have a nice nap?"

Rick's amber eyes darkened and, to Justin's astonishment, he shot a glance full of something close to anger at the Earth Mage. "It was full of odd dreams," he said, strain in his voice, as if he were trying to keep it neutral and failing.

What is his problem?

Trying to keep the suspicion out of his own voice (and suspecting he was succeeding about as well as Rick), Justin asked, "Is there a problem, Rick?"

"No." Said far too quickly.

Nikki looked from one to the other, clearly confused. "Maybe we should head back to the inn," she said finally, and appeared relieved when Rick left off glaring at Justin and nodded agreement.

"You guys go," Justin said, and sighed. "I have to go see someone."

Nikki's eyebrow went up. "Oh?"

The word held a wealth of questions in it; Justin took the coward's way out (and knew it) by ignoring them all. "I'll catch up with the two of you back at the inn," he said instead, and turned away. He heard them leave and sighed again.

Time to face the music.

Chapter 17

"The Beginnings of Suspicion"

"I don't suppose you'd mind explaining exactly what happened at the Rothman House."

The icy voice sent a chill down Tony's spine as his master stepped out of the shadows and into his home office. Andreas was dressed in his Council robes—black satin, lined and trimmed with silver; that meant he was either just returning from or heading to a Council meeting. Tony knew that either way, he was about to be reamed for what had happened.

"She offered single combat," he replied quietly, closing the journal he'd been writing in and raising his dark eyes to look at his Lord. Andreas towered over him, anger and disgust radiating out from the Shadows surrounding him in almost visible waves. "What was I supposed to do?"

"You were supposed to keep him alive!" Andreas' roar shook the windows. Tony winced.

Pointing out he was already dead would not be politic at this time, I'm thinking, he thought very privately, blessing the fact that his personal shields were very, very thick. It was the only thing that kept him alive sometimes.

Andreas continued to rage, a thunderstorm contained in the tiny office. Tony had rented a house in the midst of a small housing complex: the little condo was only six rooms total, but it was all he needed. His neighbors, mostly young executives working in the nearby Mt.

Washington Valley, tended to ignore him, and he returned the favor. Now, listening to his Lord rant, Tony appreciated their indifference. *Gods bless taciturn New Englanders, who keep their noses in their own business. It makes this much easier.*

"Are you listening to me?"

A fist slammed down on his desk, disrupting his thoughts and causing him to jump. For a blind man, Andreas had an uncanny ability to see things as they were.

The Shadow Lord reached out and grabbed Tony by the collar of his shirt, pulling the shorter man easily out of his chair. Tony's feet dangled a good two feet off the ground as Andreas pulled him up to his face; at this close distance, the Shadow Mage could see the scars crossing what once had been a handsome face, angry purple lines that snaked under the black cloth that covered the remains of Andreas' eyes. A strange smell, almost incense-like, drifted up from the Lord's clothes; Tony was hard put not to sneeze as it tickled his nose.

"I hate it when people don't listen to me," Andreas hissed. "And I hate it even more when people don't follow my instructions. Do you understand me?"

"Yes, my Lord," Tony whispered in what he hoped was a suitably cowed voice. "I apologize, my Lord. Forgive me."

Andreas snarled at him and dropped him; Tony hit the floor hard, one ankle turning underneath him. He winced in pain, but managed to pull himself up and into his chair.

"Now, I will ask you again. What happened at Rothman House?" Venom dripped from Andreas' voice.

Tony quickly summarized the events; Andreas snarled again, and the Mage moved to distract his Lord from another explosion. "However, my Lord, I believe I recognized her."

"What?" The Shadow Lord stopped mid-snarl. "Explain."

"Her face was very familiar; when I came back here, I looked at the old files." Tony opened his drawer and pulled out Teraisa Donnelly's file. "She looks exactly like one of the two escaped breeders from the last experiment."

"You're joking." Andreas had gone from angry to intrigued in a split second. "Which one?"

"Teraisa Donnelly." Tony flipped open the file: the same dark blue eyes stared back at him from her photo. "She was originally Cameron's second, but when the first spells were discussed, she objected to the whole project on the grounds that the spells were going to damage the Balance."

"Ah yes, I remember her. Alex hated her; she was a woman that didn't 'know her place,' according to him." Amusement rumbled in the Shadow Lord's voice and Tony breathed a little easier; apparently the storm was past. "She threatened to go to the government, expose the project—Alex arraigned for her to be drugged and held in the facility, not wanting to deal with her. And you think this new Mage is her daughter?"

"Can't be Donnelly. She looked about the right age for the child, if she survived." Tony paused a moment, then played his trump card. "And there were inconsistencies in her aura."

The Shadow Lord still managed to pin him to his chair with a hard stare, despite not having physical eyes. "What do you mean?"

Tony squirmed, more than a little uncomfortable. "She had all three Spheres in her aura."

"All three?"

The reverent tone in Andreas' voice only increased Tony's discomfort. "Yes, my Lord. The Shadows were dominant, but that could be because her mother was also a Shadow Mage."

"So it worked." Andreas turned towards the window, the pleasure he felt obvious. "This is very, very good news, Tony. It almost makes up for letting me down earlier."

"Thank you, my Lord." Pompous ass. "Do you have any new orders?"

Andreas rubbed his chin with one hand. "I think it's time to step up our schedule. Do you have the breeders selected yet?"

"Yes, my Lord." Tony pulled another set of files from his drawer. "Four potential Mages, none of whom has received any training, with no family or ties to anyone. Runaways are wonderful lab rats."

"Good. I want them collected this week. Let's get this underway."

"And what of Alex, my Lord?" Tony hid a very private smile as Andreas growled again. "He will not be pleased at your changes."

"I don't care. This is my experiment, not his." Steel crept back into the Shadow Lord's voice. "If he complains, tell him I said that if he hadn't made such a mess before, I wouldn't have to be involved."

"Yes, my Lord." That will go over well. "And the woman?"

"Who, the lead?" Andreas dismissed her with a wave of her hand. "If she interferes, kill her. I won't tolerate any problems this time."

"As you wish, my Lord." Tony hesitated. "One other thing, my Lord."

"Yes?" Andreas had been turning to leave—the vortex in the corner was already pulsing.

"There was an Earth Mage with the girl. One who looked far too comfortable in the Shadow Lands."

Andreas scowled. "Tall boy? Sandy hair, hazel eyes? Kind of lanky?"

"That's the one." *Interesting—you obviously know him. How many halfbreeds are out there?*

There was a new theory on halfbreeds circulating around the universities—Mages that seemed to be able to work in more than one Sphere at a time. Very rare, but they seemed to be either Earth/Shadow or Earth/Dawn. The theory was that these were the result of the union of a male Shadow or Dawn Mage and a female Earth Mage. Tony had never personally met a halfbreed, but had heard of them. Duke University supposedly had two students that were showing signs of being halfbreeds.

"Justin." Andreas spat the name out. "Don't worry about him. If he interferes, I'll take care of him." He gathered his robes and the Shadows around him. "But that tells me volumes about her and where to find her. Have a special unit prepared in the secure wing. No one else is to know what it's for. Not even my son."

Tony nodded.

"And make sure all the breeders are kept separate and don't know about each other. We can do the spells multiple times."

"That will involve a lot of time, my Lord," Tony warned. "Alex will…"

"Alex will do what he's told," Andreas snapped. "Take the time. I won't have anyone screwing this up this time."

With that, he stepped through the vortex.

Tony waited until the Shadows subsided, indicating the Shadow Lord was truly gone, and then picked up his phone. Andreas had things he wanted to do, but Tony had long ago realized that the rewards for following the Shadow Lord's dreams were iffy at best.

His son, on the other hand, had far more concrete visions…and more money.

And if you play your cards right, Tonio, you should be able to eliminate both father and son, his mother's voice whispered in his head. His inner thoughts were always in her musical voice: the lovely alto that had taught him his first spells. His mother had been a wonderfully opportunistic Mage, who had taken advantage of her Haitian background to not only learn Shadow Magic, but other, darker arts. Her son had taken her training and raised it to a true art form.

And once both Andreas and Alex are gone, Gene-Tech will be mine, he thought gleefully. And then we can truly begin to change the world to what it should be.

Tony was humming as he dialed.

"Alex? I've just talked to your father. There's been a change of plans…"

There was water falling musically in the garden, but Trimaris' thoughts drowned out the peacefulness of the scene. She sat in the midst of her flowers, the sunlight warm on her skin, and pondered Shadows.

What did you get us into, Ky? Not for the first time, she wondered what Andreas had done to warp her sister into helping him with this insanity. Did you truly love him?

She was seated in the garden she and her sister had first planted years ago, back when they were both very young and new to their powers. Kymara had laid out the garden, but it had been Trimaris who had actually coaxed most of the flowers to their full growth. Kymara had been like a butterfly, flitting from project to project for most of her life, never settling on anything.

Then she met Andreas, and seemed to settle down. We even thought it was a good thing, at first…

And then she died, and he vanished. And we had to pick up the pieces. And now…

Trimaris laid her head on her arms, which lay on the stone table she sat at. Closing her eyes, she breathed in the scent of primroses, morning glories and poppies—brilliant scents, heavy to the point of being colored. Normally the garden, with its small stream and brightly colored songbirds nesting in the arbors, soothed her, but since her meeting with Andreas, she had been unable to find any peace.

Her mind flashed back to the box he'd shown her and she shuddered, blocking the image from her memories by force of will. She'd never been so scared—trapped in cold Darkness, cut off from the Light that sustained her, she'd looked into the box and seen what awaited her. Even now, the chill of the Shadows wrapped around her, reminding her of exactly what fate held for her, should she decide to fight Andreas.

I am a Child of Light, she had wailed, and only Darkness had answered her. It had been a horrifying moment; only by agreeing to help him had she been released.

Now she wondered truly which was the greater evil.

Raising her head, she looked around the garden dispassionately, golden eyes dull. If we succeed, this will all be gone anyways, she thought. Why am I fighting the inevitable?

"Because you're a bloody wimp, that's why."

Trimaris jumped. The voice had come out of nowhere, resonating in the still garden air. She could have sworn it was her sister's.

"Of course it is." The voice sounded irritated. "Wake up, Trimaris."

The Dawn Lord watched in utter astonishment as a golden glow coalesced by the garden gate and her sister stepped out of it. Kymara looked as she always had—long golden hair loose over her shoulders, her robes pristine and her golden eyes sparkling mischievously.

"You're in trouble, Tri." Kymara sauntered over to the table and dropped into the other seat, looking for all the world like she'd stopped in for tea.

"And you're dead, Ky." This was getting far too bizarre. Trimaris started to rise, but her sister frowned at her and she dropped back into her seat.

"I know that." The flatness in her voice was another shock. "And if you aren't careful, you'll end up the same way."

This is my subconscious telling me I'm in over my head, Trimaris decided, looking at her sister. I'm having this conversation with myself.

"If that makes you feel better, go ahead and believe it," Kymara said, responding to the unspoken thoughts the way she had when they were children. "It doesn't really matter if you believe in me at all. What matters is that you listen."

"Listen to what?" Trimaris felt a chill going down her spine. Even if it was just her subconscious, it was very, very creepy.

I've lost my mind...

"Stop that!" Irritation flashed across Kymara's pretty face. "If all you want to do is sit and feel sorry for yourself, go for it. I won't waste my time here. But dammit, Tri, I need you to fix what I started." Her grin took the place of the irritation. "Just like old times."

Despite herself, Trimaris gave her sister's ghost a wry smile. That at least was a true statement: Kymara had been forever getting herself into scrapes that she didn't want their parents or Xavier, their older brother, to find out about, so she would come crying to Trimaris to fix whatever she'd done.

"Listen to me, Trimaris." The amusement faded; for once, Kymara was totally serious. "This is going far beyond what Andreas and I had planned."

"What do you mean, Ky? You'd gone pretty far. I mean, overthrowing the Council? Do you have any idea what that would have done to the Balance? The StarChild would have had no choice but to order a Cleansing." Even now, knowing the extent of Andreas' plans, Trimaris was shocked at the role of her sister.

"The StarChild is the least of your worries right now. I'd welcome a Cleansing—it would stop this insanity."

"That's not comforting, Ky!"

"It's not meant to be." Trimaris decided that she liked the blunt Kymara even less than she liked the whiny one. "Time to grow a backbone, sis. You have to stop Andreas before he casts the final spells."

"Grow a backbone?" Trimaris sputtered. "I'm not the one who started this madness and then had the poor sense to get my throat ripped out! What where you thinking, Ky?"

"I don't know," Kymara replied honestly. "I don't. But I know now what the consequences of our actions will be… and so do you."

The image in the box rose again; Trimaris swallowed and shuddered. "What do I need to do?"

"You need to stop him." Kymara rose and stretched. "If he succeeds in casting the final spells, there is at least one person who will be very unhappy."

"Oh? Who?" Trimaris watched her walk to the gate, already beginning to glow.

Kymara turned at the gate and looked back at her sister, looking like a mystical avatar. "The child that survived."

And then she vanished.

Trimaris clutched the table edge, the ice rimming her heart having nothing to do with the Shadows now. A child survived? Light above. *Now what do I do?*

Chapter 18

"A Unique Invitation"

"You want me to do what?"

Both Nikki and Rick stared at Justin, who continued to butter his English muffin casually, as if he hadn't a care in the world. Nikki's breakfast continued to cool in front of her, uneaten—she hadn't eaten last night either, Rick remembered, and pushed her plate pointedly in front of her.

She ignored it, staring at instead at the Earth Mage. "Okay, let me start again," she said, and Rick noticed the very slight tremble in her voice. "You want me to go back into the Shadow Lands, back into that ....cold, to learn how to use this gift? Why can't you teach me?"

"I can, but only so far, and not fast enough," Justin told her patiently. "You need to be taught by a master."

"A Shadow Mage." She looked extremely dubious. Rick didn't blame her.

"A Shadow Lord, actually," he corrected her. "A Shadow Lord who's already had experience in dealing with ... problem cases, if you like."

Her frown deepened. "I'm not sure I do."

"Alenya trained both Shanna and I," Justin said reassuringly. "Don't worry—she's a good teacher. One of the best."

"Then why's she so willing to train me?"

Rick watched Justin hesitate and wondered himself. He felt isolated already; knowing he wouldn't be going back with them to the Shadows made him less interested in the current breakfast conversation.

Unplugging from the scene, he and his thoughts went straight back to the rut they'd fallen into since he'd plunged the knife into Justin's shoulder. If he let himself go, he could still feel the blade in his hand; the warm, wet feeling of the blood that had slicked his fingers as he drew his hand away.

That wasn't what bothered him.

What truly bothered Rick was the Power he had sensed running with that blood; the Power had called to him, and something deep inside him had answered. It was the sound of that primal voice, something that had remained hidden for all his life, which had catapulted him straight past fear into pure terror. Not even the unbridled Shadows writhing around him in the Lands had done that.

What kind of sick bastard enjoys violence like that? He wondered for the millionth time since yesterday. *People like Robin. Not people like me!*

But you did... It was an insistent voice, one dripping with anticipation. Rick had always wondered what madness sounded like.

Funny, I never realized it sounded like Rutger Hauer.

Not even the feeble attempt at humor could lift him out of the depths his thoughts had dragged him into. Rick poked at the sausage lying on the plate in front of him, his appetite as scarce as Nikki's, and wondered how to stuff Pandora's demon back into its box.

You can't, Rutger whispered gleefully. Rick could even sort of see him (yet another clue that he was most likely losing his grip on reality) standing in the darkness of his mind, wearing a long black cape and carrying a silver walking stick. *Once that box is open, it's open, my dear boy. Nothing you can do but go along for the ride.*

Rick gritted his teeth and stabbed the sausage savagely with his fork. *Not this ride!*

"Rick? You gonna eat that sausage, or just maul it?"

Sarah's voice startled him; he jumped, and the sausage and fork it was impaled on fell to the floor with a clatter. Both Nikki and Justin were staring at him, concern on their faces; Sarah was giving him the worried expression he usually saw on her after walking up from a vision.

"Sorry," he said awkwardly, leaning down to pick up the sausage. "I guess I'm still tired—didn't sleep well last night."

That wasn't a lie, but it also didn't lessen the anxiety in their faces any, as he saw when he looked back up. Rick set the sausage and fork on the napkin next to his plate and scrubbed his hands across his face. "Look, I've got writing to do," he mumbled, and fled the kitchen.

Unfortunately, Rutger didn't stay downstairs with the sausage. As Rick sat at his desk, staring at the blank computer screen in front of him, the blonde actor strolled onto the page and smiled at him.

What's wrong, Rick? His voice oozed false concern. Aren't you happy that you turned out to have a gift after all?

"I have a gift," Rick snarled at the screen. "I have a gift for writing. I have a gift for Sensing things. Those are the only gifts I need."

Oh, don't lie to me! You've been jealous of Nikki and Justin both, because of the things they can do! Rutger conjured up a chaise lounge and sprawled on it. His khakis were perfectly pressed linen; he swung his walking stick up in the air and sighted along it like it was a rifle. And now here's your chance to do something as well.

"What, cut myself and see what happens? No thanks. Pain and I aren't friends." Rick hit the delete key, wishing his delusions were as easily erased as the words on the screen.

But you could be. Rutger abandoned his cane to look at him with his trademark piercing blue eyes. And it only hurts for a moment anyway.

Rick slammed down the lid of the laptop, shutting the actor up for the moment. He sat, his head in his hands, wondering if this wasn't the time to take up serious drinking.

That's a brilliant idea, lad! Rutger crowed, unseen but still heard. Alcohol numbs the pain, you know. Then it won't hurt when you bleed!

"Shut up!" Rick turned and pounded his forehead on his desk. "Just shut up." This last part was whispered.

Nikki and Justin exchanged glances as Rick bolted from his chair, and then rose as one to go after him.

"Don't." Sarah stepped in front of the door, the scowl on her face telling Justin that she was more than ready to use force to keep them in the kitchen. "Haven't you done enough to him already?"

"What?" Justin looked at her, honestly puzzled. "I don't know what you're talking about."

"I'm talking about how he always gets like this after going somewhere with you, Justin Greystone." Sarah spat his name out like she would a mouthful of rotten food. "You use his talent, force him into situations that make him overload and then you just drop him off and go back to wherever you came from, without even making sure he's okay! Do you have any idea how long it takes him to recover from one of these trips?"

"As a matter of fact, yes," Justin replied, stung. "And we were just about…"

"To leave!" she shouted shrilly. "To walk out of his life again, until the next time you need a Sensitive!"

"To check on him," he interrupted icily. "Having lived most of my life as a Sensitive, trust me, Sarah, I know exactly what he's going through."

The force of his words caused her to pause, but only for a moment. Her eyes narrowed again and she opened her mouth to argue, but a crash from upstairs cut her off.

Nicety forgotten, Justin shoved Sarah aside and bounded up the front steps, Nikki hot on his heels. Rick hadn't been the same since they'd gone into the Lands; Justin had thought it was just the magical overload the Sensitive had endured there. The main reason, in fact, that Justin had been against Rick going into the Lands in the first place.

That and the fact that he's mortal. But sensory overload, while explaining his episode yesterday, does not explain why he's still so freaked this morning, he thought grimly. Sensory overload usually brings on a deep, dreamless sleep, which cures it.

Oh Goddess, please don't let anything have hitched a ride back on him.

His thoughts flashed back uncomfortably to Matt, who had gone through a similar psychotic episode after being exposed to a much lower level of magic. Justin was still of the opinion that there had been far more going on with Matt than what his sister had admitted, but she hadn't wanted to talk about what she'd found in his room, and he respected her enough not to push.

Not this time, he vowed, pushing open Rick's door. I've lost enough friends.

"Get out!"

Justin ducked just in time; the book Rick had thrown at him sailed past his head, narrowly missing Nikki and slamming into the wall across the hall. The Earth Mage continued into the room, tackling his friend and wrestling him to the floor before he could throw anything else. Nikki and Sarah hovered in the doorway, unsure of what to do.

"Knock it off, Rick. Don't make me hurt you," Justin muttered, as Rick continued to struggle against him.

Rick surprised him with a harsh laugh. "Hurt me," he said bitterly. "It seems I like that sort of thing."

Justin was so surprised by the remark that his arms relaxed for a split second; Rick surged up against him, slamming his head into Justin's jaw, rocking the Earth Mage's head back and causing him to see stars. He tasted blood in his mouth and swore, tightening his hold again.

"Knock him out," he told Nikki curtly, who shuddered but reached out her hand. "Carefully."

I'll do my best.

Nikki stepped into the room and tried to lay a hand on Rick's forehead. The young Sensitive was actually foaming at the mouth, struggling against Justin's iron grip, growling low in his throat. She wasn't sure what had brought this on, but trusted Justin's judgment.

For the moment.

Opening herself to the Shadows she felt even here, Nikki finally managed to grab Rick's face in her hands and send the coolness of the Power through to him, a stream of sleep, slow and steady. Following the instructions Justin had given her before, she concentrated on the idea of sleep, deep and dreamless sleep, healing sleep.

It seemed to be working; Rick was still struggling, but not as hard, and his growls were abating. Justin kept his hold tight until his friend sagged against his arms. Nikki tilted Rick's face up and nodded at Justin.

"His eyes are closed," she said, taking her hands away and letting the rest of the Shadows go, as Justin had taught her. "I think he'll sleep for a while."

"Good." Justin shifted Rick into his arms, gave her a strange look and then laid him gently on the bed. "This will give me a chance to figure out what the hell triggered that." He looked over at Sarah, who was still hovering. "Why don't you two head back downstairs?" he suggested. "I'll join you in a few moments. And eat something."

Nikki, who was going to argue until she nodded her head and watched the room tilt a bit, mumbled agreement and dragged Sarah from the room.

"You'd better not hurt him," Sarah said venomously, before she allowed Nikki to drag her down the stairs.

"He won't," Nikki said, her words slightly slurred. She hadn't eaten since coming back from the Shadow Lands; her stomach, formerly disinterested in food, was now promising to climb bodily out of its cavity and go foraging for itself. Her plate was still untouched on the table. She took the English muffin and swallowed it in three bites, just to pacify her growling tummy.

"Here, let me warm that up," Sarah said suddenly, taking the plate and popping it into the microwave. Nikki let her, chewing instead on the sausage Rick had left on his napkin. Jonathan, ever the opportunist, sidled his way up to her and laid his warm head on her thigh, eyes pleading. The microwave chimed, and she fed him the last bite as Sarah's back was to them. The innkeeper eyed both of them as she set the hot plate in front of Nikki, but didn't say anything, turning instead to look up the stairs.

"What's he doing?" Sarah fretted. "What's taking so long?"

"He's trying to figure out what happened," Nikki told her, tucking into her eggs. "Rick's in good hands with Justin, Sarah."

"Yeah, right," Sarah sniffed. "Just like the last time."

"What do you have against Mages, Sarah?" Nikki laid down her fork, a little surprised at how clean her plate was; not even a crumb left for Jonathan, who slumped down next to her, disappointed. She looked at the innkeeper, who flushed.

"It's not Mages in general," she muttered. "It's that Mage."

"Justin?" Nikki couldn't imagine what the mild-mannered Earth Mage could have done to draw Sarah's ire. "Why? He's Rick's friend."

"What kind of friend takes a Sensitive into a heavily-haunted graveyard and then just dumps him at home?" Sarah demanded, turning around and pulling ingredients roughly out of the cabinets. Nikki had observed this before—when Sarah was upset, she cooked. "What kind of friend allows a Sensitive, a high Sensitive, to go with him to investigate several different suicide locations, and then again, dumps him at home and goes on his merry way?"

Nikki had no answer to that, other than a murmured, "I'm sure there's more to it."

"Is there?" Sarah was trembling with anger. "I have had to put him back together several times since he's taken up with Justin. I'm the one who held him as he screamed, trapped in nightmares I can't even begin to understand. The one who tended his bruises and scrapes and worse. The one who comforted him by reminding him that the real world still exists. Where was Justin during all of that?"

"Doing the same thing for the other members of our group."

Sarah flushed as Justin came in, and turned back to her ingredients. "I know you want to believe the worst of me, Sarah, but I have never abandoned Rick, and he'd be the first to tell you that," he continued, picking up the mug of tea he'd abandoned earlier and holding it in both hands. He murmured something under his breath and the mug began to steam; he sipped it and then looked at Sarah sadly. "It's just that he actually has someone to come home to. You'd be surprised at how many of us don't."

Sarah's motions slowed down; she didn't turn, but Nikki realized she was thinking Justin's comment over. His remark hit a nerve she'd been trying to ignore in her own life; now, she looked inside herself and realized that once she'd entered the Shadow Lands, she'd effectively left home forever.

I can't bring this into my parents' house, she thought somberly, feeling a wave of homesickness well up in her. If I continue on this path, I'll do it alone.

Not alone. Justin's thought was warm in the chill of her mind. Never alone.

She looked up and smiled at him, thanking him silently. Sarah's ingredients had become a quick bread; she slipped it in the oven and then turned to the two sitting at the table. "So, what did you discover about Rick?" she asked, and Justin's face became guarded.

"I'm not sure," he admitted quietly. "Something happened to him in the Shadows; something more than just sensory overload. I tried to keep him from coming, but ..." He shrugged. "I've put in a block for right now, and left him a note about it. After I get Nikki settled in, I'll come back and work with him."

"And that's it?" Sarah's eyes started to spark again.

"What do you want from me, Sarah?" The weariness in his voice startled Nikki. "I'm an Earth Mage, pretending at times to be a Healer. If I can't help him, I'll bring someone who can. That's all I can do at the moment."

Sarah stared at him, and then nodded. She mumbled something and hurried out of the kitchen. Jonathan, disturbed by her movement, got up and ambled after her.

Justin sighed and set his tea mug down. Nikki knew what was coming next. He looked at her and said simply, "Are you ready?"

No, she wanted to scream. I just want to go home. Instead, she simply looked at him. "What's in it for me?"

He looked startled. "You get to live?"

There it was, in stark black and white. She had wondered how long it was going to take him to say that. Rick had explained a bit more about the Balance last night, on the way home; if even half of what he'd said was correct, she was a walking disaster, and Nature usually had a swift way of dealing with imbalances.

"It's not just Nature you have to watch out for," Justin said very seriously, leaning over the table towards her. "Nikki, there are those out there who are deliberating your fate right now: very powerful people. If they decide you pose too great a threat to the Balance—they'll take steps to make sure you aren't a threat anymore."

"They'll kill me."

"Yes."

The word hung there, a spectral noose waiting for her to hang herself. Nikki looked at it, and debated. Only for a moment, but long enough that she knew she'd seriously considered the alternative before signing her life away with a simple nod of her head.

Heaving a sigh of relief, Justin smiled at her and offered her a hand up. She accepted, feeling like the condemned as they are helped into the electric chair. Yes, Warden, that's tight enough, thank you. Wouldn't want to twitch too hard when the current hits and fall out of the chair.

"And you'll like Alenya," Justin said. "She's a great teacher."

"Mmm." Nikki wasn't sure what to expect. Justin opened the door to the pantry, concentrated and then motioned her through. "You want me to go into the pantry?"

"I want you to go through the Gate in the pantry," he said patiently.

"Since when is there a Gate in Sarah's pantry?" she asked, looking in at the vortex swirling lazily in the semi-darkness. "She's going to kill you if you leave it there."

"I wasn't planning on leaving it there," he replied. "Wanna get a move on? They aren't that easy to hold open, you know."

"No, I didn't." Nikki looked at the vortex a moment longer, then stepped through.

There was the now-familiar squeeze as she went through the World Walls, and then she stepped into, not the pantry, but the woods of her dreams. Justin stepped in beside her, and the vortex sank in on itself and vanished.

"This way," he said, pointing to what appeared to be a random direction and setting off.

Nikki followed him, a chill feeling hardening in the pit of her stomach. Her boots crunched on the leaves as they found the same track she had followed in her dream; as they stepped onto the lawn and the house loomed above them, Nikki did what most people would do when faced with an impossibility in front of them; she burst into tears.

Justin had been expecting something along the lines of this. He started towards her, but was beaten to the punch by, of all people, his foster mother, who had appeared literally out of nowhere to enfold Nikki in arms that had once comforted a small boy afraid of the monsters in the dark.

Alenya whispered something; seamlessly, she transferred the three of them into the library, where the wards of the house settled around them. Then she let Nikki cry; inside, the storm that both she and Justin were expecting would do less damage to the Balance than outside.

But there was no storm; not yet, at least. Nikki's sobs were almost silent; only the shaking of her shoulders let him know that she hadn't finished. Justin gave into temptation and poured himself, not a glass of wine, but a stiff shot of the special brandy Kith made every year. He tossed it back, shuddered and felt the icy fire of the drink crawl through his veins.

"That bad?"

He nodded at the smoky question. "I'll tell you later. Let's get this settled first."

Nikki had drawn back as the voice flowed over her. "You!"

"Hello, Nikki." Alenya smiled. "Welcome to my home."

Nikki looked from Justin to the woman in black, and back again, feeling slightly betrayed, although he couldn't have known about her dreams. "You're Alenya?"

The Shadow Lord (she had to be, Justin had said she was) nodded, amusement coloring a face Nikki had never seen void of shadow. But the eyes, the emerald eyes: those she recognized.

"You bastard! Why didn't you tell me?" Nikki swung around and glared at Justin, who looked startled. He was doing that in her company quite a bit, and it was starting to irritate her.

"Tell you what?"

"That the woman in my dreams was a Shadow Lord!" It sounded irrational as soon as she said it, but there was no way to call it back. Justin made it worse by grinning at her; despite herself, her lips twisted into a smile.

"Nikki." That voice, the one that had haunted her for weeks, called her attention back to the person who would be teaching her. "How could he have known?"

"He seems to know everything else," she muttered rebelliously, turning back towards Alenya. "Why shouldn't he have known?"

"Indeed." She had a lovely smile, one that lit fire in her eyes. Nikki responded to the smile, feeling that despite everything, she was finally in the one spot she could call home.

And if that isn't a bizarre feeling, I don't know what is.

Alenya came over to her and cupped her cheek in her hand, raising her face to look at her in the light of the flickering mage lights along the wall. "You look so much like your mother," she murmured, and Nikki's eyes widened.

"You knew my mother?" she whispered, the Shadow Lord nodded.

"Oh yes, child. I knew her." There was a pause. "And I will tell you the entire story, I promise. You have much to learn, and that will be part of it. But not now." She looked at Justin. "The Council has agreed to let her be until it is seen whether or not she can be brought into balance."

Justin let out a breath Nikki hadn't known he was holding. "Thank God they showed some sense this time!"

"We'll see." Alenya let her hand fall. "Why don't you show Nikki to the room next to Shanna's."

"A room?" Nikki looked at both of them. "How long will I be here?"

"As long as it takes."

The sentence had a hollow clank at the end, like the key turning in the lock of a prison door.

Chapter 19

"Ahead of Schedule"

There were several emails waiting for Tony when he limped into his office a scant two days after his meeting with Andreas, most of them flagged with the urgent red highlighting he'd come to realize was standard operating procedure at Gene-Tech. There was also a handwritten note from Bret, the guard he'd been working with on the collection of the breeders.

Last two breeders to be taken next week, it said, in Bret's casual handwriting.

"Excellent," Tony murmured, setting the note on fire in the brazier on his desk. "Lord Andreas will be most pleased."

"Indeed," Alex said from the doorway, and Tony jumped, then winced at the pain that radiated from his twisted ankle. "I hope you know what you're doing."

Tony snarled inwardly, his face only slightly irritated at the interruption. "I do, Alex. Care to come in, or shall we share this conversation with the entire facility, rather than just the hall?"

Shutting the door ostentatiously behind him and locking it, Alex strode into the room and sank into the chair at the table next to Tony's desk. He had been given a new office just days after he and Sylvia had met; Tony assumed she'd complained enough. He was just happy to be out of her immediate presence; something about her grated on his nerves.

When he had a spare moment, he promised himself, he would find out exactly what that something was.

"My father's not one to be toyed with," Alex was saying, as Tony pulled his mind from the entertaining thoughts of torturing Sylvia. "If he finds out you're working against him, Tony, I won't be able to protect you. I hope you understand that."

Which is your way of saying that you won't have your ass on the firing line, you supercilious little prick, Tony thought dryly. Luckily, I already knew that.

"Don't worry, Alex. Your lily-white hands won't be anywhere near this," he said out loud. "Just leave everything to me. I know what I'm doing." And the less you know about it, the less worry I have that you'll open your mouth and fuck it up.

Which was why Alex was here, of course—Tony was positive of that. Since their conversation last week, when Tony had let him know that Andreas was moving the schedule up, Alex had been pitching one fit after another. Most of these fits had to do with his father; the ones that hadn't had focused on how much Tony wasn't telling him.

"Those new wardings are costing me a fortune in overtime," Alex said, his baritone voice sulky. "And now you're building another one. With even more protections and wards built into it. Care to tell me why?"

"No." Tony made a big show of closing the screen to his laptop and resting his hands upon it. "We've been through this already. The less you know, the less Andreas will think you're involved. You're the one who didn't want to face his anger, remember?"

Alex flushed at the implied criticism in his bland tone. "You could at least have told me you were going to start collecting breeders."

"I did," Tony pointed out. "Or don't you read your emails anymore? I sent it out last night."

A banging on the door interrupted Alex's reply; Tony started to reach out, checking to see who was there, when Sylvia hollered through the door, "Open it now or I'll blow it open!"

Tony sighed, rubbing his hand over the top of his head. I shouldn't have gotten up this morning...

She banged again, and he flipped his free hand at the door, unlocking it. Sylvia raged in, anger a visible cloud that clung to her like an ill-fitting trench coat, baggy and unflattering.

"How dare you cut me out of this project!" she screeched, waving a stack of papers in front of his nose. He wondered somewhere in the back of his mind if she'd even noticed Alex sitting there.

Probably not. "I beg your pardon?"

The papers were shoved close enough that he was mildly worried about paper cuts on his face. "I'm talking about the fact that there are two girls, barely eighteen years old, in holding cells in this facility! Two girls who, by the way, have no idea what they're doing here and are drugged up to their eyeballs to keep them from wondering about it! And when I do find out who ordered this, what do I find? Your greasy fingerprints on every single goddamn order!"

The papers were dropped as she grabbed his collar. "This is my project! I am the research lead! Not you! I thought I made that clear when you started here!"

"Then be a lead!" Tony had had enough. He surged to his feet to stand nose to nose with Sylvia. "For the past two weeks, you've done nothing but delegate! Mary's been setting up all the spells—no one's even seen you! What have you been doing?"

"Working on the advanced spells!" she snarled back. "My job as the lead, remember? I have to set up the lead spells, so the others can follow. What about you? Or have you just been ordering kidnappings?"

"And how were you planning on getting breeders?" Tony snapped, sidestepping her question. "Did you honestly think you could just send out a call for volunteers?"

"At least that way, I'd know they knew what they were getting into! Or were you planning on keeping them drugged until the babies were born, and then just letting them go?" Sylvia's voice was scathing.

"What makes you think this was the only time we'd need them?" Tony asked sarcastically. "This is an experiment, remember? Experiments have more than one stage—this way, since they're so young, we can keep the line going for years without having to find more breeders. And they're throwaways; I checked. No family or friends to miss them. What more could you ask for in lab rats?"

The horror on her face was sweet on his lips, and he couldn't stop. "Besides, my dear, let's not split hairs. You know you wanted young ... volunteers."

"You are one sick bastard." Did he imagine it, or was there grudging admiration under the revulsion in her voice?

"Thank you. Coming from you, Dr. Richards, that's a compliment." Tony sat back down and picked up the papers she'd dropped. "Was there anything else?"

Sylvia grabbed the papers and stalked out. Tony smiled and sucked up the blood from the small paper cut she'd made on his fingers. Alex had snuck out at some point in the argument, and his office was quiet again.

Finally.

———

Sylvia's stomach flipped as she listened to Tony. *He's really lost it*, she realized. *And I thought I was insane. He's so far beyond me that I can't even see his back trail anymore.*

The glee in Tony's eyes frightened her; her voice shook as she said quietly, "You are one sick bastard."

"Thank you. Coming from you, Dr. Richards, that's a compliment." Tony sat back down and picked up the papers she'd dropped. "Was there anything else?"

Nothing I'll discuss with you, you sick fuck. Sylvia grabbed the papers out of his hand and made a tactical retreat, one small part of her mind gleefully registering the paper cut she gave him as she took back the papers. The air in the office had gone stale, or perhaps it was the creepiness of the villain sitting behind the desk; whatever it was, she wanted out, and quickly.

She was proud of the fact that she didn't run down the hall to her office; her fast walk was still a walk, and she even managed to keep the shakes inside until her door was locked behind her. Then she sank into her chair and covered her face with her hands, letting the horror wash over her.

Not normally an early riser, Sylvia had been in the office since nearly 2 am, working on the first set of advanced spells they would be casting on (she had thought) willing breeders. She had been determined not to make Cameron's mistake of using unwilling breeders—his journal had detailed the problems Teraisa Donnelly, in particular, had caused them. The fact that she'd been one of his researchers had really bothered him; he had written extensively about how worried he was about the effect her Shadow Magic would have on the spells. In the end, she'd been drugged most of the time.

Sylvia taken time out around 4 a.m. to read the emails she'd been ignoring, and the one Tony had sent, blandly upgrading her careful schedule and noting almost after the fact that two of the breeders had been already brought to the facility, had started her blood boiling. What she'd found after that had brought her up to full rage. Just thinking about it now was starting to make her steam again, dispelling her horror at his casual dismissal of what he'd done.

Enough! There was too much at stake to get angry now. She'd seen the two girls Tony had "collected"; both runaways, thin and drugged out of their minds. And it hadn't escaped her notice that both were latent Mages, completely untrained and therefore malleable. There would be no problems of the sort that Cameron had had with Teraisa.

But gods, they are so young! And totally unprepared for what we'll do. How can I go along with this? Sylvia buried her face in her hands again, the anger draining away, leaving a hollow emptiness in the pit of her stomach. Unaccountably, Morgan's face rose in her mind, his dark eyes troubled, the way he'd been at breakfast that morning, when she'd gotten Cameron's diary unlocked. He'd warned her; and now, she wished desperately that she'd listened.

As if her thoughts had summoned him, Sylvia's cell phone rang, the "Imperial March" from the Star Wars movies sounding impossibly loud in her office. She dug through her purse and grabbed the phone, just as it stopped ringing. The number that flashed was Vashti's.

Now what? Sylvia dialed the number for her voicemail and listened as the message played—a simple invitation to dinner, nothing more. It was a credit to Alex's managerial style that she wondered instantly what was up.

Paranoid much, Richards? The question was only half-rhetorical. She called Vashti back and agreed to come to dinner; the Earth Mage was delighted, and said so. Sylvia asked, as always, what she could bring; as always, Vashti told her to bring just herself, and Sylvia countered with a bottle of wine.

The old game.

Once she hung up, Sylvia picked up the papers she'd taken from Tony; copies of the orders she'd taken from the guards he'd handpicked to "collect" the breeders. There were two more names on the list; a quick search of them on the 'Net had given her precious little information about them. She suspected that they too were runaways - "throwaways," Tony had called them. And probably latents; the better to provide a base for the spells to anchor to in the unborn fetuses.

Cameron had been blunt in the journal he'd expected no one else to see, and he'd made reference to how the spells sat so well with the two breeders because they were both Talented. Sylvia had been shocked to discover the identity of the second breeder: none other than Caran Masterson, Alex's own wife. It brought her opinion of Alex down even further, that he would sacrifice his marriage for the sake of this experiment. It also made her wonder. Why was this experiment so important? What contract was riding on this twenty-three years ago that he would sacrifice her for? Granted, he doesn't have a high opinion of women, but even so!

And what is fueling reviving it now?

Cameron hadn't known what the contract was; or if he did, he didn't consider it important enough to record it. Sylvia hadn't found it recorded anywhere. Obviously Alex had kept some of the records from her. Which just served to pique her interest more: she'd starting doing some digging, but hadn't been able to discover his new client.

He wouldn't be going through this much expense for no profit, Sylvia mused, running her fingers over the papers. There's someone footing the bill for this, but who? And why?

She still hadn't figured it out by the time she pulled the Jag into Vashti's driveway that night, the early twilight just shading the sky. Night-blooming cereus spilled its sweet fragrance into the evening; Sylvia took a deep breath and let the scent carry away her stress.

Vashti was in the outdoor kitchen, sitting on a low bench, a glass of wine in her hand. There were several strands of Christmas lights, the long white icicle ones, hung around the area, throwing a soft light over the scene. A fire flickered low in the cooking pit; a Dutch oven was nestled in the coals, and Sylvia tasted the tang of curry, saffron and cardamom in the air.

"Smells wonderful," she said, dropping a kiss on Vashti's soft cheek. "Thank you for inviting me."

The Earth Mage smiled and offered her the glass. "I thought I heard the car."

Seeing a second glass on the ground next to the bench, Sylvia accepted. The talk was light as twilight darkened into true night and the stew bubbled. Despite the wine and the cordial atmosphere, Sylvia could feel Vashti waiting for someone, or something—and it wasn't the food.

"Expecting someone else?" she asked finally, and Vashti smiled.

"Sharp as ever, child. I never could hide anything from you." The warmth in her tone made Sylvia smile, even as she knew it wasn't true. "I'm expecting more guests. And as the sun has truly set, they should be here soon."

Interesting. Wonder why they had to wait that long?

The answer to that question became clear as soon as the first vortex, emerald in one of the shadowed corners, began to swirl. Sylvia set her empty glass aside as the Shadows twisted and a Shadow Lord stepped into the clearing, wearing white robes chased with silver designs. Her vortex disappeared, only to be replaced in the fire by one of deep red; the Dawn Lord that entered wore a set of breeches and a tunic of dark green that accented her golden hair and eyes.

It was the final member to arrive, however, that set Sylvia's teeth on edge. Gliding into the clearing, seemingly made entirely of Shadows, the being simply radiated Power and mystery. Sylvia watched, her mouth open, as the Shadows parted and a woman she had thought dead for twenty-three years stepped out.

"Impossible!" she blurted out, shooting to her feet as Teraisa Donnelly looked at her with something that might possibly have been amusement glimmering in her dark blue eyes. "You're dead!"

"Not entirely." The woman's voice was dark as the Shadows surrounding her. "Not yet."

"Sit, Sylvia." Vashti's hand was suddenly on her shoulder, forcing her back onto her chair. "We have much to discuss tonight."

Sylvia sat, suddenly very much afraid of what she was about to hear.

She grew less comfortable as she was introduced to the other two: Haldana the Dawn Lord simply nodded at her, golden eyes unreadable, but the Shadow Lord Cassandra gave her a hard look and demanded, "This is the one?"

"Yes." Vashti's voice was slightly reproving. "And she is here of her own free will, Cassandra."

"Do you have any idea what you're doing?" Cassandra demanded of Sylvia, who shrank back from the anger in her emerald eyes. "Of the damage to the Balance?"

"Peace, Cassandra." Oddly enough, it was Teraisa who spoke. "She knows. And she is not as comfortable with it as she would like to think."

Pieces clicked into place with such a loud crack that Sylvia wondered if it was audible outside her head. "You're the ghost."

She'd thought everyone at the facility was going insane when she'd first heard the "ghost" rumors. The descriptions had varied wildly: some people had reported a dark cloud, moving through the wings, mostly the secure wing, while others had told of a brilliant beam of golden light, and the scent of roses. Depending on which phenomenon had been encountered, there was either a chill or warmth in the air.

"Partially," Teraisa said quietly. "There are many things interested in your experiment, Sylvia."

That wasn't comforting either.

"Cassandra, what was the Council's stance on the child?" Haldana asked, and Sylvia sat back to listen, wide-eyed.

Cassandra looked over at Vashti, who nodded. "The child is being trained, to see if her Gifts can be brought into Balance," the Shadow Lord said, and Sylvia watched Teraisa close her eyes, as if in relief. There was only one reason that she would do that.

Goddess above and below, a child survived. Did they all survive?

"We don't know," Vashti murmured, and Sylvia realized she'd thought loud enough for them all to hear. "Only one has surfaced so far. It increases the odds that the others survived as well."

Sylvia looked at Teraisa, her face in Shadow and her eyes shrouded. "Your daughter."

A nod, and Sylvia drew in a trembling breath. "Is she … normal?"

"Define normal." Definite amusement colored her voice. "She is healthy, and strong. But she manifests all three Spheres in her aura."

"All three?" Sylvia's head was spinning. "That's … "

"Impossible?" Cassandra's voice was still angry. "No, not if you realized what you were mucking around with, Shadow Mage. The very substance of the Summoning Spells nearly guarantees that she would have had all three Spheres in her aura!"

The clearing went dead silent at her words, not even the remains of the fire daring to crackle. Haldana and Vashti were white with horror; Teraisa's face was once more in Shadow, betraying nothing of her emotions.

"Tell me you're joking, Cassandra," Vashti said finally, and the alien note was back in her voice. "How could they have gotten a hold of the Summoning Spells?"

"Obviously from someone on the Council," Cassandra replied. "Think of what else happened twenty-three years ago."

"Kymara," Haldana said slowly. "She was on the Council, and she died right around the same time. But would she have really stolen the Spells? And why?"

"Does it matter?" Vashti asked practically. "What's done is done. Now we need to decide what to do in the present." She looked at Sylvia, who refused to meet her eyes. "The program has restarted, yes?"

Hating herself, she nodded.

"Have the breeders been collected?"

"Two have." She heard a sharp intake of breath from one of the Lords. "We're expecting the other two next week."

"And then?"

Sylvia shrugged. "According to the new schedule, the eggs will be removed at the end of next week. We should have live fetuses ready to implant within two weeks."

"And then the spells will start." Teraisa's voice was curiously flat; Sylvia reminded herself that the creature before her had already gone through most of the procedure. "The Shadow Lord and Dawn Lord will not arrive before the fetuses are three months old: they'll let the human Mages do the preliminary spells on their own."

That agreed with the timetable Sylvia had set up; she nodded.

"And if all goes well?" Haldana's voice was brittle.

Sylvia shrugged. "We should have healthy children in approximately ten months. Then we move into the observation stage of the experiment."

It sounded so cold, even to her, the trained scientist. And her stomach turned as she thought of the two girls currently in the cells, their eyes dulled with drugs, simply waiting for whatever would happen.

There were spells being cast on them even now, spells designed to keep them docile and take the place of the drugs that wouldn't be used once the fetuses were implanted. Alex was being very strict on how the girls (Sylvia hated the word "breeders") were to be kept: the spells would keep them quiet and make them care for themselves. All, of course, to make sure the fetuses were born healthy and strong.

"Do you have any idea what you're making?" the Dawn Lord asked her, shock in her voice. "You're using the Summoning Spells! How can you expect the Balance to survive that?"

"Not even the real spells, which is worse," Cassandra chimed in. "A bastardization of them, corrupting the intent even more."

"I don't know what you're talking about." Sylvia finally looked up. "I've never heard of these Summoning Spells. The spells we're using are copyrighted to Gene-Tech. They were created by the head researcher for the last experiment."

"Actually, they were given to him," Teraisa murmured. "Alex came in with them about a month before the experiment started and told us to learn them."

"Do you know where Alex got them?" Cassandra asked, and Teraisa shook her head.

"What do the Summoning Spells summon?" Sylvia asked, and there was a long pause before Vashti answered her.

"I don't think that's really relevant right now, child. Suffice it to say that the Spells shouldn't have been tampered with. Just having them in mortal hands is inviting trouble with the Balance." Vashti turned to the two Lords. "I think we need to see these spells."

There was murmured agreement, and she looked over at Sylvia. "Can you get them for us?" It wasn't really a question.

"I'll try." She saw the looks on their faces and stubbornly resisted melting into a puddle. "Those spells are highly classified—they're not to leave the facility! If I try, I could end up in her position!" Her, of course, being Teraisa, who chuckled dryly.

"She's right, partially. If she's caught sneaking the spells out, she'll be replaced. And probably killed, knowing Alex. He won't make the same mistake twice, even if he does think I'm dead." Teraisa paused, looking at Sylvia thoughtfully. "You'll be making notes, though?"

"Of course." Sylvia could see where this was heading.

"Your notes could be very valuable to us. I suggest you bring them with you the next time we meet." It wasn't a request. Sylvia realized she was getting a lot of those lately and sighed.

"I'll do my best."

There was little talk after that. The two Lords left, and Vashti headed inside for bowls for the stew. Teraisa lingered a moment longer.

"Vashti tells me you have Cameron's journal." Her voice was curiously void of emotion; Sylvia nodded cautiously, wondering where this was heading. "I suggest you read it again. The spells you work don't just affect the children you're playing God with."

She reached out a hand and touched Sylvia on the cheek; the Shadow Mage shuddered at the chill seeping from her skin. "After all, Cameron and I were both once mortal Shadow Mages too."

"And what are you now?" Sylvia whispered.

"I don't know anymore." Teraisa withdrew her hand and melted into the Shadows, leaving a very shaken Sylvia to ponder her last words.

What do I do now?

Interlude 2

"A Time Between Times"

"The Lady Trimaris, my lord."

Trimaris entered the study seconds before the butler could announce her, having pushed past him downstairs. Planting her hands on his desk (and thanking the Light that his servants were too afraid of the Shadow Lord to linger in his presence), she hissed, "And when were you going to tell me about the children that survived?"

Andreas' sharp intake of breath was the only clue she'd surprised him. He rose slowly from behind the desk, his robes whispering in the twilight he preferred, and said quietly, "I beg your pardon?"

"Don't lie to me, Andreas." She pushed herself off the desk and glared at him, too angry to be cowed by his presence. "I know about the girl at Cassandra's. Do you think I wouldn't realize who she was?"

"No one knows what she is," he replied urbanely, moving to the sideboard and pouring two glasses of wine. "For all they know, she's another damn halfbreed."

"She's not a halfbreed. She's a product of this damn experiment that you're hell-bent on recreating." The wine looked like blood to Trimaris; she crossed her arms obstinately over her chest, refusing to take the glass he offered. "So now what are we going to do?"

"Continue the experiment."

She gaped at him. "Are you insane? What will that do to her?"

"Does it matter?" Andreas sipped the wine and offered her the other glass again. "You really should try this—it's a very good vintage."

"You really are insane." Trimaris accepted the glass in shock; once she touched the cool glass, she had to fight not to fling its contents into his calm face. "If she's one of the children, the others could have also survived. We've got three walking time bombs on our hands."

"Do we?" Andreas smiled. "So far, she's the only one. And my sources tell me she has all three Spheres in her aura. If she can balance herself, she's no threat to us or the Balance." His smile deepened. "And if she is one of the children, she's just proven our experiment works."

But at what cost? Trimaris shuddered at the implications.

"But tell me, my dear," and his smile turned hard. "Just how did you find out about her?"

"You think you're the only one with sources?" she retorted, hoping her voice sounded stronger to him than it did to her. If he found out where her information was really coming from, she wasn't sure what he'd do.

Kymara had been a figment of her imagination, she'd been sure of that; but now, with Andreas confirming what her sister's ghost had told her, Trimaris felt the world move beneath her. She took a swallow of the wine to steady herself and watched the glass shake in her hand.

Are you really dead, little sister? Trimaris felt a hysterical giggle bubble up in her throat and tried to strangle it before Andreas heard. Just what I needed to make this perfect—the ghost of my sister haunting me. She turned towards the window, needing something to ground herself, and gasped.

"You're the one who wasn't even sure I existed." Kymara was leaning against the wall, a bright golden glow against the muted backdrop of Andreas' study. Trimaris looked quickly back at the Shadow Lord, who had taken his chair majestically, and then back at her sister, who grinned.

"Don't worry, he doesn't know I'm here." The Dawn Lord's ghost strolled over to her one-time lover and laid a hand on his face. "In fact, he doesn't really know much at the moment. This is between time."

"Of course it is." Trimaris felt the giggle bubble up again. "Where else would a dead Dawn Lord hang out?"

Kymara gave her sister a look of disgust. "Are you done yet?"

"Sorry." Trimaris tried to look repentant and failed. "I assume there's a reason for this visit? Or were you just lonely?"

Another dirty look arrowed at her. "No, I missed the stupid comments you seem to love to make lately."

"Going insane does that to a person, I hear." Trimaris realized she still had the glass of wine in her hand and tossed a healthy swig back.

Andreas had been right: it was a very good vintage. "So tell me. I think I'm ready to hear anything now."

"Just shut up for a moment and try to focus." Kymara's hand rested on Andreas' shoulder; Trimaris was struck by how good they looked together, even with the bandages on the Shadow Lord's face. They had been a handsome couple.

And a dangerous, deadly one.

"You have to look beyond your prejudice, Tri. He's a good man." Kymara's eyes were troubled. "You'll never succeed if you don't realize that."

"He's a psycho who got you killed, Ky. Or did you forget that fact?" Trimaris was beyond rationalizing her sister's appearance.

"I haven't forgotten. That doesn't change things." Kymara looked down at her lover again, and her face softened. "Don't hurt him more than you have to, Tri," she murmured, and kissed his cheek. "It's not all his fault. Stop him, but don't let him suffer too much."

She fragmented then, shimmering into golden shards that sparkled in the dim air as they floated down towards the rug. Trimaris watched them disappear, her mouth open and her thoughts whirling at the changes Andreas had wrought in her sister. Even in death, Kymara was still devoted to him—even as she urged her sister to stop him.

That fascinated Trimaris. She stared at him, wondering how he'd aroused such emotion in her flighty sister.

Time must have started again; Andreas frowned at her and raised fingertips to his face. "Have I turned green or something, Trimaris? Or are you staring at my handsome face?" This last comment dripped with irony; Trimaris flushed and stammered something inane in response.

He looked at her; despite his lack of physical eyes, she felt his quizzical stare. "You're troubled, Trimaris. Is there something you'd like to talk about?"

She looked back up at him, feeling buffeted by everything that had happened in the last few days. The unexpected sympathy in his voice was the last straw—it broke the dam and drained everything away, leaving her hollow. "Who are you, Andreas?" she asked finally, dropping into the other chair in front of the fireplace. The leather was warm; the heat from the flames was a welcome tonic to the chill of the Shadow Lands. "And why do Dawn Lords seem to have a soft spot for you, despite what you're doing?"

Andreas would have blinked, had he eyes; as it was, she felt how startled her question made him. "What do you mean?" he said carefully, after a moment's thought. "I'm a Shadow Lord. Nothing more."

"My sister loved you." Trimaris found the glass of wine still in her hands, amazingly enough; she watched the ruby fluid shimmer in the firelight, liquid flame. "She died for you."

"She died for us." The sympathy melted into sadness. "I still miss her. Sometimes I can even smell her perfume. Can hear her voice."

Was this what she meant? The thought rose in her mind. Or is this just another piece of his insanity?

Or mine?

Andreas was still talking, his resonant voice filling the room. "We had such plans. Kymara loved to plan things." He chuckled, remembering. "She even had names picked out for the children."

"Really?" Somehow, that didn't surprise Trimaris.

"Oh yes. The last couple of months, she fussed over the breeders like a mother hen. You would have thought she was the one carrying all three children. And she couldn't wait to hold them."

The image flashed into her mind: Kymara, seated on a couch, an infant in her arms. The child had a fuzzy halo of blonde hair and the deep blue eyes she remembered Andreas having before the accident. Tears filled Trimaris' eyes as she realized it was a natural setting for her sister; something she must have longed for, forbidden as it was.

And then, through the tears, she realized why the experiment had consumed so much of Kymara's attention.

"You're the father." The words were whispered; it was all she could do to force them out. "Those children: they're the children you couldn't have together."

Dawn Lords and Shadow Lords were unable to conceive children together: the theory was that the resulting child would be too unstable to survive. Earth Lords were rumored to be fertile with both, being the grounding forces of the Balance, but no children had ever been discovered.

Andreas had bowed his head, tacit admission that what she'd guessed was true.

"Oh lord, Andreas." The implications were stunning. "That girl is your daughter."

"Our daughter. The only offspring we could hope to have." He sighed. "I just wish Kymara had lived to see her."

The sorrow in his voice brought a lump to her throat. They sat together, each wrapped in their own thoughts, as the fire died down. When the room finally went dark, she let the tears fall.

Oh Light, what do I do now?

Chapter 20

"Lessons in Life"

"So, how goes the teaching?"

Kith and Alenya were seated in the garden, enjoying a glass of mead together as the full moon sank into shadow, when Cassandra spoke from the lower gate. Her white robes, chased with amethyst, reminded Alenya of the moonflowers Nikki was so fond of.

"It goes," Kith said quietly, as Cassandra joined them and accepted a glass from her daughter. "Not as quickly as she'd like, but it goes."

Cassandra raised one dark eyebrow. "It's been four months, Kith. Even the worst student makes some progress in that amount of time."

"She's made progress." He swirled the mead around reflectively in the glass. "Just not enough to let her go back. That's not the real problem, I'm afraid. Nor the only one."

"What is?" Cassandra's voice sharpened a bit in concern.

"The fact that she's happy here and feeling guilty about that." Kith sighed. "This is where she feels the most comfortable, but she seems to think that's a disservice to her adoptive parents."

"Oh, that." Cassandra dismissed Nikki's concerns with a wave of her hand. "She'll learn. The Council won't care about that. They want to know how Balanced she is."

"She's a creature of Shadow—especially since her mother was a Shadow Mage." Kith shrugged. "She'll always be drawn to the Shadows. But she's learning. Would your friend Vashti be willing to teach her the Earth Lore, like she did for Shanna and Justin?"

The elder Shadow Lord nodded. "Considering the level of Power involved here, she volunteered immediately."

Alenya had been sitting quietly, half-listening to the conversation, the last drops of mead from her glass melting on her tongue. There was something else nagging at her, something she'd noticed more and more as she tutored Nikki in the use of Shadow Magic.

She let her mind drift back, remembering the first time she'd tried to help Nikki ground herself in the Shadow Lands. Justin had shown her how to do it on Earth; the technique was similar, but to truly ground, Nikki had to open herself totally to the Shadows. Considering what had happened the last time she tried that, she'd been understandably hesitant.

And had failed, miserably, with a result similar to what Alenya herself had gone through at the same phase of her training. The memory came flooding back...

Nikki ran instinctively through the house, eventually bursting through a set of French doors into a garden heavy with the scent of moonflowers. Alenya had followed behind her, far enough to give the girl some room, but close enough to intercept any stray magical effects from the storm of emotion surrounding her young pupil.

"Oh Mom, what is happening to me?" Nikki wailed, slipping onto the ground and burying her face in her arms on the bench. "Why can't I do this?"

The tears tore at Alenya's heart; she too remembered how difficult it had been to master the Shadows around her. And that was for one who had grown up with them; she couldn't begin to imagine what Nikki was dealing with inside. Kith might understand, with his odd background, but Alenya could not, and that made the training even harder on both student and teacher.

After about fifteen minutes, though, the child ran out of tears. Nikki simply sat on the ground, looking up at the full moon hanging above the garden. A light breeze sprang up, and on it drifted plaintive harp notes, a quiet lullaby. Alenya, still standing by the French doors, smiled as the song dried the last few tears on Nikki's cheek, knowing exactly what Cassandra was doing.

Gradually, Nikki realized there was someone else in the sunken garden, seated beside the pool that rippled in the moonlight. The rays slid down the silver strings of the harp that leaned against the woman's shoulder, gilding the white wood of the instrument and bleaching her dark hair as it slipped down her back. Her dress was white and silky, and the breeze stirred the edges of it against the stone wall she sat on. Nikki watched, fascinated, as her long fingers caressed the strings, coaxing the fragile notes into life. Alenya watched as well, seeing her mother anew through her student's eyes.

Her face was similar to Alenya's, but slimmer, with an ageless beauty that belied her untold years. Her skin was unlined, and there was an inner radiance that glimmered in the darkness. Long dark lashes lay against her cheeks, and her half-closed eyelids shadowed her emerald eyes.

And then the Shadow Lord received her first shock. Nikki whispered softly, "Why did you enter my dreams?"

"She may not answer," Alenya said, deciding it was time to come into her student's line of vision. "My mother feels it's her right not to answer to anyone she feels doesn't need an answer."

"It is," Cassandra responded tartly, not pausing in her playing. "Age hath its privileges, after all. It's one of the only reasons to get old."

Alenya smiled and sank down on the bench, smoothing down her dress as the music started again, with a melancholy undertone that tugged at her heart. The ancient Shadow Lord played as if there was no one else in the world but her and her harp, and the gentle gurgle of the koi pond in the corner was a low counterpoint to the plaintive strings. Nikki leaned against Alenya's knee, and she looked down, startled.

"I'm going to have to die, aren't I?" The girl whispered, closing her dark blue eyes. Alenya was faintly alarmed at the dark circles of exhaustion under her eyes. "To restore the Balance, I'm going to have to die."

Alenya's hand moved to Nikki's head, smoothing the silky dark hair as she tried to find an answer. "We don't know that, Nikki," she said finally. "We simply don't know enough about you. Don't fret yet."

"My life has changed so much in the last month," Nikki sighed, leaning into the caresses. "I don't know anything any more."

"You know who you are, child. No matter what happens to you, you are still the girl raised by your parents." Alenya smiled, in spite of the fear in her heart. "You had a happy childhood, yes?"

"Yes. No magic, no shadows—just your normal, happy kid. My folks gave me everything I needed. That's part of why this is so unbelievable." Nikki sighed again, sounding so much like the other young girl Alenya had raised that the Shadow Lord smiled.

"Everything comes to an end," she said. "You cannot live in the past forever."

"The Balance is shifting, and we must shift with it," Cassandra said quietly. "Or die."

"What do you mean?" Nikki asked her, opening her eyes and staring at Cassandra. "Why is the Balance shifting? Because of me?"

"If I knew that, I would not be as worried as I am now, child." The ancient Shadow Lord closed her green eyes again, and the harp sang quietly in the background of her words. *"The Balance is not a stationary thing. We have to work to keep it alive. And yet, for all our knowledge, we know very little about what the Balance truly needs."*

"Alive?" Nikki's voice was full of wonder.

"Everything is alive, child. It all has a power of its own. You just have to learn how to use it. Your part in this song is just beginning to make itself known." A rippling stream played through the main melody, a bright tone against the deeper background. *"Once you come into your own, your place in the Balance will be clearer."*

"Alenya?"

She looked up, startled, as Kith spoke her name. He and her mother were both looking expectantly at her; apparently, she'd been asked a question.

"Umm, Tuesday?" Alenya said hesitantly, not knowing what else to say. That wasn't the answer they were looking for; Kith chuckled and Cassandra sniffed, both very aware she'd been lost in her own thoughts.

"Sorry," she sighed, setting her empty glass on the wall of the koi pond. "I was just thinking about Nikki. There's something…I don't know."

"Kith said you had a visitor last month," Cassandra repeated. "Did you want to share?"

Alenya grimaced. "Father showed up. It wasn't pretty."

"No doubt." Her mother's face wrinkled in disgust. "What did he want?"

"He wanted to know about Nikki." Alenya shrugged. "He said he wasn't happy with the Council's decision and wanted to see her himself. I refused; there's no reason to parade her around like a prize horse. Then he read me the same riot act he did when I took Shanna and Justin in and stormed out."

"Hmm." Cassandra leaned back in her chair, her emerald eyes shadowed. "That's not a good sign. Andreas has a short temper these days; if he gets the Council fired up about her, we may not have much longer." She looked at Kith, who shrugged helplessly.

"I don't know what the problem is," he said, and Alenya heard the desperation in his voice. "She has the power: we know she does. But for some reason, she can't access it here very well. She does something— and then collapses."

"It's true." Alenya rose and leaned over the placid pond, slipping her fingers into the water and ignoring the questioning nibbles of the koi who rose to the surface. "This is what happened the other day." She let Shadow dribble into the water, turning the surface into a dark, glassy mirror. Both Kith and Cassandra joined her as she fed the memory of the last lesson she and Nikki had shared into the pool; once again, she was drawn into her thoughts...

"Nikki?"

Alenya paused on the top stair, expecting to see Nikki at her mother's feet again in the sunken garden. The music was there, but only Cassandra occupied the jasmine-scented area, seated in her usual spot beside the fishpond. Alenya raised one dark eyebrow and re-entered the house, heading for Nikki's other favorite spot.

She found her curled up in one of the armchairs in the library, with one of the Mage-kittens that wandered the house asleep in her lap. Nikki's eyes were closed, and her head back against the soft velveteen of the chair; the book she'd been reading hung loosely from one hand against her knee.

Alenya stood and smiled, remembering another young girl who had frequented her library. The scene shifted as she remembered: the dark hair turned a brilliant red-gold, and the girl herself became younger. Then Nikki stirred, the book dropped, and the scene was broken.

"Time to wake up, sleepy," Alenya chuckled, as Nikki rubbed her eyes and yawned. The kitten protested as she stretched and then tumbled off her lap and stalked out, grumbling.

"Did I sleep through another lesson?" Nikki asked, suddenly alert.

"No." Alenya settled into the other chair and waved a hand. The book Nikki had dropped floated up and into her hands. "Heavy reading."

"Kith thought it might help me understand the Balance a little more," Nikki explained, running her hands through her long, dark hair.

"And did it?"

"Not yet," Nikki confessed, grinning. "The History of the Shadows was a little denser than I was expecting."

Alenya smiled and sent the book back up to the shelf with a small toss. "It put me to sleep as well."

"Then I don't feel so bad." Nikki leaned back against the chair and fixed Alenya with a solid gaze. "But you didn't come in looking for me to discuss my reading."

"No." Alenya turned serious. "I wanted to try hunting again."

Alenya refused to say anymore as she walked out the front door and down the steps. Nikki followed her down across the lawn and into the grove of trees on the other side.

"Now what?"

Alenya sank to the ground gracefully, motioning her down as well. "Now, we try again."

Nikki sat down on the ground and tried, once again, to ground herself. She drew in a deep breath, calming herself; Alenya smiled, proud of her courage.

"Very good." Alenya said approvingly. "Now, hold on to this calm, and open yourself to the Power."

Despite herself, Nikki tensed. "No, don't do that!" Alenya said sharply. "Relax! I won't allow anything to happen to you."

Drawing in a deep breath, Nikki forced herself to relax and tentatively opened her eyes. Alenya could see the Shadows swirling around her; they had gotten this far once before, but Nikki had lost her nerve. This time, she was holding on by the skin of her teeth; Alenya prayed she could keep herself together.

"See the Power," Alenya told her. "Reach out and pull it into you. Don't be afraid."

As if on cue, Cassandra's harp music, deep and slow, welled up out of the darkness—Alenya preferred to hunt during true night, when it was easier to spot the spirits of Light that were misplaced. She watched as the music worked its magic on Nikki—the girl calmed down again, taking strength from the melody.

Nikki stretched out her hand and the Shadows swarmed over it. The Shadow Lord could hear them whispering hungrily to her. "Don't listen to them," she warned. "Remember, you are in control, not them. Listen to the music."

Concentrating on the harp, Nikki drew the Shadows into herself. "Now what?" she whispered.

"We need to hunt," Alenya said. "Your current form is not suited for the hunting I do. You need to change."

Nikki narrowed her eyes. "What do I do?"

"Change."

Nikki had never managed the Change before; this time, something had clicked. She flowed into the great cat form as if it were a dress she had pulled from her closet—almost Lord-like in her instinctive use of the magic.

"Very good!" Alenya clapped her hands, unable to hold back. "Oh,

Nikki, that was perfect!"

Nikki opened her eyes, obviously still not sure what she'd done. She'd been sitting up; now, she lay along the ground. Two large black paws lay in front of her. With a startled gasp, she rose on four feet and stood blinking at Alenya.

"How did I do that?" she asked.

"Much of the true Shadow Magic is instinctive," Alenya said. "You know what to do, just not how to vocalize it yet."

She shifted her form as well, and the two great cats padded deeper into the forest. "You said we were hunting," Nikki said. "What are we hunting?"

"A spirit in the wrong place." Alenya paused and sniffed the air. "Can you smell that?"

Nikki sniffed as well. The strange odor, almost like incense, flavored the air and she wrinkled her nose. "That church smell?"

Alenya chuckled. "Yes. That's our prey."

Nikki looked over at her. "How are we talking?" she asked. "Shouldn't we be meowing or something?"

"You can if you like, but you'll sound pretty silly," Alenya said, amused. "You've only assumed the form; you aren't really a cat. You're still Nikki."

"Oh." Nikki followed her as she tracked her prey, the incense smell growing stronger. "Why are we tracking this spirit?"

"Because it's disrupting the Balance. The spirit was destined for the Dawn Lands; that's why it smells like incense." Alenya paused and sniffed again. "It's much stronger—we're getting close. Don't talk out loud any more. We don't want to scare it."

She moved into the brush and realized they were heading towards the stream. They always move towards the stream, she thought ruefully.

This one was not mutilated like the last one was—she stood in the center of the stream in a short blue dress, a sundress. The only jarring part of the scenery was the bruise around her neck.

Strangulation marks. Alenya shook her head. Poor child.

Alenya bounded out into the stream, startling the spirit. Nikki hurried after her.

The spirit broke into a run, and Alenya chased her, getting lost in the thrill of the hunt once again. She forgot about Nikki, about the Council, about everything but the fierce pleasure of the run and the taste of fear in the air. Her primitive nature surged to the front, and she growled happily.

What are we doing? Nikki's thought barely penetrated her bloodlust.

Stay back and watch. Alenya leaped forward, pinning the spirit to the ground. The woman shrieked as she landed on her face, the great cat holding her down.

"Be at peace—I send you to a better place," Alenya panted, and with one swipe of her claws, severed the woman's jugular. As before, she was drenched in blood as the woman died.

She was brought back to the present by Cassandra's murmur of approval; it was almost a purr coming from the Shadow Lord. "She did well."

"Yes, until we returned, and she could barely change back." Alenya withdrew her fingers from the pool, and the water slowly faded back to clear. "She was exhausted. Just like every other time she's tried to work any major magic here."

"And that's what doesn't make sense," Kith agreed, settling in onto the wall. "She's got mostly Shadows in her aura; a Shadow Mage for a mother—why can't she work magic in the Shadow Lands?"

"There must be some reason. Why don't you go to the source and find out?" Cassandra said smoothly.

"I doubt Alex Masterson will let me walk in and see what kind of bastardization he's created with the Summoning Spells," Kith said dryly, and Alenya chuckled, despite the seriousness of the conversation. "No matter how politely I ask."

"No, probably not," Cassandra agreed. "However, his lead researcher is having some problems with the nature of his experiments. I believe she'd speak to you." She dipped her fingers in the pool and summoned an image of a young blonde woman with short hair and a determined set to her face. "Her name is Dr. Sylvia Richards."

"Copies of the spells would be best," Kith mused. "That would tell me the most. Any chance she's brought them home to work on?"

Cassandra shook her head. "They're locked in the facility. But she should have notes you can look at."

"Better than nothing." Kith looked over at Alenya, who raised one eyebrow. "I think you should stay here, amarae."

Beloved.

The endearment, nearly a purr in his deep voice, sent a thrill up her spine. It almost made up for the remark, which she knew he was counting on.

Almost.

"I don't think so, amarae," she replied sweetly, smiling up at him.

"I'm just as interested in these spells as you are."

"And Alex Masterson may very well know who you are, especially if your father is involved," Cassandra said pointedly. There was silence at that.

"Why else would he come to you?" she continued, and Alenya, who knew her mother far too well, heard the pain underlying her words. "Kymara wasn't the only one who had an accident twenty-three years ago. Who was she involved with?"

"Andreas," Alenya breathed, as she suddenly realized what that meant. "But why? Why would he be involved in something that would do so much damage to the Balance? He's a Council Lord!"

"I don't know. I don't know why your father does anything anymore." Cassandra looked away for a moment; when she looked up, her eyes were clear. "But I would suggest that you stay far away from that facility, Alenya. Let Kith handle it, at least for now."

Alenya nodded, still in shock. Her father, the Lord who regularly made acidic comments about the need to keep the younger Lords from interbreeding with humans and keeping the Balance pure, was collaborating in this insane scheme? It didn't make sense, and the small child who had learned Shadow Magic on his knee cried out from inside her that it wasn't true.

Not her father. Not Andreas.

"No," she whispered, and then there were arms around her. Kith's arms; she leaned into their strength, still struggling to find a reason to explain Andreas' behavior. "Not him."

Not him.

Chapter 21

"Digging Up the Past"

Sylvia was curled up in her old armchair in her living room, one of the few relics left from her days with her ex-husband, sipping herbal tea and wishing it was some of the chardonnay in her refrigerator. Only wishing, because she still had work to do and the wine would definitely not help her map out the spells for the next week's castings.

Besides, things like alcohol had been affecting her oddly lately. She remembered some of the symptoms Cameron had documented in his journal, especially as the experiment had progressed, and shuddered. *Has it started already?*

Then she thought of Teraisa, and the foreign Shadows swirling in the former Mage's eyes, and the shudders became full-blown shaking. Sylvia wasn't sure which was worse: sliding towards madness, as it had become apparent that Cameron had, or winding up something less than human, like Teraisa.

Not much of a choice, no. Who would have thought that the result of a successful experiment would be getting caught in the threads thrown out by said experiment?

Because the experiment was successful—frighteningly so. Sylvia, working with more tools than either Cameron or his successor had had available to them, had tweaked the spells, concentrating the energy in a laser-like fashion, targeting the specific genomes that unlocked magical potential. If the experiment were only to create super soldiers or super Mages, they could have stopped there and had the results they wanted.

But the price they were paying was high, not only in terms of karma but in terms of people. Two of her junior Mages had already fallen by the wayside, burnt out by the sheer amount of power they were playing with. She had just come back from visiting one of them in the magical asylum they had placed them in; the man would never be coherent again, and his Talent was flaring wildly. The asylum, with its practiced magical Healers, would keep him from hurting himself or anyone else. Sylvia had gone to see what exactly had been done to him; those who had exceeded their Gifts didn't usually flare like Martin had, and she was concerned that this was one of the side effects Cameron and Teraisa had both warned her about.

She closed her eyes, the image of his burning aura seared into her brain. It was as if he stood before her again, wreathed in flares of brilliant color: blue and purple and red, throbbing and striating against a background of writhing Shadows. His eyes were wide, and his mouth twisted as he screamed words in what she thought might be Latin, or Greek; the only words she vaguely recognized was 'protecte me'— protect me. What he needed protection against and who he was calling to were things Sylvia couldn't imagine. Who knew what demons haunted Martin now?

It was as if their attempts to unlock energy in the fetuses had done the same to the Mages casting the spells. Sylvia herself had noticed that it was getting easier to use the energy around her; this side effect had at least some use. Until it fried her brain, of course.

Cheerful, Richards. You're just full of fun thoughts today.

The crackling of the fire in her fieldstone fireplace was soothing, calming her shudders; she opened her eyes, enjoying the warmth of the flames and the comforting taste of peppermint tea on her tongue. Both helped combat the chill that seemed to have seeped into her bones the last few weeks; she wondered idly if it was only the coming frost of the winter, or the endless cold of the Shadow Lands. Would she end up as nothing but Shadow herself? At least Teraisa still seemed to have most of her facilities intact; Sylvia decided she rather be alien and still coherent than locked up in an asylum, dependent on others.

But I will miss being warm, she decided, draining the remains of her tea and getting up for a refill. *At least in the beginning.*

There was a knock on the door as she passed through the hall on her way to the kitchen; Sylvia paused, wondering with a flash of panic who might be at her door this time. The only good thing was that it probably wasn't a Lord, of any variety; they didn't tend to knock.

Or use doors, for that matter.

"Who-who's there?" she called out, as the knock came again.

There was a pause, and then a male voice said, "Dr. Richards? I'd like a moment to talk to you."

She didn't recognize the voice; nor, when she looked out the peephole, did the young man staring back at her look familiar. Dark blonde hair, pulled back in a neat ponytail, and amber eyes: he wasn't one of the junior researchers at Gene-Tech, nor a guard. "Can I help you?" Sylvia asked guardedly, wondering how he'd found her. Hopefully, he wasn't press.

"Dr. Richards, my name is Rick Jackson. I'm a local writer. Can I talk to you for a moment?"

A writer. Not a reporter. How very interesting. And magically Sensitive; she could see tendrils of Power snaking out from him to Sense the world around him. As Alice had once said, "Curiouser and curiouser."

Making a decision, she unlocked the door. "Come in, Mr. Jackson. What can I do for you?"

———

She's not going to let me in, Rick thought, trying hard to keep his face calm and his projected intent innocent as the scientist peered at him through the peephole. He could feel her suspicions thick on the Shadows that surrounded her. She's not going to do it.

Then the door opened, and she stood before him, an odd combination of smile and frown twisting her pale lips. "Come in, Mr. Jackson. What can I do for you?"

He gaped at her for a moment, then recovered and flashed his smile at her. "Thank you for your time, Dr. Richards." The house was elegantly furnished and had the feel of a home that was lived in by someone with a purpose that kept them elsewhere most of the time.

Sylvia took his jacket and motioned him into the living room before continuing on down the hall, calling back over her shoulder, "I was just about to make more tea, Mr. Jackson. Can I get you any?"

"That would be great, thanks," he replied, looking around the cozy living room, a contrast to the rest of the house. A magnificent fieldstone fireplace dominated the small room; there was a worn armchair and an equally worn couch arranged on the hardwood floor around the hearth.

Obviously, this was the room where Sylvia did her relaxing.

Rick sat on the couch, his briefcase next to him, and waited for his hostess to return. The fire was a large one, even settling into coals as it was, more of a December fire than one he would have set in October; the nights were turning cold, but they weren't bone-chilling yet. He wondered if Sylvia was feeling more than just normal cold.

"So, what are you looking for, Mr. Jackson?" His hostess had returned with a small TV tray that she placed between them before sitting in the armchair. The tray had a pot of steaming tea (peppermint, if his nose wasn't lying to him) and some small sandwiches: roast beef, dill Havarti and mustard, he discovered when he picked one up and bit into it. Sylvia poured them each a mug of tea and then waited for him to answer.

"It's Rick, please," he said, once he'd swallowed. "And I'd like to talk to you about Gene-Tech, Dr. Richards."

Her face closed. "I can't talk about any of my work there. Confidentiality agreements."

"Of course," he agreed calmly. "I wanted to talk about the explosion twenty-three years ago, actually."

"I wasn't there." Sylvia sounded confused; Rick simply finished his sandwich and pulled out the articles he'd pulled from the Internet. "I don't know that I can help you that much."

Rick silently handed her the printouts, and waited while she read them. Her face went pale, then white; he was expecting that. What he wasn't expecting was what happened in the fireplace; as she read on, the flames, which had been fairly low, started to rise as she got more agitated. That was disturbing; fire magic was Earth Magic. And Dr. Sylvia Richards was a Shadow Mage.

A log popped in the fireplace; Sylvia jumped as the noise, like a gunshot, echoed through the quiet room. She looked at the fireplace and the flames roaring there, then at Rick, her eyes narrowed. He shook his head, mutely denying her unspoken accusation.

"What do you really want?" Her voice was shaky. Obviously, the stories he'd found had struck a nerve.

"I want to know what they were doing at Gene-Tech. And what they're doing now. You aren't making super soldiers for the Arabs, Dr. Richards." Rick leaned in. "You're working with Shadow Lords, and you're doing something a lot more dangerous than you realize."

She flushed, not denying his accusations, and his eyes widened. "You do realize." This was forced out in a whisper, and she flinched as if it had physically struck her. "Are you nuts?"

"That's open to interpretation."

Both Rick and Sylvia shot to their feet as a third voice joined their conversation. He stood in the hall, a look on his face that Rick couldn't decipher. There was no doubt as to what he was, though: the Shadows curled around him like possessive lovers, phantom fingers that caressed his pale skin and dark hair. His eyes were dark green, a forest at twilight, and full of Shadow. Black leather pants hugged a lean lower body, and his black shirt whispered like silk as he moved into the room.

The Shadow Lord moved with liquid grace towards Sylvia and held out his hand. She shrank back from him and he chuckled.

"Peace. I would like to see the articles." He scanned the pages that she handed him quickly, making noises that sounded like a giant cat grumping in its sleep. Rick was fascinated.

And troubled. Sylvia was visibly shaken by the appearance of the Shadow Lord here, which meant he wasn't the one involved in the project. But she hadn't denied his theories, which meant Rick had been right in at least part of his suspicions.

Justin mentioned the Council of Nine the last time I talked to him and how interested they were in Nikki. Could this be one of them? He studied the Lord as the silence stretched. Only the fire crackling broke the quiet.

When the Shadow Lord looked up, Rick decided it couldn't hurt to ask. "Is the Council of Nine finally interested enough in what Gene-Tech's doing to try and stop them?" he said coolly, but politely.

It was never smart to be rude to someone who could squash you like a bug, and Rick had no illusions about the Shadow Lord's potential.

It was, however, not what the Lord was expecting to hear. His handsome head snapped around, and those dark green eyes pinned the Sensitive with a hard look. "What do you know about the Council of Nine?" he demanded.

"Only that they're the leaders of the Lords," Rick replied, his insides churning. "And that they've been looking into the experiments at Gene-Tech, because of…" He stopped, unable to continue because Sylvia was there, and he didn't know if she knew about Nikki.

"Because of the child that survived?" the Shadow Lord completed for him, and he nodded. Sylvia's face didn't change at the comment; Rick realized she must have already known.

Does that mean Gene-Tech knows? Or is she keeping this knowledge to herself? And how did she know?

The Shadow Lord looked keenly at him. "What's your interest in this, young man? You're a little young to remember the first explosion."

"I know Nikki," Rick said, deciding to be honest. "And I'm worried about her."

This drew a faint smile from the Lord. "You must be Rick, then. I've heard a lot about you in the past four months. Should I pass along a greeting?"

Pieces fell into place with a loud clank. "You're one of the Lords training her. You're not with the Council."

"Not anymore. And yes, she has been staying with us." He turned back to Sylvia. "I've been told you're the lead researcher."

She nodded slowly.

"Good. I want to see your notes. Something's not right." Her eyes hardened and the Lord raised an eyebrow. "I was also told you would cooperate. Was I misinformed?"

There was just the slightest edge to his last word, a hint of the power that he commanded, and the Shadows around him flared. Sylvia shrank back and hurried from the room.

"How is she?" Rick asked quietly, once Sylvia was gone. "Nikki, I mean."

Kith was watching the Shadow Mage leave, noting inconsistencies in her aura that bothered him, and almost missed the question. "She's fine," he said absently, fingering the pages in his hand and wondering what he was going to find in her notes.

The boy opened his mouth as if to say something and then closed it, obviously troubled by something. Sylvia returned with a leather-bound journal and a yellow steno pad, both covered with notes. She handed them to Kith silently and then turned back towards the fire.

He sat down on the couch, laying the printouts beside him, and began to read. Kith was used to the chill of the Shadows; the cold that lay in his stomach now as he read her notes and the snippets of spells was fear, an alien taste in his mouth. These weren't just bastardizations of the Summoning Spells: these were new, very new, and they had one purpose: the melding of Magic and flesh.

This is insane. Beyond insane. He looked up and snarled at Sylvia. "Cameron's journal. Now."

She bolted from the room; the tone in his voice brooked no hesitation. Rick stared at him; he looked back at the boy, really looked at him, and got another shock.

Justin had told him of the Sensitive that had accompanied them to the Shadow Lands. What he had failed to mention was how Sensitive the boy really was. Or that there was more to him than that.

Most Sensitives had normal auras; none of the traces of magic, and only the Earth colors. Rick's was mostly normal, but for a brief moment, a flash of red reared up over his shoulder, a bloody snake that hissed at the Shadow Lord before dissolving back into the boy's aura. Kith stared, his mouth open. Rick's face got a little apprehensive; it's never good to have something powerful look at you like that.

Sylvia broke the tableau by coming back into the room; Kith accepted the worn journal without taking his eyes off Rick. Only when he felt the Earth magic still in the book did he look down. There was another long silence; when he finished reading, Kith dropped the books to the floor and buried his face in his hands.

Rick jumped when the books crashed to the floor, his nerves already stretched thin. The Shadow Lord had stared at him, gaping like a fish, then simply gone on reading. It was bizarre, not to mention mind-wracking.

"All right." The Shadow Lord's voice was weary. "I think I understand."

Oh goody. This should be fun.

The Lord looked up at Sylvia. "When do you start the major spells? The ones being done by the Shadow Lord?"

"Next month," she admitted slowly. "Both Lords should be in attendance next month."

"Both? Two Shadow Lords?"

She shook her head. "One Shadow Lord. One Dawn Lord. Like before."

The Shadow Lord's jaw dropped again. "He's gotten another Dawn Lord to help him? Lady of Darkness!"

"We need both. Every single spell calls for both a Dawn Lord and a

Shadow Lord." Sylvia shrugged. "I assume that's from the original spells."

"The original spells call for three Lords, Dr. Richards," the Shadow Lord snapped. "Dawn, Shadow and Earth. They all have to be represented. That's what keeps the damn things in Balance."

Both Rick and Sylvia's jaws dropped. "There-there really are Earth Lords?" she whispered. "Why don't…"

"Because they hold to the view that humans shouldn't be tampered with," he replied evenly. "And seeing this, I can't say I blame them."

He rose suddenly, Cameron's journal still in his hands. "I'll take this, and these." These being her steno pad. "Be very careful, Dr. Richards. These spells weren't meant to be tampered with. I suspect you already can feel the differences in yourself." As he strode into the Shadows, he threw one last shot over his shoulder. "After all, your Talent for Earth Magic is starting to look rather impressive."

The fire roared as he disappeared.

Rick turned to look slowly at her; to his surprise, she was scowling. "Damn Lords," she muttered. "Now I'll have to recreate everything I was working on."

"Are you nuts? He just told you to basically knock it off, and you're worried about notes so you can continue? What the hell is in the water at Gene-Tech, anyways?"

Sylvia turned to look at him, a strange fire in her eyes. "Those notes were for how to change the spells, not cast them, Rick. I'm not entirely stupid, but I'm also not taking on a Shadow Lord and a Dawn Lord by myself. I'll work around them, if I have to."

"Oh." There wasn't much more he could say.

"Rick." Her voice changed; a note of troubled hesitation colored it. "You know this child—the one who survived?"

He nodded.

"Is she…normal?" The last word was barely audible.

Rick chuckled dryly as he picked up his papers and turned to leave. "Define normal."

Chapter 22

"Curiosity Killed the Cat"

"Are you ready, amarae?"

Kith's voice was low and amused as he glanced at his lover. Alenya's eyes were shining. Even now, as they were poised to break into a heavily guarded and warded genetic facility, she was enjoying the adrenaline rush of the hunt. Feeling his eyes upon her, she flushed and grinned.

"Of course," she said. "I've been waiting twenty-three years for this."

Below them, the vast bulk of the Gene-Tech Scientific Facility filled the valley like a grey cancer, squatting low and long into every available crevice. To Lord senses, it glowed black and red and purple. The wards were set very specifically, she noticed.

"Masterson's not taking any chances," she said, looking down.

"He's also not warded against Lord Magic," Kith pointed out. "And that's a little worrying. Either he's so convinced that he's hidden himself away, or he thinks that Andreas will protect him."

"Why shouldn't he? Andreas must have something tied up in this to be trying again, especially after what happened the last time," Alenya said. "After all, it cost him his sight and his lady. Why shouldn't Masterson think he'll protect it?"

"True." Kith looked down in the valley again. "No reason for us to not be careful, though."

Alenya's teeth glinted in the night as she bared them in a savage smile. "I'm always careful."

They had shifted before they'd come to the facility, thinking it would be easier to sneak into the building on four feet, rather than two. They slipped through a small vortex in the trees on the other side of the hill, and approached the concrete structure slowly. The sky was overcast; a storm was building, and there were convenient shadows everywhere. The only open space was a 20-foot cleared area around the building. Kith and Alenya paused under a small bunch of trees and considered how to best approach it.

There, and Kith pointed with one large black paw to a point where the trees had encroached on the clearing. It looked like an employee lunch area—there were several picnic tables scattered under a scattering of solitary white birches. Not a lot of shadows, but the best bet they had.

We can encourage more, as well, she murmured, and he rumbled agreement. She laid her chin on her front paws and closed her eyes, summoning the Power that sang in her blood. The shadows around her began to writhe and grow. Soon, they were Shadows that flowed out from the small grove, slinking along the ground like a viscous fog.

Gently, love, came his warning. We don't want to set off any alarms. The movement slowed to a crawl as she reined the Shadows in, letting the Power ooze out of her. It seemed to take forever, but when she finally opened her eyes, there was enough darkening of the night to hide the two Lords as they snuck over to the building.

Phasing through the walls would have been easy enough, but as luck would have it, there was a mage coming in late as they sidled up to the side of the building; he wasn't paying attention to anything but how late he was, and they were able to slip in behind him before the door shut. The tardy mage headed off towards the lower security wing; Alenya and Kith paused to get their bearings before heading towards the heart of the wards: the secure wing.

Alenya noted the changes as they paced slowly down the halls: the iron latticework built into the walls themselves, the wardings that gradually grew denser as they penetrated deeper into the labyrinth, and most of all, the psychic cold that permeated the entire facility. This was a church dedicated to Science, and Logic was the chilly handmaiden that watched over the worshippers. Alenya shivered.

Don't worry, amarae. We won't be here long. Kith's mental voice flowed like warm honey through her bones, chasing the chill away. She sent thanks back over their link, reveling in the closeness.

This way, he said suddenly, turning. Then he stopped short; she nearly ran into him before she saw why he had stopped.

The other wings had been guarded, but not like this. The mage who sat behind the desk here was alert and actively surveying the area, his M-16 comfortably within reach. Two other guards, also armed with M-16s, lounged near the wall; both had active scans going. Alenya and Kith huddled back near the wall, observing for a moment.

Something jangled on her nerves: she paused and considered as the scans swept over and around her. It took two more sweeps before she realized what it was.

They're scanning for Earth magic!! A look at Kith confirmed that he, too, had realized the object of the scans. *But why?*

What kind of distraction did you cause twenty-three years ago? Kith asked slowly, and she frowned.

I blew the generators... oh my.

Indeed. Sour amusement colored his voice. *Destructive magic like that is not usually Shadow work, but Earth. I'll bet the residue was hot, as well.*

Probably. And I'd gone to great pains to make it look accidental, and Andreas was in no condition to look into the causes. To mortal mages, it probably did look like Earth Magic.

Not to mention the fact that the journal the head researcher had been keeping was saturated in Earth Magic, Kith mused. There were plans in there for how he was going to try and disrupt the experiments. *It does stand to reason—Earth Magic is magic of healing and, of all them, balancing. Masterson must know what he's doing is against the Balance. No wonder he's so paranoid about Earth Magic this time around.*

Makes it easier for us, once we can get past the ugly brothers out there. Alenya looked at her lover. *Can you get us past them?*

I think so. Kith sat on his haunches and considered the situation, head cocked to one side and just the tip of his tail twitching slightly. Then he chuckled. *You know, this could be easier than we're making it.*

What do you mean?

Do you really think Andreas left his name at the desk? Kith turned and looked at her. *Why should we sneak in? It's not as if these lackeys will know which Shadow Lord they're supposed to let in.*

You mean, brazen our way in? The audacity of the plan appealed to her sense of humor. Kith slowly shifted back into his normal form, adding a long black robe of silk over his leather pants and soft black boots. He watched as she shifted as well, her concession to formality being matching leather pants, boots and a long, vaguely Mandarin styled shirt with black-on-black embroidery. Panthers, of course, stalking dragons through a jungle.

Hand-in-hand, they strode out into the foyer, giving the guards a chilly stare as the mages came to attention. Kith's face, normally gently mellow, was hard and every bit the arrogant Shadow Lord. The guards merely waved them in, not bothering to try and stop them.

"Were I Andreas, I would flay them all," Kith muttered as soon as they were out of earshot. "You'd think they'd at least ask our names."

"This is my father you're talking about, love," Alenya reminded him. "The Lord that had all of his servants' tongues cut out once because one of them questioned him. Remember? He's not big on fraternizing with mortals."

"True." They wandered down the hall, Kith following the scent of Sylvia's magic. They were hoping this would lead them to the spells; Kith wanted to confirm that the original Summoning Spells hadn't been taken from the Grove. This was his biggest concern, and Alenya could see why. It was still possible that the fetuses could be saved without harm if they were using bastardized spells. If he had decided to use the full Summoning Spells, however, she and Kith would have no choice but to call in the Council. Most likely, the Council and the StarChild would rule in favor of destroying all four breeders and the children they carried, innocent or no.

Lady of Darkness, please let them be using the bastardized versions, Alenya prayed, as they went down yet another hallway. The doors were farther apart in this one; Kith stopped before one door and nodded at her. It was locked, but that wasn't really an obstacle; a quick twist of Shadows within it, and the door swung open quietly.

They had already discussed what they would do in the rooms; Kith went straight to the table, where there were notes and spells scattered, while Alenya rifled through the desk, looking for the files on the old experiment. She pulled a dusty folder out and leafed through it before a low whistle brought her over to her lover's side.

"I think we're in luck," he said. "It looks like the spells are variations. Not the true Spells."

"Of course they aren't," came a familiar voice from behind them. "What good would the Horsemen have done me?"

Alenya caught a glimpse of her father's face before the Shadows closed in, and then she saw nothing.

———

Andreas looked down at the motionless bodies of his daughter and her lover, his dark eyes cold. "The cells are ready, yes?" he asked Alex, who nodded. "Good. Have them taken to the newest one—the one with the extra wardings."

Alex pulled his walkie-talkie out of his pocket and barked a sharp order into it. Four guards appeared and pulled the unconscious Shadow Lords out of Sylvia's office. Once they were gone, Alex turned on Andreas.

"What the hell were they doing here?" he demanded angrily. "Dammit, Andreas, you promised me you'd keep the Council off our backs!"

"I have!" Andreas glared back at Alex, the look all the more effective with his missing eyes. "Neither of them are Council members! And if your mages have set their spells properly, they won't be able to warn any of the Council either. You're just lucky I scented their magic tonight. Your guards are slipping."

"Don't instruct me on how to keep this facility, Andreas. Just keep to your part of the bargain." Alex didn't sound mollified, or cowed, for that matter. Andreas frowned mentally: this new attitude of Alex's was not comforting at all. Nor was it conducive for what Andreas had planned for him. However, he didn't have time to ponder the implications of that thought, so he settled for a frosty sniff and stalked out.

How did they find out about this? The thought consumed him as he strode down the corridor to Alex's office. The idea that Trimaris had somehow betrayed him was ludicrous, of course; she knew exactly what fate awaited her if she did. If not Trimaris, then who? Alex?

He dismissed that thought with a shake of his head. Alex wasn't nearly clever enough (no matter what he thought) to hide it if he was plotting against the Shadow Lord. And he had his own reasons for wanting to see the experiments succeed: Andreas knew about the offers he'd been entertaining from various paramilitary organizations for "super soldiers."

Bah. The only thing these soldiers will be used for is to grind the Earth Lords into the ground.

He helped himself to the bottle of Scotch that Alex kept in the bottom drawer of his desk, noting in passing that it was nearly 25 years old. Interesting—irrelevant, but interesting.

Andreas enjoyed interesting irrelevancies.

What he didn't enjoy were surprises, and his daughter turning up at the site of his experiments was a particularly unpleasant one. He summoned a minor shade and sent it off to tell Tony he wanted to see him.

This was not a good development. Not at all.

———

Her head was pounding, and her eyes felt like sand—no, ground glass—had been rubbed into them by a three-year-old with a vendetta. Alenya groaned, wondering just what had happened; it was all blurred by pain.

"Don't groan that loud," Kith muttered. "It hurts too badly."

The cell was thankfully dim, and there was something sort of soft beneath them. Alenya lay there, trying to will away the idiot who was drumming inside her skull and to piece together what had happened.

The one image that was strongly stamped on her mind, even through the pain, was her father's face. Andreas had shown no emotion at all; not that he'd ever been particularly close, or loving, but the cold Shadow Lord that had faced them right before she blacked out had been alien. Was it the side effect of the experiments? Or was he always like this, and I just too much the dutiful daughter to see?

Does it matter? She levered herself up onto her elbow, and then sat up slowly, hoping her head would stay on. Even though he's my father, I can't let that stop us. We have to stop these experiments.

Looking up (once she'd convinced her eyes to open), Alenya looked around the cell, blinking against the wardings that screamed from every angle. Andreas hadn't been fooling around when he'd had these cells warded. Just from the brief look she gave them, Alenya could see the master craftwork in the spells.

Only the best for a Shadow Lord, after all.

Kith had sat up beside her, rubbing his temples. "We have to get out of here," he said blearily. "We have to stop him before he gets much farther."

"Why is he doing this, Kith?" she asked softly. "Why is he going against everything he's been brought up to respect?"

"I don't know, amarae," Kith said finally, not meeting her eyes. "I just don't know."

———

"I don't know," Tony repeated, beginning to get very tired of those three words. "No one's been in contact with any Shadow Lords. We've questioned everyone involved with the project."

He, Alex and Andreas were in Alex's grand office, discussing the breach of security. Tony privately thought they were making a fuss about nothing. If they didn't think the spells were enough to hold them, (and Alex had already made one sarcastic comment to that effect) Tony had a solution to that too.

No one had ever said Shadow Lords were immune to bullets, and he had a brand new Glock 9 that he'd been itching to try out.

"Everyone?" Andreas rumbled from his seat behind Alex's immense mahogany desk. Alex had already complained about that, too.

Tony was also getting very tired of Alex's complaining.

"Yes, everyone," he repeated. "All the mages and the guards. Even the guys who come and clean the damn floors. Everyone…" He trailed off.

Alex's head had come up; he'd apparently just reached the same conclusion as Tony. "Everyone except Sylvia."

"The lead?" Andreas looked irritated. "Why was she not questioned?"

"Because she's not here," Tony said slowly. "She's been working from home for the past two weeks."

"I thought it had been made clear that all work was to be done on the premises," Alex said icily, his eyes glittering. Tony shrugged.

"She's the lead," he said blandly, inwardly smiling. "Who am I to tell her she has to work here?"

Alex snarled something under his breath and grabbed the phone off his desk. "Call Dr. Richards," he snapped to someone on the other end. "I want her in here as soon as she can haul her ass in, and yes, you can quote me." Then he slammed the phone down and glared at Tony. "It was your job as her second to report her to me!" he shouted. "Dammit, you may have just compromised this experiment!"

"Nothing has been compromised," Andreas said, his deep voice rising above Alex's. "It doesn't matter what she's been doing, or who she's told. Once we have cast the spells on All Hallow's Eve, there is nothing that can stop us. Not even the StarChild will be able to stop the births without doing a full Cleansing."

"And what makes you think she won't?" Alex countered, turning on the Shadow Lord. "This puts all of us in danger. Unless you're planning on opening your home to the experiment."

"If it comes to that. The StarChild is busy at the moment: the Council will have to present a very, very impassioned plea to tear her attention away from what she's involved in," Andreas rumbled. "I can guarantee you that won't happen at the moment."

"And your daughter? We can't keep those two in there indefinitely." Tony tried to keep his voice neutral.

"Luckily, we don't need to. Once the children are born, they will be no threat to us. My daughter wouldn't slaughter helpless babes." Andreas passed a hand over his face as if brushing away Tony's question.

"So what? We just wait until the prototypes are born, and then pat the two of them on the head and say, 'Welcome to the new world order, please don't get in our way'?" Alex demanded. "Be reasonable!"

"I am!" A heavy hand slammed down onto the desk. "I will not murder my own daughter out of hand! Besides, we might be able to reason with her. With more than one Shadow Lord, we could cast the spells faster."

"Oh yes, by all means," Alex agreed, sarcasm dripping from his words. "Let's reason with her. After all, you're so good at it."

"What is that supposed to mean?" Andreas snapped, leaning forward.

Interesting. As Alex and Andreas continued to argue about what to do with the two captive Shadow Lords, Tony fondled the small black cube in his pocket and thought about certain experiments of his own.

He'd read ahead in the spells, despite Sylvia's insistence that they do things slowly, and he'd compared what they were using now to the spells Andreas had given the last team. The Shadow Lord was changing things, tweaking them just a bit. Tony doubted Alex had noticed the differences. Sylvia, on the other hand, was smart enough not only to see the differences but to guess their end results. He wondered if Andreas had thought of that.

Or does he think he can contain her too? Or does he even care?

The shrill ring of the phone finally broke up the argument. Alex grabbed it.

"Yes?" he snapped. "Where the hell have you been? Do you understand what's happening here? We've had intruders break in!" Andreas made a sharp sound and Alex glared at him, and then spoke into the phone again. "I expect you to be here, dammit! Not at home!"

Ah, the absent Dr. Richards. Tony watched Alex's face turn several shades of purple, most not normally found in nature, as a cool female voice murmured on the other end.

"You are still subject to my rules," Alex retorted. "Remember who's supplying the overhead for this project!"

Another spate of murmuring, at the same tone. One thing Tony admired about Sylvia: the hotter Alex burned, the icier she became. Watching the two of them interact was a spectator sport worthy of food concessions.

"I require your presence here," Alex said finally, and even Tony blinked at the venom in his voice. "Bring what you need for the next several months. You'll be staying here until the prototypes are delivered. If you aren't here within the next 30 minutes, I'll be sending someone to collect you." He slammed the receiver down on her objections and glared at Tony. "Call everyone in. This has just become a closed project. No one leaves site without my permission."

Tony bowed and left the office, his fingers slipping back into his pocket to caress the cube again.

———

"You son of a bitch!"

Sylvia stared at the phone in her hand, flushing hot and cold as Alex's parting words ran in circles in her head. "Staying there. And send someone for me? I don't bloody think so."

She threw the phone across the room, the anger in her filling her ears with a roaring sound. Behind her, the flames leapt up in the fireplace, mirroring her rage. The wine glass on her desk shattered. It was the noise and the shards flying that reminded her to rein her temper in.

It's happening. Shadow Mages were legendary for their calm; it was Earth and Dawn Mages who reveled in emotion. Cameron had mentioned in his journal how hard it had become to keep his feelings in check, especially around Alex. Sylvia wondered darkly if it was his own special gift: the ability to arouse unnatural irritability in his lead researchers.

"Thirty minutes," she growled. "Thirty goddamn minutes. Which gives me twenty minutes to pack and ten to get there. Providing, of course, there aren't any cops around to bust me for breaking the speed limit."

Growling to herself, Sylvia stalked into her bedroom and threw a bag together. Her things together, she went into the kitchen and poured herself a glass of water, hoping it would calm her a bit. As she sipped it, Alex's words came back to her.

Intruders? Who would intrude? Sylvia could think of a couple right off the bat, starting with the Shadow Lord Cassandra and ending with the child that had survived the prior experiment. But Alex wouldn't sound as worried if it were the child. *Did the Council decide to take action without warning me? Would they?*

Why not? Her practical side asserted itself. *You're in as deep as Alex, deeper probably, because it's your hands that are casting the spells in the first place. And you haven't had time to implement many of your changes, Sylvia.*

The phone was in her hand and she was dialing Vashti's number before the thought was done. The Earth Mage would know if the Council was moving.

"Sylvia, how good to … "

"I've only got five minutes," Sylvia interrupted hastily. "Alex has summoned me to the facility; he's closing the project. After this, I don't know when I'll be able to talk to you again. But tell me, did the Council decide to move on Gene-Tech?"

"No, not that I know of." Vashti's voice was confused. "What do you mean?"

"Alex caught intruders in the facility. He wouldn't say who." Sylvia glanced at the clock and cursed. "Warn the Council for me. I gotta go."

She hung up, grabbed her bag and keys and ran out the door, congratulating herself on buying a Jag that could outrun just about any car on the road.

Chapter 23

"Release the Hounds"

Nikki was out in the garden again, perched on the wall around the koi pond, enjoying the solitude. The colors in Alenya's garden were pale, luminous in the half-twilight that passed for day in the Shadow Lands: whites, pinks and blues for the most part, a mix of flowers she recognized and varieties that were indigenous to the Shadows. The moonflowers and jasmine were her favorites; there was a single moonflower in her hands now. The scent filled her nose, reminding her of home.

I wonder what Mom and Dad are doing now? It's October, or so my calendar says—the garden is dead, but Mom will have the porch all decorated for Halloween. She smiled, remembering the displays of past years. Dad will have been carving pumpkins for days by now. And the neighborhood kids will be whispering, wondering what sort of treats Mom'll have this year. She always has the best candy on the street.

The ache was back, but by now it was so familiar that Nikki ignored it. She had chosen her road; her path lay in Shadows now. Perhaps someday it would wind back into the sunlight; until then, she would keep her memories safe and a moonflower with her whenever she could.

Cassandra's harp stood in the corner of the garden, shielded from the slight splash of the koi pond by the trailing branches of a weeping willow. For once, the ancient Shadow Lord was not there, playing; the house was quiet.

It was a little disturbing.

Nikki turned as Justin came out of the French doors, his face troubled. Uh-oh. That's not a happy look.

"Have you seen Alenya? Or Kith?" he asked abruptly.

"Hello to you too," she replied wryly, and he glared at her.

"I'm serious. I haven't seen them at all today."

Nikki frowned. "Now that you mention it, neither have I. How odd." Then she shrugged. "They're old enough to be out on their own, don't you think? I mean, it's not like they need chaperones."

"They never just leave." Justin's voice was worried. "That's not like them, and Farnsworth said he hasn't seen them since yesterday."

She thought back. "They weren't at dinner. Cassandra said something about them having to look at something. I slept in today, but Alenya wasn't around when I came downstairs."

"Looking into something?" Justin pounced on that. "Did she say what?"

Nikki shook her head. "Sorry. And I haven't seen her either today."

He slumped down onto the wall next to her. "Great."

"They might have just lost track of time," she offered hopefully. "You never know. It doesn't always have to be bad news."

Justin shot her a dark look. "Okay, so maybe I'm wrong, but what are we going to do about it?"

Nikki had no answer to that.

They sat in silence for a bit, until Farnsworth came out. The butler had several notes, all of which he handed to Nikki. She thanked him; he bowed and left, still not saying a word.

"Does he sleep in that uniform?" she murmured, watching the stiff back of the butler vanish into the house.

"I'm not sure he sleeps," Justin replied. "He might just plug in somewhere in the back until he's needed again."

The image of Farnsworth standing in a corner, a cable plugged into his back, wasn't that hard to imagine. Nikki shuddered and looked at the three notes in her hand.

The first was from Kith and was addressed to both of them. She tore it open and they scanned the lines quickly.

Nikki and Justin, Alenya and I are going to do some further explorations into the spells that Alex Masterson was using at Gene-Tech. We may be gone several days. If you don't hear from us, go see your friend Rick—he's been looking into this too. Good luck to you.

"Further explorations where?" Justin muttered, taking the note. Nikki was already opening the second one.

This one was from Cassandra. Come to Vashti's, it said preemptively. I need to see you. Ignore any other notes you get.

"Helpful," Nikki said, laying it beside her and looking at the third envelope in her hands.

It was a plain white business envelope, with her name on it. Printed in the top left-hand corner, in stark black ink, was one word: "Gene-Tech."

"Lady of Light," Justin breathed, looking over her shoulder. "How did they know you were here?"

She shook her head and opened the envelope. Alex Masterson's script was bold and clear: the hand of a successful businessman with nothing to prove. I have the two Shadow Lords that have been training you, Ms. Jeffries, it said. I have a simple business proposal for you. Join me, and I'll let them go free. Ignore me, and I'll kill them. Come to the facility.

It was signed, Alexander Masterson.

The notes lay before them; three different sets of instructions. Nikki pondered all three as Justin watched her.

"You know Masterson's is a trap," he said finally, and she nodded. "So, we go see Vashti?"

"No."

The calm word stopped him as he was getting up from the wall, and he stared at her. "What do you mean?"

"I mean no." She rose smoothly, gathering the notes together. "My teacher left us specific instructions. We go see Rick."

"But, Cassandra said…"

"I don't care." Nikki turned and gave Justin a look that was worthy of Alenya at her iciest. "Cassandra isn't my teacher. Kith is. And I'm doing what he said."

"The fact that he told you to go see the guy you have the hots for and haven't seen in four months has nothing to do with that decision, of course," Justin said sarcastically, and then shrank back as her eyes blazed.

The fire was almost instantly snuffed; she might not have figured out her magical gifts, but the four months she'd spent in the Shadows had taught Nikki how to rein in her emotions. "No. Nothing."

She turned back and went inside.

Nothing, she repeated to herself, trying to stop the fluttering in her stomach. It's not like that.

The first and last kiss they'd shared ghosted out of memory and settled on her lips again, setting the butterflies in her stomach afire. She stopped in the hall, the notes clenched in her fist, and closed her eyes, willing the sensations away.

I have to be strong, Nikki chanted to herself. I can't let myself be distracted. We have to save Alenya and Kith.

Justin appeared at her elbow suddenly, causing her to jump and squeak. "Sorry," he said unapologetically. "If we're going to go see Rick, we'd better get going."

That's a flip, Nikki thought suspiciously, eying him. "What are you up to?"

Justin shot her a hard look. "Let's go find Rick so we can rescue my foster parents," he reminded her. "That's the priority, remember?"

She bit back a sarcastic comment and nodded. "Let's go."

———

It was gloomy at the inn; clouds hung heavy in the air. Nikki smelled the storm coming; after the unchanging weather of the Shadow Lands, the energy of the approaching tempest was electric on her skin. She shivered, enjoying the feel.

"Nikki!"

The electricity of the storm was replaced by the electricity of Rick's touch as he bounded down the steps and pulled her into his arms. His scent, equal parts Drakkar Noir and sheer maleness, surrounded her. She buried her face into his shoulder and hugged him tightly.

"I'm so glad to see you," he whispered, his lips moving against her hair. "I've been worried about you."

"Same here," she murmured into his sweatshirt. "Justin's been good about telling me what's going on, but it's not the same." Nikki pulled out of his arms, stepping back to just look at him. His summer tan, just beginning the last time she'd seen him, was faded now, his dark blonde hair longer and loose, framing a face that was thinner than before. But his eyes were the same: dark amber, warm and inviting, and full of magic.

It was hard not to drown in them. Only the fact that Justin coughed apologetically behind her broke the tableau.

"Welcome back," Rick said easily to Justin, pulling Nikki to his side and keeping one arm around her shoulders. "It's been a couple of weeks; I was beginning to think you'd forgotten me."

"You should know better than that," Justin retorted, a smile on his lips. "I only forget those that annoy me, remember?"

They grinned at each other, and Nikki felt a weight lift from her heart. The snarling between them seemed to have dissolved; whatever had been bothering Rick the morning she'd left was gone. Thank goodness. I need them both.

"Rick, we need your help." Her voice trembled a little. "Alex Masterson has Alenya and Kith."

He looked shocked. "How did he get his hands on them?"

"They went to look at the spells for the experiments," Justin said, the humor gone from his face. "He caught them at it."

"Shit." Rick looked down at Nikki, then back at Justin. "What can I do?"

"Kith left a note, saying you'd been looking into the experiments too," she said. "He said if anything happened to go look you up."

"Kith's a Shadow Lord, right? Tall guy, long black braid, tight black pants?" When Justin nodded, Rick frowned. "He was at Dr. Richards' the other night—interrupted my interview with her. He seemed pretty intent on what she'd been doing."

"Dr. Richards?" Nikki asked.

"The head researcher over at Gene-Tech," Rick told her. "The one who's running the new experiment."

"That must be why he wanted us to come see you," Justin mused, nodding. "Give us a bit more information to work with."

"Come on up," Rick said. "My notes are all upstairs."

That wasn't all that was up there. Nikki felt the Shadows gathering as they came up the stairs; she pushed ahead of Rick, her eyes narrowed. The door was partially open; she kicked it and then pulled back, watching as it swung open the rest of the way.

"Took you long enough." Cassandra's irritated voice flowed out of the Shadow hovering in the middle of the room. "Get the boy and his notes and get to Vashti's. We don't have much time." The Shadow dissolved.

The abruptness of the Shadow Lord's demands caused another flare of temper to blast along Nikki's nerves; the lights flickered and there was a sudden crack of thunder outside as she brought herself firmly under control again. Justin and Rick both stared at her; she was shocked, herself.

"What the hell is wrong with me?" she demanded, turning to Justin. "I can't do a damn thing without falling over in the Shadow Lands, but here I get annoyed and blow fuses?"

Justin shut his mouth (which had fallen open in shock) and shook his head. "Let's get to Vashti's. She'll be able to figure it out," he said. "This is way beyond me."

Rick grabbed his laptop, a file folder stuffed with papers and Nikki's keys, which he tossed to her. "It's got a full tank," he said, grinning at the mock outrage on her face. "Hey, you didn't want it to just sit, did you?"

"Jerk," she muttered, but the epithet lacked force. "At least I'll get to drive again."

"Let's go." Justin's face was still shaken. "I don't think we have much time."

Above them, the thunder rumbled again, low and angry.

It was only a short trip to Vashti's farm with Justin giving directions from the back seat, but to Nikki it felt like it took forever. As the Jeep rumbled along the dirt road to the farm, lightning flashed above them, the darkness cut by brilliant flares. She felt torn: more alive than she had before and yet more alien. The Shadows still whispered to her, but her ears were assailed by the fierce screaming of the lightning overhead, and the sullen rumbling replies of the thunder.

Will I ever truly be normal again? The bouncing of the Jeep only intensified her discomfort. I don't even remember what it was like to just enjoy where I was, without hearing things.

The farm was larger than she'd expected; they drove through a trellis arch covered with wild grape vines, bare now of their heavy bunches of fruit, and into a small yard. The wildness of the property impressed itself upon Nikki's mind—suddenly she wondered if this was what the Garden of Eden had felt like, before the Fall.

Three figures waited for them in front of the cottage that was barely visible beneath the ivy vines. One she recognized; Cassandra's white robes glowed against the dark green background, and the Shadows danced around her. The other two, a black man and woman, were wreathed in flames of red and green. Nikki suddenly realized she was looking with MageSight instinctively; something she had been trying to do for the past three months. What is wrong with me?

"Vashti!" Justin jumped out of the Jeep and ran to the small black woman. She smiled up at him as he hugged her. The black man beside her got an equally enthusiastic hug.

"Did we rush you?" Cassandra asked tartly, but her eyes softened as she looked at Justin. Nikki remembered that Alenya was Justin's foster mother; that would make Cassandra very much his grandmother. Somehow I don't see her baking cookies….

She makes mean scrambled eggs, though, came Justin's irreverent thought, and she giggled in spite of herself.

I didn't realize they were supposed to bite back! Her saucy reply made him turn and give her a wink.

"Don't worry, Cassandra—we have time, for the moment." Vashti's voice, full of warmth, brought her back to the present; Nikki felt like the small black woman was enveloping her in a handspun blanket when she spoke. "Time enough? That we will see."

"Time enough for food," Morgan said firmly, and Nikki's stomach rumbled, right on cue. The two Earth Mages led them through a smaller archway, into an outdoor kitchen. Nikki, following Rick, stepped into the yard—

And cried out as Magic flared around her. Black, red, green, gold—colors flashed in random spreads, blinding her. Nikki fell to her knees as the world spun, even the earth beneath her feet moving treacherously. Thunder crashed; when she came back to herself, she was lying on her back on the ground, shaking.

Morgan and Rick leaned over her; above their heads, she could see Justin and Cassandra. "Leave her be," came Vashti's voice, imperious; the others moved aside slowly to let her in.

She offered Nikki a hand; as she grasped the warm black fingers, Power arched above her, and there was a brilliant flash of lightning. In the brief flash, Vashti's face changed: the kindly older woman was gone, and the proud visage of an African queen stared back at her. Nikki's jaw dropped.

"You're an Earth Lord!" she blurted, and the woman smiled. The older woman was back, but that ageless face remained burned in Nikki's memory. The world shifted again; she felt firm hands holding her up, and she shook, an aspen leaf in the tempest of Power in the kitchen. "What's wrong with me?"

"Nothing, child. You're just reacting to the node here; for some reason, you are very sensitive to Earth energy." Vashti took Nikki's face in her hands and looked into her eyes. "There is a deep connection to the Earth in you. Deeper than any I have seen in a long time." She and Morgan exchanged glances that Nikki couldn't follow.

"Why didn't the Shadows do this to me?" Nikki said, as another wave of energy flashed over her.

"I don't know, child." Vashti nodded at Morgan; suddenly the world shifted as the slight black man picked Nikki up as easily as if she were a child. "But I think I can help you find out, if you wish."

Nikki looked at Justin and Rick, suddenly afraid. The crossroads she'd seen the day Justin had taken her to Alenya's yawned before her again, and this time she was standing in the middle of them. Instinctively, she knew what Vashti offered: the true knowledge of herself and her gifts. Alenya had tried to help her find what was buried deep within her, but like all the major magics she'd tried in the Shadow Lands, she'd exhausted herself before she'd reached the end.

This time, Nikki realized, there would be no failure. The Power swirling around her guaranteed that.

But at what price? The chasm yawned beneath her, tempting with knowledge. *Who will I come out as? Nikki… or a monster?*

The indecision showed both on her face and in the crashing of thunder from above; she gritted her teeth, knowing it gave her the answer, and nodded. "I can't continue like this," she said. "I need to know."

"Indeed." Vashti's amused look was illuminated by yet another flash of lightning. "Else we might never get rid of this storm."

Justin chuckled. "Don't feel bad, Nikki. It hailed for three days when I got here. I thought Morgan was going to kill me when he saw the damage to his fruit trees."

"Kill you? Oh no." Nikki felt the Earth Lord's chest move as he echoed Justin's laugh. "Hurt you greatly, perhaps, but not kill. The damage was not that bad."

"Come," Vashti said peremptorily, and motioned to Morgan. "Bring her." Then, as Rick moved to join them, the Earth Lord shook her head. "Not you. This is something she must do on her own. You cannot help her." She pointed to the laptop he carried. "You have information on the experiments. Call them up; we will look at them when I return."

When I return… The words echoed in Nikki's mind. This would be a journey that only she would take.

Nikki looked back as Morgan carried her out of the kitchen, back at Rick, who looked as lost as she felt. Then he tried to smile, and her last image of him was of that quirked half-smile, the one he'd given her the first afternoon they met.

She clung to it as Morgan went further into the darkness.

Interlude 3

"Origins"

Morgan laid Nikki on the large altar stone in the midst of the clearing he had entered; as soon as her skin touched the granite, her mind cleared, and the thunder above died to a low grumble. She lay on the stone, soaking in the calming Power of the stone; it simply was, a comforting weight in her mind.

"Everything has something to teach, child." Vashti's voice came from far away. Nikki felt like she was being wrapped in cotton wool, a dinner for a spider that she couldn't see. "All you have to do is open your ears and listen to them."

"There's too much noise if I do that," Nikki mumbled. Sweetly smoky incense curled around her; her nose immediately picked out the scent of moonflowers, adding to the dream-like state she was falling into. "Everything's talking to me at once."

A low laugh pushed her farther into the mist. "They're trying to get your attention. You've been oblivious for too long, that's all." Nikki tried to follow the laugh, but it spun away into the fog, dancing away in a twirl of green light that faded to grey as she watched. The stone beneath her was floating, a granite boat on a molten stream. Nikki lay back and fell into the dream, wondering where she would end up.

The mist was glowing, different colors in various areas, almost as if they were gates. Nikki's altar boat floated between them; she watched as swirls of Shadow, Light and Earth Magic curled around her, a benediction of the Spheres. Then the fingers of fog parted and a clearing appeared before her. She sat up, bemused, as her altar stone ground upon the clearing's shore.

Nikki slid off the stone, her legs a bit wobbly. There were nine wooden chairs, almost thrones, arranged in a circle around a large pool of still water, with an open space for a tenth chair. Black, green and golden marble blocks encircled the water; Nikki leaned over and saw only her face, pale and drawn, far too serious.

"Death is a serious matter."

The voice was clear, only slightly amused. Nikki turned from the pool; seated in one of the wooden thrones was a pale, ageless girl in robes the color of the fog swirling outside the clearing. Her eyes were the same hue, and the various shades of the rainbow moved within them. Long pale hair, blonde and nearly colorless, flowed over one of her shoulders in an endless wave that pooled at her feet. Her soft pink lips, washed with the tint of rosebuds drenched in dawn light, were curved in a gentle smile.

"Death?" Nikki questioned, the girl nodded. "What do you mean?"

"It is time for you to take your true place, Horseman." The title sent thrills through Nikki. "The Balance changes, and we've need of your skills."

"Skills." Nikki snorted, and the noise echoed from the mist. "I can't even work my magic in the Shadows, and I'm overloading on Earth. What kind of skills do you think I have?"

"You have your heart, Horseman, something no other of your kind has ever had." The girl tilted her head. "As eldest, you will lead. The others will follow. Your heart will be the best guide you have." She rose and moved to the pool with the grace of a waterfall. Power fell from her hands in droplets, ribboning the surface of the water with intersecting circles. Images shimmered in the waves; Nikki leaned back in to watch, fascinated. "The Balance lives within us, child. We all have a part to play. In the past, your kind has lived only to destroy. That will change now."

"My kind. You make me sound like some other species."

"So you are, Horseman. You are one of the Four, Servants to the Cleansing." The images in the pool coalesced; Nikki watched as the four dark riders from her dreams rode through a slowly disintegrating landscape, dragging destruction in their wake. "In times past, your kinsmen were created when there was great need, when the Balance had been so distorted that not even the Council that sits here could repair it. Their job was to sweep the Worlds clean, so that the StarChild could reset the Balance and life could begin anew."

"And now?" Nikki was fascinated.

The pale girl smiled. "And now, the Balance has changed. There is no shift. You and your siblings are more than just mindless destruction: within you are the possibilities of the future. For the first time, the energies of the Horsemen are embodied in flesh—grounded in the Earth. Balanced, in a way that only a Child of Earth can be."

One word, however, had jolted Nikki. "Siblings?" The girl nodded. "I have siblings."

"Indeed. You are Horsemen, after all. You are a group."

"And I am Death," Nikki whispered, looking up. "The eldest."

"The leader." Despite her arctic appearance, the girl's hand was warm as she laid one palm on Nikki's cheek. "Now you must take the mantle of that leadership." The other hand gestured; the fog rolled back in a gate, and a black horse, with eyes the same color as Nikki's, trotted up. "Cerberus will bear you to battle, as he has done for your kin in times past. And battle you will, child. Conceived in love, and yet designed for war: you must reconcile your various faces, gather your sibs and protect the Balance. I do not envy you this task—nor the rewards you stand to gain should you succeed."

"But we are Balanced." That tidbit sent a wave of relief crashing through her.

"Yes. You need not fear on that score. You need training, still, but the greatest training you have already received." The hand on her cheek slid to her chest, and Nikki was suddenly very aware of her heartbeat. "You can love. Never forget that."

"Who are you?" Nikki asked, as the girl dropped her hand to her side and began to walk out of the clearing. At the edge of the mist, she turned.

The fog wrapped loving fingers around her; she smiled as she blurred into the haze. "I am, child. Know that I am, and will always be." Then she vanished.

Cerberus nudged her shoulder with his soft nose, and she stroked him absently, still thinking on the girl's words.

"Conceived in love," Nikki murmured to herself. "And Balanced. That's all I need to know."

She pulled herself into Cerberus' saddle, her body settling into the proper position as if she'd done it all her life, and the great black stallion shook his head, eager to go.

"Let's go," she said to him, and the mists parted.

Chapter 24

"Breaking In"

"Think she'll be okay?"

Rick and Justin watched Morgan carry Nikki from the outdoor kitchen, into a tunnel formed by vines growing over a trellis. The concern in the Sensitive's voice was echoed by a deep sigh from Justin. "If not, we're all screwed."

There was no arguing with the truth in that. Rick turned away, putting his laptop on the table away from the firepit. Despite the frequent flashes of lightning, and a near-continuous rumble of thunder, there was no rain. Yet; the air was heavy with the promise of it.

"There is an awning we can put up, if it starts to rain," Justin murmured. "What do you have?"

Rick handed him the paper file and booted up the computer. "Not as much as I wanted, and I had to blow some favors at the paper to get this much." The screen shimmered to life; he punched a few keys, and a couple of stories jumped up. "I did find out that there was no original contract for the first experiment. Either Masterson had a private donor, or he was funding out of his own pocket."

"Not likely." Justin was flipping through the pages in the file. "Masterson strikes me as the type who holds his money very close."

"He had a private sponsor," Cassandra said darkly. "His Shadow Lord would have provided whatever funding he needed."

"Do we know why this Shadow Lord wanted these children?" Rick asked, cocking his head at her. She shrugged.

"Who knows why Andreas does anything?" she replied.

"Andreas? Alenya's father?" Justin looked shocked as she nodded.

"Do we know how many children were in the original experiment?" Rick added, and she shook her head. Vashti and Morgan had re-entered the clearing, and were bustling around at the other end of the kitchen. Something spicy was soon bubbling in a Dutch oven, and the two joined the others around the computer.

"Would these help?" Cassandra handed over two books that looked familiar to Rick; after a moment, he realized they were the notebooks that the Shadow Lord had taken from Sylvia Richards.

"Where did you get those?" he asked, and she smiled.

"Kith left them with me before he and Alenya left. Will they be useful?"

"Probably." He took the less battered of the two and flipped through it briefly. "Dr. Richards told me this had her notes on how to change the spells. She wasn't about go head to head with the Lords working on the project, but she had figured out some ways to get around them."

"That's good." Justin started to read over his shoulder. "So there are several Lords involved?"

"Yes, a Dawn Lord and a Shadow Lord," Cassandra said, shooting a look at Vashti that Rick caught a glimpse of as he raised his head. "Probably both on the Council, too."

"Not necessarily," Vashti corrected her. "Just because both Andreas and Kymara were Councilors doesn't mean that he's corrupted another one. There is nothing that says only Councilors can cast the Summoning Spells."

Cassandra conceded the point with another nod of her head. "And from what Kith said, these aren't the original spells."

Justin had been studying both books, referring back and forth. "Not only that, they aren't even the same spells as were cast the last time, I don't think."

All heads swiveled around to stare at the young Earth Mage, and he flushed under the sudden attention. "Well, I can't be sure, not without looking at the spells they're working from, but there are a lot of notes about the 'inconsistencies' your Dr. Richards was finding. Look here."

He started to point things out in the journal; Rick tried to follow along and failed as the conversation degenerated into technical babble. He took the older diary and began to page through it as they concentrated on Sylvia's book of notes.

The pages were saturated with Earth Magic, although there was an overtone of Shadow mixed in, almost the way Sylvia's aura had looked when he'd seen her. The writing was small, careful script in the beginning: the whole book reeked of a man who was dedicated to his research and his Craft. Rick wondered how a man of such principles ended up at Gene-Tech.

The ramifications of this project go far beyond what Alex is thinking, one entry began. If the spells I'm reading are correct, the use of mortal fetuses will ground any raw power we put into it. Quite simply, the use of mortal material as a background allows us to combine magicks in a stable base.

The entry devolved into more technical jargon. Rick skipped the next few pages, which were covered with formulae, and picked up again at the next entry.

Damn Alex. I should have known he was up to something. He's gotten me two women to bear the first children: a Dawn Mage and a Shadow Mage, like we discussed. That's not the problem. I wanted volunteers; he brings me the Mage I thought was going to be my second, and his own wife. Then tells me this is it—take it or leave it. But if I leave, I have to agree to a mindwipe. Damn Alex.

There followed more pages of griping. Rick flipped through them, and then started to read again as the word "children" leapt out at him.

The children are healthy. The Dawn Lord, Kymara, is in nearly every day to check on their status. She seems convinced that she will be taking them once they are born. I'll let Alex break the news to her that the children will be raised here. I'm not letting them out of my sight until I'm sure we did everything right.

"Why would she want the children?" Rick said, and the discussion stopped. Justin raised one eyebrow; Rick read the passage out loud and then asked his question again.

"Maybe she and Andreas were planning on taking over their training themselves," Morgan offered.

"But why?" Rick repeated. "Why not let the scientists take over that part?"

No one had an answer. Rick flipped through the journal again, hoping to find more. Towards the end, Cameron's journal took a darker turn; the experiments were going better than he had expected.

The fetuses are like sponges. They soak up all the magic we throw at them; the changes to the DNA have apparently allowed them to acclimate to nearly unlimited power. This fits right in with Alex's plans; I know the Russians have offered him a lot of money for Mages they can control. The only question is how quickly we can get a second batch up and running—and if we can do it without the Lords.

"Holy shit," he breathed. "They were trying to do an end run around the Lords." Vashti, Cassandra and Morgan were still deep in the other book and didn't hear him, but Justin did.

"What?" Justin grabbed the book out of his hands and read the paragraph. "I'll bet that pissed off Andreas." He continued to flip through, while Rick frowned.

"I wonder if that's why he died," Rick said, pulling his computer towards him and tapping a few keys. "That's one of the last entries, right?"

"Not really. There's another month's worth of notes here." Justin craned his neck to see the screen. "What did he die from?"

"Car accident. Ran his car off the road in Franconia Notch—ended up in Echo Lake."

"Wonder if Andreas even knew they were trying to get around them."

"Maybe not, but that's not the odd part." Rick called the other story up. "Look at this."

An old newspaper article came up. The article carried a large photo and a banner headline that screamed, "Twelve people still missing in Facility catastrophe!"

"Remind me to never ask a Shadow Lord for a distraction," Justin said feelingly, scrolling through a description of the fire that had ravaged the facility. There had been numerous fatalities, mostly mages and researchers caught by the flames.

"Is that what this was supposed to be?" Rick muttered. "Overkill just a bit, don't you think?"

"I don't think she meant for the fire to happen. She said she blew the generators; I'll bet Masterson skimped on the building code and this was the end result." Justin tapped a key and another part of the story appeared. "So what's the odd part?"

"There's no mention of infant bodies."

Justin scrolled quickly through the rest of the story. "You're right."

"Which means both breeders got out with their babies." Rick rubbed his chin thoughtfully. "Wonder where the other one went."

"And if she delivered successfully," Justin added.

"She did."

Nikki's voice was calm, steady; as she walked into the clearing, everyone straightened and looked at her. She returned their gazes serenely; for the first time since she'd discovered her Talent, Rick realized she was at peace with herself. Her aura was quiet, no longer flaring around her; and it was predominantly green, although a darker green than most Earth Mages he'd seen. Fingers of Shadow and Light wove through it, not battling for supremacy but mated together.

She was Balanced.

The realization slapped him across the face. From the stunned looks on everyone else, they had come to the same conclusion.

One perfect dark eyebrow arched. "Is there a problem?"

Vashti was the first to recover. "I take it the searching was successful."

Nikki nodded.

"And?" Justin asked. Rick was too stunned by the changes in her to do more than stare.

"It was successful." Obviously she wasn't going to share the experience. "What have we come up with so far?"

"Not much." Justin shook his head. "The only thing we can really say is that for some reason, they've changed the spells that were used the last time."

The second eyebrow climbed. "Why?"

He shrugged. "We don't know. Only that they are. And Dr. Richards was apparently trying to mutate the spells yet again, to keep them from damaging the Balance."

"They won't hurt the Balance." The words were said with complete confidence; now it was Justin who raised an eyebrow. "They can't."

"Care to share how you know that?" There was just the slightest touch of sarcasm in his voice, and she smiled.

"They're basing all their spells into the unborn fetuses. Mortal fetuses. Children of the Earth."

"And Earth is a Balancing Magic." Rick grabbed Cameron's journal again. "Look at this." He read the passage aloud, and Nikki nodded.

"Exactly," she said. "I'm not a Shadow Mage with Earth and Light Magic worked in; if anything, I'm an Earth Mage, with a heavy tendency to use Shadows. This explains why it was so bloody hard for me to do anything serious in the Shadow Lands—not the right power source."

Cassandra gave her a keen look. "Is that truly what you are? Just an Earth Mage?"

Nikki returned her look coolly. "Does it matter?"

"I think it does—if for no other reason than the Council will want to know," the Shadow Lord said softly. "You are still a concern to us."

"I've passed beyond the Council's jurisdiction," Nikki replied, and a second look of shock rippled over Cassandra's face. "Kill me now, and the Balance will be forever distorted." There was a deeper tone underlying her voice; Rick didn't recognize it, but it caused all three Lords to stop and stare at her. "Let me do my job, and we'll all live to see tomorrow."

There was a moment of silence, broken only by a brilliant flash of lightning and a sharp crack of thunder.

"What's tomorrow night?" Justin said suddenly. He'd been looking at Sylvia's journal again; now, he looked up, a frown on his handsome face.

Rick checked the calendar on the laptop. "October 31st," he said. "Halloween."

"The time the Walls between Worlds are thinnest," Morgan said, and exchanged a look with his sister, who nodded.

"There's something they're planning for then," Justin said. "Listen to this: Alex just brought in a new set of spells. Does he have any idea how long it's going to take to integrate these? And why a specific date? Now I'll have to scrap everything I had scheduled for All Hallow's Eve to put these in. The entry's dated three weeks ago."

"Does it say anything about what kind of spells he brought her?" Cassandra asked, and Justin, after flipping through a few pages and still frowning, shook his head.

"From what I can piece together from the formulae she's got here, it looks like some kind of binding spell, but that doesn't make sense." His brow wrinkled in thought. "What's he binding them to?"

"Himself, maybe?" Nikki guessed. "But why?"

"To make sure what happened before doesn't happen again?" Rick said, and everyone went still. "After all, Nikki, your mom and the other woman broke away, and there's nothing dragging you back to the facility. But if Andreas binds these unborn babies to him now, if for some reason these women escape, the children would be forced to find him."

"Drawn to him," Nikki murmured, and her face paled. "What a horrible man."

"No, not necessarily, but a damn practical one." Rick shook his head, admiring the sheer bullheadness of the Shadow Lord. "At least he learns from his mistakes."

"How can you admire him?" Nikki turned on him, eyes blazing, and the flames in the firepit leapt up behind her. "He's creating children to be used as soldiers in this damn war of his, and you admire him?"

"I admire his work ethic," Rick said coolly. "Not the results."

She glared at him a moment longer, obviously trying to find something else wrong with that comment. The flames danced, and then began to die down as she brought her temper under control and turned away from him.

"The stew!" Morgan's sudden yelp was comically dismayed. He grabbed an oven mitt and pulled the Dutch oven out of the fire, brushing off the hot coals on top quickly, muttering under his breath as he put it on the stone wall surrounding the firepit. Vashti brought him a spoon and he carefully pulled the lid off, letting curry and saffron-scented steam billow into the air. His face was worried as he lifted a spoonful to his lips and blew on it carefully; it seemed the entire clearing was holding its breath, waiting for his verdict. After tasting the stew, his face relaxed. Then he turned and shook the spoon at Nikki.

"Don't you know that stews can be destroyed by sudden heat?" he scolded her. "And then what would we do for dinner? You need to be careful when making stew! How do you think you're going to save the world when you can't keep your emotions in check enough not to burn stew?"

Nikki shrank back from the accusing spoon, and from behind Morgan, Rick saw Vashti roll her eyes. "It's stew," she told her brother, taking the spoon from his hands. "If it were soufflé, I'd worry. Now, where were we?"

Justin was trying to smother a smile; Rick guessed this was fairly commonplace.

"Well," the young Earth Mage said, turning back to the computer, "I'd say if we were looking to break out Alenya and Kith, tomorrow night would be the night to do it. They'll all be distracted with this new set of spells."

"Can you get past a full facility?" Vashti asked. "Sylvia called, right before you got here. Alex Masterson has called in all the personnel on the project and locked the site down. She was on her way over there."

"Why would he do that?" Nikki looked over at Rick and Justin, who both shrugged. "Because he caught Alenya and Kith? That doesn't seem reasonable."

"You're assuming he's a reasonable man," Justin replied. "And that he's in control."

Nikki fished out an envelope from her pocket. "This has no Shadow residue on it," she told him. "So Andreas didn't write it. That doesn't leave too many others."

"You don't know that," Justin argued. "Andreas could have ordered him to write it."

"What is it?" Cassandra interjected, plucking the envelope from Nikki's hand. She read the note, growling low in her throat, and then passed it to Vashti. "When were you going to tell us about that?"

"The note?" Nikki shrugged. "I don't know; I'd almost forgotten I had it. I'm not planning on giving myself up, so the note is really unimportant."

"Not necessarily." Vashti was fingering the paper. "Alex definitely wrote this: his scent is all over it."

"You know Alex Masterson?" Nikki asked her, and Justin's jaw dropped. Rick just watched, caught up in the emotions brewing in the clearing.

"Oh yes, I met him years ago, at a meeting of Earth and Shadow Mages." She smiled at the expressions on Nikki and Justin's faces. "Didn't you know? Alex Masterson is a Shadow Mage."

Alex Masterson is a Shadow Mage?

Nikki felt like she'd been hit by a truck as Vashti's words registered. But how? And why?

"That makes his work even more inexcusable," Cassandra said, her voice hard. "Any trained Mage knows the importance of the Balance. What he is doing is diametrically opposed to what he was taught."

"You hope," Justin muttered, the shock replaced by a cynical look. When Cassandra glared at him, he shrugged. "Hey, I'm just calling it as I see it. There are a lot of Mages out there who care only about the almighty dollar—and Masterson's got some very lucrative contracts out on this experiment."

Rick nodded agreement at that and pulled another file up on his computer. "Very lucrative. If even one of those kids is born healthy, he'll be set for life."

"Oh?" Nikki shook herself out of the fugue she was in and looked at the screen. "Those are contracts!" She gave Rick a hard look. "Where did you get these?"

He grinned, proud of himself despite the nature of the discussion. "I have coooonnntacts," he drawled out, and she chuckled. "Seriously, I had some friends who owed me some favors over at the Union Leader. They got these for me."

"This is pretty serious," she said, looking at the names on the contracts. "I'm surprised the Leader isn't writing a story on it."

Rick looked sheepish. "I promised them a scoop if they'd hold off," he admitted. "They're not going to run anything for another two weeks."

Justin chuckled dryly. "Let's hope we're around to see it."

"True." Nikki read the contracts briefly, noting the number of zeros in the dollar amounts. "Alex Masterson's going to be a rich man, if he lives."

"Is that the plan? Kill everyone there, grab Alenya and Kith, and then get out?" Rick looked at her. "It's direct and has a lot of charm, but I think it could use some refining."

She let the screen blur in front of her as she pondered his words. The Horseman inside her agreed dispassionately with his analysis. Dead bodies don't talk back, and not only would a clean sweep stop the immediate problem, but it might make others think twice before playing God.

But what about the innocents there? Her human side stubbornly reasserted itself. Not everyone there is a monster!

They know what they're doing is wrong. The Horseman was implacable. The Balance must be preserved.

Only one of the experiments is pushing the boundaries of the Balance, her human side said angrily. The others aren't.

The place must be closed.

"Well, that I agree on," she muttered, and shook her head.

"You cannot kill everyone," Cassandra said, and Rick raised an eyebrow. "Alex and Andreas, and whoever the Dawn Lord is, must be brought before the Council to answer for this. They must pay for this hubris."

Morgan growled agreement, and Vashti nodded. Nikki sighed, suddenly feeling very old.

"Let's worry about that after we get Alenya, Kith and those children out of there," she said, pushing herself away from the table she'd been leaning on to look at the computer. "How are we going to get in there?"

Vashti and Cassandra exchanged glances. "I think we can get you a guide," Vashti said finally. "She'll meet you there."

"This Dr. Richards?" Can we trust her? After all, she is working for Masterson.

Vashti shook her dark head. "No, Sylvia's probably being watched. But this…person should be able to get you in unnoticed."

Interesting. What other Lords are going to pop up and help us out in this? Nikki's skeptical side kicked back in. Does she think we're going to trust them just because she vouches for them?

What option do you have, child? Vashti's mental voice was cool in her head. Or are you bound and determined to do this alone, and die uselessly?

She and the Earth Lord locked eyes; in the end, it was Nikki who looked away. "Can you get in touch with her?" she asked, and Vashti nodded.

"Good, it's settled." Morgan started handing out bowls of stew. "Now eat. You'll need a good meal in you before you do anything." He winked at Nikki. "Gotta keep your priorities straight."

Nikki accepted the bowl, shaking her head and smiling. "You're all insane."

"Of course we are." Morgan gave her another wink as he passed a bowl to Justin. "How else do you think we've survived so long?"

Chapter 25

"Beginning of the End"

"Are you done yet?"

Tony's question was more irritable than he intended; Alex's head snapped up, but at least he stopped his damned pacing.

"If this goes wrong…" Alex began for the umpteenth time, and Tony closed his eyes to pray for patience.

I still need him, he chanted silently to himself. If only for the money and this place, I need him.

But not for very much longer.

"It's not going to go wrong," he said out loud, and Alex snarled at him. "How many times do we have to go over this? The spells are in place. Andreas suspects nothing. After tonight, we can stop worrying about whether or not we'll lose the children."

"But are you sure?" Alex whined, and Tony's fingers tightened around the pencil he was holding.

"As sure as I can be. I'm not omnipotent, but barring any catastrophic events, yes—I'm sure." And if you ask me one more time, I'll jump up and strangle you, and to hell with what I need you for.

Something in his face obviously got through; Alex clamped his mouth shut on his next question.

However, he started pacing again, and Tony ground his teeth together in frustration. At least he's not talking any more, he said to himself, trying to bring his anger under control. And I can try really hard to block out pacing.

Unfortunately, the office wasn't quite as big as Sylvia's. If his plans went right, he should be able to appropriate her's very soon, though, and, if he played his cards right, maybe Alex's too.

That mahogany table in his office would be a perfect place to lay her out before I slit her throat, he thought fondly. Her blonde hair and pale skin would glow against the dark wood, and the blade would catch the last rays of the setting sun through his picture window.

Ahh, yes. The plans I have for you, Dr. Richards...

His daydream was abruptly interrupted by the heavy feeling of a portal opening. His office was only lit by candles; Tony preferred to spend the day before a major spell casting soaking up the element of his magic. Now, he and Alex both watched as the Shadows began to spin in the corner, darker than the rest of the room. Andreas' portal opened slowly; by the time the Shadow Lord stepped through, the arms of the spiral were caressing the edges of the room.

"An entrance, as always," Alex sneered. "One of the days you'll actually have to just come into a room, rather than make a production of it, and you'll probably have a breakdown."

Andreas gave Alex the same look Tony usually gave a small child: one promising utter death and destruction if said small child came within twenty feet of him. Alex glared right back at him; idly, Tony wondered if the coming night was making him feel bold. And if Andreas would squash him like the bug he was.

And if Andreas would let him watch said squashing.

"Why don't you go make yourself useful, Alexander, and make sure everything is set for tonight?" Andreas rumbled. "There's a storm brewing; I want to make sure we have no repeats of the last time we attempted a working like this."

As if to underscore his words, there was a violent crack of thunder in the sky above. Even through the wardings and the concrete of the facility, Tony felt the power of the storm coming in, and shivered. Andreas' antipathy of Earth Magic had spilled into the Shadow Mage, and the raw, uncontrolled energy swirling in the air above him was slightly worrying. However, he was confident in the protections he and the mages underneath him had placed around the facility.

Alex snarled something under his breath, and the Shadow Lord fixed him with an evil glare. "Are you still here? I thought I gave you something to do."

Matching gazes with an irritated Shadow Lord is not the best way to ensure a long life. Alex wilted before the eyeless glare and hurried from the room, muttering to himself. The moment the door closed behind him, Tony found the glare transferred to him. "Are we ready?"

If one more person asks me that... "Yes, My Lord. The breeders are in good health, the spells have been distributed and all the principals are here."

"Good." Andreas pulled a small roll of sheets out from under his robes and handed them to Tony. "We're adding these to the spells tonight."

Tony unrolled the sheets and pulled one of the candles on his desk closer, so he could read the spidery handwriting. This was an old, old spell—and one he recognized.

Well, well, well. Even the noble Shadow Lords will stoop to Blood Magic if they think it will suit their purpose. I wonder who his sacrifice is. Tony looked up at Andreas, a vicious grin on his face. "Of course, my Lord, these can be integrated easily. May I ask who the sacrifice is?"

"There will be several." Andreas handed him a larger version of the onyx cube Tony usually carried in his pocket. "I want the male Shadow Lord subdued. Unconscious would be best. My daughter is to be contained within that. Keep her in the cell. I don't want her to see anything."

"So you'll be sacrificing the Shadow Lord." Tony raised his eyebrows. "There's a lot of power in that sacrifice."

Andreas grunted. "Enough to bind the child to me."

"The child? What... Oh, that child."

Andreas nodded. "She'll be here tonight. I know it. If I have to, I will bleed Kith dry to bind her to me. Once I control her, we'll use some of her blood to bind the children to me. That way, no one will ever take them away from me. Not even those damned Earth Lords. She's Shadow through and through: her Shadows and blood will erase the Earth in them."

Tony's jaw dropped. "Yeah, if it doesn't shred the Balance first! Andreas..."

"Are you arguing with me?" The quiet menace in the Shadow Lord's voice brought him up sharp.

"Be reasonable, Andreas. Even a Shadow Lord's blood is not going to be enough to pull that off." Tony fought to keep his voice steady—Andreas was more unstable than he'd realized. "You'd have to have several..." His voice trailed off as he realized what his Lord was planning. "Alex. You're going to sacrifice Alex."

Andreas nodded. "Very good, you pick things up quickly. Yes, my son has served his purpose. Now it's time for him to actually contribute in a positive manner to this project."

Damn. This evening is going to be far more interesting than I expected. Especially if we somehow manage to pull it all off. Tony smiled up at Andreas. "What do you want me to do, my Lord?"

Andreas' vicious smile matched the Shadow Mage's. "Well, to begin with..."

⁂

Sylvia sat in the center of her office, her door securely locked and a single candle lit in front of her the only spot of luminescence in the room. Like Tony, she was preparing for the spells to be cast that night by soaking in Shadows. Unlike Tony, who seemed immune to the changes wrought by the spells they were using, the Earth Magic that she'd felt growing in her was thrilling to the storm brewing outside. Her Shadow calm was battling with the exhilaration of the Earth Magic; a small part of her mind wondered if this was why Cameron lost his mind.

I can understand it. Shadow Magic is control-based; from what I remember of Hesper's lectures, Earth Magic is more emotion-based. This goes against everything we're taught. Her soul ached to fly with the storm winds above; she watched flashes of brilliant color swirl against the darkness of her closed eyelids. Just remaining in her body was a struggle.

"I must say, you're dealing better with it than Cameron ever did."

Sylvia opened her eyes; part of the room was even darker than dark, and Teraisa's amused voice came out of the Shadows gathered there. There was a hint of the former Shadow Mage's dark blue eyes, but Sylvia wasn't sure.

"Thank you, I think." The Shadows swayed in ironic acknowledgement of her sarcasm. "To what do I owe this visit?"

"My daughter will come here tonight."

Sylvia sat up straight, all humor falling away. "Is she nuts? This place is crawling with Mages! Not to mention the fact that the Shadow Lord is making his first appearance tonight."

"Just the Shadow Lord?" There was an odd note in Teraisa's voice. Sylvia nodded.

"The Dawn Lord's part doesn't come in until next month. This is a new set of spells: only Shadow Magic involved." Sylvia cocked her head. "Does this have to do with the prisoners in the cell that suddenly I'm not cleared to see, despite the fact that I'm the lead researcher on the project?"

"Yes. Andreas is keeping two Shadow Lords in there."

"Shadow Lords?" Sylvia was so surprised that she fell backwards, catching herself at the last minute from puddling on the floor. "He's keeping Shadow Lords in that cell? Where the hell did he get two Shadow Lords?"

"They came to him." The amusement was back in Teraisa's voice. "After he visited, Kith decided to come and look at the original spells here. He brought his lover, who happens to be Andreas' daughter."

"Andreas? That's the Shadow Lord."

The Shadows nodded. "He and Alex caught them in your office, looking at the spells."

"No wonder Alex was ready to shit kittens over the phone." Sylvia rose from the floor in a single fluid movement and strode over to her desk, settling her soft pants and shirt as she went. She preferred to cast in yoga outfits—the soft cotton clothing allowed her maximum movement and were cooler than the robes most Mages wore. Her bare feet padded on the concrete floor. "So why does your daughter care?"

"Andreas' daughter is her teacher."

Sylvia had picked up her water bottle and taken a swallow; Teraisa's comment caused her to nearly spew the contents of her mouth all over her desk. "Goddess above and below, what a tangled mess! Does Andreas know this?"

"Naturally."

"So, he's got his daughter and her lover in a cell." Sylvia took another sip of water. "And he knows the child survived. So, what, did he send her a message?"

"Alex did. Offering to let them go in exchange for her."

"I hope she knows it's probably a trap." Sylvia was positive of that. "No way is Alex going let two Shadow Lords go."

"She knows. That's why she's coming."

Sylvia paused at that. "I'm sure there's logic in there somewhere."

There was a long silence, and then Teraisa sighed. "Do you know what the original spells summoned, Sylvia?"

"No. I never could figure that out." Sylvia waited, wondering if she really wanted to know.

"Were you ever taught the legends of the StarChild and the Horsemen?" The Shadow Mage frowned and put her water bottle down. "The myths about the Cleansings and how in times of trouble, the Council would summon the Four Horsemen, beings of pure destruction, to prepare the Lands for the Cleansing? Every apprentice learns that. If there were Earth Lords, I might believe it."

"Your friend Vashti is an Earth Lord," Teraisa said quietly. "And the spells you're tampering with are the spells to summon those Horsemen."

The color drained from Sylvia's face completely. She stood in the darkness, surrounded by Shadows, and shivered. "You're bluffing."

"Why should I?" The Shadows parted, and Teraisa stepped into the room. Sylvia stepped back from the tall woman, with her ice-pale skin and the Shadows writhing, barely contained, in her dark blue eyes. "Even with your changes, you cannot stop them, Sylvia. You are fooling yourself if you think you can. But my daughter is so much more than what they ever dreamed she could be. She will stop this madness."

"She's not a Horseman. Those are legends." Sylvia's voice shook.

"Every legend has a basis in fact," Teraisa said. "Even this one. Andreas screwed up. The child he wanted to control will be his downfall."

"And then what?" Sylvia demanded. "We've gone too far now to stop. What happens to the children still here? We have to finish these spells or the Balance will consume them all!"

Teraisa hit her. Sylvia didn't even see the blow coming. The cold fist caught her in the mouth, knocking her backwards over her desk. As she lay there, blood metallic in her mouth, trying to clear her head, the former Shadow Mage leapt over the desk and landed on top of her. One clawed hand grabbed her chin and forced her into eye contact; Sylvia gritted her teeth in pain as the tips of the claws pricked into her skin.

"I care nothing for the children in this run!" Teraisa hissed, and the Shadows surrounding her echoed the hiss. "Do you understand me? Nothing. The only thing I care about is making Andreas and Alex pay for what they did to me. If you move against my daughter, I will include you in my vengeance. Kymara got off easily. I will not be so merciful next time."

Sylvia remembered the shredded throat on the Dawn Lord and decided that if that was what Teraisa called mercy, she wanted none of it. "If you break my jaw, Andreas will know someone's around," she croaked. "He'll be looking for you."

Teraisa snorted, but the pressure eased on her face. "Just be warned,

Shadow Mage. The only one who needs to come out of here alive is my daughter. Anyone else is expendable."

The Shadows swarmed over both of them; when they retreated, Teraisa was gone. Sylvia remained where she was, pulling her knees up to her chest and hugging them, for a very long time.

Andreas had taken over Alex's office again, preferring the large leather chair to complete his preparations. The office had changed very little in the ensuing years; then again, Andreas had spent very little time in the facility during the other experiment. He and Kymara had always prepared for the spells the same way: dinner, either at his house or in her garden, then lovemaking, right up until they were due into the Spell Chamber. Now, preparing in his cold study just didn't seem right, so he came to the Facility and prepared himself instead.

Perhaps when Trimaris joins us, it will be easier, he thought sadly. For right now, I must go on.

Once again, the errant scent of roses drifted across his nostrils. Kymara had always smelled of roses; the scent followed her wherever she'd gone, marking her passage. After she'd died, he'd torn out all the roses he'd coaxed into his garden for her: all but one bush, the bush she'd planted for him. He hadn't been able to remove it. It still bloomed in the shadow of his house. When the windows were opened, it was like she moved through the rooms again.

Bah, I'm acting like an old man, in love with the past, he thought irritably. Alex must have brought in roses or something.

When he looked mentally around the room, however, he found no vases of flowers. Just the scent, naggingly familiar, which moved on a breeze that wasn't there.

"Poor Andreas."

Her croon startled him: a voice he'd only heard in his dreams for the past twenty-three years. Andreas probed each cranny of the room. Nothing.

"Why do you do this?"

I'm truly losing my mind, he thought frantically.

Then he felt a soft touch on his cheek; the warmth of a summer's day flooded his bones. Andreas moaned.

"Will this truly bring me back?" Her voice was a soft, warm breeze against his ear, as it had been when she shared his bed. "Or is it all for naught?"

"Kymara..." his voice was a strangled whisper. "My love..."

"Our child survived, Andreas. Our child. What more do you need?" The murmur thrilled his senses. She had the sexiest voice, especially when she whispered.

And they had taken it all away from him. The fire in his bones turned to ice as he remembered her blood on his hands, her throat torn to pieces and her beautiful skin stained with the remains of her life. Anger turned the regret into his mouth to acid.

"I want revenge," he snarled, and the hands withdrew. "I want the life back I had."

"The past is dead, Andreas. Leave it be."

"I can't!" he cried. "I will destroy the Earth Lords that murdered you and took my eyes. That child should have been raised by you. She was our daughter! They took it all and hid behind their precious Balance to justify i."

Andreas rose suddenly, gathering the Shadows around him. "Even now, they seek to stop me. You are dead, Kymara! This is another Earth Lord deception!" He rushed from the room.

In the center of the darkness, a single golden light glimmered. The shimmer grew, and Kymara stepped into the room.

Tears, like precious moonstones, dripped down her face. Kymara sank to her knees in the darkness, her aura a halo of light around her, and wept for what was about to come.

Chapter 26

"Storm Winds Rising"

Nikki pulled Rick up behind her on Cerberus; the black horse tossed his mane and stamped his foot, eager to be off. Like the last time, when she'd gone back into Rothman House after Francesca, Nikki felt a fierce excitement burn through her veins; despite the seriousness of the situation, a savage grin seemed burned on her lips.

Justin put his hand on her leg; she looked down into his concerned hazel eyes, the grin fading. "Are you sure you're ready for this?" the young Earth Mage asked seriously. "You know I'll go with you, if you need."

She shook her head. "We've been over this, Justin. You're our ace in the hole. The Council Lords can't get involved because of the potential damage to the Balance. If we're caught, we'll need you to come bail our asses out."

This brought a weak smile to his face. "Hopefully you won't need me." He patted her leg one last time, and shook Rick's hand. "Good luck."

Nikki urged the great horse forward. Cerberus leapt into a run, the wind bringing tears to her eyes. Formed of Shadow, Earth and Light, the stallion simply hitched a ride on the storm winds, letting the swift puffs of Power eat up the miles between Vashti's and the Gene-Tech facility. She felt Rick's arms tighten around her; the simple gesture reminded her of the tight hug her mother had given her back in Kingston that morning.

She and Rick had driven down to her home after the meeting at Vashti's broke up; she'd wanted to see her parents one last time, before heading into something it was doubtful she was going to survive. She owed them an explanation, if nothing else.

Lara had cried, and Marc had been incredulous at her story; in the end, it was Cerberus himself who convinced them, showing up in the garden, pounding his hoof into the ground insistently. After that, there hadn't been much discussion; Nikki had bid them goodbye, and collected some small things to bring back with her.

One of them banged against her breastbone now: an angelic amulet, given to her when she was very small and afraid of the dark. Her mother had threaded the silver chain through her fingers and whispered, "The Archangel Michael will protect you, little Nikki. The darkness will never triumph over him."

Heavenly Archangel, guide us now, she prayed, feeling the little medallion cool against her skin. Even though I walk in Shadows. Keep the true darkness from our backs.

"Do we know where we're meeting this guide?" Rick asked, his lips touching her ear in an effort to be heard. The warmth of his breath caused her to shiver.

"Somewhere right outside the facility," she called back. "But then I think I'm changing the plan."

"What?" She heard the slight note of panic in his voice and smiled.

"Trust me. I'm not sure yet. I want to hear what she's got to say."

Cerberus' hooves only touched the ground at certain intervals; with the winds blowing as hard as they were, the journey to the Gene-Tech facility took only about 15 minutes. He settled them down on the backside of a hill above the structure. They slid off his back and stretched.

"We'll know this guide how?" Rick muttered, running an impatient hand through his blonde hair. Nikki turned to grin at him and her jaw dropped as she gazed over his shoulder.

He turned, following her eyes. A cloud of Shadows was moving towards them, vaguely human-shaped, and definitely not randomly. Nikki and Rick exchanged glances.

"How do we know it's not something Gene-Tech put out to find us?" he hissed, and she shrugged.

"I could rip it to shreds, but if it's our guide, that wouldn't be the best thing to do," Nikki murmured.

"Can you put up something to protect us while we wait for it?" he said, and she nodded.

Closing her eyes, Nikki reached, not into the ground, but into the storm above her, looking for the swirling energy that raced in the atmosphere. She pulled a piece of it down around them, encasing the three of them in the tempest. And then they waited.

The Shadows continued to move towards them, never veering from their path. Nikki tensed, trying not to look scared. Behind her, Cerberus snorted.

"Well, well, the child has grown teeth." The voice coming out of the mass of Shadows was dark and amused. "Peace, Nikki. I have no quarrel with you."

"Pardon me if I'm not reassured." Nikki kept the winds swirling around them.

"Peace. Vashti sent me to guide you in." The voice was still amused.

Nikki and Rick exchanged another set of glances. Rick shrugged, leaving the decision up to her.

Thanks, she thought sourly at him. Can you pull any sort of feelings off it?

Not with your shield up, he replied. Once it's down, maybe.

Wonderful. Nikki sighed, and looked out at the Shadows again. Oh, hell, I guess I can always try and put us back together if it decides to jump us. This is getting us nowhere.

Agreed.

She loosened her grip on the winds; the tempest swirled up and away from them, leaving the two of them standing in front of the Shadows. With her shield down, she could feel the laughter coming from the darkness in front of them.

"Good. Now we can begin."

"Are we ready?"

Alex's voice echoed through the Spell Chamber, magnified by the sound system. Alex himself was seated in the antechamber, watching through the reinforced window. Sylvia felt his voice resonate through her; the vibrations set her jaw aching again.

Tony had given her bruised face a curious look when she'd come in, but hadn't said anything. She'd given curt orders, making sure everything was set up the way she'd had it laid out. Now, everything was set; she looked at Alex and nodded. All they needed was the Shadow Lord to make his appearance.

"Is the Shadow Lord here, Alex?" she called. "We're wasting time."

"Don't get your panties in a bunch," he snapped back. "He'll be in there momentarily."

She growled a bit before clamping her teeth down on her temper; the storm winds were stroking her to an impatience she'd never had to deal with before. Tony shot her another quizzical look; this time, Sylvia didn't hold back her snarl. Her second actually took a step back from her; the small involuntary action warmed the dark part of her soul.

The door opened, and everyone turned. There was no doubt that he was a Shadow Lord; the Shadows draped over him like adoring fans, intent on his every breath. His tall body was held arrogantly erect; despite the black bandage stark against his pale skin, his face was handsome, far more so than she'd expected. He was dressed in what she assumed were his casting robes: black satin, from the looks of them, with a softer black lining.

Sylvia was expecting to feel awed. She was not expecting what happened next.

He came over to her, moving as confidently as a man with his sight. "Dr. Richards?"

"Lord Andreas." She bowed her head: a greeting of mortal to Shadow Lord, a sign of respect even if he could not see it. Hesper had made sure she knew the intricacies of dealing with Lords. "Is everything to your satisfaction?" There was the faintest scent around him: smoke, and something woody.

His fingers caught her chin, forcing Sylvia's face up. The pressure against her new bruises made her hiss in pain; surprisingly, he shifted his fingers, tracing the outline of one gently. "Playing a little rough, Doctor? I am surprised." Listening to his voice was like wading into a warm bath and finding the water was over her head. She didn't mind drowning when the temperature was right.

The insinuation made her blush, causing the bruises to stand out even more. His fingertips continued to trace the outlines of Teraisa's handiwork, an intimate gesture that had her flushing even more. "And yet, were I to guess, I would say these were given to you in anger. Who could you have angered, Doctor?"

His fingers were raising her internal temperature to near melting. "I ...I don't know, Lord Andreas." Her voice rose a bit on the last words. It took all of her concentration not to puddle at his feet.

Sylvia despised herself, even as she leaned into his caress.

"Such a pretty face." Was that concern in his voice? "Let's keep it that way, shall we?" Or a threat? Sylvia couldn't focus enough to tell. "Don't play any more games alone in the dark, Dr. Richards."

He gave her a final stroke on the cheek before his hand dropped and he moved off to inspect the breeders. Sylvia stood rooted to her spot, trying very hard not to tremble noticeably.

Was that an invitation?

The door to the cell opened abruptly; before either Kith or Alenya had a chance to react, the barrel of a rifle swung in and fired off two shots. The sharp point of the dart was a simple pricking, nothing more; but when the fog cleared, she was on the floor of the cell, every muscle in her body aching.

She was alone.

For nearly four hundred years, the comforting presence of Kith had sat in the background of her mind; even if they had been separated by distance, they had always been linked. The emptiness was too much for her to bear; the small cell soon echoed her shrieks of anger and pain.

"Let me out of here!"

Alenya pounded on the walls until her fists were bruised and bloody, focusing on the pain to drive the feeling of isolation away. Her only consolation was that wherever they'd taken him, Kith was doing the same thing.

Hopefully, he's getting to pound on something that screams!

Very little sound penetrated the wards on the chamber, but apparently it was too much for the guards to bear. The door opened again, and a cube was tossed inside. Just as her mind registered what it was, the Shadow Cube opened.

"Noooooooo!"

Only the Shadows that enveloped her heard.

Whatever their guide was doing was working, although it was hell on Rick's nerves. The center of the Shadows was cold, although nowhere near as cold as the Shadow Realms. It tinted his entire viewpoint like a bad pair of sunglasses. With his Sensitivity, everything carried a halo; Shadow Magic and wards flashed everywhere.

Jesus, Mary and Joseph, what was this guy expecting, World War Three? Rick closed his eyes as they crept past the guards at the entrance to the secure wing. The flaring of Shadows around the man was too brilliant: the icy edges of the wardings he was tied into cut at Rick's sight like razors. *There's more magical firepower guarding this place than I've seen since Shanna got her dander up and took out Lucien.*

And two city blocks. But let's not think about that.

Are you done? Nikki's question was tart. *I can't fix on either of them if you're worrying out loud like that!*

Sorry. Rick retreated farther behind his shield, thinking very privately that four months in the Shadows had given her a comfort level with magic that was far beyond even his jaded views. Nikki grinned sideways at him and then settled back into herself, trying to latch on to Alenya or Kith's scent. They were far enough beyond the entryway that she stopped, to give herself more room to work with; Rick stood just behind her, scanning the area for any more guards.

Masterson's going to have guards everywhere, he reminded her. *We can't take that long.*

I know that. Her mental voice grew even tarter. *And the sooner you let me look, the sooner I'll be done!*

Peace, children. The voice in the Shadows was muted and reproachful. *I can only mask so much. If you continue, the Shadow Lord might notice us.*

How are you masking us? Rick thought, very quietly to himself. *Shadows can sense Shadows—what aren't you telling us?*

If their guide heard him, it made no reply. Instead, it simply asked, *Where do you want to go? The warded cells are down this way.* A lazy arm of Shadow drifted towards one end of the wing. *The Spell Chamber is that way.* Another arm spiraled out in the opposite direction. *I can't split myself to hide the two of you going both ways. So which should it be?*

Rick and Nikki looked at each other; he could see the indecisiveness in her, and sympathized. *He'll have them in the cells, probably. And we'll need them to help us stop the experiments,* Rick said to her. *I'd say the cells are our best bet.*

She nodded, clearly not happy over letting the spells continue, but agreeing with him. *But as soon as we find them...*

He slipped a hand into her's. *Then we stop Andreas.*

How cute. The Shadows began to move down the hall, forcing them along. *Just don't expect Andreas to fall before you and beg for mercy. It's not in his nature.*

The warded cells were bright enough to start Rick's head pounding; even with the darkness of the Shadows around him, the sigils pulsed and flared, shouting their warnings. Shadows and Earth Magic coiled around the final cell, and he snagged Nikki on the shoulder.

What do you want to bet that's the one? He said, pointing to it and the three guards stationed in front of it.

Her reply was dry. What gave it away?

How do we get them away from there?

Leave that to me. Just get ready to get them out. Nikki's hand slipped out of his; before he could grab her, she'd stepped out of the protections of their guide and into the hall. Rick swore and jumped out after her.

Three machine guns swung up, trained on them. Nikki smiled, and something within Rick responded to that smile with one of its own, even as he shuddered away from the mayhem implicit in it. He involuntarily stepped back as she raised her hands, and Power answered her call.

Magic flowed from her fingers, Shadows of green and blue and red, Earth-flavored Darkness that swarmed over the guards. They sank to the ground, the energy of life literally sucked out of them; Rick shuddered as they continued to fall in on themselves as Nikki drained them dry.

"Was that really necessary?" he forced out, his gorge rising as the corpses collapsed into piles of dust. She turned, and the alien look in her eyes, compounded of Shadow and the lives she'd taken, made him take another step back.

Her voice was nearly unrecognizable. "What did you expect? I take no prisoners."

As she turned back towards the cell and raised her hand again, Rick realized there were only the two of them in the hall. Their guide was gone, and so was their veil of secrecy. Nikki reached out and grasped the wards; a swift yank, and her Magic ripped the wards in two. Alarms went off all through the facility; Rick groaned and did something he'd thought he'd never have to do again.

As Nikki broke open the door and went inside, he reached into one of the piles of dust and picked up the M-16. Slipping the strap over his head, he settled it comfortably across his shoulder before heading inside.

She was crouched beside Alenya, who was wrapped in Shadows that looked slick, like glass. As he entered, Nikki looked up at him, the Power in her eyes still glowing. "I can't break this," she said, anger in her voice. "If I do what I did to the wards, I could kill her. Where's Kith?"

"We're going to have a ton of guards here very quickly," he replied. "We need Justin."

"Call him." Nikki rose and then registered the gun in his hands. "What are you doing with that?"

"What I have to." The gun felt uncomfortably good in his hands. He squashed that thought and jerked his chin towards the door. "Go deal with Andreas. Here." Rick reached into his pocket and pulled out the talisman Justin had given him. "And try not to slaughter Masterson. As soon as Justin can get here and free her, we'll join you."

"Good luck." And before she could go, he grabbed her and pulled her close. Her lips were cold, chill with Shadows and death, but her taste was as sweet as he remembered from before. Time stopped; it was only Rick and Nikki, balanced in perfect harmony, joined in a small pocket of peace in the midst of the chaos swirling around them.

The kiss broke; she looked at him, the Power in her eyes glowing now with life, not death. "A promise," Rick said, and jerked his head towards the door again. "Now go be a hero."

Nikki nodded, and left. Rick pulled his cell phone from his pocket, hoping to hell he had a signal. The display glowed: two bars.

Thunder cracked again above them. Rick dialed.

<hr />

"What is going on?"

Andrea's voice thundered above the klaxons screaming. Lights flickered: more impressive to his MageSight was the mass of Power streaming throughout the facility. Something large was stalking through Gene-Tech, and it was headed directly for the Spell Chamber.

"Damn you, you said you were prepared for this!" he shouted at Alex, who was cowering behind the safety glass. Andreas turned back into the room; Sylvia was stock-still, drawing Power around her, while Tony stood as if frozen in shock. "Go and find out what that is!" the Shadow Lord snapped, and Tony jumped. Sylvia ignored him; the Shadows around her writhed out and wrapped around the breeders. The shields she wove impressed him with their strength; he decided to let her protect his interests and snapped a Shadow of his own at Tony. "I said go!"

The Shadow Mage scurried for the entrance, but before he could go much further, the iron door blew inward in several pieces, knocking him back into the center of the room. He ended up at Andreas' feet, bleeding from a cut on his head.

Shadows boiled into the room, climbing out from the doorway over the walls; Shadows that tasted of mortal anger and hatred. Fear began to inch icy fingers into Andreas' heart—what kind of beast was this?

"The kind you created." A large piece of Shadow flowed into the room, rearing up above him. "Look deeply, Shadow Lord. Look at what your hatred has wrought." The Shadows split, and out stepped someone he had thought never to see again. As if his eyes worked normally, he watched the nightmare grin viciously and raise clawed hands. "Remember me?"

"You." It came out as a hoarse croak.

Teraisa Donnelly bared her teeth in a savage smile. "Oh yes. Did you really think I wouldn't be back? It's time to pay for your misdeeds, Andreas. I'm going to make sure you suffer."

"You can't threaten me." Andreas reached down and grabbed Tony's arm, yanking him aside as she hissed at him. "I'm a Lord of the Council of Nine. You'll never survive challenging me."

"Last time, I was content with taking your eyes," she retorted. "I was more concerned with getting my child out. This time, there's nothing to stop me taking your entire existence."

"Nothing except me."

Andreas almost didn't recognize the voice, filled with steel as it was. Light erupted in front of him; when his MageSight cleared, there was another familiar figure standing between him and the darkness. Kymara, her aura blazing, faced Teraisa, her entire body ready to fight. "I will not allow you to do this," the Dawn Lord snarled, and even Andreas took a step back at the venom in her voice. "Haven't you destroyed enough?"

"I? You took my life and warped me into this creature that stands before you!" Teraisa retorted. "My daughter will never have the normal life she should have, because of your meddling. You cannot pay enough!"

"You knew what we were doing! And you knew why! You had your chance to leave, but you couldn't just walk away!"

There was movement at the edge of the room; Andreas turned and saw the final straw that broke him.

She stood in the remains of the doorway, glowing with Power and youth. Wrapped around her were fingers of Shadow, Light and Earth, perfectly Balanced within her. Determination, anger and horror mixed in her aura: he knew, in that instant, what she would do. Tony had been right. The experiment had succeeded, beyond all their dreams.

And now it would kill them all.

Chapter 27

"Lunacy Ascendant"

"What the hell is going on here?"

Everyone stopped. Nikki stepped into the room, not really registering the four Shadow-shrouded stretchers or the pieces of iron door on the floor. Her attention was focused on the center of the room; more importantly, on the woman standing in the midst of the Shadows, who turned slowly around to look at her.

Blue eyes met blue eyes; there was acknowledgement, love and hate that flashed over a link too deep for most people to even realize it was there. Teraisa raised her chin defiantly.

"Don't interfere," and the voice was the smoky voice from Nikki's dreams. "I have to finish this."

"And let him win?" Nikki barely recognized the words coming out of her mouth. "Do you truly want to become the monster he's created?"

"Better than letting him get you."

"Why don't you let me make that decision?" Nikki moved forward, putting herself in the middle of the tableau, hoping desperately she could do what she thought she could. The storm screamed above; she latched onto the Power, letting it flow through her as she turned her back on her mother and looked squarely at the two Lords who had caused her to come into being.

Kymara glowed with Light energy, dancing like a flame caught in a hurricane lantern. Nikki realized she could see through her; with a start, she recognized the Dawn Lord truly was a ghost. How bizarre, she thought irreverently.

The Shadow Lord behind her was solid, however, and Nikki focused on him as the threat. Andreas stood tall and proud; the hood of his cloak was thrown back, and the black bandages across his eyes did little to detract from his appearance. He was handsome and deadly, a large snake waiting for her to get within striking distance.

"Why?" There was a wealth of pain and hurt in her question. "Why did you do this?"

"We had to." It was Kymara who answered, not Andreas, who seemed content to let his dead lover talk. "There was no other way." She drifted forward and laid a warm hand on Nikki's cheek. "You were the answer to everything we wanted, child."

"Don't touch her." Teraisa's voice grated from behind Nikki. "You cannot have her."

"No one would understand," Kymara continued, as if she hadn't heard Teraisa. "But it worked. You worked. We were right."

"It worked." Andreas' voice was a masculine version of Alenya's. Nikki closed her eyes, wondering why there was a lump in her throat. I cannot let them talk me out of punishing them! Her fingers clenched around the talisman Rick had given her. This has to end.

"It doesn't matter," and her voice sounded loud, like a child's. "You broke the law."

"We had to." Kymara's voice pleaded with her to understand. "We had no choice."

Nikki opened her eyes. "I don't care." I can't care.

With that thought, she threw the talisman to the ground.

Justin sat in the midst of Vashti's meditation grove, trying to keep himself centered. His cell phone was lying open in front of him, although he had vain hopes it would actually ring. Rain pounded down around him; his personal shields were keeping himself and the phone dry. The tempest howled overhead: one of those hundred-year storms New England seemed to get every ten years or so. The sheer Power in the air, added to the fact that it was All Hallow's Eve, made the World Walls so thin as to be naught but transparent rice sheets. Even here, in one of the bastions of Earth Magic, Justin could see layers of the Shadows and the Light, realms that hovered just out of reach.

On an ordinary night, it would be a thing of beauty, Magic to be studied and observed. He would have enjoyed it.

Now, he feared it.

What is going on there? The thought was wearing a groove in his mind. *Why haven't they called? I should go…*

No, I promised I'd wait.

Somehow.

The first bars of "Ned on the Hill" filled the clearing. Justin grabbed his phone and nearly hung up on Rick in his haste. "What's going on?"

He could only hear every third or fourth word, as the lightning flashed around him, and thunder rumbled. But he heard the important ones: "Help" and "Come here."

"I'm on my way." He snapped the phone shut and jumped as a hand came down on his shoulder. "Shit, Morgan, don't do that!"

"I'm sorry." The Earth Lord's voice was unapologetic. "You must go?"

"They need me." Justin accepted the hand up; with his shields gone (he'd lost them when Morgan startled him), he was soaked within seconds. "I need to get there fast."

"We can help." Behind Morgan stood Cassandra and Vashti, who both nodded. "You cannot hope to make it there in time otherwise."

"What are you going to do, Gate me in?" The question was sarcastic. "You'll never get through this storm interference."

Vashti's expressive eyebrows climbed her face. "Do not lecture me, young man. I've been doing this for a lot longer than you. Besides, we have powers you can't even dream of."

Justin bit back his retort and allowed them to encircle him. Cassandra hadn't brought her harp: when she began to sing, a throaty Jack Daniels-soaked alto that wrapped around him, he realized the harp was for her enjoyment. She didn't need it any more than Nikki needed someone holding her hand. Vashti and Morgan raised their voices as well; her clear soprano (another surprise) and his deep baritone wove around the Shadow Lord's melody, creating a web of sound that he could almost see. The notes twined together; the web picked him up and cradled him against the storm. Just as he was beginning to relax, the magic tightened around him.

This is not the way I'd choose to go! Justin struggled to breathe against the crushing pressure as the song continued to tighten. His eyes went dark; the thunder crashed and lightning flared against the backdrop of black. And then everything stopped.

"Justin?" It was Rick's voice, coming from very, very far away.

The rain was gone; he stared up at a roof, made of steel and concrete. Iron lacings imbedded in the structure stung against his magical senses; Justin took a deep breath and hissed it out as it burned in his bruised chest. "Remind me not to ask favors of my teacher again," he grumbled, sitting up with Rick's help. "At least I'm still in one piece."

"That was an impressive entrance. I didn't even think you'd gotten my call." Rick hauled Justin to his feet with a grunt. "There's so much damn interference here—I thought the bars on my phone were an illusion."

"The important words got through." Justin rubbed his eyes and then shook himself. "What's up?"

Rick simply pointed behind him. Justin turned; what he saw chilled his blood more than a dip in a Shadow-laced pond.

Alenya lay against the back wall of the cell, wrapped in the glossy Shadows of a Cube. He'd heard of the devices; created for use in the Realm Wars, before the creation of the Council, Shadow Cubes trapped Lords in a glass-like dimension, cut off from their power sources. They were used as traps—not even Shadow Lords could break out of them. I should have known a Lord who cares as little for the Balance as Andreas would be using these.

He knelt down beside her and touched the bonds thoughtfully. Rick watched. "Any ideas?" the Sensitive asked.

"Several, but I'm not sure which to use." Justin hummed thoughtfully, and the bonds vibrated. "How much time do we have?"

"Not much." Rick's dry voice made him look over. The M-16 in Rick's hands hadn't registered before; now, it chattered briefly before Rick ducked back inside the cell. "Not much at all."

"Where did you learn…"

"Questions later." Rick fired another brief round. "Work now."

Justin turned back to Alenya, hoping Rick had enough ammunition to buy him some time.

———

The talisman lay on the ground, an innocent-looking doll with long yarn hair and a charming expression stitched on her dark face. Nikki wondered about Justin's predilection for using the little dolls, but decided to ask him later. Kymara had backed away from her when she'd thrown the talisman down; now, the Dawn Lord hovered, unsure of what to do.

"Don't you understand?" Nikki said. "You broke the cardinal rules of being a Lord. You have to protect the Balance. That's what the Lords exist for."

"What about me?" Kymara demanded. "What about my happiness? Why should I be denied what I want, simply to protect the Balance?"

"You're a Dawn Lord! What could you possibly want that you can't have?" Nikki's fists clenched as the storm howled through her.

Kymara turned back and looked at Andreas, who stretched his hand out to her. "His child," she whispered, tears running down her face, and everything fell into place for Nikki.

"You weren't making soldiers." She looked at the two with new eyes. "You were making...offspring."

The room was silent, except for the rumble of the storm above. Everyone stared at Andreas and Kymara.

"Yes. That was all we wanted." Kymara's shoulders sagged. "But it was all taken away."

"All you wanted." Alex entered the room through the other door, the sneer on his face imbedded in his voice. "Yet I'm the one that did all the hard work. What about what I wanted?"

Nikki watched him enter, her eyes narrowing. "Alex Masterson."

"In the flesh." He gave her a mocking bow. "Welcome home, Miss Jeffries."

"My home is in Connecticut," she snapped back. "Just because I was created here does not mean it's my home."

"But it will be." Alex's smirk grew as Tony slide to his side, Shadows wrapping around him protectively. "At least until my buyer comes up with the rest of the money. You've got an army to lead."

"You've got the wrong girl." Her fists clenched. "I work alone."

"Mostly alone," came an amendment, as Rick came through the door, his M-16 held confidently low. Justin and Alenya were behind him; the Shadow Lord took one look at her father and snarled.

Nikki spared him a brief smile as he settled in beside her, then turned back to Alex. "Mostly alone," she agreed. "I don't do armies."

"You will." His smile had teeth in it.

<hr>

Only Justin's shoulder was keeping her upright; one of the side effects of a Shadow Cube was that it used the energy of the victim to keep it active. But hate and rage confer energy of their own, and Alenya was feeling none too charitable towards the Shadow Lord that had sired her. "He's not here," she hissed. "What did you do with him?"

Andreas couldn't hear her, but Justin did. "What are you talking about?"

"Kith. He's not here." Her eyes were fixed on her father, but her mind searched constantly for her lover, and the link they'd shared. "I can't touch him."

Her foster son scanned the room. "He might be in another cube somewhere."

She moaned at that. "We have to find him."

"We have to stop this first." Justin adjusted her weight on him. "Or else all hell breaks loose."

———————

"Don't be a fool, Alex." Andreas' voice was deeply sarcastic. "You can't hope to control her. You can't even control your own pathetic powers."

"Care to test that, Father?" Nikki figured the sneer was a permanent part of his face. "You never tried to find out, did you? And that's what's going to cost you."

"What are you talking about?" Andreas frowned at his son, who raised his arms. Shadows flowed from them, dark and powerful; Andreas stepped back, astonishment writ large on his handsome face. "When did you learn to do that?"

"You should have made a little more certain about your lovers," Alex said. "You never know when a halfbreed might turn up." And Tony echoed his nasty smile. "My mother was a Shadow Mage—did you know that? She didn't practice much, but after you left her with me, she rediscovered her Talents. Revenge has a way of doing that to you."

"That's why you contacted me: so you could get revenge? You've certainly taken long enough." Andreas straightened up. "And now?"

"And now you've outlived your usefulness, old man." Alex laughed; the sound grated against Nikki's nerves. "I'd let you go, but you'd probably just run to the Council. So you'll have to come with us. I've got the other Shadow Lord stashed away, but who knows if I'll be able to use him." He nodded at Tony. "Take her."

Tony reached up and touched his fingers to the cut that still oozed blood. He brought the crimson-tipped hand back to his mouth and sucked at it, that nasty smile boring into Nikki. "With pleasure."

"Just keep her in one piece," Alex snapped. His Shadows continued to swirl, whirling into a vortex. "Her price goes down if I have to patch her up."

Tony just laughed. The Shadows around him took on a reddish tinge, and Nikki felt a chill run down her back.

"Nikki, he's using Blood Magic!" Justin's voice rang out behind her, just as Rick's M-16 chattered and Tony raised his hands. The bullets glanced off harmlessly; he swore and tossed the gun aside.

"Stay out of this!" she ordered, her eyes beginning to glow again. Her own Shadows answered, rising up around her to stand off against Tony's. Rick shouted something, but the Power had taken over; Nikki heard nothing, saw nothing but the Mage in front of her.

"Let's go," she snapped, and her Shadows flowed forward. Tony sneered and waved her magic aside; his blood-infused Shadows slammed into her's, and she stumbled back at his strength. "Oh no you don't."

Nikki reached into the storm above; her Shadows were suddenly blue and green, with winds swirling in them. They locked with Tony's bloody Shadows, a struggle that resembled two titanic wrestlers, each trying to get the other to submit.

"You cannot hope to win, little girl," Tony mocked her, pulling a small knife out of his pocket. "With all the victims around here, I can feed these Shadows all the Power I need."

"Try me, asshole." Nikki pointed upwards. "It's a tempest out there. I'll wager Mother Nature against you any day."

"You're on." Tony reached out randomly; his fingers encountered hair and he yanked Sylvia over to him. "Let's see what this does."

And he shoved the knife into her side.

"We've got to stop that Gate," Rick said to Justin, who nodded. The Earth Mage slipped Alenya's arm from around his shoulder; the Shadow Lord slumped to the ground, still focused on her father. Then he looked at Rick, who nodded.

"Where's the talisman?" Justin asked him.

"I gave it to Nikki." They both looked at the young Horseman, locked in her struggle—the small doll was on the ground in between her and Tony. "Can we trigger it from here?"

"We can, but she'll get caught in the back blast." Justin swore under his breath.

Rick's eyes hardened. "Will it kill her?" The ice in his voice startled Justin.

"No, but she won't be real happy with us."

"Then do it." Rick reached behind his back and pulled a pistol from his waistband.

"Where the hell did you get that?" Justin asked. "And how the hell do you know how to fire a gun?"

"Misspent youth." Rick gave him a tight grin. "This I got from one of those guards you knocked out. I learned from the last time not to go into a situation without a backup weapon." He cocked the gun and aimed. "Trigger the talisman."

The first bullet hit Andreas; the Shadow Lord was turned towards his son, and not looking. Red blood blossomed on his shoulder; Rick cursed his lousy aim and lined the gun up again.

"No!"

The voice was female. Rick was thrown back as Light hit him hard. Kymara's scream echoed in his ears; Light wrapped around him, tightening. The gun fell from his hand; already cocked, it went off and the bullet hit something. He wasn't sure what, but the sound of a bullet hitting flesh was unmistakable.

Thunder crashed, anger incarnate. The lightning flash and Kymara's rage-filled eyes were the last things he saw.

"I'll kill you!" Kymara screeched, her fingers tightening the Light around Rick. Justin jumped at her, but the Dawn Lord was insubstantial; he went through her and tumbled onto the floor. "You can't hurt me—and I won't let you hurt him!"

"They can't, but I can."

She turned, looking for the voice, and was shoved to the ground. Teraisa hovered over her, the hate in her eyes matching that in Kymara's. "And now, this ends," she ground out, and leapt at the prone Dawn Lord.

Clawed hands, the same ones that had ripped out her throat twenty-three years ago, clutched at her. Cold flooded her: Kymara screamed and lashed out, letting the boy go in favor of the enemy in front of her. Light flared, and was smothered by Shadows. The two rolled on the floor, each fighting for an advantage.

"I will send you to the deepest pit of Hell I can find," Teraisa growled. "I will bury you in the blackest depths I can find, and you will never get out to bother anyone again."

"Only if I don't burn you to a crisp first, bitch," Kymara shot back. "Light always vanquishes darkness!"

"Not always." Teraisa stopped their roll, sitting on top of the Dawn Lord. Her hands, already wrapped around Kymara's throat, began to tighten, the claws digging into ghostly flesh.

"No!"

Justin shook his head, trying to clear the cobwebs. Everything went fuzzy, then fell abruptly into focus. The Spell Chamber had descended into chaos.

Alex was in the corner, anchoring a Gate and watching the mess around him. Andreas was slumped over; apparently Rick's shot had hit lower than they had thought. Rick himself was unconscious; and Kymara and Teraisa were struggling nearby. Alenya was still sitting where he'd left her, and Sylvia...

His eyes were drawn to the center of the room, where Nikki and Tony were locked in their battle. Sylvia was at Tony's feet—a red line of Blood Magic linked her to his Shadows. Nikki's Shadows were full of storm energy, but her own stamina was beginning to fade.

Dammit! If I trigger the talisman now, she'll never break free in time. Justin ground his teeth together. Now what?

As he pulled himself to standing, he could feel the energy swirling from the storm outside. The World Walls were thinning even more; Shadows and Light were leaking in, mixing with the Earth energy of the gale to strengthen it even more. And, he realized suddenly, so was the fight in here.

Shit, if we don't stop this soon, there may not be a facility left! He had to make a decision. Looking over at Alenya, he found her emerald eyes on him...

She nodded.

All right. Justin straightened his shoulders and called his own Power into play. So be it. Casualties of war.

Justin began his own chant, his voice lost in the howling of the winds above.

The small doll on the floor began to twitch as energy was fed into it. Justin had set a spell into it, knowing that even if they had been captured, no one would have ever taken it away from Nikki as a threat. The trap spell had lain dormant, its magical signature so subtle that it was all but unnoticeable. Until now.

Rainbow light suddenly shot upward from the doll, spraying the room and shredding the Shadows. The blinding spokes burned Power from the air, clearing the playing field. Justin wondered what it would do to the breeders—that was something he hadn't considered.

Casualties of war, he reminded himself grimly, knowing it was sophistry and hating himself. Don't stop.

The glow intensified; he closed his eyes against the brightness, wishing he could close his ears against the screams that started. Another stream of Power joined his; after a moment, Justin recognized Alenya's touch and accepted the help.

And then a third stream joined them—one he didn't recognize.

Don't stop, came Nikki's voice, and he nearly lost his hold on the spell as her Magic wove in between theirs. Or we'll lose them all.

The rainbow had thrown Nikki and Tony to opposite ends of the room as it surged up between them. She'd realized what it was; but before she could join in, something else pinged on her heightened senses: Alex's Gate. It was still up, and he was taking advantage of that fact.

He'd grabbed Tony and thrown him through; as the light moved towards him, he snarled and reached for the nearest breeder.

Oh no you don't! Nikki inserted her Power into the rainbow, wrapping herself around Justin and Alenya's combined Gifts. She climbed to her feet, feeling for the Darkness that was Alex....

And found it.

It was like walking through hip-high waves; the Power swirled around her, through her, giving her energy but taking speed. She plowed forward, reaching out with the rainbow, targeting the spokes of the Gate, trying to shut it down before he escaped. But then she realized what he was doing, and rage exploded through her.

One breeder was already through; he'd headed for the next closest when he became aware of her.

"Going somewhere?" Nikki asked, and punched him.

Alex stumbled back, spitting teeth. "You're just like your bitch of a mother," he spat. "Never seeing the big picture."

"Coming from you, that's a compliment," she retorted, and pulled her fist back again. She could have shredded him with magic, but she wanted something more visceral, more satisfying: like beating him to a pulp.

That was her undoing.

She got in one more good punch; felt his nose crunch beneath her fist. Alex's foot betrayed him; he fell backwards, and his head cracked against the floor. As he lay there, stunned, she raised her foot to crush his windpipe, grinning in triumph.

Nikki, no! He has to tell us where Kith is! Alenya's voice cut through her like a knife, and her foot hesitated.

It was enough to give him a chance to grab her ankle and yank her off her feet. Stars danced in front of her eyes when her head hit; the next thing she knew, bright pain exploded in her chest. The stars cleared, showing her the hilt of the dagger Alex had shoved into her as he leaned over her.

"Sorry, love, nothing personal," he panted, pulling back just a bit and leaving the dagger in her chest. She could see blood dripping from the fingers he'd cut; feel it landing on her cheek. "But if you won't help me, well—you're not much good to me then, and I don't want you coming after me."

The pain was good: it cleared her mind, giving her something to focus on. "Then you shouldn't have done that, love," she said, and pulled the dagger out. The blood on her chest was warm; she could feel her heartbeat, and it brought a savage grin to her lips. The shocked look on his face was icing on the cake. "Didn't you pay attention, Alex? You were playing with the wrong spells: and you got a Horseman for your troubles." A quick reversal and she shoved the dagger up into his belly and twisted. "And Death doesn't die that easily."

Behind and above him, the rainbow continued to work at the Gate, trying to shut it down. Chunks of Shadow fell to the side, and the swirl slowed, but did not stop—not yet. She wondered idly, in a corner of her mind, why not.

Alex's eyes were wide with pain; as she twisted the dagger even more, Shadows erupted from the Gate and dragged him through. Nikki let him go; as the Gate closed, the rainbow finally broke through it.

"No! No!" Alenya's scream echoed through the room. The adrenaline high was starting to fade; Nikki was aware of two things as she lay in the midst of the chaos.

One, that although her chest hurt and she was still bleeding, that Alex had missed her heart somehow. And two, that it wasn't over.

Not yet.

Epilogue

"Seeds of Tomorrow"

"How odd."

Nikki paused at the gate to the inn, looking over the remains of Sarah's garden. A light snow had fallen the night before; the rose bushes were tightly bundled and had a crown of silvery white. The landscape was white and untouched; clean, in a way that only new-fallen snow can be. It was a bandage that hid the scars from the monster storm that had hit only one week before.

It was soothing to her nerves, still recovering from the incidents of that night.

She'd been unconscious for several days following the fight, as her body worked to repair the knife wound Alex had gifted her with. During that time, everyone else had been busy: Rick and Justin had even managed to sneak back into Gene-Tech and snatch some of the files from Alex's office. Then they'd taken a page from Alenya's book and blown up the generators; this time, by non-magical means, according to them.

"What?" Justin hovered at her elbow, quietly solicitous, as he'd been since she'd woken up. She was about to punch him if he didn't stop.

"It's so different in the winter." Nikki looked around at the inn, dark and warm and inviting in the early twilight. "I wonder if I'll ever get to actually enjoy the summer here."

"Probably." Justin grinned. "I don't think Rick's going anywhere for a while, and Sarah won't be happy if you don't visit once in a while."

Nikki blushed. "Anyways," she said, starting up the stairs to the porch, "you two better have some interesting information for me. I need to know where Alex went."

His face lost its good humor. "You and me both," he said quietly. "We need to find Kith."

Alenya had retreated to her great house after the battle, going into her workroom and barricading the door. Only Farnsworth had been allowed in. He had reported to Cassandra that she was constantly casting scrying spells. Trying to find Kith.

Nikki stopped and put her hand on his arm. "We'll find him," she said. "I promise."

"I know."

Sarah opened the door, holding Jonathan back from jumping on them. "Welcome back," she said, and the warmth of her greeting washed over them. Her smile was genuine; Nikki felt like she'd finally come home.

"Thank you." To her surprise, Justin dropped a friendly kiss on Sarah's cheek as he went past, as if she were his cousin instead of Rick's. Nikki raised an eyebrow.

That's a switch. What was he up to while I was training with Alenya? She was curious, and voiced the question as they went up to Rick's room.

Justin laughed. "Sarah and I had a long talk, and worked stuff out. A lot of her anger at me was for the wrong things. It's cool now."

"Good." She started to say something else, and then Rick filled the doorway to his room and her mouth went dry.

He was dressed simply, the same as he'd been before: jeans and a tee-shirt, his long dark blonde hair loose around his shoulders, his dark amber eyes with circles under them, as always, hinting at long nights writing. His frame—lean and wiry—lounged in the doorway, more comfortable in himself than many people she knew.

"Hey handsome," she said softly, her heart thumping in her chest.

"Hey beautiful." Rick's voice was equally low; they stood looking at one another for a moment, and then she rushed into his arms.

Drakkar Noir enveloped her, combined with the masculine scent that was Rick, and she burrowed her face into his muscular chest, trying not to think about how close they'd both come to dying. His arms tightened around her; Nikki squeaked out a laugh as he crushed her into him, the barely-healed wound in her chest protesting.

"Hey, hey, don't hurt her! I'm not dragging her back to Vashti's to get her lungs healed again," Justin protested, but there was an ear-to-ear grin on his face. "You try explaining it to them!"

Rick's arms loosened, but he still held her close. "You had me scared," he said softly to her, his breath warm on her ear. "I thought you'd died."

Her chuckle vibrated through both of them. "And how does Death die?"

"Let's not try and find out." They stood there for a moment, just soaking up each other's presence, until Justin coughed.

"Yeah, yeah," Nikki grumbled, and Rick laughed. He pulled her to his side, keeping one arm around her, and gestured to Justin to head into the room.

"Good Lord, what book died in here?" Nikki asked, looking at the explosion of papers over what used to be Rick's desk.

He grinned. "My editor just sent the revisions back. I was just working on them." Watching him move to the desk and shuffle the papers back into some order gave Nikki a pang of conscience; she, too, should have been working on revisions by now. She wondered what her publisher had thought of the brief email she'd sent them, letting them know her book idea was on hold indefinitely.

At least they hadn't given me an advance, she thought to herself, and her chest ached again. I'd've felt really guilty then.

Rick turned back to them, a set of files in his hands. "Here's what we managed to get from Gene-Tech before it went up in flames."

Nikki accepted the files and sat cross-legged on his bed. Justin claimed the chair as Rick climbed up beside her.

"What happened? Tell me." She looked at them, prepared for the worst.

"It was a mess, Nik." Rick sighed, shaking his head. "Andreas and Teraisa were both gone when we went back; we'd taken you and Dr. Richards to the hospital as soon as the Gate was gone."

She nodded—old news.

"Since Kymara didn't have a body, we're not sure what happened to her. There were three women there: Vashti checked all of them. They and their unborn children are safe, and the spells weren't far enough along to hurt them."

"Why didn't you take them to the hospital with us?" Nikki interrupted.

"And say what? 'Hi, we just found these women while breaking up an experiment that's illegal on three interdimensional planes but not in the United States, and we'd like to make sure they're okay?'" Justin gave her a look of disgust. "Yeah, that would have gone over real well."

Nikki giggled in spite of herself. "Okay, point conceded." Then her face hardened. "What about Alex?"

"We don't know." Rick took her hand in his. "That Gate could have gone anywhere."

"We have to find him!" she insisted. "He's got to stand trial before the Council." Guilt over the fact that she had been quite intent on killing him stopped her from saying any more.

There was an awkward pause, and then Rick said, "What about from your end?"

"The Council's in an uproar," Nikki replied, glad to be on another subject. "They searched Andreas' house and found pictures of the end of the old experiment, but no Shadow Lord. And since we don't know which Dawn Lord he was working with, and none of them are admitting to anything, they're stuck right now."

"Leaving us with nothing." Justin rubbed his chin with one hand. "Except those files there."

"Well, there's precious little in them, other than the fact that Alex Masterson was one sick bastard," Rick said, letting Nikki's hand go and reaching around her for one of the files. "The second breeder in the original experiment was his wife, Caran Masterson. According to this, she was carrying twins."

"Twins. Two more children." Nikki leaned back against the headboard, clutching one of his pillows. "Dearest goddess."

"Only two?" Justin's voice was sharp.

"According to the notes, yes." Rick looked up. "Why?"

It was Nikki who answered him. "Because there are four Horsemen. That's how everything stays in Balance."

"And if there were only three children..." Justin let the sentence trail off, knowing they all understood the consequences.

"Then we're screwed." Rick sat back, stunned. "Holy shit."

Nikki was shaking her head. "No. We're not." They both looked at her; she frowned, knowing she was right, but not sure how. "There are four Horsemen. We just have to find them."

"And how are you planning to do that?" Rick asked her, and she shrugged.

"I don't know. But I have to."

THE TALE CONTINUES:

2009

DARK MOON SEASONS

Valerie Griswold-Ford

A Dark Horseman Novel

2010